"This is some of the most evocative writing about childhood that I have come across. Gladstone's recall and rendering of that lost time is remarkable. He has an extraordinary memory for detail as w~'' e nuances of moments that we have all lived through, but h-~ part, forgotten."

  —Joseph Olshan ~a's Heart

"This compelling story of one , place in the world having grown up in an od ~ a familiar deep tone way inside my soul. Eminently 1 ~ hard to put down."

  —Paul Zaloom, Obie Award-winning performance artist

"George Orwell wrote 'A child which appears reasonably happy may actually be suffering horrors which it cannot or will not reveal. It lives in a sort of alien underwater world which we can only penetrate by divination. Our chief clue is the fact that we were once children ourselves, and many people appear to forget the atmosphere of their own childhood almost entirely.' Jim Gladstone not only penetrates this underwater world that Orwell describes, he takes us deep below the surface and holds us there, caught between laughing and crying."

  —David Sanders, *Writing Aloud*, WHYY Radio, Philadelphia

"Growing-up-gay stories are a dime a dozen. This one gives us an imaginative, kaleidoscopic new take on that eternal journey toward the moment when a kid decides whether to live or die."

  —Patricia Nell Warren, Author of *The Front Runner* and *Billy's Boy*

"This is a sharp book, full of sad-funny feelings. Starting from the candy wrappers, toy parts, and over-loved stuffed animals scattered on childhood's floor, Gladstone traces a young man's journey to self-sensitivity, with hilarious and painful turns along the way."

  —Mike Albo, Author of *Hornito: My Lie Life*

"This book is sweet and true and surprisingly honest in a world of worked-up horseshit. It made me think very much of my gay brother and the feelings he had when he was growing up. But I related to all the characters in the book. I have met people like them. I've even been a few of them."

  —Susan Werner, Songwriter

## NOTES FOR PROFESSIONAL LIBRARIANS AND LIBRARY USERS

This is an original book title published by Harrington Park Press®, Southern Tier Editions, an imprint of The Haworth Press, Inc. Unless otherwise noted in specific chapters with attribution, materials in this book have not been previously published elsewhere in any format or language.

## CONSERVATION AND PRESERVATION NOTES

All books published by The Haworth Press, Inc. and its imprints are printed on certified pH neutral, acid free book grade paper. This paper meets the minimum requirements of American National Standard for Information Sciences-Permanence of Paper for Printed Material, ANSI Z39.48-1984.

# The Big Book
# of Misunderstanding

# HARRINGTON PARK PRESS
*Southern Tier Editions*
Gay Men's Fiction
Jay Quinn, Executive Editor

*Love, the Magician* by Brian Bouldrey

*Distortion* by Stephen Beachy

*The City Kid* by Paul Reidinger

*Rebel Yell: Stories by Contemporary Southern Gay Authors* edited by Jay Quinn

*Rebel Yell 2: More Stories of Contemporary Southern Gay Men* edited by Jay Quinn

*Metes and Bounds* by Jay Quinn

*The Limits of Pleasure* by Daniel Jaffe

*The Big Book of Misunderstanding* by Jim Gladstone

*This Thing Called Courage: South Boston Stories* by J. G. Hayes

*Trio Sonata* by Juliet Sarkessian

# The Big Book
# of Misunderstanding

Jim Gladstone

Southern Tier Editions
Harrington Park Press®
An Imprint of The Haworth Press, Inc.
New York • London • Oxford

Published by

Southern Tier Editions, Harrington Park Press®, an imprint of The Haworth Press, Inc., 10 Alice Street, Binghamton, NY 13904-1580.

© 2002 by Jim Gladstone. All rights reserved. No part of this work may be reproduced or utilized in any form or by any means, electronic or mechanical, including photocopying, microfilm, and recording, or by any information storage and retrieval system, without permission in writing from the publisher. Printed in the United States of America.

PUBLISHER'S NOTE
This is a work of fiction. Names, characters, places, and incidents either are the products of the author's imagination or are used fictitiously, and any resemblance to actual persons, living or dead, business establishments, events, or locales is entirely coincidental.

Cover design by Anne Winslow.

**Library of Congress Cataloging-in-Publication Data**

Gladstone, Jim.
    The big book of misunderstanding / Jim Gladstone.
       p. cm.
    ISBN 1-56023-383-4 (alk. paper)—ISBN 1-56023-382-6 (alk. paper)
    1. Young men—Fiction. 2. Suicidal behavior—Fiction. 3. Gay men—Fiction. I. Title.

PS3607.L34 B64 2002
813'.6—dc21

2001051525

For my parents,
Henry Aaron Gladstone
and
Sheila Margolis Gladstone

*Beyond any book,*
*Beyond all words,*
*I love you.*

# Acknowledgments

This book could not have been written and published without the moral support and artistic sensitivity of two dear friends and gifted writers, Tina Barr and Kelly McQuain. I am forever grateful.

If I can be called a writer, it is only thanks to invaluable mentoring and encouragement over the years from Bonney MacDonald, Peter Landry, David Warner, and Rachel Simon. If I am called a friend, I hope I meet that role with the standard of excellence set by Mike Gaebler, Rose Marie Morse, Armando Maggi, Ina Stern, Jacki Sufak, the two Robert Drakes, Regina Gillis, Matthew Hart, Lori Sabian, Larry Smith, Rob Goldstein, and Jay Quinn, who is also appreciated for a plethora of less important reasons.

It has been a pleasure to work with the entire team at The Haworth Press, including Margaret Tatich, Peg Marr, Jennifer Durgan, Jennifer Gaska, Sandy Sickels, Marylouise Doyle, Josh Ribakove, and Bill Palmer. The savvy guidance of Morse Partners has been invaluable to me, as has the professional support provided by John Talbot, Anne Winslow, Lynn Kendall, and David Sanders, of Philadelphia's Interact Theater Company.

In their own way, each of my four aunts—Diane Margolis, Bonnie Kay, Judie Brown, and Susan Gladstone—has been a remarkable personal supporter during the genesis and writing of this book.

Finally, there is my compatriot Jeff Abrahamson. In inimitable and irresistible style, he helps me work out all the bugs in my programming.

FALL 1987

Heat from the shower filled Meredith's bathroom, fogging over the mirror on the medicine chest. My hand trembled, and the pale yellow pills rattled against their amber vial, a delicate percussive soundtrack of dilemma.

*Did I have to end my life to end my childhood?*

For the past few months, I'd slipped into a wrinkle between the two. Meredith had led me through the looking glass, into a charmed neighborhood known as the Elbow Bends. There, in a network of narrow, cobblestone Philadelphia alleys, a thrift-store-clad cadre of would-be artists, experimental musicians, and layabout trust-fund babies had made me feel welcome, unpressured. And one impossibly alluring Portuguese expat had loved me, truly, as best he could.

In his ad hoc coffee shop, called the Copa Mà, amid the safety-pinned earlobes, the ridiculous sideburns, the wise chatter, and the passing grip of Eugenio's hand on my shoulder, I'd found the comforts of a small town tucked within life's unbounded sprawl. The Copa was furnished with tiny wrought iron tables, potted geraniums, and an improbable leather daybed where Meredith, my oldest friend, made herself a fixture, allowing the ashes on her Marlboros to grow precariously long before tapping them into her espresso saucer. The Copa was a place of dreams without plans—a place where every stranger was a potential friend. For a few months there, I had felt a rare steadiness.

Then everything had begun to shake again—to rattle me out of my holding pattern.

Even before the night the lights went out in the Copa, the night Eugenio lost his power, I had begun to feel uneasy. In the early evenings, I sat alone at a table in the corner, isolated from my new acquaintances, blowing into a mug of bitter-edged cocoa, hoping to hide behind the shroud of steam that rose around my face. From

1

across the room, Meredith caught my eye through this mist, smiling hello as she shook her head sadly, no longer bothering to repeat the same advice I had been rejecting since the first day she'd brought me to the Elbow Bends.

"You've got to go back," she had urged. "You've got to help him."

When I finally heard her, it was almost too late. I stood in Meredith's row-house bathroom. In a fog of shower steam, I tipped the open bottle to my lips. The pills would roll onto the stippled terrain of my tongue, then silence it.

I would no longer have to be the boy I was.

But I could never grow up to tell his story either.

Weeping, I dropped to my knees and read the name on the prescription label. My father's name. Then I sent the pills swirling into a vortex of Ti-D-Bowl blue.

Later that same evening, the night my life began again, I packed my blank book, a few clothes, and Meredith drove me home.

We didn't speak as we rolled out of the Elbow Bends. I put the oldies station on the radio and we hummed together, off key, to "Bye Bye Love" and "The Wanderer."

The disc jockey announced "American Pie," and I remembered the rainy gray Chevrolet my father had when I was a boy. Once, we were driving on a Sunday afternoon, and when Don McLean sang his line about the Chevy and the levee, Dad turned to me from the wheel with a sly grin. Our eyes met, and I thought I felt our souls lock in some ineluctable harmony.

My father and I were together, caught inside a sad, beautiful song.

Now we drove along the Schuylkill River, where Mer and I had once watched my brother Lewis lead the high school crew team to victory. Illuminated by strings of tiny white bulbs that burned from dusk to dawn along their rooflines, door frames, and window casings, the boathouses on the river's east bank were reflected in the water, glowing and wavery. To me, these shimmering night images were more real than the buildings themselves. By day, the houses seemed bereft, without their dream-like doubles rippling below.

Blanketed in weariness, I let go and let the car carry me. Fear and familiarity blended into exhaustion. We rolled across Route 1, the border between city and suburbs. The Pathmark. The school yard.

Bell's Pharmacy. I ticked off the landmarks to myself, all the way down to the last left turn. Meredith slowed as we moved onto the unlit gravel.

No Thru Traffic, read the sign. Private Road.

She stopped by the lamppost at the edge of the lawn. I stretched, groggy, a toddler who has napped his way home from a day at the seashore. Here I was again, 801 Roslyn Avenue. In the late October light, Meredith stood with me by the driveway. I stared over my father's cars at my brother Lew's old basketball pole, the weather-beaten net almost completely torn from the rim, but still hanging on, somehow. Mer pointed to the television, flickering through the living room window; my father was no doubt sinking into another night of ESPN.

"Josh, do you want me to go in with you?" she asked.

"Go on. I'd better do this myself," I said, holding back a wave of panic.

"I'll call." She pulled the car door shut. "Say hello to Harris for me."

I walked up the flagstone footpath. Two chipped plaster lions with green lichen tooth decay flanked the arched oak doorway with its small stained-glass window of multicolored diamonds, like the pattern on a jester's tights.

Through the leaded pane, I could see my father. The remote control had slipped from his hand as he drowsed on the couch, alone in the dream house he'd bought for us all. I couldn't bring myself to ring the bell and rouse him, to embrace him in the doorway, to carry myself across this long-avoided threshold.

I crept around back to the entrance to my mother's long-abandoned office. My father had left a key, wrapped in plastic, under the mat.

"Welcome home, Becca," read its wishful paper tag.

I spent three days there before I spoke to my father. The office that had briefly housed Mom's psychology practice had its own bathroom, and I snuck into the kitchen for food when I knew Harris was at work. In the little office where my mother once planned her escape from this house, I began to dream my way back in. Beneath a shelf of outdated *DSM* volumes, I slept fitfully on the couch where her patients used to lie. But most of the time—twelve, sixteen, eighteen hours a day—I sat at her desk, furiously filling the long-blank pages of a leather-bound notebook I'd carried for years.

"You've got to go back," Meri had urged. "You've got to help him."

She'd meant my father, of course. And I would try. But I'd also gone back to help myself. To end my childhood, after all. I would live through my twenty-two years once again. I would set them to paper and set them to rest.

~~~

On a Tuesday night when I was four years old, I awoke to find the bedroom aswarm with giant animals pulled on leashes by clowns and ballerinas. My brother Lew slept soundly, oblivious to it all. The scene was washed in pastel green and lavender, a waking dream that hung around me like wallpaper. Whales swam across the room. Baby blue hippopotami danced out the door.

I followed, stepping into the hallway, taking careful hold of the banister. The parade glided beside me, along the angled staircase wall. It was like a movie that I carried in my head and somehow projected onto the broad, flat surfaces from which our house was constructed. There were no boundaries between my imagination and the world.

Inching downstairs, I glanced nervously from side to side. On my left, the beautiful parade. On my right, in a yellow-shag-carpeted living room full of comfortably battered furniture, my parents, looking up from their easy chairs in sudden, intense concentration on me. I frantically shifted my gaze back and forth, sensing that either side of my vision might suddenly slip away: I'd either abandon my parents or be left behind by the cavalcade.

I stared at the wall, absorbed in the panoramic rush, trying to remember how to make my voice work. I touched my tongue to my lips. They were cracked with dryness. My parents walked up the stairs together. Mom sat on the step above me and touched a fingertip to my curls. Dad stood on the step below, towering over us both.

"What do you see, honey?" Mom asked as I stared at the wall. "What do you see there?"

My father looked at the wall and saw nothing. He locked eyes with my mother and slowly shook his head.

"I'll tell you what *I* see," he said sternly. "I see a little boy who's up well past his bedtime. And I think I know what I'm going to see next. I'm going to see that same little boy turn right around, march back to his bedroom, and hit the sack without any more monkey business."

He stared at me.

I raised an open palm to him, as if offering a piece of invisible fruit. "Thanksgiving," I croaked, throat parched. "Thanksgiving parade."

My mother pressed her palm to my forehead and tried to swallow her gasp.

My father's voice drew tight. "What the hell is going on?" He was frightened and angry at the same time.

"Harris, shhhhhh . . . ," my mother whispered. "Joshy has a high fever. We'll make it all better. You really do see the parade, sweetheart. It's called a hallucination."

She looked up to make sure my father understood.

"Daddy's going to carry you upstairs," she instructed.

Peeled from my sweat-soaked pajamas, I slouched at one end of the bathtub, swaddled in terry cloth, sweating and shivering. My parents scooped warm water over me with their palms as I told them about watermelon jugglers and lemon-yellow lions and a walrus that blew soap bubbles from its nose.

My mother smiled at me, asking questions about the marvels I could see. My father sat on the edge of the toilet seat, wincing and tugging at his eyebrows.

"They're going away, Daddy," I reassured him through chattering teeth.

The bulbous balloon creatures, the marchers, and the clowns dissolved into the water that had condensed on the tile wall. The droplets glowed with color, then faded to transparency, sliding down into the shallow pool where I sat.

"They're all gone now." I hated to see my father scared.

As he wrapped me in a towel and carried me out of the bathroom, I stared at his reflection in the medicine cabinet mirror: shaking his head in wonder, swallowing in relief.

Dad slipped me under my covers without even putting clean pj's on me. He quietly pulled a chair up near the head of my bed, not wanting to wake Lewis, and slid a storybook from the shelf. As my father read to me in a soothing, barely audible whisper, I fell asleep again, naked.

~~~

My father always hated returning to his own boyhood home. But until I was five, when Grandpop Josh and Gram Sara moved to

Florida, we went to their tiny row house by the reservoir for dinner each Sunday night. My father groused, but my mother insisted that these extended family gatherings were important for Lew and me. Her own parents were gone; her father had died when she was only thirteen, the same month that my father stepped into her life.

The centerpiece of my grandparents' table was a ceramic figurine, an old balloon seller whose grave expression balanced the colorful cheer of his wares. I always insisted that he be turned to face me. Through the meals, I listened to my father bicker with the man he'd named me after and tried to lose myself in the glaze of the Balloon Man's eyes.

After dinner, Grandpop Josh rose with a groan, growing animated and cheerful as he ushered me toward a walk-in hallway closet he had commandeered. Wealthier men might have had their toolsheds or workshops or private dens, but, to me, an invitation into Grandpop's cedar-smelling closet was worth more than anything in the world.

"C'mere, Josho McGosho," my grandfather beckoned, hoisting me atop one of the two bar stools he'd set along the old wooden door that he'd sawed in half lengthwise and bracketed to the wall to serve as a makeshift desk. He presented me with a dazzling assortment of coins, tipping each one into my quivering palm from its own tiny glassine envelope. There were etched metal portraits of kings and queens, animals, landmarks, and ships at sea. From Turkey and Zaire, Russia and Haiti, they shone with princes and poets and a bare-breasted voodoo priestess. (There were a good half dozen of that particular coin.)

My grandfather was fascinated with foreign cultures and peoples. His coin collection started with a few American gold pieces, but he grew bored with the notion of building a miniature Fort Knox. Instead, he opted to gather single specimens of the most beautiful, unusual, and exotic international coins he could find. Their face values and resale values mattered little to him. Focusing on a rare African coin through the magnifying lens of his loupe, my grandfather could run from his own life as fast as the antelope engraved on that silvery disc. With her tight fist and Gibson breath, Gram Sara kept a fusty reign over the rest of their home, but Grandpop Josh could always slip into his closet and travel from malaise to Malaysia in moments.

The narrow shelves above my grandfather's desk were lined with broad-mouthed goblets and oversized brandy snifters heaped with his collection of matchbooks. There were swizzle sticks, too, by the highball glassful; not generic red-and-white striped straws, but stirrers topped with tiny plastic yield and stop signs, seahorses, and starfish. Some had ovals custom emblazoned with names in gold letters: Gaslight Lounge, Dew Drop Inn, and Rockin' Bob's Speakeasy.

From a very young age, through some inexplicable pop osmosis, I sensed that the swizzles to be most coveted were the gleaming black ones tipped with the molded plastic bust of a rabbit's head. From a jumble of brighter, more childlike ornaments, the black rabbits leapt to the front of my mind.

Staring at the curved glass walls of the snifters, squinting to see through my own bent reflection, I could also make out matchbooks that carried the sign of the rabbit, each one emblazoned with the name of a different city. Chicago rabbit, San Francisco rabbit, Columbus rabbit, Shillington rabbit. It was several years before I realized they were souvenirs from Playboy Clubs.

I was never sure which objects in Grandpop Josh's collection were personal mementos and which were professional samples. Through overheard conversations, spats, and ranted monologues among the adults, I understood that my grandfather had been in the wholesale food service business, a traveling salesman of restaurant supplies. Swizzle sticks and matchbooks were his daily grind.

~

Over the years, family heirlooms have a way not just of collecting dust but of gathering wool and knitting their own histories. By the time I was twelve, the old matchbook collection lived under my bed in a green Hefty trash bag, and I imagined elaborate scenarios of my grandfather's past.

In Cleveland by day, he would sell two gross custom-printed "Johnny's Corner" matchboxes. Then, at night, he'd return to the bar to enjoy a few cocktails, bantering with the customers about what a fine gentleman the proprietor was, what a swell operation he ran, and, "Hey, John. Set these good people up with a round of manhattans. Johnny's manhattan, now there's a good strong drink. Have a few rounds, you don't know if you're in Manhattan or Cleveland or Paris, France."

I imagined the customers laughing and Grandpop flirting with a green-eyed woman who batted her lashes, teetering on high heels. When Johnny saw my grandfather at work, effortlessly convincing the clientele that the Corner was the jumpingest joint in town, he'd remind himself to order up some of those fancy printed cocktail napkins and a case of after-dinner butter mints the next time Josh Royalton came calling.

Which was the whole idea, of course. And the very reason that, after a closely clocked forty-five minutes, Grandpop was out the side door and off to one of the other five saloons he would visit that night, proclaiming each "the hottest spot in Cleveland." He had mastered the art of waving a cigarette around to deflect attention while secretly slipping a turkey baster out of his coat pocket to suck off the lion's share of each of his drinks, so as not to be entirely soused after a full evening's rounds.

Still, after a good night's work, I imagined that Grandpop was pretty blotto. When I pictured his company Caddy, even the fins had dings. As a teenager, I began to suspect that a fair share of those teeter-heeled bar women had their false lashes bent into oblivion between Grandpop's inebriated driving and the orange polyester bedspreads at the Howard Johnson's where he stayed. My grandfather was a swifty, a smoothy, a city-hopping rabbit.

It might have been possible by talking with my father to have verified, debunked, or otherwise interpreted my impression of his father's life. But how important could this information really be? Over time, my actual, factual family tree grew far less real than the deeply ingrown baobab of my imagination.

Harris, for his part, wasn't interested in telling anyway.

"Your grandfather was like a Chinese box," he once grumbled with a wistful shake of his head, offering no further explanation.

Grandpop Josh, the Chinese box man. Enough said.

And, in a strange sense, it was enough.

In my father's oddly strained tones, there were so many nuances, so many trapdoors, secret openings, and hidden flaps, that, while I couldn't quite conjure up my grandfather as a person, I sensed a power in him that I longed to share.

My father loved Grandpop Josh, almost in spite of himself.

"Your grandfather was like a Chinese box."

It was a disdainful, awestruck, proud, and pitying phrase, the emotions stitched into an indivisible patchwork that I imagined myself wearing like the silk kimono my mother's older sister, Aunt Binnie, had shipped to me from her travels abroad.

"Japan, Becca!" Dad had ridiculed Binnie's trip. "While we're trying to get it together to move to a suburb with better schools, Binnie is getting divorced and spending a fortune to gallivant around like some Jewish American geisha girl!"

"Well, she's different from us, Harris," Mom replied plainly.

When my father responded with an exaggerated nod, she realized she'd sounded more in agreement with him than she'd intended.

"But," she made an attempt at amendment, unnoticed by my father, "what's so wrong with different?"

~

As a boy, I considered my mother a first-rate chef. Each Monday through Thursday evening, she would serve an entree, a vegetable, a starch, and—every night, without fail—a big bowl of Musselman's applesauce.

Mom made meatballs with crushed gingersnaps instead of bread crumbs; she doctored rectangles of frozen flounder into edibility with mushrooms and Italian dressing; she sauteed chicken chunks with spinach and chopped red pepper. My father's favorites were shrimp scampi and T-bone steak, which were generally reserved for him and Mom on Friday nights, when Lew and I ate frozen pizza and they dined privately an hour later, softening their week of lawyering and child rearing with a meal that began with Gallo and finished with the Pepperidge Farm Distinctive Cookies.

After tucking us into bed and sharing their special dinner, our parents became what Lew and I referred to as "the Friday night jigsaw freaks," laboring endlessly to reconstitute a picture that someone had foolishly cut into 1,000 knobby little pieces. Dad once explained that this was what they had done on their first date. At ages fifteen and thirteen, they sat on the glider on Mom's front porch and built their first puzzle: a goofy-eyed baby boy in a sailor's cap.

"That was a long time ago," I remarked. "Aren't you bored with it yet?"

"Guess not," said Mom, after Dad reached over and began to knead her shoulder.

~

Most weeknights, when Lew and I heard the Chevy roll up the driveway, we leapt—as if scripted—from our sprawled positions in front of a *Gilligan's Island* rerun and bolted for the kitchen door, clamoring, "Daddy's home! Daddy's home!"

It had somehow evolved into ritual: the mad scramble, the slam of the screen door, the jubilant shouting for our father. Mom stood at the sink chopping onions as we dashed by.

"Hi, sweetie," she would greet him, wiping her hands on a red-and-white checkered apron. "How was work?"

"Pretty good," Dad would say perfunctorily, pulling her into a chesty embrace that made me feel embarrassed.

On Friday nights, this greeting drama was extended with an extra act. Releasing Mom from his clutches, Dad would pop the brass closure on his briefcase and, with a magician's flourish, produce a brown paper bag. Gripping it in his right hand, my father would slowly reach in with his left and, inch by inch, slide out the puzzle of the week.

From mounds of spaghetti to safari gazelles, from Snoopy and Woodstock to Alpine ski runs, our father seemed to pick images indiscriminately. Each week's particular end point was less important than the rigorous teamwork of assembling the cardboard pieces to achieve a perfect match with the picture on the box top. Dad would shake the puzzle box, pieces tumbling over one another inside with the rhythmic sound of a railroad train. He would thrust the churning cardboard engine toward Lewis and me, pressing us to volunteer our opinions of each week's picture.

Chug-chug-chug came a photo of the Miami Dolphins' star quarterback about to release a pass.

"Cool!" shouted Lewis. "Bob Griese!"

"Boring, boring, boring," I complained.

Roaring down the track, a bouquet of spring flowers.

"OK," I'd say. "Not awful."

"Yes, awful!" cawed Lewis. "Girl stuff. Flowers. Eck."

"Don't be silly, Lew," Mom said gently. "Flowers are nice."

"Hey, keep out," snapped Dad. "This is our guys' game!"

Mom took a half step backward, blanching at his reproof.

One week, the puzzle express brought three halved eggshells. But where one poured natural yellow yolk, the identical white shells to its left and right released bizarre bright centers of crimson and shiny blue.

"Wow!" I cried. "Coolo! That's the best one ever, Dad." What a clever ruse. What a lovely, twisted image.

"Blue eggs?!" Lew yelped. "It's a trick. No such thing as blue eggs. Red either!"

"Must be such a thing as blue eggs, buddy," argued Dad, winking at me. "We've got the photo to prove it right here. In fact, if you're good, Mom's going to make us some nice blue scrambled eggs for brunch on Sunday."

"No way! You're lying!"

Dad's eyes narrowed down to ferocious little slits. "You watch your mouth, young man. Don't you ever accuse me of lying."

"Harris," my mother chided, "leave him be." But as often happened, her voice was shoved aside by us, three bickering boys.

"Next week, we're having green!" I proclaimed, proud to be conspiring with my father. "Green eggs and ham!"

"There is no such thing!" Lew screwed up his face, turned up his volume, and stamped his Keds-clad feet. "No green eggs or red eggs or blue eggs."

"Robin's eggs are blue," I chirped.

"And their breasts are red," Dad stage-whispered to Mom, feigning a grope as her eyes flared.

"Duh, Josh! Robin's eggs are blue on the outside," cried Lew. "That's just the shells."

Dad shook the puzzle box with a loud rattle. "Well, maybe this picture is just the outside, too. Maybe the blue and red eggs are only on the box top."

I forced a laugh but was starting to lose my sense of reality. Was it possible that the puzzle pieces formed a different picture than the one on the lid?

"Maybe when Mom and I put it together just right," Dad continued, "the yolks will all be yellow."

"Na-aah, Daddy!" Lewis hollered, turning red himself. With tight, furious little fists, he pummeled the puzzle box. Dad swooped it over Lew's head and then dive-bombed it back toward him, hundreds of bits of shrapnel tumbling over one another inside. Lew swung again, too soon. His fist landed against our father's thigh.

"Up to your room, young man!" Harris screamed. "You know there's no hitting in this house. You'd better learn to control your temper, you big baby!"

Whimpering, Lew couldn't seem to move.

"Honey," Mom bent down to him. "Run and wash up for bed. Go on. Brush your teeth." She closed a hand on Dad's shoulder.

"Ma," Lewis turned and whispered on his way out, "are you really making blue eggs?"

"Up!" Dad hollered. "March!"

I got to stay downstairs for a few more minutes, until Lew was done in the bathroom. While Mom finished cooking their steaks, I sat quietly at the table, admiring my father as he read the paper. I didn't ask about the eggs.

~

Lew and I shared a bedroom. The head of his bed was right by the hallway door. He could spy out and see if anything was going on. With his tough temperament and strong, compact body, I felt like Lew was guarding us through the night. Our beds formed an L-shape, with my head pressed up in the corner of the room. I felt protected in my sleep: small, ferocious brother to my left, walls to my right and behind my dreaming head. My feet were exposed, but I didn't think that any bad guys would be too interested in them. I was safe.

Each night, between the time we washed up for bed and when our parents came to say goodnight, Lew and I acted out adventures with our favorite stuffed animals. Mine was a baby-aspirin-colored rabbit named Orangey. Lew had a bristly stuffed rhinoceros named Rhino. We shared a beat-up old elephant that had been Dad's when he was a kid. It jingled when you shook it and was called Flappy-Bellsy-Earsies.

Usually, we played river riding. We would pretend that our pillows were rafts and kneel on them, holding our animals. The bedspreads were water. Usually, Flappy-Bellsy-Earsies fell in and started drowning. He would trumpet for help and spray from his trunk. Orangey and Rhino saved him, and Lew and I gave them a reward. We were all millionaires then, and we built the pillows and sheets into our giant mansion.

"You watch yourself, Flappy," Lewis often warned. "We can't keep saving you forever."

After playing for fifteen minutes or so, we would hear the surge of water in the pipes, deep in the walls of our home. That meant Mom was at the sink with her lemon Dawn and orange plastic scouring ball. Dad was spread out over the white Formica kitchen table, reading the *Evening Bulletin* as he removed his private stash of Milanos from their neat, pleated tissue cups, drinking a tall glass of cold milk.

When Mom's washing was done, the water in the walls would stop. On a ten-beat count, their footsteps would be halfway up the stairs. In three seconds more, they'd be in our room.

"Here they come!" I'd whisper.

We pushed all our toys aside, lay flat on our backs, and stared up, wide-eyed, at the blank white ceiling.

As they stepped into the room, Dad would ask Lew if he had brushed his teeth.

"Uh-huh."

"Are you sure?"

"Yes."

Normally, my father gave him a cold, mistrusting stare and left it at that. But one Friday night, he grabbed my brother around the chin, squeezing until his cheeks flushed red. I turned to my mother and clutched Orangey, afraid that Lew's jaw might shatter.

"Open up!" Dad hissed. "Open your mouth!"

Lew pressed his lips tight; they went white and bloodless. From deep in his throat, he growled at our father, like a bulldog pup.

"Lew, please," Mom pleaded in a whisper from behind our father. "Please."

Instantly, Lew's mouth dropped wide open, his sudden obedience to our mother as much a slap in Dad's face as a sign of his victory.

Harris dug into his pants pocket and pulled out his key chain. A tiny penlight dangled from the ring. Clicking it on, Dad shined the beam over Lew's lips, into his mouth, searching for evidence.

"Oooooh, what's this? What's this I see?" he taunted, reaching into my brother's mouth with the scary index finger he'd bent crooked in a teenage baseball dislocation. I heard his nail scrape against Lewis's back teeth and felt my mother's hand grip my shoulder.

Dad withdrew his gnarled finger with a flourish, shining his light on the calloused tip.

"What do you see there?" He bellowed at Lew.

What I saw were two black specks—on the pedestal of my father's callous, right by his yellowing nail, two tiny black specks.

"Fig seeds!" My father proclaimed, victoriously.

My mother looked to the floor, shaking her head in disappointment.

"What did you have for dessert tonight, Lewis?"

"Canned peaches."

"I'm about to start spanking *your* can, mister. You know what I'm asking. What else?"

"Cookies," Lew snapped, tough as Rhino the rhino.

"Fig Newtons, Lewis!" our father roared, pounding fists on the mattress, terrorizing. "From your filthy mouth, it looks like you had Fig Newtons."

He raised his left hand and brought it glancing down against Lew's temple. My brother released a canine snarl. He was raging at our father for humiliating him in front of Mom and me, raging at being hit, and raging, finally, because tonight—as he did on about half of all nights—Lewis *had* brushed his teeth.

I had seen him do it. But, somehow, I couldn't speak up.

After Dad turned out the lights, I curled in my blankets and decided that, in the morning, I would teach our mother how to listen to the pipes. She could monitor us in the bathroom the same way we listened to them in the kitchen:

*When Lew goes up, and I'm still downstairs, you listen for the water in the walls. If you hear the water running for a few minutes once, that's him washing his face. Then you can hear a change, like a creak: that's when he turns off the hot water and leaves just the cold on for him to brush his teeth. Then, when I go up, it's the same thing. Keep track, Mom. If you listen, you can stop Dad when he's wrong.*

My mother slipped back into our room a few minutes later. Lewis was already asleep.

"I'm sorry about tonight, Joshy," she consoled me. "We love you very much."

"We love you," she had said, as if they were one person.

And I realized that there was no point in explaining anything.

She covered me up and kissed Lew on the forehead.

I lay awake for hours that Friday night, thinking about our parents beneath us, deep in concentration, working on their puzzle.

~

When Dad left for work at ten on Saturday mornings, I went up to our bedroom and sat at the salmon-colored Formica desk, peering out through the shutters. Lewis and the neighbor boys played rough-touch football on our front lawn.

Laid out on the desk were two slips of paper that I'd picked up at the 7-Eleven on the way home from school the day before: the week's top forty hit lists from radio stations WFIL and WIP. Most of the titles on the lists overlapped, but I had to hear each song on each station. I would sit at my desk and do this important paperwork on Saturdays, just as my father was doing his paperwork downtown at his office.

The orange plastic AM transistor radio I'd received for my eighth birthday had quickly become one of my prized possessions. Each weekday morning for years, I'd stood in my parents' bathroom as my father prepared for his busy day's work. The silver dial on his black transistor was kept tuned to the all-news station, which sounded especially resonant and authoritative bouncing off the pale blue bathroom tile. Although I never spoke a word as he washed and brushed his teeth, my father nonetheless made a point of hushing me when the sports scores came on.

Lew stayed back in our room during my early morning sessions with Dad. He emulated his beloved athletes with a daily routine of push-ups, sit-ups, and chin-ups on a bar Dad had hung for him in our bedroom closet.

"Why do you always watch Dad go to the bathroom?" Lew would ask me.

"I'm not watching him go to the bathroom. I'm listening to the radio with him."

"You mean he never pees?"

"I guess he pees, sometimes. So what? You've seen him pee."

"I do not watch him pee!"

"What about 'Make an X'?"

"That doesn't count; it's a game."

Often, before sitting down to dinner or taking off on a car trip, our father would corral Lew and I into a bathroom.

"OK, it's duel time. Let me see my guys make an X."

We would stand at opposite sides of the toilet bowl and simultaneously release our streams of urine so that their trajectories crossed, forming a lopsided liquid rendering of the letter X. After we shook off and zipped up our flies, Harris would unfurl his own elephant's trunk of a penis and project a thick, percussive cable of fluid into the toilet. This diagonal slash across the bowl reminded me of the bright red universal "No" symbol we'd recently learned in school. No smoking. No litter. The obliteration of our X.

"Yeah, 'Make an X' counts!" I snapped at Lew. "Besides, that's not what I go in there for anyway. I like to listen to the radio with Dad."

I loved standing beside my father, as the AM broadcast filled the room, punctuated by the hiss of lemon-lime Gillette issuing forth in a Dairy Queen swirl on Dad's palm. My father applied the lather to his scratchy bristles—a pure white mask over dark shadow.

The razor cut its swath through the cream, revealing fresh pinkened strips of face, almost boyish. After every stroke, there was the trickle of water, washing away a bladeful of white, studded with prickly pinpoints of beard. I was mesmerized, watching those little pieces of my father's body go swirling down the drain.

By the time I got dressed for school, Dad was in a dark blue suit that gave him back the power that shaving momentarily took away. He leaned over Lewis and me, reeking of Skin Bracer as he kissed our cheeks and asked for a spoonful of cereal. With a mixed mouthful of my Mini-Wheats and Lew's Apple Jacks, he kissed Mom, standing by in her pink velour bathrobe. He snapped up his briefcase and stepped out into the world.

"Love you!" he shouted as the screen door clattered shut.

"I can't eat any more of this," Lewis complained to me, waving his spoon over his cereal bowl. "Dad's face stuff makes my nose gag."

Save for those few minutes before breakfast on school days, my father's radio rested silent in the master bath, the airborne dust of dried toothpaste and shaving cream gradually accreting around the control knobs, tarnishing the chrome. My own transistor always sparkled for me, though.

Saturday mornings, as Lew and his friends rough-and-tumbled outside, I sat at that desk in our bedroom, watching over the squadron of noisy boys in the front yard. I checked off a song on the WIP top twenty, navigated back and forth between stations for a few minutes, then checked off a song on WFIL's list. I felt a sense of mastery. I was in control of a serious situation, while outside they were merely playing. I scoffed when neighborhood fathers stopped out front to throw a pass or two with the boys, thinking that they should be working, like my dad and me.

One Saturday, the number one song on both stations was called "You're So Vain," by a singer named Carly Simon. As I twisted away the hours trying to catch the less frequently played eighteens, nineteens, and twenties, I heard this Carly's voice sing to me over and over again. I was Joshy, the neighborhood kids were Richie and Johnny and Billy, and singing from the radio was Carly—a boy who probably wanted his parents to call him Carl like I kept begging mine to call me Josh. He sang to me, privately, and I was seduced by his sweet, urgently mysterious voice. Carly, Carly, Carly. I listened to his strange, beautiful tune again and again. The words made enticing nonsense: images of changing weather in a mug of black coffee, dancing with one's own reflection, a flowing scarf made of apricots.

Once, Mom had laid fresh apricots among the strawberries and slices of pound cake for her bridge club. I had never seen them before. Setting a pair on my small palm, I rolled their furred weight up onto my fingers, then down to the heel of my thumb. Afterward, I ran my hand across my cheek, grazing my lips and picking up their faint, still ripening scent.

The only apricots I'd known before then were the dried ones that came in a crinkly plastic bag. I ate them like secrets, sticky side to the roof of my mouth, leather to my tongue. I pressed them hard to my palate, never biting, never speaking, letting them fall apart until the sweetness could not be avoided.

On the Saturday of "You're So Vain," my father came home from work with a paper bag. I wondered if we were headed, pathetically, toward two-puzzle weekends. But then I saw the logo on the bag: Sam Goody. All day long I had heard shouted commercials for the Sam Goody music stores. I felt a chill of excitement. My father and I had both worked at our desks all day. Now our worlds had overlapped again.

"What'd you get, Dad?" I relished our communion.

He grinned his tightest, most devilish grin at Mom and Lewis and me as we gathered around the kitchen door. Then, without a word, he slid out a record album, inch by inch.

She wore a big floppy hat and a come-hither grin. A tight blue T-shirt on full, hard-nippled breasts. Mom turned away and turned on the water in the sink. Lew said, "Who's the lady?"

And I read, bewildered: Carly Simon, *No Secrets*.

~

My father gave us a book once, *The Big Book of Safety Fun*. It was scary, no fun at all. Careless stick-figure kids called the Nit-Wits stuck their fingers in sockets, were bitten by dogs, and got run over by cars. The picture that scared me most was a little stick boy who stepped into a shower without first testing the water temperature. The Nit-Wit screamed, his bottom bulging crimson in the scalding downpour. Some nights, thinking of that image, I would run the shower so my parents would hear it, but I'd never step under to wash.

One night, when Lew and I were seven and eight, our mother started to shower in our bathroom, even though she and Dad had their own, attached to their bedroom. I'd rarely heard my parents disagree, and, that evening, as I molded Play-Doh monsters in the den and eavesdropped, I thought they sounded like Lewis and I arguing over which cartoon to watch or who got the prize in a new box of cereal.

"I know you have to get up and go to work, Harris," Mom argued with Dad in the kitchen. "But I have to be up early, too. The boys need help getting ready for school."

My father coughed, as if there was some minor irritation in his throat.

"Harris, all I'm saying is that maybe half the time you could let me shower and get ready for bed first."

"Why don't you just use the one in the kids' bathroom while I'm using ours?" my father suggested.

"Why should I schlep my stuff down the hall? Why don't *you* use the boys' bathroom?"

"The showerhead is too low. I wouldn't be able to get my head underneath. You're smaller. You use the kids' room. OK? That's a fine solution, I think."

Hours later, we cracked the door to our bedroom and crouched together at the head of Lew's bed, watching my mother's distressed shuffle down the hall. Her beige bath sheet, her blue hair towel, and her bottles of special grass-smelling shampoo and conditioner were awkwardly balanced in her folded arms.

"Goddamn it," she muttered. It made me nervous. If Dad heard us use language like that, we'd be punished.

We heard a trickle of water as Mom began adjusting the temperature. Through our cracked door, Lewis and I spied Dad coming out of their bedroom in socks and pale blue boxer shorts.

He paused outside our room, staring directly at our narrow spy crack. We reared back in panic, but he didn't say a word. He raised his eyebrows in our direction as we tried to freeze ourselves into invisibility. Then he turned and gave a halfhearted knock on the bathroom door before pushing it open and stepping in.

"Harris! Get out of here. Let me take my shower, would you?"

"I just wanted to make sure you were OK, hon."

"No. I'm not OK. I'd be OK if you didn't have to feel like you had to control everything in this family. But look, I'm showering here. I'm doing it your way. Now leave me alone."

"Wait a minute, Becca," he sounded wounded. "Do you really think I'm trying to take control of everything? I just want things to run smoothly. I don't— "

"Harris, I don't want to discuss this while I'm standing here naked. Get out!"

Backing into the hall, Dad smacked his hands together and scowled. He looked just like Lewis did after getting sacked playing football in the yard. He reached back and pulled the bathroom door shut. Almost shut. He left a crack, just like the one in our door. As he disappeared back down the hall, he chattered in the same goblin voice he used when he pressed a flashlight under his chin to give his face a lurid glow at Halloween: "Don't do anything I wouldn't do, little boys!"

I remembered then how our father had told us that, when he was ten, Grandpop Josh gave him a gold-edged deck of French playing cards. Dad still kept them in the top drawer of his dresser. Each card featured a tinted black and white photo of a naked woman with huge breasts, cupid lips, and alabaster skin. He ceremoniously showed them to us one Sunday morning while Mom was out grocery shopping. Lew and I were thrilled to swear that they would remain a secret between just the three of us.

Now, my brother and I sat silent on the bed for a moment, listening to the rush of Mom's shower.

"Do you want to?" I asked.

"I'm not gonna," Lewis blurted. "She'd get really mad."

"He'd probably get mad, too! He'd come right back out and catch us and punish us for looking."

"But Mom would believe us if we told her he told us to, right?"

"But he didn't really tell us to."

"That's not fair!" Lew's face turned beet red.

"I don't think this is the same as those ladies from Paris," Lew grumbled, unsure of what to do. "They're probably a hundred years old by now. Or even dead."

"Don't talk like that about Mom."

"Like what?"

"I just don't want to, OK?"

"Yeah, me either. I think."

"Do you think Dad would really get mad?"

"Maybe he'll think we're chickens if we don't. "

"Wait! I know," Lewis exulted. "Let's have Flappy do it!"

"Yeah! That beat-up old doll used to be Dad's anyway."

I pulled our bedroom door halfway open, and Lew faded back across our bedroom floor like Johnny Unitas, preparing Flappy for a jingling pachydermal spiral. The stuffed elephant hurtled across the hallway, where it smacked against the bathroom door, swinging it open another few inches. The doll sagged forlornly on the hallway floor, no noise from Mom indicating that we'd disturbed her. I tiptoed out, grabbed Flappy by the trunk, and carefully closed the bathroom door, twisting my neck so I wouldn't see inside. I pulled our bedroom door all the way shut, too.

Then, before we said good night, Lew and I kicked Flappy-Bellsy-Earsies around the floor, stomped up and down on him, and buried him in the dirty clothes hamper.

~

A week after Mom started showering in our bathroom, Dad invented a game called the Royalton Varsity Bellyfights. Lew and I would call downstairs to him when we'd stripped down to our underpants getting ready for bed. Then, we happily marched into Mom and Dad's bedroom where our father arrived to position us on opposite corners of their enormous mattress.

"Ladies and gentlemen of the Kingdom of Bellyuppus," Dad would announce, eliciting giggles. "You see before you two of the finest young men ever to set foot on the planet Earth, let alone this bouncy, bouncy bed.

"Young Lewis is a quarterback, a pitcher, and can belch the entire alphabet with unparalleled grace. And Joshua can do things with a magic marker that the world's greatest artists can only imagine. Someday, they will both reach the heights achieved by their own glorious parents and be able to assemble virtually any one-thousand-piece jigsaw puzzle under the sun.

"But tonight, ladies and gentlemen, you will see them face off against each other in the most bulbous, the most gelatinous, the most indigestible competition known to man: the Bellyfight!"

And at that, we hopped to it. Clasping our hands behind our backs and refraining from kicks and head butts, we puffed up our guts and repeatedly bumped abdomens until one of us lost his balance. We both had weak eyesight and wore plastic tortoiseshell glasses. I glanced from the bed to the full-length mirror on Dad's closet door, watching us bounce up and down, grinning and bopping our tummies together in white briefs and spectacles.

Flopped on the bed after one particularly tiring round, I was struck by an intriguing possibility.

"Since Lew has an outtie belly button and I have an innie, maybe they really can button together!"

"I bet it'll work," giggled Lew, rolling off of his back and straddling my legs with his knees.

"OK, now you have to aim it really perfect," I said.

"You too!" cried Lew.

Dad cleared his throat.

Lew and I cupped our hands under our guts and tried to shift our bellies into perfect alignment.

"All right, I think you've got it, Lew. Now lower yourself. Don't crush me. Houston, prepare to button!"

Lewis and I both began to laugh hysterically as he lay atop me and slid his abdomen back and forth trying to get a perfect match.

"Is it in?" I was cracking up.

"I think we're buttoned, Dad!" Lewis cheered.

"Okay," I cried. "Now let's stand up without coming undone."

"Ready, Josh— " Lew sputtered with laughter, "one—two—three—up!"

We were halfway there when I lost my balance and plopped back down to the mattress.

"No problem, Button Brother, let's do it again!" I enthused.

"No, guys, I think that's enough of that game," Dad ruled.

"OK, OK. Round three of the Bellyfight," Lew countered. "Who knows, Joshy. Now that we're thinking about it, we might accidentally get buttoned in the middle of a fight."

"No. Enough with Bellyfights." Dad sounded bugged at us. "It's time to go to bed."

"Did I do something wrong?" I wondered.

"Just brush your teeth, all right?"

Every night, between washing my face and brushing my teeth, I got caught up in my own reflection. I leaned in close to the medicine cabinet mirror and stared at the two miniature versions of myself staring back out from my reflection's brown eyes. In this communion of infinite, identical boys, I would dip into a moment of trance. Then, catching the green night-light in my peripheral vision and sensing my father silently observing my foolishness, I ran cold water on my open palm and smacked myself hard on the cheek.

"Snap out of it, Joshua!" I chided.

It was during one of these brief lapses that the skeleton story came to me.

Earlier that week, I had dug up a plastic skeleton from the bottom of a Frankenberry box. It was the same glow-in-the-dark green as the phosphorescent night-light. I'd wiggled my hand down through the cereal pieces and grabbed the skeleton's cellophane wrapper. As I brought it up to the surface, I remembered my mother's frequent warning: "Don't play with plastic bags. You could suffocate and turn blue." Or eerie green, I then suspected.

Long ago, I imagined, the skeleton was a bad boy. His tiny family lived in the General Mills monster cereal factory where regular-sized people made Count Chocula, Frankenberry, and Boo Berry. One day, he was playing with the mini-marshmallows and he found a big cellophane sack, as long as his whole body, like the plastic on the clothes hangers my mother brought home from the cleaners. The boy pretended it was a sleeping bag and crawled inside. Unfortunately, It was too much like a sleeping bag and he really did fall asleep in it. The plastic pulled in tight around his mouth and nose, just like his mother had warned him. Dreamland, forever. The cereal factory workers buried the boy at the bottom of a box, still in the bag that killed him. They shoveled the cereal over his body like earth in a grave.

That night, I tossed and turned for hours, wide awake but dreaming of the tiny dead boy, rotting inside his own bedtime tomb. I crept across our room to make sure the closet door was shut tight on my fancy holiday clothes that hung there, sheathed in sheer, deadly plastic. I turned around the dinosaur model on the desk so its eyes wouldn't stare at me.

Lewis snored contentedly in his bed, oblivious to my agitation. "Why does he have it so easy?" I wondered angrily. "Why isn't his life full of scary, complicated thoughts?" When Dad yelled at Lewis, it hit my brother with the momentary explosion of a water balloon, but then everything seemed to dry off. When my father showed disdain for me, his words and actions seeped inside, running all through me, like twisted rivers. I clenched my jaw and held on to my pillow for dear life.

The next day was Wednesday, the day of the week when the third-grade boys were bused over to the high school for swimming lessons. I carried my dark blue swim shorts, my Charlie the Tuna towel, and a little black comb in a plastic bag that said "Anderson's shoe store." The changing area at the pool was thick with a humidity that carried the intermingled smells of chlorine and teenage perspiration. High school boys weren't scheduled for swimming when we kids came in, but their feet and armpits and scrota haunted the locker room.

The adolescent atmosphere provoked my anxiety. My mother always said to be wary of strangers, particularly teenagers, who seemed to me not regular humans of a certain age, but an altogether different and dangerous species. Walking home from school, I always crossed to the other side of the street if someone I judged to be a teen was approaching: this included most boys and men between twelve and twenty-five. (Girls weren't included unless they smoked or wore anything with leather fringe.) My homeward path on any given school day was a wild, frightened, zigzagging line.

In the locker room, damp in the vapors, my mind went back and forth on itself. "I'm scared," I worried. And then, in response, "Don't be stupid."

Scared, stupid, scared, stupid; I was one and then the other in an endless loop. Standing there dazed before the gunmetal-colored lockers, I got lost in the dirty grout between aqua tiles, oblivious to the boyish chatter and rat-tail towel fights around me. A high echoing laugh followed by the smack of a swinging door finally brought me back.

"I'm the only one here!" I suddenly realized. All the swirling thoughts in my head gave way to the more immediate fear of being late for role call. I stripped off my clothes, tugged on my trunks, and ran—although the signs said DO NOT RUN—across the clammy locker room floor.

I slipped into the pool water's chemical glow, sliding into place amidst the line of boys along the wall. After calling out "Here!" in response to our names, we all gripped the edge, extended our legs, and kick, kick, kicked. The flutter kick, it was called. Stretch out your ankles and beat your feet like butterfly wings on the water. All of that seven-year-old energy, concentrated into the feet, exploding in neat sharp splashes from hundreds of little-boy toes.

When the coach called "Halt!" our legs drooped down into the bathtub-warm water. Breathing heavily, we let go of the wall and stood on the bottom, our chins barely above water as we bounced on the balls of our feet.

The water cut our heads off from our bodies. Our fleshy faces, pink and brown, bobbed atop the pool, a disembodied flotilla, while below, cast in chlorine-tinted submarine light, our necks and torsos, hips and legs stood headless and translucent. It seemed to me that the high school pool, lapping over its edges and wetting the surrounding floor, was an enormous X-ray machine. Beneath the head of each of my classmates was a glowy green phantom of bone. Inside each child, I saw a seven-year-old skeleton, a drowning or plastic bag suffocation just waiting to happen.

"No wonder they call it the dead man's float," I whispered inside of my head, knowing I was onto something important. I stared up at the distant ceiling. I would not look underneath.

~

The following Saturday night, our parents were out at the movies. Janice, the sitter, was ensconced in the downstairs den, watching *Bridget Loves Bernie* and yapping with her girlfriends on the phone. I was already changed into my pj's when Lew scooted in from the bathroom in his underwear and glasses, a vestige of minty foam around his mouth. The corners of my eyes almost tickled as I watched Lew yank down his briefs, then hop around comically as the elastic band caught around his left ankle for a moment.

Before he put on his pajamas, Lew would take his glasses off and rest them on top of his penis. He called the resulting long-nosed character Weelore Dickinson and spoke for him in a squeaky, high-pitched voice.

"Good evening, Philadelphia, this is Weely D. with the evening news. The weather report is rainy. Yes, indeedy-do, lots of yellow rain expected. Just don't get any on the seat, if you know what I mean! This is Weelore Dickinson, signing off!"

I wheezed through gales of laughter at this brazen ridiculousness. My brother was so much less self-conscious than I.

"Dare you to run outside!" I challenged.

"OK."

"I mean like that, nude."

"OK."

"You wouldn't."

"Watch me."

"Yeah, I will. And so will old Mrs. Diamond on her porch and everyone else who's outside."

"I'm not scared."

"Sure you're not. What about Lisa? Bet Lisa bites your balls off."

Lisa was the ill-tempered, ill-named male German shepherd that belonged to the Browns next door. I was terrified of him although I figured I would act nasty, too, if my parents had named me Lisa.

"Do you dare me or not?"

"Yeah, I dare you. I double-dare you."

"Adios!" Lewis yelped as he bolted, demonstrating a bit of his Sesame Street Spanish vocabulary.

My jaw hung slack as I watched the smooth white halves of Lewis's tush rise and fall. He bounced down the stairs, unlatched the front door, and exclaimed "Abierto!" as he swung the door open, then zipped out onto the lawn, running until I could no longer see him from the head of the stairs. The night air, scented with mowed grass and lilac, climbed the steps in Lew's absence. I clenched my teeth and growled, imitating Lisa.

An infinite twenty seconds later, Lew barreled back into the house, slamming the door.

"Cerrado!"

He sprinted up the stairs, tossing his head back and panting from the giddy exertion. He dove onto me, naked and laughing.

"I won, I won, I did it! I won the bet!"

"OK, OK, already, you won. Big deal. Running around naked in front of people."

"What did I win? What's the prize? "

"Get your pajamas on, Lewis! The prize is that Mrs. Diamond didn't call the cops on you."

"I don't care. I don't care anyway if there isn't a prize! It was fun! You should try it sometime, Joshy, if you aren't too chicken!"

Pj's on, Lewis sat on his bed, Indian style, doing funny little dances with a toy I had given him as a gift the week before. A plastic skeleton.

"Skelly-ton! Skelly-ton! Bony, bony, fun, fun, fun!"

"Knock it off, Lewis, or I'll take that back," I said, knowing that there was nothing I wanted less.

"Such a sourpuss!"

"Shut up and go to bed."

Lew went silent, but as we lay there in the dark, I could still feel a gnawing tension. I squeezed my eyes shut to make things calm down, but the squeezing made thunder in my head. I thought of the skeleton, the dead boys, all the time my father had begun to spend coaching Lew's Peewee softball team.

"Hey, Lewis," I whispered.

"What?"

"You know the little green TV plugged in by the bathroom mirror?"

"You mean the night-light?"

"Well, sure, it's just a night-light if you don't know the secret."

"What secret?"

"No, no, never mind."

"Come on, you brought it up."

"Well, do you remember what midnight is?"

"You mean when the big hand is, uh . . . " Lew was just learning to tell time.

"Right, when the big hand and the little hand line up at twelve in the nighttime."

"Yeah, midnight."

"Well, at the stroke of midnight, the green screen of the night-light turns into a TV."

"No way."

"Oh, yes! And do you know who appears on that screen? Not Scooby Doo, not Big Bird."

"Mister Rogers?"

I caught myself before I burst out laughing and broke the mood. Then I brought my voice down to the quietest whisper and conjured up words and images from a commercial I'd seen for the Creature Feature.

"No, Lew, it's none of those friendly guys. The one who appears in the haunted TV is . . . Satan!"

"Well, well, who is this Nathan guy?"

"Not Nathan!" I sputtered. "Satan! The devil, the evil one, Beelzebub!"

"What does he do, Joshy? What would he do to me?"

"Oh, don't worry, Lewis. He only kills little boys who are in the bathroom when he appears at the stroke of midnight. So don't be afraid, buddy. Just don't go pee at twelve. Everything will be just fine . . . "

I let my voice trail into mumbling fake sleep. But I knew I'd be asleep for real soon enough. I smiled into my pillow, thinking of Lewis, squirming, maybe even wetting his bed. For the first time in over a week, I felt calm. I felt clever. I felt like my father that night.

~

After our navel maneuvers, Lewis and I were afraid that bellyfights had been sunk for good. This was cause for considerable dismay, because although Lew and I often got along, and Dad loved to play ball with Lew, the bellyfights had become the one activity that all three of us could enjoy together.

"Why do you think Harris got so angry at you guys?" I made Orangey ask us after several sadly fightless weeks.

"Grouchy old Harris. Who ever knows what will make him mad?" Lew had Rhino reply. "He tries to organize some fun and then he messes it all up."

"I don't know," I said seriously. "I must have done something wrong, Lewis."

"Geez, Joshy. You didn't do anything. We were having fun. That's all we were doing. And all of a sudden, it's like Dad thinks, 'Too much fun!' "

As sensible as Lewis seemed, I couldn't quite accept the notion of my innocence. When Dad suddenly canceled that last bellyfight between rounds, I'd felt beams of disapproval shoot from his eyes, vibrating under my skin as I marched toward the hall bath. In the following days, he would only glance at me sidelong, never meeting my eyes head on. But when I looked away, I felt penetrated by his stare.

One night, perhaps sensing my melancholy, Lewis reached under his mattress and yanked a strand of elastic from a hole along the edge of his fitted sheet. Twanging one forefinger against the rubber band as if it were an upright bass, Lew crooned a familiar lyric:

"Ai yi yi yi, I am a Frito bandito. Ai yi yi yi!"

He threw his head back and tweaked the ends of an imaginary waxed mustache, getting ready to improvise a riff.

"I eat Fritos Corn Chips wherever I go; the rest of the wordies I just do not know; and Harris Royalton should suck my big toe!

"Ai yi yi yi, Harris the Belly bandito. Ai yi yi yi, Daddy can be such a creep-o!"

A moment later, Dad pushed open our door.

"How about a bellyfight, fellas?" he asked enticingly, as if his banishment of the sport had never taken place.

Lew looked at me, eyebrows jumping. He believed that our wishes had come true. Our father had realized how stupid he was being. As Dad turned his enthusiastic smile to me, I thought differently. It seemed unfair that he could just turn things on and off at whim. Why did he stop the fights? Why was he starting them again? And why didn't he have to explain? Without an explanation, I was terrified. I might do something wrong again. Still, I agreed to join in, not wanting to disappoint Lew.

The pipes sang with Mom's dish washing as we followed Dad down the hall and took our familiar corners on the bed.

"Ladies and gentlemen, welcome to the Royalton Varsity Bellyfights. You see before you two of the bellyachingest boys in creation." There was a seriousness in Dad's tone as he introduced us once again.

"Young Joshua is a brilliant student, bringing home all 'Outstanding' marks on his most recent report card, not a single 'Satisfactory.'" Lew grimaced, knowing that he had quite a few S marks, even one S– on his last report. "Joshua is also quite skilled at numerous other challenges of the intellect and the imagination. His stories have been known to make the entire Royalton family laugh out loud at the dinner table until milk ran out of each and every one of our beautiful Royalton noses, even Mom's nose, which, of course, is not a Royalton nose by blood."

"Not a Royalton bloody nose!" I joked.

My father laughed.

"Like I said, ladies and gentlemen, Josh has his own wacky way of seeing things."

"What about me, already?" Lew complained from his corner.

"Ah, yes, Lewis," Dad went on. "Our Lew is a hulking marauder of tremendous physical prowess. On the diamond he can whack a ball deep into enemy territory. He can do a half-twist from the high diving board and swim twenty laps without running out of breath. And in football, he crushes the opposing quarterbacks like flies. Some kids may fear the rigors of competition, but not my Lew. The athletic arena is where he proves his strength and worthiness."

In moments, my brother and I were slamming up against each other on the bed, pounding our guts together with more venom than playfulness. And as we bounced and butted that night, not taking the time to laugh at how silly we looked or to feel the pleasant tickle of soft white skin against skin, play eroded into one-on-one combat. My only real strategy was to back off, hopping to the corners of the mattress as Lew pursued me.

I didn't want to fight.

"Lew looks like a natural," Dad fueled him with play-by-play commentary. "Joshua is on the retreat, but Lewis is charging toward him. Somebody's gonna get flattened!"

Now it was two-on-one combat.

Furious as I felt, I felt even more helpless. The next time my brother slapped up against me, I let myself fall backward onto the mattress.

"Yesss!" Lewis cried as my father hoisted him into the air. "I am the champion. Lewis Royalton is the winner."

"Atta boy, Lew. Go wash and brush now."

My father turned to me. I was splayed out on the bedspread in a mix of sorrow and disbelief.

"What's wrong, Joshy? You're not gonna be a sore loser, are you? You've won plenty of times before."

"C'mon, Dad. You know this was different."

"How so, kiddo?" he acted as if he really didn't understand what he was doing to us.

"You were rooting for him. You wanted him to cream me. You . . . you weren't even being funny; you were just being mean." I buried my face in the covers, trying not to cry.

The mattress sunk as my father sat on the edge of the bed and rubbed my shoulders. "I think you're exaggerating this in your mind a bit, Josh. It was the good old bellyfights, back in action. You know I'd never do anything to hurt either of you guys. I mean, I'm sure I'm not a perfect dad, but I try my best. Sure, I was rooting for Lewis. And for you. I root for both of you every minute of every day."

There was such conviction in his deep voice and such wet sincerity in his blue eyes I suddenly found myself questioning everything I was so sure of a moment before. Either my father was flat-out lying or I was somehow crazy, as if the lenses in my tortoise-shell frames had, rather than making my vision clearer, somehow distorted all my perceptions of the world. Lying there, my father seated at my side, gently stroking my shoulder and watching over me, I was awash in self-doubt. My father went downtown to do business. He could drive a car. He could inflict punishment and offer rewards. His shoes were so large, I could put both my feet into one of them. He was the biggest person in our family.

I offered a weak smile.

"That's what I like to see, buddy. There's no reason to feel bad. You know I love you." He walked two fingers from my shoulder down to my belly, drawing a shiver and a giggle from me. "I forget, Joshy. Are you ticklish?"

I started to laugh as he jiggled his index finger into my navel and scrambled the rest of his fingertips over my tummy like a frantic ten-legged spider.

"No, I'm not ticklish!" I laughed. "That must be Lewis!"

"I don't think so!"

I wriggled madly, his hands now flying over my chest, ferreting into my armpits, dancing on the dirty soles of my feet.

"I'm not ticklish! I'm not ticklish! Maybe you're thinking of Mommy!"

My gut began to cramp from the gales of laughter. I wheezed, breathless.

"You think your Mom's ticklish, huh? You think I get her on the bed like this and give her the tickle torture?"

Gasping so hard I couldn't form words, I saw Dad's spark-filled eyes and toothy grin hovering over me, like a a corrupt politician in an editorial cartoon. Over his shoulder, I saw Mom push through the bedroom door carrying a basket of laundry.

"What are you guys up to?"

"Well, I'm not tickling Joshy," Dad said, laughing himself now. "Because Joshy, you see, is not ticklish." He dug into me again, wriggling his fingers with a relentless staccato pulse.

"Honey, I don't . . . ," Mom sounded nervous.

"It's OK. Really. We're having fun."

I couldn't catch my breath. I started pushing at my father's arms to get him off of me. I cried out to my mother but no sound came. "Help me, Mom!" I heard in my head, but only rasps of hyperventilation met my ear.

When I looked to my father's eyes, I saw glee matching my panic. I stared up at him and began to spit through clenched teeth. His upper lip curled in disgust as rivulets of saliva struck his face. His enormous palm crashed down on my cheek, knocking my glasses askew. My mother gasped.

"You get to bed immediately, young man!" my father shouted. "You're showing a real talent for ruining a good time tonight. That's twice! I don't want to hear another word out of you, understand? Three strikes and you're out, buddy boy."

Stepping out into the hall, I glanced back to see Mom sitting on the easy chair with her mending kit. She bit her lower lip as our eyes met. I turned away, remembering that she thought spitting was a filthy habit.

~

Rain spattered against the bedroom windows, a continual tattoo, a mysterious call to action. The dinosaur model on the desk stared at me, trying to transmit a plan that would set things right. Ever since the night of the bellyfights two weeks before, I'd felt increasingly estranged from my father. As lightning broke in the late autumn sky, I watched streams of rain racing down the panes. Through the window, all our neighbors' homes were reduced to gray, blur-edged forms, none too solid, buffeted by the storm. Lewis had conked out almost immediately upon hitting his pillow that night. He was no more comfortable than I with the windy tumult outside, but, as ever, he flipped some internal switch and plunged into sleep, removing himself from waking worry. I kept rising from my bed, pressing my face against the window, trying to understand the source of my discomfort.

"A little water never hurt anyone. You're acting ridiculous." I could hear my father say. We had been walking home from the drugstore one afternoon when a shower broke. I pulled my body taut, shoulders up to cheeks, willing my flesh tighter to my skeleton, trying to reduce myself to a single edge, a weather-cutting blade, passing paper-thin between the raindrops.

"Look at you! What is it you don't like them calling you in gym class? What's that name they call you?"

I looked down at my mud-splashed sneakers and muttered, "A spaz."

"Well, Joshy, plain and simple, you do look like a spaz. Relax, son, it's only water."

I walked around and around our room. I looked down at Orangey, resting on the floor by the hamper. He was no longer of use to me. I turned to look at Lew again. He breathed heavily, clutching Flappy to his side. Just weeks before, we had crushed that elephant, ground him into the floor with our heels. Yet here he was, embraced again, easing my brother into sleep as I stood apart from them, wide awake and all alone.

I didn't realize I'd been staring into the hall through the crack in our door until I saw my mother walk by in her pink bathrobe, towels and bottles cradled in her folded arms. My father had recently asked her why she didn't just leave her apricot scrub and herbal shampoo and special soaps in our bathroom.

"Harris, you keep thinking I'm going to switch over to your side about this. It's the kids' bathroom; I'm a guest—probably a guest they'd rather not have. You're the one who should be interested in having a naked woman in your bathroom! Look in their tub: water guns, plastic boats, Crazy Foam. Bugs Bunny brand toothpaste. It's the kids' room!"

"Awww, Becca. It's not like seeing your Summer's Eve or Tampax is going to hurt them. Who knows, they might even learn something."

"What about me? What about how I feel when I have to get washed in that little Disney World? Sometimes it feels like I'm just another kid to you."

"Hey," he raised his eyebrows with lecherous affection. "Here's looking at you, kid."

"You're something else. Do you know why my stuff is staying in our bathroom, Harris? Because that's where it belongs. It's the master bathroom, and we're the masters of the house, you and me. When we do buy a new place like we keep talking about, this showering down the hall is coming to an end. And, in the meanwhile, every night that I have to carry this crap down the hall reminds me never to give in again."

On that windswept night, as rain rushed from the sky and steamy water showered onto my mother's naked body, I saw a frightening but strangely simple way to escape from isolation, to be part of something more important than my trembling self. I would take on the mission that Lewis and I—for all our father's prodding—had felt to be somehow terribly wrong. I might be trampled underfoot like the elephant, but perhaps I would emerge trumpeting, triumphant.

The coast was clear. I took three strides down the hall to the bathroom door and turned the knob as slowly as possible, avoiding the hair-trigger click that could give my game away. Alone here, without Lewis, I had no need to fear his infectious laughter. My brother had a tendency to get giggly during the explanations of men and women, penises and vaginas, that our parents had recently begun to present to us in awkward conversations over dinner. I was more solemn. I would be able to control myself, to maintain my silence. I pushed the door open just wide enough so I could crouch, almost kneeling, on the tile floor, staring ahead at the shower doors. The vision before me had little to do with the lurid images my father had intimated Lewis and I would see. This was nothing at all like the French playing cards or even the *Playboy* magazines at our barber shop. Through the condensing steam and the pebbled glass of the sliding doors, my mother neither aroused nor daunted me. Blurred by glass and mist, her body was more landscape than sex, she was inexact and peach, a fuzzy-edged form, a calming apparition of warmth and moisture.

Despite the prickly interchanges that often preceded her evening showers, my mother seemed remarkably at peace here, in this cabinet of cleansing indoor rain. She moved her arms slowly, turning her body gently into the water and humming off-key.

The song was "The Twelfth of Never." My parents had the Johnny Mathis version on one of their few record albums. They called it "our song." They'd danced to it at their wedding. On Sunday afternoons, when they completed the weekend's jigsaw puzzle, they would turn on the little brown phonograph in the den and sweep around the room to their tune.

"The Twelfth of Never" was a mystery to me. It told of a love that would last until a date that didn't exist. Did this mean the entire romance was somehow nonexistent? All the exactitude of my parents' puzzle building seemed compromised by the vagary of the tune they used to celebrate it.

I left my mother lathering her hair and found my way back to bed without turning on the light. I got up again to stare at Lew for a moment through the darkness, trying to understand why we'd tortured Flappy. I can't imagine how my father suspected we would feel after spying on Mom, but I felt no guilt at all. I felt as clean as if I'd been showered myself. Outside, the rain tapered to a drizzle.

Moments later, still standing over my brother, I peered out the crack in our door to see Mom emerge from the bathroom in her robe, still humming, her head wrapped in a towel turban. I heard their own bedroom door swing open then and my father step down the hall to meet her.

"I thought I heard something wonderful." He smiled gently, then took the bottles and jars from her arms, placing them in the roomy pockets of his own dark green robe. "Are you still mad at me?"

"Harris, I don't always understand you. And, yes, every time I take another shower in the kids' bathroom, I get a little bit mad at you. But I'm also mad about you, honey. I know you mean well for all of us, even if you don't always know how to express it. But everything will work out, I think. I'm still singing our song."

Then they danced, down the hall, into bed.

~

One December night, Dad was working late. Mom let Lew and me bundle up in the blankets and pillows of their big bed. She sat on the love seat writing season's greetings cards, looking up at us from time to time to smile as we cheered on the Claymation TV villains, Snow Miser and Heat Miser, as they threatened to put an end to Christmas.

Ours was one of the few houses in the neighborhood not spangled with tiny colored lights. Most of our schoolmates—even the other nominally Jewish kids—celebrated Christmas, but Lew and I were more than satisfied with Hanukkah's eight nights of gifts. Our parents favored blocks, balls, books, and board games over the heavily advertised and highly breakable Christmas booty our friends received. Returning from Saturday outings to the bowling alley or a matinee on those dark December afternoons, I took strange pride in driving down our neighborhood's sparkling streets, the windows decorated with candy canes and cut-out cardboard snowmen. I delighted in our difference. Ours was the house unstrung with twinkling bulbs. We had shadows beneath our eaves.

My parents had never been practicing Jews, but they objected to the hackneyed commercialism of Christmas. Less vaunted and thus less pre-conceived, Hanukkah was an improviser's delight. One year, Mom served "the traditional Hanukkah cheese fondue." Another time, Dad took us all on "the traditional Hanukkah tour of the U.S. Mint." One particularly memorable December, the first night of Hanukkah was ushered in not just with the truly traditional menorah of candles, but with Valentino and Nureyev, "the traditional red-nosed Hanukkah turtles."

Val and Nury were the only pets of our childhood, silver-dollar sized creatures who lived in a shallow acrylic lagoon, complete with a tiny plastic palm tree. Dad had picked them up at a nearby pet shop and Mom had graced each turtle's face with a cherry dot of Maybelline nail polish. Every day, when we got home from school, Lew would demonstrate how much he loved little Val by placing the turtle in a Dixie Riddle Cup, then filling the cup with water and drinking the water out over his amphibian pal.

It was barely a month after Hanukkah's end when, one afternoon, we found Val and Nury bobbing motionless in the basin of their lagoon.

"I think they're dead," I said.

"Are not," Lew insisted, prodding them onto the ramp that led up to their palm tree with a trembling forefinger. They slid back into the water. Nury listed onto his back.

"Joshy," Lew's voice broke, "it's not fair."

I had rarely seen my brother so openly tender.

"I love them," he whined. "Even if they're dead, I still love them."

"Guess you'll be skipping your special beverage today, huh?"

"Stop making fun of me!" Lew ran to our room, crying hard.

Our mother had been standing in the den, looking on. Having noted the turtles' passing earlier in the day, she'd wanted to give us a moment alone with them. Now she stepped in and laid a hand on my shoulder.

"That wasn't very nice, Josh. Let's go make sure Lew's OK."

He was lying on his bed, staring at the ceiling.

"I'm sorry, Lew," I blurted, frantic to have him accept my apology. "I didn't mean to tease. It just came out. I'm sad, too."

"Dead, dead, dead. What is the point of anything if it's going to end up dead?"

"Remember what you said downstairs. How you still love them even it they're dead."

"Lew, honey," Mom stepped in. "You have to remember the good things. All the fun you had with the turtles. That doesn't go away. You can keep it in your memory forever."

He squinted his eyes in concentration.

"In school, we had to tell about our fathers. And I only remembered the good things."

"Sweetie, we're talking about the turtles."

"Michael Boyd had fish," I offered. "And when they died, he flushed them down the toilet."

"Can I?!" Lew was suddenly enthusiastic. "Mom, can I flush them down the toilet?"

Furrowing her brow in puzzlement at Lew's sudden mood swing, she consented to his request with a shrug.

I trumpeted taps through pursed lips. Lew laughed and pushed down the silver handle. Valentino and Nureyev raced in circles, headed down to turtle eternity.

~

The year I was ten, my parents exchanged no Hanukkah presents. Their big gift to each other would be a new house.

For the past six months, we had all spent several hours each weekend exploring homes that were up for sale.

"Dad, do they take the basketball pole with them? Or does it stay here?" Lew asked.

"It stays, pal. It's stuck into the cement."

"All right! I vote for this house."

While my parents examined kitchens and gutters and master suites, I felt the guilty thrill of wandering through other children's rooms, half-convincing myself that the rules of privacy that applied in our house had no relevance in these strangers' places.

One boy with Phillies and Eagles posters on his walls had babyish Spiderman Underoos in his dresser drawer. Another had a sprawling electric train set that practically covered his bedroom floor. A teenage girl in one house had an oval woodburned sign on her door: "Missy's Pad." Inside, she had pink shag carpet and black-light posters of unicorns and elves like they sold at Spencer Gifts in the mall. I shut myself inside and flipped on the special lamp to see the posters' violet glow. I snarled in Missy's mirror to see my bright purple teeth. Cool. Satan.

In one house, I had to go to the bathroom. I went in the parents' room. In a basket next to the toilet were some magazines, *Playboys*. I knew I couldn't sit in there too long, but I flipped through as quickly as I could, examining Miss May and the month's two other naked ladies. I thought it was funny how, in addition to lounging around on silky pillows, the bunnies talked on the phone, typed, and arranged flowers without any clothes on. I supposed these were the kind of ladies that Grandpop Josh had met on his sales trips, the sorts who worked for bars and bought his swizzle sticks.

I flipped away from the naked women and settled on a fashion spread, "For the Debonair Playboy." Men leaned against sports cars in ties and dress shirts, shiny shoes and suspenders. Then, when I turned the page, they were sprawled across the hoods in tiny striped and polka-dotted underpants. After seeing my father in only the drabbest of briefs and boxers, I was startled to see these handsome models wearing Underoos for grown-ups. So was the kid with the sports posters still babyish? Shoving my erection down between my legs to force out the last bit of pee, I quickly zipped up and flushed. I ran to find my family.

I grew sick of wondering if we would move into one of these houses. Sick of wondering if everything would change. Our parents had told us that Lew and I would have our own rooms in the new house. This was supposed to excite us, but, despite the recent strain in our relationship, I felt reluctant to be split from my brother.

One Sunday afternoon, as we left Ricklin's Hardware with a bag full of screws and spackle, my father said he wanted to show me the newest contender. It looked like a mansion to me. Not like any of the other houses we'd visited. No aluminum siding or tar paper shingles. A big stone home set back on a deep green lawn. There was a small stained glass window in the front door. Twin plaster lions flanked the stoop. On television, I'd seen houses like this one only by night: The wind would whistle in the trees, clouds would roll by the moon, and then, inside, a grandfather clock would strike; a phantom would glide down a hallway; a sheerly clad beauty would bolt up in bed, convinced there were prowlers about.

"Dad, is the real estate agent meeting us out here or inside?"

"Neither, Joshy. We're just taking a look for ourselves. There's not even a sign up yet, see? I just noticed the listing in the paper this morning."

Huge trees arched above us in a cloak. There was just a curb, no sidewalk between us and the lawn. As my father took me by the wrist, tugging me onto this half-acre of green, I felt like a trespasser. I imagined a crooked-toothed Southern groundskeeper in a high window, firing buckshot at my buttocks and shouting, "Git off our propuhty!"

"Dad, we're not allowed to go walking around here. It's private."

"Don't worry!" He was quick to brush off the rules he so stridently enforced when Lewis and I went into each others' drawers. "Look at the size of this lawn. It's practically a park."

"It isn't a park, though, Dad. And we're not supposed to be here."

"Cut out the whining," he said sharply, before drawing a breath and adopting a gentler tone. "When I was a boy," my father swept his arm about us, "this was where the rich people lived."

"Grandpop's cousin Sammy, who owned the restaurant supply business, lived here with his wife, June. They had Ping-Pong and a pool table and the linoleum on the basement floor had a shuffleboard court printed on the tiles. How about that?"

On and on he went in bitter-edged reminiscence. Despite an occasional downward glance, I don't think he was even talking to me anymore. It was as if some trapped door inside of him had popped open, letting a gust of long-dormant thoughts come whirling out.

"Thing is, Sammy and June and their girls lived on the same street of row houses as us until I was your age. Then boom! They're in the big house. Now, your Grandpop, he said he was robbed. Grandmom told him to take it easy, wait it out, and he'd get what was coming to him. But there was nothing coming. And when he realized he'd never get his own big house, he stayed out on the road more and more. Your grandfather was always away, you know. Never had any time for me. I hope you boys appreciate all the attention I give you."

Dad stared longingly at the heavy oak door, leaning down and petting one of the plaster lions.

"This place is great, isn't it? It's part of my past, Joshy. Maybe part of our future, too, huh?"

"C'mon, Dad," I pleaded. "Can we go home already?"

~

That spring, like each one before it, our parents took us to the Philadelphia Zoo. Like every family, we saw ourselves in the monkey house. Adults hunched over young ones, sweetly but sternly protecting them from danger. The animals picked and poked at one another, shrieking and slapping. Some swung wildly about their cages, greedy for whatever sense of freedom they could find within their barred parameters. Others sat sullenly in the corners.

"Hey, fellas," Dad pulled us aside and whispered. "Get a load of that gorilla's penis!"

"Big as his banana!" I snorted.

My mother shook her head and made eyes at my father.

"Do people really come from gorillas?" Lew asked.

"Think about Dad." I replied, drawing an ugly stare from him. "I only meant how your body's all hairy, Dad," I explained with a shrug of feigned innocence.

Winding along paths lined with giraffes, peacocks, penguins, and camels, I frequently lost focus on the intended attractions and turned my attention to the hundreds of pigeons that made the zoo their home. As they stumbled along singly or bunched in dithering clusters to peck at litter, I saw the color in the pigeons' wan gray feathers; iridescent green and purple necklaces that threw vaporous light, surrounding the birds with an aura of lilac and jade. I smiled to their gulping pigeon music, explaining to myself that they swallowed their songs, not yet ready to unleash strange and challenging melodies on the simpler creatures that surrounded them.

On Saturday mornings, Lew and I watched the cartoon perils of a pink-clad aviatrix named Penelope Pitstop, constantly pursued by a snaggletoothed hound named Muttley and his evil master, the wax-mustachioed lothario, Dick Dastardly. Buzzing through the sky in his WWII prop plane, there was only one thing more important to dastardly Dick than his cravings for Penelope: a secret message, held tight in the talons of a heroic but speechless carrier pigeon. Each week's program opened with a turbo-charged instrumental theme song, climaxed by Dick's five-alarm, top-of-lung holler: "Stop that pigeon now!"

"C'mon, Joshua," Mom called out, catching up with me as I strayed a few yards down the path, following the birds. "Stick with the rest of us."

"Sorry, Mom," I said, offering no complaints or resistance. There was no use trying to explain. I packed up my mental dovecote for the moment.

"Joshy, you are so weird sometimes," she said, shaking her head. "All the animals in the world and you zero in on those filthy winged rats?"

"That's mean, Mom." Lew zoomed to my defense. "Josh can like pigeons. Alex, in my class, his family has Uncle Waldo's Ant Farm. That's what they keep for a pet: ants!"

"Hey, boys," Dad suggested. "How'd you like to keep your Aunt Binnie for a pet?"

Lew laughed, first at the pun, then at Dad's notion of poochifying our mother's glamorous, emotionally distant older sister.

"We could put her on a leash, make her crawl around on all fours. Give her some big old bones to chew on . . . "

"Harris!"

"Dad! Dad!" I entered the fray. "Instead of dog fur, she could wear her mink coats around the house!"

Then I noticed my mother's face, gone jagged with anger and isolation. Invited into our father's joke, Lewis and I had ganged up with him, leaving her alone, outside our family. I caught my brother's eye.

"I didn't really mean it, Ma." Lew grabbed hold of her wrist. "I was just joking."

"Me too, Ma. Aunt Binnie's OK. She sends us really good presents."

"And what about you, Harris?" she asked, jutting her head toward him, now protectively flanked by two of her boys. "As these guys are so quick to say when they get in trouble together: 'You started it.'"

"Sahwwy, Mommy. I'm a bad wittle boy."

His delivery was wicked. Nobody laughed. I wasn't sure whether Dad was making more fun of Lew and me, or Mom.

"Come on, guys," Mom said. "Let's go to the Children's Zoo."

"No way!" objected Dad. "That's for babies!"

"Harris, the Children's Zoo is for children. That's what these smaller members of your men's club are, if you'll recall."

Lew and I zipped down the elephant trunk sliding boards into the barnyard-styled petting corral where chickens ricketed underfoot and dingy sheep dominated the landscape. We jumped back, laughing, when they bleated at our touch, then we sauntered over to the adult-lined fence and imitated their whine of complaint to our parents.

"Awww," exclaimed Dad, oversweetening his voice. "My little sheepies."

"I think they're the shepherds, honey," corrected Mom.

"We're centaurs!" compromised Lew, a big fan of the Hercules cartoon.

"Well, whatever you beasties are, I want to get some good shots, so go back there and mingle amongst your kind. Good, good guys . . . Right . . . each of you stand there beside one and I can keep the four of you in one frame. One, two, let's see a smile now, one big happy flock!"

"Now guys, walk behind them. OK. OK. Good, good. Now lean forward and reach your arms as close to the heads as you can. Good, just reach up and set your hands down on their shoulders. Good. OK— now. Keep your hands there. Now step right up to their tushes."

"Harris! Are you sick?"

"Shhh, shhh!" Dad was laughing. "Look up at me and flap your tongues out guys. Like you're panting. All right, here we go: One, two, uhh, uhhh, aaaaaah!"

We laughed at Dad's groans and funny faces, not sure why Mom had sat down on a bench a few yards away, looking away from us toward Noah's Ark, shaking her head in silence.

The chiming of a carillon signaled our exit from the petting pen and the start of the nature show. In a small amphitheater, Lewis and I reached out to touch the skin of a live boa constrictor, saw a baby chimpanzee drink from a bottle, and learned about the dangers of raccoons with rabies in some Philadelphia suburbs.

"Not where we live," Mom whispered when Lew glanced at her nervously.

It wasn't the raccoon that made me skittish but the crow. Jenny the Zoo Lady reached into her draped wooden box with a three-foot pole, then withdrew it, mounted by the screeching creature. She called it a mynah bird, but it was crow enough for me. It looked just like the ebony-drenched pallbearers that lined up along the telephone wires on my walk home from school most days, staring down at me and calling out their dreadful premonitions. I imagined their talons pulling conversations out of the wires, then reducing them to the absolute blackest secrets. "Caaaaaw! Caaaaaw!" They would scream, broadcasting intimate privacies.

The previous November, Lewis had taken a long strip of brown construction paper and, at one inch intervals, used Scotch tape to attach crow feathers he'd found on neighborhood lawns. He taped the strip closed in a circle to make a headband.

"Look, Josh," he'd explained to me. "I can wear it like an Indian at Thanksgiving so the holiday will be more real. Usually Mom only invites white people."

From the moment he showed me his project, my mouth went dry, and I felt sweat beading on my forehead.

"Couldn't we make feathers out of different colored paper, Lew? So it would look brighter and more like a holiday?"

"I thought of that, but I like using real feathers. It's more Indianish this way."

"Lew, can I tell you something secret? Promise not to tell? Promise?"

"What is it?"

"I'm scared of those feathers. I feel sick around them."

"Why?"

"I don't know. Please don't think I'm dumb." Suddenly tears burned down my face. "I just hate them. I hate them, I hate them."

"Joshy, please don't cry. Come on, let's start cutting paper, OK? You can make one too. You can be an Indian, too."

"Raaaaaaaaack! Raaaaaaack!" The mynah bird cried at the Children's Zoo.

The mynah, the crows, that raven Mr. Dibbins read about in Halloween assembly, crying "Nevermore"; they were so frighteningly forward in their darkness, so direct in their speech that I couldn't bear them. I had come to believe in a world where indirection ruled, where meanings were pieced together subtly, always wavering, nothing ever confirmed as definite or true.

"Dr. Jekyll here sometimes mimics human speech, but usually he just makes bird sounds. He comes from Southeast Asia," said Jenny.

"Raaaaaaaaack! Raaaaaaack!"

I glanced at my parents, my brother, and the other families all around us, calmly watching and listening to Jenny and the bird. My stomach heaved and my forehead grew clammy as it occurred to me, more strongly than ever before, that maybe nothing was wrong with the world and everything wrong with me.

Just the night before, as they were putting together a scene from *The Wizard of Oz,* I had asked my parents whether they thought that if the same company made two puzzles with the same number of pieces, they might use the same jigsaw pattern. Was there a piece in this puzzle of a crash-landing house that was an exact match for a piece of the merry-go-round they'd built the week earlier?

"That would mean," I suggested, thrilling at the prospect, "that you could actually use some pieces from each box to put together a perfect rectangular puzzle with a completely mixed-up picture."

"Where in the world . . . ?" My mother looked at me like I was a man from Mars. "Joshy, you think too much!"

Jenny walked up the aisle of the amphitheater extending her pole, so everyone could get a good, close-up look at the bird. Lew stood to get a better view. I turned my head in the other direction.

"Honey," Mom said, tapping me on my shoulder. "Don't you want to see Dr. Jekyll?"

I turned for just a moment and the bird caught my eye dead on, two cold, truth-telling beads above a piercing yellow beak. Dr. Jekyll spread his wings malevolently, glared at me, and cawed.

"Hell-o! Hell-o!"

The audience laughed and laughed.

~

I was sitting alone at a small round table in the school lunchroom when Lew approached me.

"Tell Mom I'm going to Donny's after school, OK?"

"OK," I muttered.

"Why don't you come over to the Goodmans', too?" Lew coaxed. "Donny and Robby got a new Creepy Crawler set. You can make your own monsters."

"You know I'm not going over there."

"For how long, Joshy? Robby's your best friend."

"He has to apologize for this whole thing. Until then, I'm still on strike."

In honor of my lack of coordination in gym class, Robby had recently christened me with a nickname, Weeping Flower. Somehow, I had managed to tolerate this. But it turned out that Robby had taken things to a higher level.

A week earlier, as Robby and I sprawled on the Goodmans' living room floor one afternoon playing Ker-Plunk! and watching *Ultra Man,* his father, Uncle Howard, came home early from work. Like the fathers of many of the children Lew and I socialized with, Howard Goodman was another lawyer who worked with my dad. Uncle Howard, Uncle Jerry, Uncle Alan, Uncle Ben, and all the rest had known one another at least since law school—some from as far back as grade school. Virtually all of the adults I knew were linked in this network, tied to one another by a collective Philadelphia past. Dad called the men from the office his partners, just as I'd heard him refer to Mom as his partner. Whenever I ran errands with my parents, it seemed like someone they knew came up to say hello every five seconds. There seemed little choice but to try and fit in.

Howard Goodman came home from work that afternoon calling, "Hiya, honey!" to Aunt Betty upstairs. He chatted with Donny, who had been playing with his Lite-Brite set on the kitchen table. Then he wandered into the living room where he spotted me splayed on the carpet with Robby.

"Hey, hey!" said Uncle Howard. "It's the Weeper! How's tricks, Joshua?"

The Weeper? It was like being smacked with a plank. Robby had told his father about Weeping Flower. Which, in turn, suggested that my father now knew that my whole school considered me a pussy. And so did the father of every family we knew.

"Hello, Uncle Howard," I said curtly, standing up. "I'm going home now."

"C'mon," complained Robby. "You've gotta finish the game."

"I do not. The only thing I have to finish is being your friend. I'm on strike. I'm on a friendship strike." I grabbed my schoolbag and slammed out the kitchen door.

Two weeks later, despite the fact that the name-calling had slowly died down, I held my ground. Robby had to apologize or I wasn't talking to him. This meant that I was eating my lunches alone, my usual table mates continuing to sit as a group, Robby heading up the banter and gross-out jokes about the cafeteria food. Lew invited me to sit with him and Donny and their third-grade friends, but I knew how that would look. The Royalton brothers: Lew and Loser.

I was an outcast, but I had participated in the casting out. Proud to be the odd and brainy stranger among my peers, I was, at the same time, ashamed of the weakling status that accompanied the identity I'd claimed for myself. Unlike Lew, who had begun anticipating the likes of scouting and Little League, I had little interest in being a child anymore. I wanted to read grown-up books, eat grown-up foods, and have grown-up conversations. But the children and the adults I knew were all bound together in the trickiest of knots. To be cut off from the school yard was to be severed from the entire world. A constant stream of strange ideas bubbled up and soaked through my head. I was no kid, no adult. I could not identify myself. I was angry, sad, and, somehow, exuberant.

"You don't want me?" I longed to scream at them all. "Well, I don't belong to you anyway. I am an alien on your planet!"

Nonetheless, I encouraged my brother to belong. I told Lew he should go play Creepy Crawlers at the Goodmans' without me. I walked with him as far as the 7-Eleven that day, then headed home for another sequestered afternoon of reading and radio and staring out the window.

I heard the first crow's call as my brother and I turned off in opposite directions. The closer I got to home, the louder the screeching grew. It seemed there were hundreds, thousands, beating their wings to darken the sky—animals and weather all at once.

"Caaaaaw! Caaaaaw!"

They were crowding the wires, lined up in dark regiments. My insides churned; my skin shivered with sweat. I rushed onto our block, huffing and puffing, only to find that the surface of the earth had changed. All the way to our house, the lawns and sidewalks were plated in black sheen, a caul of feathers everywhere. The crows screamed above my head, gleamed below my feet, and left nowhere to run but home. I put fingers in my ears, squinted my eyes shut, and tore through their wicked music, across their disembodied parts.

I pounded at the kitchen door and my mother came, trailing six feet of curly yellow phone cord. Receiver still to her ear, she gave me the "Shhhh" sign as I collapsed, ashen, into a chair at the kitchen table.

My mother hung up the phone and stood for a moment facing the wall. Her face was pink and mascara-smeared when she turned to me.

"Oh, sweetie," she said, lips trembling. "I have really sad news."

Goddamn crows made my mother cry.

"Honey," she cupped my cheeks in her hands. "Grandpop Josh died today."

Mom called Aunt Betty to send Lew home. "Don't tell him what's happened; just hurry him along."

The phone rang and rang. Dad's partners at the office had all heard the news, now their wives were calling to console my mother.

"Only sixty-four. So young," my mother lamented to Aunt Cookie, Aunt Barbara, Aunt Estelle, Aunt Ruth. "No, not that I can think of right now. I'll let you know if there's anything you can do. Thank you. Thank you." She dabbed her eyes with a paper towel from the roll above the sink.

Every time Mom rested the receiver in its cradle, it rang again. Our yellow kitchen telephone had become death's hotline. Aunt Myrna, Aunt Elaine, Aunt Liz. Then my real aunt called—Aunt Binnie, Mom's older sister, to whom I was bound by blood, not business.

"Oh, Binnie," Mom cried, "I can't even remember what I felt like when Daddy died. Since I met Harris when I was thirteen years old, I've thought of Joshua as my father. And now he's gone, too . . . "

Mom's voice became a series of gulps, then a wracking sob, aching for the lost fathers. Unable to listen, unable to help, I stepped out of the room and sat at the foot of the stairs. Again, the phone rang.

"Joshy! It's for you."

"Hello?"

"I'm sorry, Josh." It was Robby.

"You mean you're not going to tease me anymore?"

"What?"

"You know," I turned away from my mother and dropped my voice to a whisper. "Weeping Flower."

"I meant I'm sorry that your Grandpop died."

While embarrassed at my selfish miscomprehension, I still seized on the opportunity at hand.

"Well, Weeping Flower died today, too, okay? So don't ever bring him up again unless you want Grandpop Josh's ghost to come haunt you! I have his name, you know. He looks out for me!"

I started to cry.

"Hey, Joshy. Josh. Don't cry, OK? I know what it's like. My Grandmom Rose died last year. Ma says she got Gram's secret recipe for blueberry pancakes, but it isn't really right. They don't taste the same. They've never tasted the same."

"Robby!" I heard Aunt Betty trying to shush him. "That's not going to make him feel any better."

"Hang on a second," Rob told me, setting the phone down on the table. "It's true, Mom! What? Do you want me to lie? Grandmom Rose is gone and now Josh's Grandpop had to die, too. I hate it. It sucks!"

"I've told you not to use that word in this house!"

"Suck! Suck! Suck! Your pancakes suck, too, Ma!"

Robby picked back up. "Josh, I gotta go. Don't cry too much, man."

I ran to the bedroom. A few minutes later, Lewis pounded up the stairs. He dove onto my bed and we grappled with each other, weeping and wrestling, pressing into the soft bulk of our pillows. I let my brother jam me hard against the mattress, boring his shoulder into my chest, wondering just how much I could take. Then, accidentally, he pushed me off the bed. I fell in slow motion, as in a dream, falling the height of my brother, myself, my father and grandfather, each standing on his elder's shoulders, a tower as tall as the house we lived in. My head hit the floor with a loud but painless crack. I wondered what it would be like to die.

I thought of how I'd messed up the bellyfights, how I'd spit in my father's face, how I was so bad at sports that Dad had to deal with the embarrassment of his partners at the office all calling me Weeping Flower. I thought of Mom's scared faces when I mixed with my pigeon friends and her constant worried pleas for me to try to be more sociable with the neighborhood kids and not spend so much time alone in my room. Who would want to raise a child like me?

"I don't think," I told Lewis, "that I really want any kids."

Our conversation was cut short by the familiar sound of the car pulling into the driveway. "Daddy's home," I whispered to Lew and, instead of our usual thunderous run, we crept quietly to the kitchen, turning to stare at each other every few steps. Mom and Dad were wrapped tightly around each other, humid air blowing in through the still open door. Tears from one's eyes ran down the other's cheeks as they pressed themselves into each other.

"Oh, Harris," she cried. "Poor Dad."

"It's gonna be OK, sweetie," my father sobbed back. "Everything's gonna be OK, Becca girl."

Lew and I inched toward them, still unnoticed. "What do I say?" I had asked my mother earlier. "What should I say to him?"

"Oh, Joshy, don't worry," she'd smiled under cried-out eyes. "Say whatever you feel inside."

"Sorry, Dad," I began to mumble. But nothing needed to be said. Lew and I were suddenly tangled up in their arms, crying along, all four of us Royaltons together, in a wet, aching dance on the lemon-scented linoleum. Hands and shoulders and sniffling noses, we circled round a common hollow. For a piercing moment, before the twinge of guilt arrived, I wasn't really sorry at all. I was as content as I'd been in months. Everything seemed to have shifted. I was happy in the face of death.

Late that night, we flew to Miami. Out the airplane window, wraith-like clouds floated above the tiny lights of earth. My father opened his briefcase, his face quickly changing from sorrowful to serious. He began shuffling through Grandpop's paperwork on his tray table, punching numbers into a calculator and taking notes. Dad had been Grandpop's lawyer. He did his investments, his insurance, and, I realized then, his will. Dad was in charge of whatever finances I had, too. He and Mom put something away for Lewis and I each year on our birthdays, but I never asked how much, never wondered how it might be invested. I happily took my two dollars allowance each week to buy Slim Jims and Wacky Packs and left the rest to Dad. My father took care of everyone.

Lew drowsed beside me, Flappy at rest in his lap. Mom was on her second tissue packet of the flight. She wanted Dad to talk to her. She could not switch off her grief and become a model of efficiency.

"I keep thinking," she said, "That Dad probably couldn't have chosen a way he'd better like to go."

Grandpop had been at the dog track with some other men from his condominium when a fistful of heart attack took him in a quick minute.

"Oh, yeah," my father muttered, half-smiling, but shaking his head from side to side. "Out gallivanting as usual. Never at home with the wife and kid."

"Harris," Mom said, gently pulling him out of his time warp. "There hasn't been any kid at Josh and Sara's for fifteen years now. And you know how your mother lords over their apartment. Thank goodness he was out with his buddies."

"I guess so. That's good, honey. Listen, just let me go over these papers for a bit, OK? I want to have everything in order to explain to Mom."

My mother blew her nose.

Glancing nervously at Dad as he worked, I tried a few calculations of my own. He was thirty-five and his father was dead. I was ten. Would I be ready for my father to die twenty-five years from now? I knew thirty-five was supposed to be grown-up, but it seemed to me that I would always be a kid, Mom and Dad watching over me. I couldn't imagine being thirty-five, as old as my father. It would be the twenty-first century. We would all be talking on picture phones and flying around with jet packs. Maybe people wouldn't die anymore.

But if people kept on dying, my secret wish was to go before my father. When he died, all the world would be thrown into chaos. I didn't want to see it. And my own death would allow me—with my weak body and my strange thoughts—to get an early escape from his stares, his grip, his questions. Perhaps I would get to spend more time with my grandfather when I died. Strong and loud and logical, my father was surely built to outlast me. He would survive as a tent pole, standing in the center spot; on each side of him, a useless drape of canvas where once a Joshua Royalton had stood.

Lewis and I had never visited our grandparents' high-rise condominium in Miami before. We fell asleep almost immediately in the guest room. When I woke the next morning, Lew was still sleeping.

Through venetian blinds, sunlight striped him like a tiger. I patted my hair down in the full length mirror, then opened the door it hung on, thinking I was headed to join my parents and Gram in the living room. As I pulled the door open, a light clicked on automatically. This was not the living room. It was my grandfather's treasure room from Philadelphia, transferred in its entirety to a slightly larger closet. It was the cave of wonders.

I didn't want to invade Grandpop Josh's privacy, but in the wake of his death, I felt a sense of invitation. I imagined him there with me, pointing out the highlights as I dug into cigar boxes full of exotic coins, sifted through piles of matchbooks, admired volumes of *National Geographic* photographs from around the world. In the lower drawer of a file cabinet, I found a small pile of *Playboy* magazines along with a huge slip-cased volume, *My Secret Life.*

"A long-buried Victorian classic," it said on the cover. I scanned a random paragraph, finding the words "buttocks" and "cock." My head buzzed with all the places I could go, all the things I could do. On one wall, smiling over the room's whole cache was a gilt-framed print of the famous movie star Marilyn Monroe laid out completely nude in a sea of rumpled red satin sheets. Stretched out so comfortably, looking up at me with bright, glassy eyes, she reminded me of another photograph I'd often felt compelled to examine. My parents had a book called *The Best of LIFE.* It was a collection of photographs from a magazine that had gone out of business. Over and over, I'd returned to that book to look at one stunning black and white shot. A tall, beautiful woman wearing a long, autumn coat laid on her back, staring up and smiling in oddly composed contentment. Instead of rumpled satin, she rested on crumpled metal. She had leapt from the observation deck of the Empire State Building, landing on the roof of a parked car.

"Hey, Josh," Lew had risen from his bed and wandered over to the half-opened closet door. "What's in there?"

Instinctively, I kicked shut the drawer full of *Playboy*s, then swung the door wide open. "Check it out!"

"Whoa! Boobies!" he exclaimed, his reaction to Marilyn swift and simple. "Has Mom seen this?"

"Who cares about boobs, Lew? Look at this stuff. Stamps, coins. It's like buried treasure." But it wasn't buried. It was escape and ad-

venture and Grandpop Josh, zestfully present, just two days before
we would watch his body lowered into the ground.

"Well what's the big deal? It's the same old junk room Grandpop
had in Philadelphia. He just moved it down here with him."

"Don't call it junk," I insisted.

"Grandmom calls it junk. Dad calls it junk. Last night, I saw the
dining room out there—it's the same stuff from their old house where
Dad grew up. Grandmom was even having her same old bad breath
drink, you know, with the little white onions floating around in it.

"I thought when old people moved to Florida, they got to live different, have fun all the time. I thought there would be little cabins
around a swimming pool and everyone would wear sunglasses and
bathing suits and eat oranges all day. I thought Grandmom would be
drinking out of a coconut, like on *Gilligan*."

"Well, maybe it's a bit more like that on regular days," I offered,
weakly. "It's a funeral now, remember."

Still, to me, little was lost. I was sunshine drunk in my grandfather's tiny museum; his closetful of secret life. Each matchbook
could be read as an adventure story. Each swizzle stick would stir up
memories. Exotic stamps were for urgent letters yet to be written and
every coin was a penny for your thoughts.

"My thoughts," I thought. Mine, because Grandmom called them
junk. Dad called them junk. Even Lewis, my own brother, had
learned to call them junk. I started to cry.

"It's all right to be upset," Lew said, putting a hand on my shoulder.
"Is it sadder, Josh? Is it sadder when you have the same name as the
one who died?"

~

Dozens of friends and relatives milled around the apartment over
the next three days. There was Cousin Abe Levitsky, who once
bought his kids a Shetland pony that ended up eating the carpets off
the floors. Great-Uncle Mush tried to amuse Lew and me by redefin-
ing his chief talent—"I'm not farting, I'm burping out my tushy!"
Tipsy Great-Aunt Rip bickered with Gram Sara over the last of the
sweet vermouth, and neighbors upon neighbors from up and down
the halls of the apartment building dropped in, more interested in the
platters of chopped liver and cold cuts than in offering solace to my

grandmother. When a fat delivery man came from the deli, Grandmom insisted he sit down and have a drink with her in the kitchen.

"We'll have to go dancing sometime, now, Mort. You can hardly turn down a lonely widow."

Telephone pressed to his ear, my father weaved absently through the mourners, as if tethered to some other world by the phone cord. He would pleasantly greet some long-forgotten relative, then dial another call, taking notes on a little pad as he talked, occasionally eyeballing Lew and I across the busy room, winking and giving us the thumbs-up as if to say, "We'll be out of here soon, fellas."

"C'mere a minute, guys," said Dad's cousin Herbie, the slow one, waving us up to the buffet table. "Do you know what this is?"

He pointed to a pile of oval, reddish meat slices next to the potato salad.

"It's tongue! It's the cut-up tongue of a cow."

"No way!" cried Lew. Herbie laughed his stupid laugh.

"We grossed him out, little Joshua! Gimme five!" I held out my palm and he slapped a slice of tongue onto it. I felt myself gag and winced in repulsion.

"Don't drop it," laughed Herbie. "Hold your tongue, Josh! Ever hear that 'spression? Hold your tongue!"

"One more thing," said Herbie, peeling the meat from my palm, rolling in into a tube and popping the whole thing into his fat-lipped mouth. "Follow me."

He marched us down the hall and into the guest room where we'd been spending the nights. Then, Herbie reached for the door to my closet.

"Hey, who said you could go in there?" I blurted.

"Don't worry kid, it's OK. I been in here to see it a million times." He kicked open the door, pointed to the gilt-framed picture and then positioned himself, standing in profile, his face alongside the portrait.

"Yeah, so what?" crabbed Lew, who seemed as bugged by the guy as I was.

All of a sudden, Herbie unfurled a never-swallowed slice of cow tongue, letting it hang from his mouth as he made googly eyes and sloppy, wet lapping sounds at the naked Marilyn Monroe.

"Get out of here!" I shouted. But it was me who ran, leaving Herbie and Lewis laughing in the closet. I went out to the apartment's balcony and stared down at the eerie green swimming pool, water lapping at its edges, nine stories below.

I had assumed we would leave within a day or two of the funeral. But my father explained that he had business to settle for Grandmom. The week began to drag on, and I retreated to Grandpop's office, refusing to go swimming with Lew and Mom, and avoiding the living room, where Gram and Dad snapped at each other bitterly. There was a clock radio in Grandpop Josh's closet, and I turned up an oldies station to drown out their arguing.

Once, I turned around to find my father leaning in the door frame, watching me pile coins on the desk and silently moving his lips to the words of a novelty song.

"I'm a lonely boy," he mouthed along to the croaking voice of Clarence "Frogman" Henry on the radio. "I ain't got a home."

"Hey, Dad."

"Hey, Joshy. I remember this song. I was seventeen. Preparing for my college entrance exams. I was really nervous about getting a scholarship." He paused, suddenly flooded with long-forgotten detail. "Jesus. I remember. Your grandmother came into my room when I was studying one Saturday. Didn't knock or anything. She was carrying two martini glasses. Handed one to me. She'd already had a few in the kitchen. 'Get up, Harry,' she says. 'You're working too hard. Let's have a dance. You take out the trash every night, you look after the little kids in the neighborhood. Your father's never home, for chrissakes. You do everything around here. That makes you the man of the house. So have a drink, Harry, and give the lady of the house a whirl.'

"She just flopped forward into my arms then, dead weight. And I remember this song was on the radio. 'Frogman' Henry. He changes his voice from verse to verse, right? First he's a boy, then a girl, and finally he's a frog, all singing the same words. 'I'm a lonely guy. I ain't got no home.' I danced my mother out into the hallway, stepped back in my room and stood there with my back against the door. Swallowed that horrible martini in one gulp."

"Kind of like when you let me try your beer once?"

"Joshua!" he laughed. "Heaven forbid! Heaven forbid I ever twist you up like my parents did to me." Then looked down into my eyes and asked, terribly seriously, "You're OK, aren't you, pal? Are you having a happy childhood?"

"Duh, Dad," I squirmed, taken aback by his question. "Are you having a happy parenthood?"

"Well, I mean, things are sometimes . . . I just wanted to make sure . . . "

"I wish you didn't have to fight with Grandmom."

"Me too, honey. Me too."

The next afternoon, Lew and I stayed with Gram Sara while Mom and Dad went to an appointment at her bank.

"Would you like to play Go Fish?" I asked as she splashed another finger of gin into her glass.

"Why does he have to leave me like this?" she grumbled.

"Everyone has to die sometime," Lew stepped up beside her chair, sweetly repeating my parents' soothing words. "We should be glad he didn't have to be sick for a long time."

"Not your goddamn grandfather." She rattled her ice loudly, grimacing as she took a long gulp. "My son. Off he goes with her again. Just like his father. Running around and leaving me behind. Always acting so sweet, that Becca girl, goddamn it."

"What's she talking about, Joshy?" Lew whispered to me.

"Dunno. I think she's drunk. I hope they get back soon." I turned back to my grandmother. "So would you like to play, Gram? Fish? Or War?"

She made a harsh guttural sound, then stuck a liver-spotted finger into her glass, swirling around the liquid.

"Hey!" suggested Lew, brightly. "There are stirring sticks in Grandpop's closet!"

"Shut. Up." I said through gritted teeth, clamping a hand on his shoulder.

To my great relief, our parents walked through the door then, my mother carrying a bag from Burdine's department store.

"I brought you something, Mom." She handed a gift box to Gram, who opened it, warily, then lifted out a shiny blue scarf.

"Hermès, Mom. You always said you wanted one."

"So you're giving me what I want, Rebecca Micklin?" Gram Sara stood suddenly, her chair toppling backward as she shook a gnarled hand in my mother's direction. "Always so sweet, aren't you, Becca? So caring and generous?"

"Mom," my father tensed. "Would you please sit down and relax? Becca thought this might cheer you up a little, that's all."

"That's all, is it?" Gram's voice rose and splintered as her face pulled into a sour knot. Lew and I glanced at each other, stepping backward from the dining table.

"You're going to give me something now, Becca? You think getting a goddamn bolt of Parisian silk can make up for what's been taken from me?"

"Jesus, Mother. Bec's not trying to make up for Dad. She just thought—"

"Harris," Mom swallowed. "That's not what she's saying."

Mom rushed to Gram's side, reaching out to embrace her.

"Oh Sara, I feel terrible. Please don't feel that way. Harris is your son. You love him like I love my boys. Nothing can ever take that away from you, Sara. I never meant to—"

"For God's sake, Mother." Dad was angry, shocked.

"God has nothing to do with it!" the old woman snarled, whipping his face with the scarf. "Just you and your own holy father. Your holier-than-thou father."

"Please, Mom," he squirmed, catching Lew and I from the corner of his eye. "Calm down. You're embarrassing the boys."

"I'll calm down when I damn well please," she barked, reaching for her Gilbey's bottle.

And then, with a sharp, single cough, Gram Sara collapsed onto the dining room table. Mom dropped to the floor, weeping. Dad ran for the telephone. A whole generation of Royaltons had passed.

"Thank God!" said Lew as we plopped into molded plastic airport chairs four days after the second funeral. It was finally time to go home.

They let me keep a few favorite matchbooks, and I hid two *Playboys* at the bottom of my suitcase. Although he'd arranged for most of the apartment's contents to be sold, my father had surprisingly laid claim to the coin collection, shipping it home by UPS in a half dozen shoe boxes sealed up with electrical tape.

"You always said they were junk, Dad."

"Maybe, but I might be able to sell them for something."

"Dad! You're not supposed to sell them." These were the world's most valuable coins, Grandpop had once explained to me. You could spend them without ever giving them up. They could be used to play the jukebox of your own imagination.

"Well, don't worry about it now, Josh. I'm not going to have time to do anything with them for awhile. Guys, your Mom and I have some great news. Some happy news after all this."

"What?" asked Lew, excited.

I knew. Even before they said it, I knew.

"We finally bought a new house!" Mom cheered. "There's a big yard, a playroom right off of the kitchen, and a huge basement for you guys to play in. And you'll each have your own big room."

"Cool!" enthused Lew.

I forced a smile. This is what my Dad had been doing on the telephone amidst everyone else's grieving. He was scraping together the shattered bits of nest egg that Grandmom and Grandpop had left behind, trying to hatch a new life for the rest of us.

As we flew through the sky that night, I thought about the snails in my class terrarium, how they crawled around with their houses on their backs. I had asked Miss Loquasto why they left silver trails behind them when they moved.

"What's the point?" I'd asked. "They never need to find their way back, do they? Everything is with them, wherever they go."

"We are now beginning our descent," announced the pilot's voice over the loudspeaker. Out the window, I saw tens of thousands of houses, each an identical dot of light.

~

My parents gave us a tour of our new house. It was the one my father had wanted most. The one with the plaster lions by the front door. The one I'd imagined was haunted.

My bedroom, in the rear left corner of the house, was as far as possible from my parents', diagonally opposite. Through windows on two sides of my room, I looked into the boughs of an enormous oak tree, squirrels leaping from limb to limb. The tree seemed to hold my room aloft even more than the house's walls did.

In the floor of the linen closet outside my room, there was a hinged wooden flap covering a narrow three-foot chute. Each night, Lew and I would drop our dirty clothes in and they'd tumble downstairs.

"Bombs away!" we'd yell. "Sweat socks away!"

There was another door—with a latch to keep the dirty laundry from spilling out—on the end of the chute downstairs, next to the washer and dryer in the playroom.

I had my own blue-tiled bathroom, halfway down the long hall, directly across from Lew's room. Lew had his own bath, like Mom and Dad's—right in his room. But something was wrong. There was a second door on the other side of Lew's bathroom. We pushed it open and found yet another bedroom, as big as Lew's and mine. It was right at the top of the stairway, closer to Mom and Dad than any other room in the house.

"A big guest room! This must be the White House," Lew marveled as we stepped inside. "Hey," he wondered, smiling up at me, "why can't Josh and I have these connecting rooms?"

I didn't say a word. Just days before, I would have seconded Lew's request in an instant. For the better part of a year, I'd been lamenting the separation our parents had promised us. But now, having seen the isolated place they'd assigned me, I craved it. I felt an urgent possessiveness. I would be a gyroscope in a box, spinning in private treetop delirium.

"Well," said Mom. "Dad and I have something to tell you. This isn't a guest room, guys. Somebody's coming to stay."

Dad stepped up behind her, reaching around to cross his arms beneath her breasts. "My steady girlfriend's going to have a baby."

Our father shone as if lit from within. Pressing his cheek against Mom's, he beamed as though something lost had been found. She gave him a peck on the forehead, amused, it seemed, by his adolescent zeal.

"Holy shit!"

"Lewis!" Mom hollered. "Watch your mouth."

"Yeah," I cracked. "The baby might hear."

"When, Mom, when? Is it a boy or a girl? What's its name? Can I teach it stuff?" Lew was a flurry of questions. "Whoa-ho! Sorry Joshy, guess I ended up with the best room in the house!"

"About six months." Dad patted Mom's belly. "We're not going to find out the sex until it's born."

Lewis giggled at the word sex.

"That's not a funny word, Lew. How do you think the baby was made?" This was typical of my father, taking advantage of even the slightest available context to parade the world of lovemaking before us. Since the time we were six and eight, we'd heard his discomforting routines, usually over dinner.

"You already told us this," we'd protest, as he swallowed another bit of meat loaf before launching into the latest lecture. While he did find room for educational details about birth control and reproduction, Dad was never abstract. He offered no seeds and eggs, no generic genitalia. My father taught no impersonal lessons.

"My penis gets all hard—it's called an erection—because your mother is so sexy looking and because she wants me so much," he would begin. "I slide my penis into Mommy's vagina. It feels really good to both of us. I get on top of her and push and push it. She grabs my butt and helps pull me inside her. After a while, it feels all tingly, full of pressure, like it's going to explode. And then, it happens. Like a big sex sneeze, the sperm shoots out of the hole in my penis. That feels the best. It's called coming. Oooh, baby!"

Standing in the new house, he told us again, with gnashing teeth, sound effects, and pelvic thrusts, holding tight to our mother and future sibling. Then he cast his eyes along the hallway of rooms, down the gently curving staircase to the harlequin stained glass in the front door.

"How did I get so lucky?" my father laughed with tears in his eyes. "How can we have all this?"

The next afternoon, sprawled on my new bed and lost in *The Hound of the Baskervilles,* I was startled by the sound of a pebble against the window. I jerked my head up to find Lewis crouched on a high limb of the oak tree. I opened the window and pleaded with him.

"Get down from there! It's dangerous!"

"It's easy," he said. "Come on out, I'll show you. Just a little higher and I can see the school roof."

In the backyard, Lew demonstrated how to grab on to a branch and pull up, but, strain as I did, I didn't have the strength to boost myself onto even the lowest limb. Frustrated at being weaker than my younger brother, I returned to the tree alone many afternoons, gradually hoisting myself into the lower branches, but too timid to make the risky maneuvers that would lend me the widest view.

~

My mother became fast friends with Ellen Cleyskil after they met at the PTA during our first September in the new neighborhood. Although their friendship struck me as unlikely at first, I was grateful for the window Ellen provided into an unkempt other world. The Cleyskils' house was a clamorous, ramshackle affair, teeming with artwork and oriental rugs, unpacked boxes of flea market finds, old books and newspapers and magazines in crazy teetering piles everywhere. The five Cleyskil kids, from Raphael, a year older than me, to three-year-old Ulana, noisily charged up and down the house's two mammoth, bare wood staircases at all hours of the day and night, a tribal procession of raven hair, ruddy cheeks, flannel, and tattered lace.

Ellen was a painter whose densely colored and darkly humorous canvases of barnyard animals and family members hung, big as billboards, in every alcove and hallway. Her kitchen was a place of rising yeast and delicious homemade improvisation: eggplant-macaroni-pumpernickel stew, served not at the sit-down family dinners so central to life in my own home, but in a sort of perpetual grab-and-go buffet.

Ellen's roly-poly husband, Alexander, the medical director of a small psychiatric hospital, was inexplicably nicknamed Frisbee. The first time I met him, Mom and I were lingering at the Cleyskils' house late one afternoon over homemade doughnuts and coffee.

I turned on my stool at the butcher block kitchen table as he walked into the room, stubble-faced and puffing a pipeful of cherry tobacco. I stood up from my chair, stepped toward him, and extended a hand as my father had taught me.

"Nice to meet you, Doctor Cleyskil. I'm Josh."

He squinted at me through his round wire rims.

"Well, it's nice to meet you, too, Joshua. Call me Frizz, though."

I glanced over at my mom, who simply gave me a shrug and a smile. So Frizz it was from then on, despite my father's persistence in referring to the Cleyskils as Uncle Alex and Aunt Ellen. Not that Dad actually felt that kind of secure, dyed-in-the-wool affection toward the Cleyskils. In fact, he thought they suffered from some mild but immensely unsettling form of lunacy.

"What a pair of wackos!" he declared, rolling his eyes and laughing in disbelief, after dropping by the Cleyskils' house with Mom one Saturday afternoon. "It's chaos. Junk thrown everywhere, that slobbering Saint Bernard wandering wherever it feels like. Did you hear him say the kids have no bedtimes? Geez, I hate to think how that pack is going to turn out. Just being saddled with those goofball names is a handicap to start out with."

"I think the children have beautiful names," Mom replied. "They're very warm, interesting people, and they're certainly not hurting you. Live and let live, Harry."

"Fair enough, babe. As long as we don't have to live together!"

Despite Dad's lack of interest in socializing, my mother was irresistibly drawn to the warm ferment of Ellen and her home. Clippings from the Cleyskils' greenhouse started appearing on our own kitchen windowsill.

"Josh, have you ever heard about this?" my mother asked, snapping an aloe leaf. "It's related to a cactus. If you get burned, you can smear this goo on to make it feel better."

"Yeah, cool. It's a plant from the succulent family."

"No, honey, it's from the Cleyskils'."

Almost embarrassed, as if I'd made my mother sound dumb, I explained what I'd meant.

"You know what else is funny, if you think about it, Ma?" I went on, "is that even though they're related, cactuses and succulents are kind of opposites. The outside of a cactus can prick you; the inside of a succulent makes you feel good."

"Joshua, how do you get all this stuff in your head?"

Such moments were awkwardly prideful. Although it felt smart to be a step beyond my mother, It also made me wonder which of us was leading the way down the garden path.

~

Our teachers told us to skip after-school activities and rush right home. We sprinted over dandelion-dotted spring lawns.

"It's a brother," Lew shouted.

"A sister!" I cried.

Dad took an unsteady breath and bit his lower lip.

"The baby was born with its heart on the outside of its chest," said our father. "It's wide open. Anything can touch it, and anything that touches it can make it sick." Lew and I sat on the living room couch. He stood above us, staring down intently, as if somehow a third child might materialize, tucked safely between us.

"Can't they do that open heart surgery stuff on babies?" Lew asked.

"Sometimes, sweetie. The doctors are going to do whatever they can. There are a lot of problems, though. The brain is pushing too hard on the eyes. We don't know what the vision will be like. Other problems, too. It's a mess."

"What? What else? We don't care if he's deformed or handicapped or whatever they call it, we still want him," insisted Lew.

Dad smiled tightly and pressed the heel of his palm against his cheekbone. As if he'd pushed a button, his skeleton suddenly went out, and he slumped to his knees, falling onto the couch between us, weeping. Lew and I placed open palms on our father's shoulders, rubbing them in circles meant to save him.

"I don't know what I'd do without you guys." He wrenched words from his tears. "You and your mom. Do you know how much I love you? We're the Royalton family. That's all we are. I don't want to lose this baby."

"We love you, too, Daddy," comforted Lew over the sobs, gently patting the top of our father's head.

"We're still a family, no matter what happens," I offered, instantly embarrassed because my words sounded more like the *Free to Be You and Me* album than the gnarl of real emotion I was feeling. It was as if I was outside my body watching the three of us, not sure what the scene was really about. Dad and I already knew that the baby would die.

Ellen Cleyskil had quietly stepped in from the front hall. "Harris, she's probably going to be awake any minute. You ought to get back to the hospital."

"You boys are really special, you know that?" she said with a genuine smile, chucking Lew under the chin and winking at me. "Your mom is one lucky lady. If I didn't have my own kids, I'd scoop you up in a minute."

"Not on your life!" Dad laughed ruefully, standing and stretching his back. "Guys, I know you're going to be good guests now. You're going to sleep over at Aunt Ellen's house, OK? I'm going to stay with Mommy and the baby tonight. We'll try to call. And I'll definitely see you tomorrow."

"Dad!" I called to him as he walked to the car. "You didn't tell us what the baby's name is!"

"It's a girl," he said solemnly. "Her name is Cora. Your mom picked it. A real Cleyskil name, huh, Ellen? Little Cora Royalton."

She lived for nine days.

Lew and I weren't allowed to visit. We never saw her. But I imagined Cora, and I cradled her in my mind. She was very much my sister; her wet heart open to the world, her vision strangely distorted. I always wondered whether they sent her the way of the turtles, or if they gave her a real funeral, like Grandmom and Grandpop's.

~

I was glad that my mother, in the midst of her grief, thought to send Lew and I home with Ellen on the night that Cora was born. The Cleyskils were a happy distraction for me. Raphy, the only older boy who had ever paid me any attention, showed me his new chemistry set while Lew roughhoused down the hall with eight-year-old Essex. Later, while the four of us ate dried figs and played Parcheesi, Avi, the five-year-old, came screaming past us in the living room, beating his fists against Clovis, the Cleyskils' gargantuan Saint Bernard, who sauntered along obliviously, gnawing Avi's beloved Superman action figure to shreds.

Lew and I were assigned to the double bed of a rarely used guest room crowded with dusty boxes and rolled-up carpets. As I opened the door to the hallway bathroom to wash up, Raphy emerged wet-haired and practically naked.

"Hey, g'night man! I'm sure everything will work out." He punched my pajama-clad shoulder with a grin, teeth as white as the elastic band of his underpants. His sister Rosalie honked away on the floor above us, practicing saxophone.

"Dad didn't call like he promised." Lewis twisted next to me in the bed. "This place is a mess. I hope we can sleep home tomorrow night."

"I'm sure we will. I'm sure everything will work out." I echoed Raphael while secretly wondering about where I would rather sleep.

~

After Cora, my mother had to go to a doctor once a week.

On a Saturday afternoon, as he watched a Phillies game on television with Dad, a commercial for heartburn relief set Lewis off like a bomb. He was red-faced out of nowhere, crying and throwing punches at our father.

"What's wrong with Mom? Did that messed-up baby you made get Mom sick, too? Why does she have to go to the doctor all the time?"

"Whoa, whoa! Ease off, champ." My father grabbed Lew's wrists and steadied his furious shaking. "Mom's just fine. It's not a doctor for anything that's really wrong. It's just someone to talk to about your problems."

"C'mon, Dad, tell me the truth." Lew protested. "No lying in this house, right?"

"Are you accusing me of lying?" Our father's voice bristled.

"But Dad, you always say we should tell you what's bothering us. Why can't Mom just talk to you?"

"Well, you know, pal, I actually think you're right. Mom and I have been able to work out each other's problems since we were teenagers, for God's sake. But if she wants to see Dr. Friedman, too, I suppose that's OK with me. I just want her to feel better, so things can get back to normal around here."

"Is it true?" Lew looked up from his baseball card collection as I passed the open door to his room later that evening. "Mom's not sick? Dr. Friedman just talks to her?"

"Yup. He's called a psychiatrist. He shows people inkblots and asks them about when they were little kids and stuff."

"I don't get it."

"Me either, exactly. But lots of people think it works."

Six months earlier, caught up in a notion that I was probably a space alien swapped for Josh Royalton rather than the true product of my nominal parents' sexual intercourse, I had broken down, shaking and sobbing in their bedroom. Mom had made me an appointment with this same Dr. Friedman. His office was a small, wood-paneled room in the same house where he lived. An elfin, fiftyish man with a nose sharp enough to give you a paper cut, he swung wide arcs with his index finger as we conversed. It was as if Dr. Friedman wanted to create the impression that our dialogue was a symphony he was conducting. But I lost confidence in him at the Rorschach.

"What do you see here?" he asked. Two erect penises, I thought.

"Two blue giraffes," I said.

"And here?" Mega-vagina, obviously.

"Butterfly," I said.

He called my mother in for a chat after our appointment was over. I wondered whether he had read my mind to figure out my real thoughts. But I had totally faked him out.

"Well, Dr. Friedman would be happy to see you another time if you want," said Mom on the drive home. "But he says you're just fine. You're a pretty normal kid."

Right. He was totally worthless. Then again, if I was doomed to be an alien after all, I supposed it was advantageous to be an alien who was smarter than human doctors. Dr. Friedman was a good guy, though. When I'd mentioned how Dad always tried to be in control of everything, he didn't get mad. He said it was pretty interesting. I wondered if Mom talked to him about stuff like that.

When she went to her Friday afternoon appointments, Mom dropped us at Kurt Franco's house. He was a new friend of Lew's who lived right at the end of Dr. Friedman's cul-de-sac. Kurt was a blocky, pug-faced kid who, years later, got kicked out of high school for selling barbiturates. I'd stand aside and watch as they played football on the lawn or street hockey in the driveway.

"Your brother is such a fag," I overheard Curt remark to Lew one day. "I bet you can kick his ass."

Picking us up after her appointments, my mother was ashen and distracted. She'd turn the radio to the news, setting the car abuzz with information, nodding or making little grunts at each story the announcer presented, as if intent on shifting her focus from herself to some more real world. She would drive without a word, Lew and I equally quiet, the newsroom typewriters a bed of percussion beneath our silence.

Mom would take us to the drive-thru at Jack in the Box. Her therapy session over, now it was our turn to talk to the clown.

"One Super Taco and onion rings and a Coke," I'd yell at the looming plastic face full of static, its fiberglass hair as orange as the pool of oil my taco would soon leak onto our kitchen table.

"One regular hamburger, *completely* plain," Lewis specified. "No ketchup, no pickle, nothing. Completely plain, OK?"

The clown would confirm, and the pimply kid at the window would give us a burger dripping with condiments.

"We'll scrape it off." My mother would try to placate Lew back at home. But this was not an acceptable solution.

"These people are morons!" my brother would holler, stomping around the kitchen. "Its not like I asked them to do *extra* work, like give me mayonnaise or something that doesn't usually come on it. I asked them *not* to work! Don't give me a pickle! Don't give me ketchup! Why can't they follow the easiest rules?"

Lew was an average student, except in math, where he excelled. My brother took great pleasure in the way that digits would combine and divide correctly, controlled by preordained formulas that always worked out right. Unrequested ketchup symbolized intolerable disorder. It was chaos on a bun.

"Josh, you can have it. I'm not touching it." He yanked open the refrigerator door.

"Guys," Mom exhaled, exhausted and uninterested, "eat whatever you want. I'm going to go take a nap. Tell Dad I'm upstairs when he gets home."

"I'm making a bologna sandwich!" Lew yelled after her, as if she'd been the one who perverted his burger. "And I'm making it the right way!"

It was almost scary, the way Mom was acting. Always so gentle and overattentive, she was fading away from us now. Dad, too, had seemed different—distant—since the baby, paying more attention to Mom and less to us. It was as if the mathematical formula that added up to the Royalton family wasn't working quite right. Everything was afloat. I wanted to exercise a little control of my own.

"Lew," I asked, feigning innocent curiosity. "What *is* the right way to make a bologna sandwich?"

"White bread, two slices of bologna, a little mustard—yellow, not that brown French junk," he proclaimed as he assembled.

"But I like lettuce and tomato on mine."

"So?"

"So are you saying that my sandwich is *wrong?* Like, you're right and there's something wrong with me? Like I'm some kind of freak, because I don't like my bologna sandwich exactly the same as you?"

"Shut up, Josh," he muttered.

My thoughts accelerated as my brother fumbled with his sense of order.

"Dad likes lettuce and tomato, too, Lulu. I guess me and him are freaks together, huh?"

"Don't call me that, asshole!"

"Now, now, Lulu. Watch your tongue," I chirped in a prissy falsetto. "You know we're not allowed to say that word in this house, Lulu-belle."

"I'm gonna kill you!" He clenched teeth and fists.

Just as Lew was about to lunge at me, our father pulled in the driveway. We looked away from each other, sat down at the table, and began eating, silently.

"Hiya, pals. Everybody have a good day?" Dad asked, swinging open the kitchen door. The relief hung as thick as the tension.

~

Mom started dropping me off at the Cleyskils' instead of leaving me with Lewis at Kurt's on Fridays. I sat in the kitchen watching Ellen cook or played with the younger kids or just wandered around the house, looking at the paintings and paging my way through stacks of illustrated books on topics from ancient Turkey to modern dance. One week, when Mom came in to pick me up, Raphael had just casually sat down across the table from me and dealt a hand of gin, as if we were in the habit of playing cards together.

"Rats! We were just getting started. Can Joshua stay over next Friday night?" Raph asked my mother. "Maybe we could hang out on Saturday, too?"

"If Josh wants to. And if it's all right with your mother." She raised her brows at Raphy, surprised that any child would offer an invitation without first asking for parental permission.

"It is," he said, certainly. "It's not like we have organized plans around here, you know."

He chuckled at the lovely shambles around him.

"*Really?*" Mom tried a rare touch of irony. "I hadn't noticed that, Raph. C'mon, Josh, gotta go now."

My mother laughed aloud as we walked down their hilly front yard to the car. "Just don't decide to move in or anything," she joked. "Your father will have a fit if you run away to join that circus."

The next Friday night we lay on the floor of Raph's room watching television.

"What girls do you like?" he asked.

Patti LaBelle wailed her way through "Lady Marmalade" on Don Kirshner's Rock Concert.

"*Voulez-vous couchez avec moi ce soir? Voulez-vous couchez avec moi?*"

"She's from here," I said, pointing to the native Philadelphian singer in her neon green mylar space suit.

"She looks like an alien. You can't even tell what language she's singing." Raph's T-shirted shoulder nudged against mine. "C'mon. What girls do you like?"

"Caroline Levy—she's pretty cute." I guessed.

"Cool. You can have Caroline." Raphy offered his approval. "She's good for a fifth grader. What about in my class? What sixth grade girls do you like?"

I tried to remember which girls were supposed to be most popular in Raphy's class. "Stacey Vickers?"

"No way, José," Raphy said, clamping a warm hand on my neck. "Stacey's all mine, Josh. Don't even think about it."

"Oh. OK."

"You think you're gonna steal Stacey from me, Joshua Royalton?" he growled, leaning over my chest.

"No, Raph. It doesn't matter— "

But he dove onto me then, and we started to roll, tumbling in our T-shirts and underwear, Raph gently threatening to kick my ass and make me pay if I ever made a move on his girl. He smelled of milk, wet wool, and Saint Bernard. He grabbed, headlocked, and finally pinned me with a kind, balletic violence. Straddling my chest and laughing, his white briefs at my eye level, Raph wiped back his sweaty hair and smiled down at me.

"You OK?" he asked.

"Uh-huh."

"You like to wrestle?"

"Sometimes."

"Are you ticklish?" he asked.

"No," I said firmly, flashes of the final bellyfight threatening to move in on this new game.

"I'll bet you are," Raph countered, sliding up my shirt and spidering his hands over my torso.

"No!" I yelled, afraid I would spit at him, lose him forever. "No!"

But it was OK. I laughed as he touched me. I reached up to Raph's belly, tickling back. Once again, we entangled, skin against skin.

There we were, together. It was me and Raphael and Lewis and Dad. All of us, roiling and rolling away.

Come morning, Raph had big plans. We were going downtown on the bus.

"What's there to do?" I wondered aloud.

I had visited my dad's firm in one of the dozen or so dull, gray office buildings of Philadelphia's modest, unimpressive business district. And every spring, I had been dragged with my schoolmates to see the Liberty Bell and Independence Hall. The city was where our fathers went to work and where they'd worked to get away from. My dad and mom, all the partners, all the aunts and uncles, had grown up on the Philadelphia side of City Line Avenue. They called themselves successes when they'd crossed over into suburbia.

It would be years before I found unexpected happiness in the heart of the city my father shrugged off at the end of each day. Raph's idea of downtown was the Gallery Mall. As part of an ongoing series of misguided development efforts, the municipal government had opted to finance the construction of this suburban-style shopping complex in the midst of the city. The adventurous promise of a trip to the city seeped away as we spent several hours trudging from the upscale Slim Jims of Hickory Farms to the marked down books at B. Dalton, from puppies at Pet World to "Colonial Corn Dogs" at Ye Olde Food Court. It felt good to be at Raphy's side, but I was drained, having tossed all night. And I was dumbstruck at the contrast between the exotic universe of his life at the Cleyskils' and Raph's gregarious affinity for all things Kay-Bee and Gap.

Our final stop of the day was Spencer Gifts.

"Whoa! Check it out!" Raph exclaimed, grabbing my shoulder and pointing to a display of the brand-new, pre-ubiquitous Farrah Fawcett poster. The toothy, toothsome star of *Charlie's Angels* beamed at us in gold tresses and a red maillot. I knew exactly what I was supposed to feel. But I didn't feel it. Farrah in her crimson swimwear was another generation's take on Grandpop's red satin Marilyn. But Grandpop Josh's painting had a holy, romantic air, hidden away in a closet shrine, revered in its heavy gold frame. Here, in just one store, were dozens of poly-bagged angels, rolled up and ready to go.

"I gotta get this. Hang it right over my bed, you know." He pumped a fist up and down in front of his crotch, raising his eyebrows at me. He slid one of the plastic sheathed tubes from its box and held it at an angle, protruding from his groin. "Boi-oi-oi-oing!"

"C'mon, let's go catch the bus," I prodded. When we'd wrestled the night before, I'd hoped that Raph would somehow leave his impression on my body, an all-embracing tattoo that I could carry about as armor. Now, I wanted to hurry home and be free of him.

I did go back for more, though. On other Friday nights, raging, I cannot deny I went back. Even without a whit of romance, I took sad, intense pleasure in our friction.

~

"Hallelujah!" my father cried when I walked in after that first overnight with Raphy. "The prodigal son has returned, set free by the artsy-fartsies!"

"Hey, Dad," I grumped, my relief at getting away from Raph quickly dissipating. My father was in the playroom behind the kitchen, hammering something. "What are you doing in there?"

I stepped into the room to find him lifting a glued-together jigsaw puzzle from a box piled high with them. It pictured an array of antique pocket watches. While Mom and Dad had not built a single new puzzle in the months we'd been in the new house, Dad had clearly spent most of this Saturday resurrecting their former accomplishments. The white walls of the room had become a mosaic of random images: ships at sea, political campaign buttons, Rockwell paintings, those eggs with the multicolored yolks.

"Your mom's been up in our room all day. Says she's not feeling well. I've been meaning to do this for awhile. Maybe it'll cheer her up when she comes down. Help me with this level, would you Josh?"

I held the silver box with its liquid window along the upper edge of a teddy bear picnic, my father straightening the image until the level's bubble held steady between my fingers. He nailed one skinny brad into each of the puzzle's four corner pieces.

"Looks like you're finally doing some decorating, too, huh?" My father pointed to the narrow tube I had set aside when I went to help him. Raphy had insisted that I buy a poster, too. Not a Farrah, of course; she was Raph's property. "What do you have there?"

"Poster."

"I knew you weren't swinging around a baseball bat, Joshua. A poster of what?"

Not able to bring myself to say it, I unrolled the image for him: fashion model Cheryl Tiegs in a minimal lavender bikini, backed up against a wall. My father beamed.

"Well, he might be a little weird, but the kid's got good taste. She doesn't have boobs like your mom, though, huh, Joshy? I got you beat there." He winked at me.

With four bits of adhesive putty, I stuck Cheryl Tiegs over the head of my bed. Finally, I'd made a statement on my own blank walls. Then I sat there, Indian style, staring at the poster, hoping to be stirred. I flipped my radio on, then off again quickly. It was the top of the hour; no music to be found, only annoying newscasts.

~

The summer before seventh grade, a new kid moved into the neighborhood: Doug Spanner, from Georgia. Even though he was in Lew's class, his heavy accent and devil-may-care attitude made him the center of attention for the whole school from the first day of classes that autumn. Doug was the only sixth grader who the popular guys in my class let into their street hockey games after school. Doug set off cherry bombs in the cafeteria, lifted packs of Tic Tacs and Bubble Yum from Bell's Pharmacy. He was even unafraid to sneak a peak in the girls' room at school.

The low ceilings of the Albert Riggs Middle School were simply big rectangles of acoustic tile balanced on a metal grid. Mrs. Reston once got overexcited during a map talk about India and thrust her pointer skyward, dislodging one of the tiles, which came slapping down to the floor like an overstarched flying carpet.

In the few minutes between the end of morning classes and sixth grade lunch, I tagged along with the hockey guys to the third-floor boys' room. Doug, having somehow sneaked back inside from recess, leaned jauntily against the garbage can, spitting arcs of tobacco juice into the sink. He smirked at us all and flashed his big, stained Chiclet teeth.

"All righty, boys, it's playtime."

I was usually assigned to play lookout, lurking by the bathroom door to make sure no teachers were headed our way. The others boosted Doug on top of the white porcelain urinal. He could have climbed up himself, but Doug didn't want to get any residue from the ammonia-smelling toilet cake on his new black Adidas.

He reached up with both hands, knocked a tile out of place, grabbed hold of the metal gridwork and hoised himself through the hole. As he pulled up, his feet pushing off the urinal's chrome handle, the sound of Doug's muscular "Oof!" and the roar of rushing water sent a surge of adrenaline through me. I glimpsed away from my lookout crack in the bathroom door to see only patch-kneed jeans and sneakers dangling from the neat rectangular gap overhead. Just where the rest of him became engulfed in the shadows above us, I could see a pale band of belly as Doug's bright red T-shirt tugged out from his belted jeans.

"I'm closer—I'm closer," he stage whispered, narrating his own motion as he arched his upper body over the dividing wall and reached for the girls' room ceiling. "I'm closer—I'm closer—I'm touching it."

My mind clouded with a vision of dexterous pink fingers gingerly setting down on top of a thin foam tile and resting there, dangerously, only five feet above the braided hair of a tinkling neighborhood girl.

The swoon was broken by Doug's grand finale. He pounded a fist on the tile and send it tumbling down on our victim's head. As the girl broke into a scream, he whooped a Minnie Pearl "Howwwww-deee!" and we buckled over laughing as he proudly descended from on high with another punctuating flush of the urinal. Swaggering from the boys' room, we choked back giggles and tossed off daredevil pleasantries to any adults who passed our way.

"Lovely day, isn't it, Vice Principal Lawrence?"

"I suppose so, Mr. Spanner. Shouldn't you be down at lunch by now?"

"I sure am looking forward to art this afternoon, Miss Wolfert."

"So am I, Joshua. We'll be working with modeling clay."

Doug shouldered me into the corner of the stairwell as the other guys charged by on their way to the lunch line one day.

"Guess what I saw, Joshy-boy?" he asked, crushing me up against the wall.

It felt good to lean in to his whisper, taken into his confidence.

"What?"

"Maybe I shouldn't tell," he teased.

"C'mon Doug! I can keep your secret."

"Well," he worked at suspense. "What I saw was . . . Mallowe's hairy pussy!"

Melanie Mallowe was, as our teachers whispered among themselves, the most *mature* girl in the seventh grade. Which is to say, she had returned from summer vacation sporting tremendous breasts. She was as big as Miss Wolfert, the art teacher. For years, Miss Wolfert had been nicknamed Booby Wolfert by the students, a moniker I feel certain she used to her advantage in maintaining order over each year's bevy of smart-ass yet easily intimidated boys on the cusp of pubescence.

Even the likes of Doug had a hard time doing more than getting mealymouthed and settling themselves down when Booby Wolfert sashayed their way, tilted back her hairdo, thrust forward her cleavage, and asked, in a bedevilingly sultry whisper, "Now, baby, do we have a problem here?"

When Melanie Mallowe had brought her new breasts to school in September, we all grew squirmy and uncomfortable. Here, personified, was the treacherous mountain pass we were all in the process of traversing. And now, Doug had spied her hirsute hidden treasure.

"I saw it; I saw it; I did," he boasted in his best Foghorn Leghorn drawl. "The bearded clam! Leave it to beaver!"

"How?"

"She *showed* it to me. Before I sent the tile flying today, I lifted up the corner and peeked down in the stall."

"Geez, Doug, she coulda screamed. She coulda had Mr. Lawrence paddling your butt in a minute."

"I've had my butt paddled plenty," he curled his upper lip. "Don't matter to me. Anyway, she could hardly tell who it was just by my eyeball in that little bitty corner. But she wasn't exactly chasing me off anyhow. She was sitting there, but it didn't sound like she was peeing or anything yet. She hears the tile lift and looks up to the ceiling and sees me. I was gonna shit myself. But then she smiles. And then she gives a little wave. And then—you're not gonna believe this!—she runs her tongue all over her teeth like the Pearl Drops lady on TV. She bends back and arches up to the ceiling so I can see it."

I didn't exactly believe that this was all true. But Doug's boastful confidence was exciting. He pressed into me and whispered. "It was right there. I could have practically touched it. Mark's brother was right, by the way: it smelled like a tuna sandwich. Speaking of which, you better get your butt to the cafeteria!"

Before running off in another direction, Doug Spanner shot me a dashing farewell wink. I felt certain I could recognize him by just a sparkling eyeball.

~

Lewis and I retreated into our separate rooms that year. Thanks to Dad's newfangled puzzle decor, the playroom had become a no-man's-land, sitting empty, an unvisited memorial. The drawers and cabinets were packed with our old building blocks, plastic cowboys and astronauts, Chutes and Ladders, Candyland. Upstairs, Lew struggled over his reading assignments and charted the NCAA basketball standings on his corkboard. I kept to myself, listening to the radio and playing deejay to the oak tree squirrels on a stereo set I'd received for my birthday.

I spent hours poring over books—my own, of course, but especially selections from a secret cache I'd discovered. My parents had bookcases in the living room, but it was in the basement that they warehoused hundreds of funky, dog-eared treasures. In old cardboard boxes, I found *Peyton Place* and Arthur Hailey, Robert Ludlum and *In Cold Blood.* I also found the sex books.

Even at twelve, I knew to laugh at *Sane Sex Living, Sane Sex Life,* published in 1929, a book that, I gleaned from its inscription, had been Grandpop Josh and Gram Sara's primer, which they then passed on to my parents.

"This book is not to be shared with those outside of the medical profession," admonished an introductory passage. The volume instructed that the average testicle is the approximate size of a horse chestnut and that some women pride themselves on long, luxuriant pubic hair that, when combed out, hangs as low as the knees. I sprawled on my bed, chuckling maniacally.

"What's so funny?" Mom yelled in from the hall one afternoon, clearly pleased to hear me in good spirits. "Can I get in on it?"

According to its avocado green cover, *Everything You Always Wanted to Know About Sex But Were Afraid to Ask,* had sold millions of copies. It was as cruel and compelling a book as I have ever read. Between my father's dramatic reenactions and our school nurse's slide shows, I felt fairly well versed in the field. But this book had two chapters that drew me like flypaper.

In "Male Homosexuality," best-selling sex authority Dr. David Reuben described typical homosexual activities: dressing as a woman; sucking a man's penis in the bathroom of a bowling alley; inserting a light bulb in the rectum.

"No names, no faces, no emotions. A masturbation machine might do it better," wrote the doctor. Such were the facts. Clearly, this was not about me. Yet, for some reason, I found myself hoping that my parents had skipped this chapter. I hid the book at the back of my underwear drawer so that Lewis would never stumble across it.

The next chapter—"Masturbation"—provided enormous relief. Here, Dr. Reuben declared my recently discovered sport of choice both fun and harmless. Even better, the doctor pointed out the benign normality of occasional naked wrestling with Raphy.

"The sexual pressure that builds up in adolescent boys is tremendous. It has to find some outlet," wrote Dr. Reuben. We were young; real sex was unavailable, yet we had undeniable urges. As long as Raph talked tits and pussy as he gripped our cocks in a single fist; as long as we hung poster girls to smile down on our panting grapple; as long as I didn't find it so incredibly comforting to have his swelling chest press into my skinny ribcage, then we were—both of us—normal.

I came straight home from school each weekday, hunkering down in my room to splice together a soundtrack for my life. I stitched songs found on records and the radio into cassette tape tapestries of operatic personal melodrama. On the stage of my bedroom, Elton John's "Philadelphia Freedom" tugged against Billy Joel's "You're My Home." *Fiddler on the Roof's* "Tradition" faded into Donna Summer's "Love to Love You Baby" as I humped a pillow in front of my closet mirror.

My mother had begun to go out by herself almost every afternoon, visiting Ellen or studying at the library.

"What are you studying for, Ma? Need any help?"

"I didn't really mean studying, honey. I'm just doing some research. Looking some things up."

With the run of the house these afternoons, I took the onanistic grand tour: Suede couches in the living room! Refrigerated air in the kitchen! Shag rug in the den! Wall-to-wall mirrors in the powder room! All-out perversion on my parents' own bed! I was the hound dog of puberty, secretly marking my turf.

Before going home one afternoon, I stopped at Bell's Pharmacy to buy a pack of gum. Shirley, the heavyset, perpetually silent check-out clerk whose name I knew only from her plastic tag, was out from behind the counter and hollering up a storm.

"Your parents or the police!" she was demanding. "I need a decision now."

I sidled up beside the "Get Well Soon" cards to get a better view of what was happening. Shirley was dressing down Bobby Nizer, an awkwardly gigantic boy, over six feet tall in seventh grade, his voice as deep as a man's, his head an acne-covered rectangular block. Bobby's father was the township dogcatcher; his mother, an orange-vested crossing guard. In our well-groomed, upper-class suburb, Bobby was among the ignored; the kind of kid nobody really liked and everyone felt a bit sorry for.

"What's it gonna be, kid?" Shirley asked him, shaking the *Playboy* that he'd attempted to shoplift in Bobby's face.

"I dunno." He clenched his jaw. "Call my mother, I guess."

Shirley delivered the news by phone and sent Bobby home to suffer whatever consequences might await him.

I walked back to the magazine rack, grabbed a copy of *Penthouse,* and returned to Shirley's counter. I slapped it down loudly, along with three one-dollar bills.

"You wanna bag for that?" she asked, unfazed.

"Nah," I said cavalierly, before zipping the magazine into my windbreaker as I stepped out the door to head home. By the time I hit high school, my night table drawer would be packed with naked women.

My mother had begun to express concern about how I was spending my after school hours.

"Josh, it's not healthy for you to just hang around the house every day. You need to interact with your peers, honey. You've got to learn to socialize."

"I know how to be sociable, Mom. I'm very sociable. Let me play you some tapes."

In addition to my music mixes, I had been recording my increasingly frequent contributions to radio talk shows. I would call in and effect a variety of adult voices to ask questions or offer comments on the day's topics. Between my bouts of masturbation and disco lip syncing, I angled in on discussions of home improvement and thirty-year mortgage rates. I was really on the radio, sharing my thoughts about downspouts and decor with the masses.

"My husband and I did the most darling thing in our rec room," I chirped in a southern-twanged falsetto to Marge Dotson, the Interior Queen, on WWDB one afternoon. "We took dozens of beautiful jigsaw puzzles we'd built together and used them to decorate the walls."

"Well that's a super idea, Josephine. It's always great to combine your own hobbies with your design scheme. Your home is a way to express yourself! So many folks today just go for packaged themes and trends that don't speak to them personally. Funny story: A lovely lady from Broomall's kids came home from visiting her ex-husband for Thanksgiving. They tell Mom the walls of Dad's new Mister Macho pad are covered with moose heads and antlers. And you know what, Josephine? The man doesn't even hunt!"

I glanced up at Cheryl Tiegs and winced.

On the less popular shows and stations—especially during open forums when I didn't have to think up a comment about a particular subject—I used different voices to get on the air several times over the course of a four-hour broadcast. Sometimes I didn't even disguise my voice.

"Hi, this is Josh in the western suburbs. I heard you talking about good gifts for Mother's Day. I always like to write a poem for my mom. This year, I did one called 'Ode to an Everything Pizza.' Would you like to hear it?"

I imagined tens of thousands of listeners sitting rapt as I delivered my rhymed couplets about silver anchovies and cloud-white mozzarella.

After hanging up, I called back in immediately. "Cheers!" I deepened my voice and tried out a British accent. "This is Charles Pufflethwaite. I am a professor of poetry at LaSalle University, and I want to commend that young pizza boy, Joshua Royalton. He's already writing at a college level."

"I may be thirty, and he may only be a kid," I offered in the velvety tones of Claire from Mount Airy, "but he sure knows pizza. I swear, I was drooling! How can I get a copy of that great poem? I'll pay five dollars for it, and I bet lots of other listeners would, too!"

"Well, what do you think about that?!" asked Lorraine Jones, the program host. "We've launched ourselves a real literary star! So call us back if you're still out there, Joshua, I need to get some information."

"I just want to say how flattered I am, Lorraine. It's really just a little nothing I scribbled down. You and your listeners are the greatest!"

"Well some of them seem to think it's you who's the greatest, Josh."

"Thank you, Lorraine. Thank all of you so much."

My mother sat silently at the edge of my bed, head nodding in concentration, lips pursed in concern. I thought she was about to speak several times, but eventually she just stood and paced my carpet in an arc.

"What is it, Mom?" I asked, not understanding her consternation. "Are you mad at me for sharing your Mother's Day poem? I didn't really make copies for anybody. You have the only one."

"Oh no, Josh. I'm not angry. I'm just a little confused is all. You're a pretty complicated kid, you know that?"

Her vocabulary had changed in therapy. I was no longer weird or strange, just complicated. Nonetheless, I couldn't tell whether my mother considered this complexity a point of pride or a problem to be solved. I wasn't even sure of my own opinion.

"I still think we ought to come up with some activity you'd like to do with other kids, Joshua. Otherwise I'm afraid you're going to end up awfully lonely."

"I guess so," I muttered, pulling at a loose thread on my comforter and thinking that I'd arrived at awfully lonely quite some time ago.

~

Lewis joined Little League that spring. Dad came home early a couple times a week to help coach the team. He had urged me to go out for baseball, too.

"You sit around doing nothing all afternoon, Joshua. Come get some exercise."

"Dad, I wouldn't even make the team if I auditioned."

"Josh," Lew tried to speak gently, his eyes nonetheless rolling involuntarily, "it's called trying out, not auditioning."

"Whatever. I'm not going to. I'm a spaz, anyway."

Lew laughed. My father hollered at me.

"I'm not going to listen to that bull, Joshua. If you want to play baseball, you can play baseball. It's all a matter of determination."

My father believed his own words of wisdom. After all, he had dreamed precisely and prospered. Out of row house nowhere, he'd imagined himself into his idealized home and family. So I could play baseball, and Lew could be valedictorian. Harris Royalton believed we could all dream ourselves into being, and that all of our dreams would be at one with his own.

The Ed's Sunoco Panthers played their games on Friday afternoons. Once the season was under way, my father insisted that, rather than go to the Cleyskils' during Mom's appointments with Dr. Friedman, I come out and sit in the stands to cheer his boys to victory. While I resented my father forcing me to take part in Little League, even peripherally, I was secretly relieved. I didn't want to see Raphael Cleyskil anymore.

A month earlier, Ellen had been in the midst of telling me about quinoa, an unusual grain she was thinking about trying in some recipes. Raph ambled in through the back door, the upturned collar of an indigo jean jacket framing his coral-lipped smile.

"What's for dinner, Ma?"

"I'm just fine. Thanks for asking. And how was your day, Raphael?"

"Sorry. Hey, Josh." He swigged milk straight from the carton, a capital offense in my house. "So how *was* your day, Ma?"

She said something about her studio and the dog and the vet. I lost focus and, against my better judgment, found my attention drifting toward Raph. He was my most tangible connection to all things Cleyskil, to an artistic family that made things up as it went along, rather than following plans. When he stood close to me, I still wanted to slip into his skin.

Raph asked me to stay over again that night, and I instantly agreed. But when his friend Bailey Jergens arrived after dinner, all chin-stubble and piggy eyes, I felt the bottom go out of my gut. At first, I had no real reason to dislike this bulky boy. In fact, I got a good laugh from his thrift-store service-station jersey, its oval name patch reading "Dick." But I wanted no outsiders in this house. I wanted to be among Cleyskils.

A beat-up pool table had materialized in the endless labyrinth of upstairs rooms, and the three of us played a few games, each giving little Avi a shot when he begged to be included. We ended up in Raph's room, the new Kiss album on the turntable. Bailey sat on the edge of the bed, absently rubbing his crotch through army pants.

"So, uh, what's next?" he asked, glancing at Farrah on the wall.

Raph laughed nervously.

"What's up?" I wondered. "What's going on?"

"I'll go first," he said to me, standing up and walking over to my chair. "Doesn't bother me. I'm just getting, not giving. Nothing wrong with that."

"Wait a minute, Bailey," interrupted Raph.

"Why wait? I'm ready now. C'mon, Josh, Raphael says you give one hot blow job. So let's get to it."

"What are you talking about?" I flushed red and stared at Raphy.

Had I not discovered *Everything You Wanted to Know About Sex* and the *Penthouse* "Forum" several months earlier, I would not have even known what a blow job was. I had never done it to Raph, although I had, unsuccessfully, tried to do it to myself in a painful bit of bedroom contortionism.

"It was kind of a joke," Raph muttered under his breath so Bailey wouldn't hear.

"Yeah?" I spat, angry but still blushing. "What kind of joke?"

The older boys stepped out into the hall. I wondered if Raph was telling him that I had chickened out, insisting that I really had done it before.

"Sorry about that, man," Raph said, coming back into the room alone now, his friend gone home. "I guess I thought you might go a little further."

"But why was Bailey here?"

"Why not? He's a cool guy. I mean, we're all horny, right?"

"Raphael, you don't understand. I'm not just horny. I mean, I like . . . I feel . . ."

"You're pissed at me, aren't you?"

"Yeah, I'm pissed!" Betrayed. Lost. Abandoned.

"Well, come on, then," he coaxed, crouching down, beckoning with his hand. "Take it out on me, dude. Wrestle me!"

"You don't get it, Raph! That's not what I want. I never wanted to *wrestle*."

As the other boys took the field on Friday afternoons, I sat in the bleachers, waiting until my father looked at me before cracking open a book with a flourish to let him know I wasn't paying attention.

"Are you Lew's older brother?"

A boyish man with a strangely familiar oval face gave me an almost bucktoothed smile.

"Yep. Taught him everything he knows."

"Well, he's a mighty fine ballplayer. Oh, sorry, I'm Paul. Nice to meet you. I'm Harris's co-coach."

I liked the way he casually said "Harris" to me, instead of "your dad" or "your father." A few minutes later, I looked up from my paperback, *Jaws* (it had much more sex than the movie), to see the Panther left fielder dropping back to catch a fly. His face was shadowed by the bill of his black cap, but I recognized the boy's broad, rounded shoulders. He timed the ball perfectly, plucked it right out of midair.

"Way to go, dude!" Lewis threw his arm around him as they jogged in to take their turn at bat.

"That's my guy!" cheered Paul. "Good grab, Dougie!"

It was Doug Spanner. His father, Paul, looked exactly like him, almost more like an older brother than a dad. Such a troublemaker in school, always benched in gym class and getting into fights, Doug's interest in the uniforms and strict schedules of Little League took me by surprise. Yet there he was, sitting next to Lew, turning from the bench to wave up at me. Taking Doug's lead, my brother grinned and waved, too.

"Hey, guys!" I yelled as they took to the field again. "Let's go, Panthers! Way to play baseball!"

Harris heard this and shot me a happy wink.

After a massive trouncing of the Earl's Amoco Orioles, the five of us went to Pizza Town USA for a postgame celebration. I almost said something to Mom when we came home afterward, because I'd noticed the fathers eyeballing Diane, the slinky tube-topped waitress. "Move it in, move it out, shake it round and about," the jukebox played Johnnie Taylor's "Disco Lady." Doug was staring at Diane too. He kept elbowing Lew, who, while prehormonally oblivious, occasionally stage whispered "Jell-O Mama!" just to prove he was in sync with the prevailing sentiments.

When Dad gave Lew permission to have Doug sleep over that night, I coughed on a bit of pepperoni. After the three of us played endless hands of gin and Johnny Carson had bid all a good night, my father marched us upstairs, setting up the cot for Doug in Lew's room.

"Nighty-night, Joshy boy!" Doug joked as they shut the door behind them.

Alone, in the dark, I felt a pang of jealousy. But Doug was friends with both of us, I reassured myself. He could only be in one room. My envy was soon supplanted by a haunting calm. A sense of inevitability.

Slipping under the covers, I suddenly decided to remove my Fruit-of-the-Loom briefs. I flung them across the room and lay there, naked. The weight of darkness pressed me flat against the pale blue sheet, damp beneath my back. The red digits of my clock radio burned 1:17. I heard them creep out of Lew's bedroom and into the hall. They tuned their voices down to mere breath, speaking to each other in word-shaped exhalations. I swallowed hard on my own anxious laughter.

"I will lie still," I repeated to myself. I watched a film of emotion-charged images projected on the burnt orange screen of my closed eyelids: Doug's legs dangling down from the ceiling, my father shaving, a flock of crows blackening blue sky. I heard the boys tiptoeing across my carpet.

"Lewis," Doug whispered, just feet from my bed. "Shine the light."

As I shut my eyes, the narrow beam of my brother's penlight swept over my covers, then flushed my face. It was a physical presence, this beam along my body. My groin pulled tight when it crossed the blanket there. The soft hairs above my upper lip were set dancing just before the beam touched my eyes, turning burnt orange to warm marmalade.

For these seconds, every sense was heightened. Trying to lie still, I wanted to jump out of myself. I squinted tighter, and blood rushed to my groin, hardening me. Yet I was unembarrassed, strangely powerful. I exerted some magnetic force over Doug.

"All right," he whispered. "We're almost there."

I felt the light now, crossing my waist again. I sensed Doug's pink fingers reaching toward their goal. I believe I could actually feel him pinching the sides of my top sheet before raising it up, like a tent. I swallowed as the light touched and rested on my bare erection. They might be better at baseball, but there was satisfaction in knowing they were still fifth graders; that I still had some kind of edge. Fearfully, I allowed myself to indulge the narrowest possible opening of my eyes.

They were staring at me now, seeing the curls of new hair, the thickness. I wished that they wished they could be like me. At the same time, I felt pinned down and helpless. Gulliver, perused by Lilliputians.

"Geez. This is too weird," complained Lewis, suddenly forgetting to whisper.

"Shush! Keep the light still."

For an hour, or a minute, we were transfixed.

"Let's go already," Lew whined.

"Yeah, uh . . . all right," Doug muttered, half-consciously.

Doug Spanner let go of the top sheet. It dropped to my body and sent a breeze across my skin. I kept my eyes closed and my mouth shut. They were gone.

Then I heard Doug Spanner's laugh. His feet pounding back down the hall to my brother's room. Doug bounced, raucous, on Lewis' bed. He hollered a familiar greeting.

"Howww-deee!"

~

"Hello, Dolly! Well, hello, Dolly . . . " I tried to project my singing voice to the back of the Community Auditorium.

"Ouch! Cut it out. What are you doing?"

Carmen Rae, the volunteer impresario behind this Family Playhouse production, was jamming four stiff fingers into my gut, just below the ribcage. It was bad enough that Carmen was always touching me—stroking my hair, patting my ass—but now it really hurt.

"Josh-u-ahh," she declaimed, dramatically elongating my name and sweeping her arms about for emphasis. "We must always sing from the di-a-phragm! Di-a-phragm!"

She jabbed my midriff again with each syllable, then grabbed hold of the long gray-streaked braid that hung down to the middle of her back, and whirled it around like a cowgirl caught on the end of her own lariat.

"Do you know what the diaphragm is, Joshua? Hmmm? Naughty, naughty! I wasn't thinking of the diaphragm you're thinking of. I have psychic powers, you know. I can read your dirty boy mind." I almost laughed out loud. Though older than my own parents, she acted like a wild teenager.

"I have a dirty boy of my own at home!" crowed Carmen. "Not to mention the one I'm married to!"

Some of the neighborhood women in the chorus giggled, others muttered disapprovingly among themselves. Finally, Carmen got around to explaining the advantages of singing from the gut to me and the others. After a few minutes of vocal exercise, the song really did sound better. It was all about resonance, Carmen said. It was all about vibrations.

"Don't forget to exercise your diaphragms, ladies!" she taunted, lighting up a Viceroy as chorus rehearsal came to an end. "And how about recruiting some men for this chorus? Why is it they're interested in the leading roles or nothing? See you Tuesday, girls."

"Such prigs," she muttered to me as they filed out. "Hello, Dolly, my eye. You know, I was almost on the plane to join Das Mufti Wana once. The world famous Albanian dance-puppetry troupe? They wanted me. Recognized my vision. My mother was sick though, the old goat. Had to watch her wither in a Tuscaloosa hospital instead of making my mark in the Eastern Bloc. I did work Vegas, though, Joshua. Lead showgirl in 'Pasties Akimbo!' at the Mirage. Played my own solo on an ice-blue marbleized grand piano."

She glanced disdainfully at the battered upright she was leaning against, grinding her cigarette against the bottom of a glass ashtray in furious little circles.

"Well, I gotta get on home to the menfolk, Joshua. You staying to work stage crew? Well, I'll see you tomorrow. You can read lines for whoever's missing. And Joshua, don't forget darling, my Family Playhouse antimantra: Federico Fellini, Federico Fellini. Chant to yourself a hundred times before sleep. We are artists, you know. In our souls, we can transcend the mediocrity that surrounds us!"

In her fancy straw hat, as big around as a flying saucer, Carmen Rae strode out of the auditorium, wickedly self-possessed. I shook my head, simultaneously fascinated by her exotic, ever-altering resumé and put off by her imperious condescension. Would-be doyenne of our community theater, she barely deigned to be part of the community. I couldn't imagine what it was like to live with her. That would be one screwed-up family. Part of me suspected she was making up the whole story, about a husband and a son my age. I'd never run into any kooky Rae kid around.

But I still thanked heaven for crazy Carmen. And for Ben Ricklin, from the hardware store, who volunteered to design and building the sets. And for all the actors and chorus members and backstage techies and everyone else involved in Family Playhouse.

Years later, my mother would explain that it had actually been Frisbee Cleyskil who'd raised the curtain on my new social life. My radio tapes had seriously rattled her and, while she bemoaned my strange frequency to Ellen one afternoon as they picked radishes from the Cleyskil garden, Frizz ambled in among the stakes and vines to offer a suggestion.

"You know, Becca, Josh may just be looking for an art form," he observed. Frisbee's voice was like a rusty hinge. It often swung open to insight, but it did so creakily. "I've got a few patients, schizophrenics— "

"Frisbee!" Ellen blurted, setting a hand on my mother's back to keep her from tipping over into the zucchini patch. "Joshua is not seriously ill. You've seen him getting along with Raph. He's just fine."

"Oh, gosh, Becca, I didn't mean to startle you. I wasn't saying that Josh was schizophrenic. I mean he's not, is he? As far as you know?" Frizz plucked a nearby tomato, biting into it like an apple.

"Ai-yi-yi, the absent-minded professor!" Ellen mussed her husband's hair. "How about finishing with that helpful advice you stepped in to dispense?"

"Oh, right. So, one patient of mine kept smearing her shit all over the ward. But when I gave her paper and a watercolor set, along with a little encouragement—*boom!*—it stopped. And she made some pretty good paintings that month."

"She went back to the, uh— " my mother faltered, " —the feces after a just month, though?" she asked.

"Oh, no," Frizz reassured. "She killed herself."

"There are other cases, too," Frizz continued. "I had a guy playing with his body hair all day, twisting it, knotting it. But pointed in the right direction, he's a macramé genius. You know those gimp lanyards the kids like to weave? Well, he makes them for all the inpatients now, color coded to indicate their meds. See, here's my wristband; green-and-white barrel stitch means I'm on two hundred milligrams of Valium."

"So what does all this have to do with Joshy?"

"Well, if he's acting out all these different personalities, Becca, maybe he'd enjoy getting involved with theater."

"You know, Frizz, that actually does sound like a good idea."

"Well, howdy doo!" Ellen cracked. "There's a method to his madness after all."

"But y'know, Bec, the art form is just a channeling of the symptoms. It's not a cure for what ails."

"Honey," Ellen shook her head hopelessly. "You keep forgetting. You're just sharing an idea. Josh isn't one of your beloved crazies."

"Ladies, ladies, it's *you* who keep forgetting. Everything is relative. Everyone is crazy!"

He shuffled out of the garden, munching his tomato.

The first week of June, only ten days until the gala premiere of my first big show, Carmen Rae was unhinged.

"Y'know, gang, I should have run off with that aerial act. Benny Dangle and his Flying Spangles. I could be twirling spread eagle over Tokyo tonight. Or I could have stayed on with the Ozark Mountain Shakespeare Fest; I'd be working in the service of the good Bard himself. But no, no, my *straaaange* path brought me here. Here. To the station-wagoneering, lip-glossing, low-fat soft-serve frozen-yogurt-eating capital of suburban America, USA!"

"Still, I didn't give up! I said to myself, Carmen Rae, why don't you share your talents with that little theater and grace this community with some *art*? Well, here we are, ladies and gentlemen. Or should I say ladies and ladies? And ladies. And more ladies. Here we are, performing a timeless classic based on Thornton Wilder's renowned story, 'The Matchmaker,' and, beyond the lead characters, we are utterly, absolutely matchless. Not a flicker of dick in sight. As that great lady of the stage, Clara Peller, once asked: 'Wherefore art the beef?'

"How is our grand finale going to have any real meaning—how is it to convey the piece's leitmotif of romantic coupledom, if the stage—and, in effect, the very imaginative world in which the story takes place—is choking with single women?" she paused. "And Josh, of course. Our savior."

I laughed. Carmen Rae meant no insult. This was theater. I was as likely the manly savior as she was the great director.

"If it means that much to you, I'll join in for the finale," volunteered Ben Ricklin. "My crew members will, too."

Carmen Rae bowed her head, lifted her long batik skirt, and sank to the ground in a gargantuan curtsy. "Bless you, good sir. May Thespis smile upon you. And Carol Channing, too."

The next evening, as I took my place for the last number of chorus rehearsal, two warm palms pressed down over my eyes.

"Guess who?" challenged a familiar voice. His breath on the back of my neck somehow permeated the skin, curling into my head like a vapor.

"What are you doing here?" I whirled around, happy but bewildered to see Doug Spanner here.

"I'm an all-singing, all-dancing, soul-kissing, pussy-licking musical extravaganza, Joshy boy! Or hadn't you heard?"

I glanced timidly around, hoping the women around us hadn't heard. Mrs. Botchkin shook her head in disgrace.

"Apple doesn't fall far from the tree, does it?" she asked me. I shrugged, not getting her point.

"Don't you guys have Panther practice today?" I asked Doug, still trying to figure out what he was doing at the community hall.

"I went already; that's why I'm late."

"What do you mean, late?"

"Duh. I mean that's why I'm late for rehearsal. But it looks like I'm right on time for my scene, the grand finale. My mother said the show needed a little more . . . " He ground his hips and flashed that hillbilly grin.

"I didn't know your mom was in the chorus."

"Chorus! Ha! My mama, the diva? Carmen Spanner? She'd never. You know, I think she's got a crush on you, Royalton. She talks about you all the time. If you ever want to trade parents, call me immediately."

"Holy shit! She's your—but her name is Carmen Rae."

"Aw, you got me. I ain't her son; I'm her hired gigolo. Duh. Ever hear of a stage name, genius?"

Sometimes the obvious things take the longest time to notice. Buried in Carmen's affected, erudite accent was a faint echo of Doug's unbridled twang. They shared mischievously twinkling eyes and bracingly fresh mouths. And their shared talent for yarn spinning and cheap, effective drama was unmistakable. Clearly, they had everything it would take to drive each other mad.

"Hey Duggle-bug!" she stuck her head backstage to greet him. "Now, I want to see energy, virility, and oomph from you guys! Not a lot of men here; I can't afford to have the two of you sitting around pulling your puds."

Mrs. Botchkin flushed beet red.

Doug's presence made the last two weeks of rehearsal fly by. As we rehearsed, I thrilled at the opportunity to cast off Joshua Royalton and roam the stage as a stouthearted townsman, a normal person.

For the finale, Doug and I sang in a kickline with Mrs. Botchkin between us as Dolly descended a grand white staircase. Down she came, iridescent hoopskirt wide as a satellite dish, our choreographer, director, and star: the fabulous Carmen Rae. Each night of the run, she would give her husband, Paul, a dozen different flowers to throw at her, one by one. The lily, then the tulip, then the rose, as if she were being showered by myriad fans. We continued to sing through two refrains as she stood in a glowing spot, the only illumination on the stage.

"Don't matter if this chorus is men or women or children or whatnot," Doug whispered in a harsh rasp. "She'd put out the lights on all of them."

Opening night, my parents rushed to me, arms outstretched, as I emerged from the backstage corridor. Mom handed me a pair of cream-colored roses in a cone of silver paper.

"I knew it would do you good to get out of the house. You looked great up there, really confident," my father enthused, pulling a miniature bottle of sparkling cider from his trench coat pocket. "Here. I didn't know if your mother's flower was the right thing for a guy, so . . . "

"Thanks, Dad. Thanks!"

My father didn't realize that his acclaim itself was the only gift I needed. I kissed my mother's cheek.

"I love the roses, Mom. It's a tradition, you know, flowers on the first night."

"I didn't know you could sing so well!"

"You dance just like me, though," joked my father. "Clunkety clunk clunk."

"I really am a pretty sucky dancer, aren't I?"

"Don't sweat it, Josh," he reassured me. "You're the best-looking partner Selma Botchkin's had in many a moon. So tell me, son, did your character get any nookie off of hers?"

"Harris!"

"Hey, Mr. and Mrs. Royalton," Doug greeted my parents as he wandered by.

"Doug! Doug!" my mother called him over. "You were wonderful, honey. From baseball to Broadway! A real renaissance man. This is for you." She handed him a single rose of his own.

"Really?" he asked, stunned. I nodded at him, smiling at my mother's generosity. "Well, all right!"

Doug thrust up his bloom like a torch, throwing his head back and marching proudly out the door to the parking lot. At the other end of the corridor, Paul leaned against a wall, lingering in shadow, as Carmen greeted a steady stream of well-wishers.

"Well, all right!" she cheered as a township commissioner peeked down her cleavage, planted a kiss on her cheek, and popped the cork on a bottle of Asti Spumanti. "Here's to the Family Playhouse."

Lewis came to see the last show, on Saturday night. Singing and dancing were not high on his list. Our parents had taken us to a touring production of *Annie* that he squirmed all the way through and deemed, "Totally girlie pukey." I pulled him aside at home before Mom drove me to the auditorium that afternoon.

"When I came to the first Panthers game, I brought a book to read instead of watching you and Doug. It's OK if you want to do that."

"You don't mind? Cool. But isn't it dark in there?"

"I seem to recall," I said in an eerie, all-knowing tone, "that you have a little penlight."

Lew ended up watching the whole show in a state of amazement. This was his first encounter with Carmen Rae. Afterward, he told me she seemed less like Dolly the matchmaker than "Lolly, the queen of the hookers." Later still, I learned that he'd picked that line up from Dad. The cast party—in subdued, suburban fashion—would be a brunch on Sunday morning. Lew and I invited Doug to sleep over after the closing performance.

"That's perfect!" clapped Carmen Rae. "Commissioner Leery has invited Paul and me out for a little carousing. He's come every night, you know."

For all the rush of final curtain calls, there was a calmer, but equally intense pleasure to sprawling out on the living room floor with my brother and our friend. We played Clue as King Kong stomped through the late show on TV. My father eventually came downstairs in his pajamas to rustle us up for bed. I knew he planned to put the cot in my room this time. Lewis would stay alone. I could have Doug Spanner to myself. It could be like I'd wanted with Raphy. I knew Doug would try anything. But as much as my hormones hollered, my heart knew that he was no more my dream of Raphael than Raph himself had proved to be.

"Dad," I said. "Besides the cot, why don't we get out the sleeping bag? Lewis can stay in my room, too. We'll be three brothers tonight."

~

"Damn it!" my father yelled. "I can't figure out what's wrong with this thing."

Our central air had been mysteriously shutting off at random intervals throughout the last week of August. It usually came back on in an hour or two, so Dad had been reluctant to call in a serviceman.

Still, the thought of leaving the house with anything amiss unnerved him. He seemed particularly agitated as we walked out to the car.

Each year, on the day before school started, we drove out into the countryside of the Lehigh Valley. Dad would turn on the oldies station, leading us in sing-alongs with Frankie Valli, Lesley Gore, the Supremes.

"I can't hear you guys!" he shouted from the front seat, coaxing us to join in with the Righteous Brothers's "You've Lost That Loving Feeling."

"Lew and I formed our own group this year, Dad. The Royalton Brothers. And we've lost that singing feeling."

"Yeah," laughed Lew. "You know, it's gone, gone, gone!"

"C'mon, this is a tradition, guys. Don't be spoilsports."

"I'll sing with you, Harry," Mom said, shaking her head at us.

"Dad, can we close the windows and turn on the air?" Lew asked. "It's getting really hot out."

"I can smell butter melting on the cornfields, Dad."

"You guys are being a little obnoxious," said Mom. "This is *your* day, remember. Try to have some fun."

"If it's our day," snapped Lewis, "then why can't we have the windows up?"

"This is *your* day, Ma," I retorted. "You're the ones who invented it. A drive in the country, la-di-da! How fifties. It's like *Happy Days* or something. It's like Lew and I are tagging along on one of your old dates."

"Would the three of you knock it off? Becca, quit egging these babies on."

"Hey, Dad!" I barked. "Mom's arguing for you, not against you. Can't you hear?"

We drove silently for a while. My parents stiffened in the front seat and Lew made a continuous show of wiping perspiration from his brow. Family outings had lost their charm. I remembered the past spring vacation, a miserable trip to Walt Disney World. Mom and Dad announced it over the dinner table one night, passing around snapshots of an earlier visit to the Magic Kingdom, when we were eight and seven.

"Oh!" Mom pointed. "Look at Lew and Pooh."

"Remember Space Mountain?" asked Dad. "How I went twice because neither of you would go unless I'd hold you in my lap?"

Lewis and I locked eyes in appalled commiseration.

Back in Fantasyland as teenagers that spring, we gave each other the same moody look. Mom talked with a young couple we'd met in the line for her favorite attraction, the Peter Pan ride, while Dad knelt to the ground, absorbed in chatter with their fat-cheeked two-year-old stroller urchin.

I heard a bird singing just over my left shoulder, but poking my face between the branches of a small tree on the side of the walkway, I discovered not a nest, not a bird, but a four-inch-tall speaker, lashed to the trunk with wire, broadcasting an endless loop of prerecorded tweeting.

"Look at this, Lew! Fake nature."

"I wanna go home," he groaned in my ear. "I wanna play lacrosse."

I wondered how they kept pigeons away from all those winding paths, all that dropping popcorn. But the only birds around were the robot parrots in the Tiki Room.

*"Caaaaaaw! Caaaaaaw!"* Not even thinking, I burst out in a crow's call next to Tinkerbell's Ice Cream Kiosk. People turned and stared. Goofy, too.

"Joshua! What's wrong? What are you doing?" my mother grabbed me by the shoulders and put her face in mine.

"I'm OK—I'm OK," I said, feeling a huge smile break across my face.

"Well, good luck with yours," Dad said to the young couple as they rolled off with their toddler.

"Meet you back here in a few," I said. "I have to go to the bathroom."

I jerked off in a stall under Cinderella's Castle.

That night, after our parents had monorailed back to the hotel, Lew and I rode Space Mountain five times in a row.

Now, a few months later, in the family Oldsmobile rather than Disney's silver shuttles, our heads flung forward as we came to a screeching halt.

"Goddammit! I missed it; didn't I, Becca? I missed the damned exit. Everything is so screwed up today."

"I'm not sure, Harry. It's OK; if we missed it, we'll turn back."

"You boys have got me so distracted with your sourpuss act. I swear . . ."

Eventually we found our traditional spot, the riverside deck of the Great American Grill. Cradled in pastel-colored inner tubes, other families waved at us as they floated past, bobbing off toward the horizon.

"Well, fellows," Dad clinked his knife against his water glass. "I've been waiting all day for this moment. I have a major announcement to make."

He reached an arm around Mom's shoulder and pulled her tight to him.

"Honey," she nudged him. "Why do you have to be so dramatic?"

"This year it's not just the two of you who are starting class tomorrow. The really big news is that Mom's going back to graduate school."

He kissed her on the lips, then stared at her, displaying a huge jack-o'-lantern grin. She stuck out the tip of her tongue and gave a tiny, dismissive wave of her hand.

"Cool," said Lew, with a friendly smile. "What are you gonna study?"

"Oh, I get it." I interrupted before she could answer. "That's what you've been doing in the library all those afternoons."

"You got it, honey. I'm going to get a degree in psychology, Lew. In a couple years, I'll be a counselor, sort of like Dr. Friedman. I start next week at Temple, downtown."

"Neat." I smiled at her. "Hey, Dad, can I have your potato salad if you're not eating it?"

"My potato salad? Can you have my potato salad? I can't believe this!"

"Geez, sorry," I apologized without knowing why. "What's wrong?"

"What's wrong," he snapped, slamming his palms down on the table and toppling a plastic cup of Coke. "What's wrong is that I tell you guys one of the biggest, most exciting, most momentous pieces of Royalton family news of all time and all you can do is say 'neat' and 'cool' and 'Can I have your potato salad?' Everything's changing around here! How about a little excitement for your mother? How do you think you're making her feel?"

"I feel just fine, Harris," Mom said calmly as she blotted up the spilled soda with a napkin.

"Mom, I think its great and all," I said. "I didn't mean to . . . "

"Don't worry guys, you didn't do anything wrong. I know you're happy for me." She tapped Lew's nose with a fingertip. "And I'm happy too. This is just normal life," she said, glancing at our father as he rose, head shaking, to visit the men's room. "It's hardly the Second Coming. We'll meet you inside, Har. Wow, it really is baking out here. Soda's getting all sticky even before I sop it up. Let's hit the road and get out of this heat, huh?"

We wound our way homeward through the valley, quietly watching the sky bruise purple with dusk. The rising moon and setting sun floated together overhead. My father tuned in the Phillies on the radio, the cheering crowd mixing with the air conditioner's cool relief. He drifted away from us, into an easier game.

"Three up, three down!" I heard the announcer call. "This is going to be a tight one all the way."

In the waning nights of summer, beneath its arching canopy of trees, Roslyn Avenue was illuminated by swirls of fireflies that seemed to have adopted our house as their vortex. Approaching home, we saw not so much a house of stone as a wavering net of phosphorescence. In younger years, I'd filled mayonnaise jars with these creatures and laid in bed, trying to read by their light. Now, I wanted to read the light itself, as if it were Morse code. We pulled into the driveway, and I stared at the blinking caul around our house: Light, dark. Safety, danger. Love, loss. I wanted fireflies to offer answers. I wanted all the mixed messages unmixed. I wanted a family less complicated than nature.

My father had barely stepped through the kitchen door when he whirled back on us. "Damn it! Goddammit, what did I tell you all? This whole place is falling apart!"

"Harry?" Mom asked, frightened, as we clambered inside, "What's the matter?"

The house was sweltering. The air had never come back on. A pair of yellow gladioli in a glass vase on the kitchen table drooped forlornly, their petals brown and curling. My father stomped aimlessly around the room, scratching at his head with both hands. I opened the refrigerator door.

"I think I'll sleep in here tonight."

"Joshua!" Dad hollered. "I do not find this a bit funny. I do not find anything funny about this whole damned day."

"Josh, Lewis," Mom cut him off, "go make sure you have all your school stuff ready for tomorrow. You ought to get a good night's sleep. Harry, don't worry, I'll call the service right now. They'll have someone out first thing in the morning. Why don't you go switch into some comfortable shorts and watch the rest of the game up in our room. I'll bring you up some ice cream, OK?"

Minutes later, as we lifted the hinged flap in the linen closet floor to dump our clothes down the laundry chute, Lew and I heard our mother in the playroom just below us. The sound, a sort of gulping and wheezing, was muffled as it rose through the week's accumulation of dirty socks and T-shirts. My brother and I glanced at each other in the sticky heat, wondering whether our mother was laughing or crying. Never mind that our parents always felt free to interrogate us based on their slight, speculative mind-reading efforts; we were eavesdropping here, it would be wrong to holler down the chute to ask if everything was OK.

Anxious given the day's delicate balance, we walked down the hall to the top of the stairs. If Mom's voice drifted up to us through this public space rather than the secret passage of the chute, we could run to her in solace or solidarity. Her muffled tones suddenly escalated to house-filling paroxysms of emotion, an unbreaking stream of whoops and hoots and that gasping, breathless laughter that there is no way to stop even though it hurts so much.

To our mother's primal cry, we rushed, uncharacteristically immodest, clad only in our sleeping briefs, as if we were little boys again, not teenage creatures with shoulder blade pimples and stripes of hair from our navels to our necks.

She pulled us into her, one son curled in each arm. Shaking and laughing, in the center of the playroom, her face damp with sweat and tears that flowed more freely than the viscous glue which had softened and weakened in the 90-degree heat of the day. At our feet, face down, lay the guts of a hundred puzzles, mostly still assembled, but molten on the surface and pliable to the touch. Still nailed to the walls were the corner pieces, four disconnected anchors for each image that had weakened and dropped away.

"What's going on?" our father demanded, running through the kitchen to the playroom. "Oh my God."

"I'm going to go to bed now," said Lewis, crisply extricating himself and giving each of my parents a quick peck on the lips. "Night, Josh. Don't forget to set your alarm extra early," he called back as he dashed upstairs. "Bowey High starts at the crack of dawn, ha ha!"

"That's right, you're in high school now," my father said, slowly shaking his head, either at me or the broken puzzles. "So here we are, three adults amidst the wreckage."

"Oh, honey," said Mom, leaning into Dad. "It's not so bad. It was an old hobby. We haven't built a puzzle in years and this room's gone to waste. We certainly weren't spending any time in here looking at them."

I suddenly remembered another lost hobby, another lost room. What had ever happened those heavy shoe boxes of my grandfather's exotic coins, exhumed from that Florida closet, but never seen since? I wanted to ask my father if he had followed through on his threat to sell Grandpop Josh's precious treasure. But, clearly, the time was not right. Dad knelt to the carpet and lifted a cornerless fallen image, flipping it from its gray cardboard back to its colorful front, sticky with half-molten puzzle glue.

It was a picture of Victorian houses, perched on a San Francisco hillside. My father set it on the card table and, as gently as I have ever seen him do anything, he began bending it up from the edges. The softened glue allowed what was once a flat and brittle image to be transformed.

My father bent as far as he could without breaking. He formed a delicate, oddly scalloped bowl.

"Consider this a piece of art for your new office, Becca. We're going to remodel this room for you. No more studying at the library, hon." He forced a too-bright smile. "I'm going to make sure you have everything you need right here."

"I'm sorry about this whole mess, Harry."

"It's not your fault, Bec. This lousy heat—I guess we'll have to sleep nude tonight, huh?"

"G'night, guys!" I beat a quick retreat before he got gross.

After midnight, my stomach slightly unsettled, I wandered down to the kitchen for a glass of ginger ale. I stepped into the playroom without turning the lights on. Sitting on the sofa, I stared at the wall ahead of me, watching the blackness turn to gray until I could make out the corner pieces, hammered in place.

"Start from the four corners," had been my father's main advice on puzzle building. "That's your foundation. From there, everything will work out fine."

My eyes drew lines in the darkness, forming rectangles with connections far stronger than the ones that held jigsaw pieces together. I thought of Ellen Cleyskil, daubing at her canvases, never solving any puzzle, but layering on the rich ambiguities of art.

I must have somehow understood even then. We Royaltons were inextricably bound, no matter what space might come between us.

~

Since moving to Roslyn Avenue, my parents, in a quiet, connected reflex, had slowly separated from the social circle of Dad's co-workers and their wives, because these couples had begun to separate from each other. During college, I met the occasional classmate who would empathize with me over the somehow perverse propriety of growing up with well-to-do suburban parents who were at least somewhat happy in their marriages. It must have been even stranger for my parents to see their own friends' uncouplings, more than twenty years in the making.

"Well, I guess we must be doing something right, huh, honey?" Dad joked at the dinner table just after they told us that Uncle Howard and Aunt Betty Goodman were kaput. Mom dragged the tines of her fork through a puddle of applesauce on her plate. The splits seemed to come at regular monthly intervals then, as if my parents had been given an unwanted subscription to bad news: Uncle Stu and Aunt Judie, Uncle Richard and Aunt Susan, Uncle Matt and Aunt Donna, on and on—my parents pulled away from them all, wanting neither to choose sides socially nor to immerse themselves in their friends' double-edged tales of hidden domestic cruelty and newfound freedom.

Six months after Howard Goodman left home, my parents told us that Robby had been booted from his private school, leaving a trail of obscene spray paint and marijuana smoke in his wake. Mom and Dad frowned in unison; Lew and I earnestly following suit. Even my mother, one foot now perpetually dipped in the brook of psychobabble, had trouble empathizing with the family shrapnel exploding around us.

"I just can't understand it," she said, plain and simple. Divorce, delinquency, drugs—all manner of vice struck us as foreign currency. We were freakishly upright people.

Meanwhile, Lew and I had begun to shy away from Doug Spanner, overcome with discomfort since we'd learned more of our friend's family history.

"Doug's taking a trip," Lew had announced over dinner one night. "He's going to visit his father."

"What are you talking about?" Dad asked. "He lives with his father. Doug and Paul look exactly alike. Hadn't you noticed?"

Of course I had.

"His other father. Check this out." Lew shook his head to indicate that, yes, this was indeed as crazy as it sounded to Dad. "When they lived in Georgia, Carmen was married to this other guy. Someone her own age. Paul was a college student who did odd jobs at their house."

Like a *Penthouse Forum* story gone haywire, Carmen got pregnant by her yard boy, then, for five years, before fleeing with Paul in tow, let her husband and Doug believe themselves father and son.

"Pretty sick, huh?" asked Lew. "Sometimes I think we're the only normal family around."

The Spanners weren't around much longer. Rumor had it that Paul's losing his job in the county auditor's office was directly connected to Carmen's drunken phone calls to Commissioner Leery's wife, in which she offered a comparative rundown of the two women's sexual skills.

Still, although months had passed since Lew or I had spoken with Doug, the Spanners' flamboyant dysfunction retained a certain magnetism for me. I wouldn't admit it to my father, but I was sorry to see them go. On the Saturday morning of their move to Missouri, I convinced Lew to walk over to the Spanners' house with me. I brought along a bag of Philadelphia soft pretzels for their cross-country drive.

"One last picture of this god-awful neighborhood," Carmen said, handing Lew her Instamatic as she grinned deliriously, huddling with Doug and Paul on the front stoop.

As his parents slipped inside to make one last check that nothing was left behind, Doug ambled over to my brother and me. Stepping between us with that ever-confident smile, he draped his arms around our shoulders.

"Lewis and Joshua Royalton," he addressed us, "may your lives be abundant with poontang. No, really. Party hard, guys. Try not to worry too much, OK? You're high school studs now. I want a postcard every time you get laid."

Lew blushed.

"Are you gonna be OK?" I asked. Doug's discouragement of worrying was altogether lost on me. "I mean, is everything all right with your parents and all?"

"You know," he clucked his tongue, "when I first met you all, I thought your family was goody-goodies. Turns out you're just good."

"Fuck!" he laughed. "I'm think I'm gonna miss you geeks."

As the bridge of Doug Spanner's arms fell from our shoulders, I caught my brother's eye. We would all miss one another.

"Say goodbye to your Mama and Daddy, Joshua!" Carmen called as the car rolled away. "I expect great things from you. Federico Fellini! Federico Fellini!"

Generously oversensitive, my mother took great pains to make sure Lew and I were not unduly worried on the frequent nights that our dinner conversation turned to the slop of other families' troughs. Years of Dad's lurid bird-and-bee peep shows were now supplanted by Mom's cloying romantic balm. From as late as my sophomore year of high school, I can remember her chiming reassurances.

"You guys understand that just because people don't always get along doesn't mean they don't love each other, don't you? When Dad and I argue, that doesn't make you think we're going to get divorced, does it?"

"Right, Mom!" cracked Lew. "Right after Ron and Nancy Reagan!"

"As the song says, boys, your Mom and I are together until the Twelfth of Never," Dad waggled his eyebrows like Groucho Marx. "And, Bec, I'm willing to extend my commitment to the Thirteenth!"

"Harry, sometimes I think you ought to be committed right now."

"Why, babe, because I'm so crazy for you?"

"El yucko," grumbled Lew.

"Take it upstairs, dudes," I seconded.

And they did, my father crooning in her ear as they left the room. I washed the dishes. Lew swept the kitchen floor.

"Hey, Josh," he asked over the rush of the kitchen faucet. "I need to ask you something, OK?"

"Sure, Lew." We'd been avoiding real conversation for months. "What's up?

"Well, have you ever done it?" he wondered, tremulously.

I gave him a blank stare.

"You know, had sex?"

"Shut up!" I felt the muscles in my face pull tight, an unexpected mask of self-protecting anger. "That's none of your business."

"Geez! Don't be such a baby. I was only asking a question."

"You're the baby. You're the one who doesn't know anything about sex. Tiny baby Lulu."

"Jerk!" He flung down the dish towel and stormed, red faced, from the room.

I stared into the black rubber maw of the garbage disposal, ashamed of myself. Daily life had begun to lead my brother and me down separate paths. We'd been spending less time with each other, rarely talking. This night, Lew had reached back toward intimacy, and I'd snapped at him in a foolish, defensive reflex.

"Fuck you, asshole," I snarled at my reflection in a soapy knife blade, remembering how Lewis soothed me with Frito serenades in the darkness of our childhood bedroom. Now, my brother had turned to me for guidance, and all I'd managed was to lash at him, seething. I felt unfit to lead.

I lost Lew that night. And it would get worse before it got better. As my brother raged on the athletic fields and I hid out on stage, it became so much easier to float apart than to grapple in the untrained and inarticulate way of loving brothers. Standing alone that night, listening to the water run over my hands, I prayed that my mother's assurances about my father and her were true for all the members of the Royalton family. That despite our differences, there would be no divorces.

Dad made good on his vow to turn the playroom into a private office for Mom. The washer and dryer were moved to the basement, the bottom of the laundry chute plastered shut. My father assumed that my mother's new space at home would keep her at close hand in the coming years.

"We're growing up," Dad would cheerlead at dinner. "But we're growing together."

In fact, when Lew and I were home at all, rather than immersed in extracurricular activities or out with new friends, we cloistered ourselves in our separate rooms, studying hard in our quest for the college grail. Mom took her studies even more seriously. Her office became a retreat; a room divorced from the rest of our house.

One night, as we were starting to clear the table after an excellent dinner of flank steak, baked apples and, nonetheless, applesauce, Mom set a box of assorted Pepperidge Farm cookies on the counter.

"Well, what do you know, guys?" Dad said, grinning and bringing the box to the table. "Old traditions die hard."

"Oh, no, Harris," she said. "That's for my study group. They're coming over at eight. It's Wednesday nights from now on, remember?"

"Oh, right. I forgot." He paused. "Well, do you have to give them those cookies, Bec? I've kinda been looking forward to them since I noticed them in the cupboard."

"You've got to be kidding, Harris. Go to the grocery story and buy your own box if it's so important. Just have a Fig Newton or something, for God's sake."

As Mom's classmates arrived, my father sat on the living room couch, feigning absorption in ESPN while furtively glancing over his shoulder to take in each guest's arrival: A bald guy with a walrus mustache, a reedy woman in spinsterish horn-rims, a prim, chubby woman, Leanne Lindsay, who had been on a PTA committee with Dad.

"Hi, Harry!" she said, poking her head in with a laugh. "Thanks for letting us schoolkids invade your house."

"My pleasure," he noted, rising. "A guy's got to support his family's interests."

As Mom led Mrs. Lindsay back to the office, the doorbell rang again, and I answered it.

"Hey, I'm Josh. Are you here for the study group?"

"Sure am," said a young man with jug ears. He reminded me of old photos of Dad. He was much more handsome though, with his sandy blond hair and protruding Adam's apple.

"I thought I might have got the directions wrong when I saw this place. Kind of a mansion, huh? I keep forgetting that grad students aren't all fresh out of college. Oh, geez, sorry, I didn't introduce myself. I'm Darren. Darren Arblum."

"So, Becca, she's such a cool person." He smiled at me. "She's your Mom?"

"Yes, she is," said my father, stepping in and extending a hand. "And I'm his Dad."

Waves of paranoia filled the room, buzzing from Dad but reverberating, full force, in me. Were Mom and this new friend bound to offer some twisted reprise on the saga of Carmen and Paul Spanner? Would I be taken from my father, abducted by Darren?

"Impossible," I scolded myself. "Why can't you keep your crazy head in check?"

"Hi, Darren!" Mom stepped back into the foyer. "Glad you made it. C'mon back; we need to get started."

~

As the rest of us grew busier with school life, my father turned back to his partners. He dug into his work, keeping later hours, taking on new clients, "socking away enough money to help you boys pursue your dreams." But he also became a tourist, paying visits to old dreams of his own. In the homes of his law school classmates, he saw fresh new marriages coming to bloom. He saw second chances at raising children.

Dad would come home from work, snapshots in hand, bubbling over with anecdotes about Jerry Minskoff's twins, Howard Goodman's three-year-old daughter.

"Look at that Tracy chewing on the football! Howie says she's very coordinated for her age. A real athlete."

"Geez, Dad," I groused, half protective of the kid, half jealous that my father had toddlers on the brain. "She's a baby for chrissakes. Give her a chance to figure out what she wants to be on her own."

"Hey, better she be a jock than a juvenile delinquent like her step-brother Robby."

"You know, Dad, maybe Robby turned out bad because Uncle Howard stepped all over their family."

"I'm sorry, Josh. You're right. I don't mean to act like I think it was OK for Uncle Howard or Uncle Jerry or any of them to do what they did to their wives and kids. But that was years ago now. Life goes on, right? You've got to give a guy a second chance."

"Fine, Dad. Life goes on. But the past is still there, isn't it? You don't get born again or something. All the old shit is still there, too, right alongside the new shit."

"If you weren't so damned smart," he laughed, "I'd tell you to watch your language. So listen, philosopher king, I guess there's no chance you'd be interested in joining me for Zak and Ari Minskoff's hockey game Saturday morning?"

"Good guess, papa-*san*," I bowed to him. "But do give my love to Jer's buxom wifette."

"I know, I know. Shelly's a real ditzball. So when are you and your brother going to introduce me to some more sophisticated women? I know high school's not the same as when Mom and I were kids, but teenagers still date, right?"

"If you want to know something about Lewis, ask Lewis." I snapped. "And I'm not dating, OK? And if I was it would be none of your business."

"Hey! Relax." He mussed my hair. "I'm not trying to push you. I just don't want you to miss out on the stuff that really makes life worth living."

~

I won a lead role in the Bowey High Players' spring production that year, Oliver Goldsmith's *She Stoops to Conquer.* In a purple brocade vest, riding boots, and a phony pigtail, I stepped nervously out of the wings for my first scene, deafening myself to the embarrassing little intake of breath and single unrestrained clap that signaled my mother was in the audience. It was a tavern scene, and upon my request to see the bill of fare, the innkeeper brought me the large leather portfolio I'd rehearsed with dozens of times. This night, however, when I opened it to peruse the menu, the listings of boiled beef and shepherd's pie were accompanied by a special dish: a lurid close-up photograph of a fat, veiny penis en route to a stubble-circled mouth. I could feel the pranksters peering in from the wings, biting down on the heels of their hands to keep from laughing. I sensed my parents in the audience, watching me.

Without cracking a smile, I buried that bone. I denied its very existence. I jammed it down deep below my consciousness and carried on. Haughtily cocking my head, spouting on in my ridiculous mockery of a British accent, I marched blithely through to the end of the show, winning my lady and accepting my applause. When the curtain came down, I was suddenly surrounded by the older guys in the cast and crew: High fives, slaps on the back, "Way to keep cool, bro!"

I was an actor, now. My ability to ignore that photograph had conferred new status upon me, assuring me an honored place in the pantheon of high school dramatics.

The next morning, Saturday, I went to the library to research a term paper and was met with further kudos on the show from my classmates. Arriving home exhilarated by this first great high school success, I ran to the giant oak in the backyard, convinced that I could finally conquer it. I hoisted myself onto the easy first branch, then took a precariously wide step upward. I grabbed and shinnied and swung until I found myself higher than I'd ever climbed before. My bedroom window hung just above. With a few, slightly shaky maneuvers, I would be there, looking in like the squirrels. I pulled myself up with a victorious grunt.

I saw my night table drawer, wide open. My father sat on my unmade bed. He was staring at a *Penthouse,* masturbating.

That night, after everyone was asleep, I crept outside and dumped all my magazines in one of the battered aluminum garbage cans by the driveway. I sprayed in a stream of the lighter fluid Dad used for the grill. And, for the first time, I struck one of my grandfather's heirloom matchsticks, black wood with a gold tip, from a box marked Wolfy's Velvet Lounge.

Lying in bed afterward, I tried to recall the slick, shiny photograph that had been hidden in the menu during the play. But even in imagination, it would not come back to me. There had been a rawness to those five burning seconds on stage that transcended anything I'd felt before. But that was smoke now, too. It was time to get on with the show.

~

"Where is your brother always disappearing to?" Mom asked as we sat at the kitchen table one late February afternoon. She had stepped in from her office for a study break and a cup of Celestial Seasonings. But seeing me home early from a short rehearsal day, she quickly scuttled her personal time. Anxiously gnawing a knuckle, she tucked into family worries. During lacrosse and baseball seasons, my brother attended practice each afternoon. But after school during winter months, he was often, unnervingly, off the Royalton radar.

"He's not getting into pot, is he, Joshua?"

"I don't know," I muttered, knowing full well that our parents had far more interest in being paranoid about drugs than Lew and I had in actually trying them. Lew was heavily invested in body-as-temple athletic aesthetics, and I simply had no interest in seeing the world any weirder than it already looked to me.

"We're not doing drugs!" Lew had responded to their hectoring once, as if that should be enough. "Quit asking about it."

While my brother grew taut and withdrawn, I polished my anecdotal skills, regaling my parents with colorful tales of my drama club friends, our sometimes drunken sponsor, Mr. Pell, and our after-school mischief at the Roy Rogers fast-food restaurant down the street from school. My parents exulted in my openness. They felt attached to my life.

My father mistakenly believed he could bring Lewis back home by keeping him in the house. So when my brother was late for dinner, or when he got a C, or when he forgot to take the cans to the curb on trash day, he was grounded. He would hole up in his room, door shut tight, stereo blasting the oblique, tuneless music of Yes and King Crimson. But my father never got what he wanted out of these punishments. Dad might be able to hold my brother captive, but Lew could still keep his feelings to himself.

I was jealous of Lewis. All my life, my emotions had floated right up to the surface for my parents to see, alive and thriving like water striders on a pond. Now, desperately afraid of my inner feelings, I performed a willful submersion with funny stories over family dinners, witty participation in class, and endless banter with the kids at drama club parties. My parents and schoolmates were charmed. Feeding off their approval, I ate away my own insides. My feelings became so private that they eluded even me.

I wanted to know what was going through Lewis' mind as much as my parents did. It was as if I'd inherited some congenital illness, a prying virus. I resented my brother's inner life, wondered how he'd learned to keep secrets. Most of all, I wanted to know if the rumors I'd been hearing were true.

"How did your brother get to be such a ladies' man?" Evan Farr asked me as we'd waited our turns to audition for *Oklahoma!*

"What do you mean?" I was taken off guard.

"He's seeing Jennifer Dulcey. I mean, geez, he's only a sophomore. She's a junior. I'm a *senior,* for God's sake. A pretty studular one, too. *I* want Jen Dulcey. Do something about it."

Do something about it? I hadn't even heard about it. I'd knocked on Lew's bedroom door that night.

"What do you want?" he said curtly, opening the door just a crack.

"Can I ask you something?"

"What?"

"C'mon. Can't I come in for a minute? Please?"

Begrudgingly, he let me in for the first time since I'd snapped at his questions over the dishes months before. Questions, I supposed, that must have had to do with Jen Dulcey. I felt like I hadn't seen my brother's room in ages. The same old football and hockey posters hung on the wall, the corners curling a bit, the stars now retired from play. It was as though Lewis didn't update his room because he no longer really lived there. He was at home inside of himself.

"So, what is it? I have to study. Fucking Dad's going to kill me if I don't get at least a B on this algebra test tomorrow."

"Well, I heard that you're, um, going out with a girl at school. Is it true?"

"Oh, geez! Who's telling you that? It's none of your business, Josh. It's just none of your business."

"So you are?"

"Just forget it, OK? I'm not talking about it."

"But, c'mon, its family stuff."

"It's *my* stuff! What do you mean family stuff? Because Dad is always riding our butts about 'When you gonna get a girlfriend?' That's crap! Why the hell should he feel proud if I have a girlfriend? It's like he wants to us to make him feel like a teenager again. And Mom, she just smiles and goes along with whatever he wants. You and Mom are idiots. At least I *know* he's holding us prisoner. And I'm not staying. I going. I'm gone."

"But what about me? I'm not Dad. Can't you tell me about Jen?"

"Forget about it, Josh!" he hissed. "No way you'd keep quiet. You're on their side now. Mr. Straight A. Mr. Sharing-Caring Bullshit Happy Family. You can get your own girlfriend if you want to make Dad happy."

Evan approached me at lunch the next day. "Did your brother agree that Miss Dulcey deserves a more cultured and sophisticated man?"

"I guess she likes jocks," I quipped, deciding to burnish Lew's reputation even if he hadn't offered official confirmation. "You need to find a girl who's interested in drama fags."

"Very funny, Royalton. Just wait. The girls in this school will come to their senses yet."

"Don't worry. You'll find someone, Ev. You deserve it, man."

"So do you, Joshua. You should bag a supermodel like the ones you have hanging in your bedroom."

I laughed. Evan hadn't been over in awhile. Months before, I had replaced Cheryl Tiegs with the grinning image of my favorite performer, the absurdly clean, strangely brainy comedian, Steve Martin. When he jerked around on television, a blankly sexless marionette, It was easy to imagine there was no body at all beneath his crisp, white suit. Even his dirty jokes seemed immaculate.

~

It was an October Saturday in my junior year of high school when the tree surgeons came, ArborRx painted on the door of their truck. But the driver, in jeans, workboots, and an unbuttoned flannel shirt over his clinging thermal tee, looked less like a doctor than a stripper. As I'd flipped through late-night cable the previous summer, the Chippendales and their grittier imitators seemed to be on every channel. The driver's two buddies shared their boss's beefy, smiling, shave-overdue charisma. I imagined cranking up the *Deliverance* soundtrack on my boom box and watching the three of them disrobe to "Dueling Banjos" right there on our wide front lawn.

With their ropes and power tools, they headed down to the foot of our driveway. I ran up to my bedroom and pulled the blinds. All day, I stayed there, the roar of their chainsaw rattling my windows. Sitting at my desk, distracted from my homework, I gravitated to the floor where I pored over a shelf of my old children's books: *James and the Giant Peach; The Big Book of Magic;* and an old favorite picture book, *Tikki Tikki Tembo,* in which a small Chinese boy, trapped at the bottom of a well, must wait endlessly to be rescued because the townspeople have such difficulty pronouncing his long and compli-cated ancestral name. I remembered my father reading that book at my bedside, placing his hand on my chest to still me as I shook with laughter at the child's plight.

I lost track of the passing hours until the din of the chain saws sub-sided and the radio I'd left playing quietly that morning became audi-ble once again. "Urgent, urgent, urgent, urgent. E-mergency," I found myself singing along to a crummy Foreigner song. I went to my bed-side window and reached for the blinds, taking a deep breath of antic-ipation.

My mother was starting a private practice in her office and was having a separate entrance built, so her patients wouldn't need to pass through the house. Wooden stairs and a landing would be built out back, where the great oak had stood. On the ground, two stories be-low my bedroom window, I saw a squirrel, utterly confused, skittering around the oval plane of stump that hours before had been his home.

~

"Josh, would you grab those crunchies? My hands are full with these flowers."

Getting up from the kitchen table where I sat with the newspaper one night, trying to solve the Jumble, I followed my mother and her vase of gladiolas into the office. In addition to her clients, Mom con-tinued to host study groups on occasion, other psychologists who would compare case notes. I never met them. They used the private entrance.

"Hey, Mom," I asked, setting the basket of pretzel knots on the table in front of her couch. "Does that guy Darren Arblum still come over?"

"Darren Arblum?"

"Yeah, you know. From your old group. Nice guy. Blond. His ears stick out like Dad's used to . . . "

"Oh, Darren. That was a couple of years ago. I didn't realize you'd met him."

". . . he had a really prominent Adam's apple. I actually think he was closer to my age than yours . . . "

"Josh, honey, I know who you're talking about. I remember."

"So, does he come around anymore?"

"No, he actually only came a couple of times. Transferred to another program, I think."

"Oh," I said, turning to go back into the house. "OK. See ya."

"Wait a minute, sweetie. Come sit a bit. I feel like we haven't talked in awhile."

On a strange impulse, I locked the door between her office and the kitchen before pulling a chair up to my mother's desk. She opened a drawer and handed me a yellowed photograph. There were two little girls; the elder maybe nine, precociously elegant in a dark, tailored coat, kneeling down and tickling a finger under the chin of a pudgy bunny-suited toddler. The Philadelphia Zoo's great gray elephant statue stood behind them.

"Do you recognize them?" she leaned toward me, brown eyes imploring.

"The little one is you?"

"And the big one is Aunt Binnie. Our parents used to take us on a zoo trip every year." She smiled. "Sound familiar?"

"So where's Dad?"

"What do you mean?"

"Oh, duh. I guess he took the picture."

"Don't be silly, Josh. My father took the picture."

"Your father died."

"Honey," she said, furrowing her brow. "I didn't lose my father or find your father until I was thirteen. This picture was taken when I was three. I did have a life before Harris, you know."

I had never thought much about my parents' early childhoods. My father had always brushed off discussion of the subject, implying that his life began and ended with Mom and Lewis and me. My mother was suggesting broader possibilities now, other families past and future.

"I know you don't remember Binnie. She was nineteen and had just married Hilton Lazar when my Daddy died. She was always very chic and fashion conscious, much more than I. You can see that in the photo. You can also see that she loved me. My father had objected to her marrying Hilton; he was older, he was rich, and he was taking her away to California. Then, when Binnie got divorced—this was before anyone got divorced—well, Harris and I really just cut ourselves off from her. I don't think you've seen her since you were four or five."

"I do remember her, Mom. She came to the old house. She brought me that double kaleidoscope, with one outer-space scene and one undersea." It had shimmered and sparkled on the outside, the fanciest thing anyone had ever given me.

"I can't believe you," she exclaimed in happy astonishment. "I'd forgotten that myself."

I wondered if she'd also forgotten how Dad had taken the gift away from me as soon as Aunt Binnie left. "That rich bitch doesn't know what a family is. She's not going to come stepping in out of nowhere to spoil my kids."

"I've been talking to Binnie on the phone," Mom confided. "Almost once a week, for a few months now. We're very different. But we're even more the same. She's my sister. I miss her. I think I may even go visit. Regardless of what your father thinks. Can you imagine what it would be like for you and Lewis to be cut off from each other's lives? Terrible."

I nodded solemnly.

"We're still family. All the time and distance in the world can't change that." She paused for a moment, deliberating. "Joshy? Why did you ask about Darren Arblum?"

"No reason."

"What makes you remember him?"

"I don't know. The Adam's apple, I guess. I always notice them."

"Is that attractive to you?" she asked, gently.

"I guess," I blushed. "I mean, on a girl. I have to do homework; can I go now?"

"Of course, I don't want to hold you back. It was nice talking."

I rushed upstairs and dove into the A section of my American Heritage dictionary. There it was: "The slight projection of the throat formed by the largest cartilage of the larynx, usually more prominent in men than in women."

I was relieved not have lied to my mother.

Girls did have Adam's apples.

~

"You've got to seem like an interesting person," my father stressed, urging me to take on more after-school activities for the benefit of college admissions officers. "You need to make yourself appear complex."

I joined French Club, which was a joke. All you had to do was sit around and talk once a month. By regularly bringing a quiche or some *patisserie* (Oreos counted) to the meeting, you could pretty much guarantee yourself election to the board senior year. With my voluntary special presentation, *"Et toi? Fromage-phile ou Fromage-phobe?"* complete with Brie on Ritz crackers, I handily locked up a board position as *secrétaire*.

I also began to pen movie reviews for *The Bowey Bugle*.

"Piece of shit!" groused Evan, kicking scornfully at the asphalt as we walked to his car after Steve Martin's persona-breaking turn as a romantic tragedian in *Pennies from Heaven*. "He's supposed to be funny."

"A WILD AND COMPLEX GUY" touted my article's headline.

"Good job," said my father after reading the piece. "One per issue and maybe you'll get to be an editor next year. Tell me that wouldn't look great on your applications? I don't know about this movie, though. I thought he was hysterical in *The Jerk*."

"He doesn't always have to be the same, does he?"

After that, I tried to focus on comedy, writing a sketch for the Bowey Rock-A-Rama, a program oddly born of the high school guidance office. Our delusional counselors figured that they would offer a creative forum to the miscreant likes of Benjy the Deadhead and Mike Cochran, who had a punk band called Angst-Kebab. Given an opportunity for public acceptance, they might be dissuaded from drug-addled evildoing in the community.

Evan arranged for the drama club to present skits between the musical acts. My contribution was a jungle-themed game show parody called Wild Guess. The loincloth-clad emcee would swing in from the wings on a vine; his bikinied assistant, Jane, would strike seductive poses and wax poetic over Turtle Wax and other glamorous parting gifts. A pygmy judge would fire poison blow darts at contestants who gave incorrect answers.

Perhaps inspired by Carmen Spanner, I created the role of the Tarzanesque host for myself. I would do push-ups and sit-ups every day until the show, then shock the school with my studly physique. I could already see my parents beaming with pride as I swung onstage, calling out to Jane with a breast-beating holler.

One late January afternoon following rehearsal, Evan and I sat in at the Roy Rogers restaurant eating fries with some of his senior friends. I playfully flirted with fat Rhonda Lelch, who was playing one of the contestants in my skit.

"Darling, have I mentioned that you're looking extra crispy this afternoon?"

"Now stop that, you handsome devil!"

"May I escort you to the Fixins Bar, milady?"

"Would you two cut it out?" groused Evan. "You're ridiculous."

He loosened the cap on a squeeze bottle so the next unsuspecting Roy's customer would release a sloppy belch of mayonnaise onto his burger.

Evan had been in a dark mood for the past ten days. After years of complaints about date deprivation, he had finally begun a fling with Jessie Elfman, only to see it collapse after less than a month. Jessie was generally recognized as one of the coolest girls in the senior class, right up there with Jen Dulcey, smart and pretty without being stuck up. But after his exultation when she accepted his first invitation to a Saturday night movie, Evan's genuine appreciation of Jess was quickly overshadowed by his indulgence in the bragging rights that he felt came with dating her.

"Irreconcilable differences," Jess had sniffled to me over the phone on the night of their breakup. "Mainly differences of opinion as to whether or not a certain eighteen-year-old boy is the center of the universe."

Evan called a minute later. "What a cunt," he snapped. "After everything I did for her."

Still fuming after almost two weeks, Evan couldn't bear my lampoon of romance with Rhonda. When she got up to use the ladies' room, Evan wrinkled his face in repulsion at her ample behind and hissed at me.

"At least I had a real girlfriend, Royalton. What have you ever done besides waste your time goofing with Miss Goodyear there?"

"Screw you," I snapped, defensively, "I'm going to have a girlfriend."

"When?" he asked, smirking and glancing around at the rest of group.

"Valentine's Day!" I blurted in unchecked wishfulness.

Since the end of elementary school, when we either had to bring a card for everyone in class or none at all, Valentine's Day had been a trial for me; a trial, in retrospect, at which I withheld essential evidence from myself. For weeks ahead, each shop-window Cupid, each heart-shaped box of chocolates, each single long-stemmed rose paired with a spray of baby's breath filled me with a flow of rich, thick feeling that I desperately wanted to share. I strained to consider every girl who passed my way, but I gave no cards or flowers. And in the evenings, after Dad gave Mom her bouquet, I would lie on my bed, staring at the ceiling, that rich, thick feeling curdling into grief.

Given this sorrowful history, even I knew the vow I'd just made was highly dubious. Rhonda returned to the table.

"Hey, get a load of this, Rhond. Josh says he's going to have a real girlfriend by Valentine's. That's just three days after the show, Joshy. Do you think someone's gonna see you up there in that Chippendale jungle outfit and fall in love?"

"Cut it out," complained Rhonda. "Let him alone."

"No, Rhonda! Come on, I'll bet you, Evan." I extended a hand in false bravado. "Five bucks."

"Don't, Josh," Rhonda pleaded. "That's a dumb idea."

"No, it's not," countered Evan, with a smirk and a handshake. "Tell you what, I'll give you ten bucks if you actually pull this off."

"Why do you let him treat you like this?" Rhonda whispered angrily as Evan stepped away to get another root beer. "There's nothing wrong with you. You're allowed to be whoever you want, Josh."

Rhonda's sympathy had always made me a bit uneasy, and I felt a twinge of nausea there at the table, watching her blithely spoon a quart of mashed potatoes into her pretty, bloated face. I could never understand why she didn't go on a diet.

"Why do you eat that stuff?" I asked, accusingly. "It has no flavor. It's like eating hot snow."

"I like it, honeybun. Upholstery for the full-figured woman."

That night, staring in my bathroom mirror, I dreamed up another game show skit: The Rhonda Lelch Treasure Hunt. After a contestant got through the preliminary quizzes, he would get to participate in the showcase finale. A silk canopy would be lifted to reveal Rhonda, lying nude on the stage, a great manatee of rippling flesh.

"Before our program began," the host would explain, "five valuable gifts—from a microwave oven to the grand prize check for $25,000—were each placed in one of Ms. Lelch's skin folds. Now, friend, you have a choice to make! Good luck."

I laughed, then slapped myself hard in the face for this cruelty.

It was not until dress rehearsal for Rock-A-Rama that the blow dart pygmy actually participated—Louis Lowen, who Evan had recruited from his calculus class. In addition to being a math whiz, Lou worked out in the weight room. He looked great in his little grass skirt.

"Hey! You wrote this skit?" Louis asked me when we met backstage, both of us wearing more goose pimples than anything else. "It's really funny. You're one twisted dude!"

"I guess so," I swallowed nervously, pulling away from the hand he slapped on my shoulder. "Thanks for helping out."

On show night, I reported for makeup, a process I detested. The performers lined up against a corridor wall, sitting in folding chairs. The girls in the makeup crew seemed to change with every show, which meant there were always unfamiliar hands touching and rubbing my face.

"No way we're getting makeup!" Benjy the Deadhead protested to our faculty sponsor, Mr. Pell. "Benjy and the Branflakes are about roots music, natural beauty. We're not Alice Cooper or Kiss or something."

"I dig your groove, Ben. But this isn't the same as performing at a party. Under the stage lights, your faces will get all bleached out with no makeup. No one will even recognize you. This will just bring out your features—your natural beauty, if you will—so that you look like yourselves rather than blank-faced nobodies."

"OK, you're next," a short, blonde girl pulled up a chair to face mine. "I've seen you in plays before. Do you know what your base is?"

"Medium bronze," I told her, as she reached into her kit for the compact and sponge. "I have to warn you. I squirm a lot. I'm Josh Royalton, by the way. I mean, I know you said you've seen me before. But— "

"Close your mouth a minute so I can get your cheeks there. Good. Good. Pleasure to meet you, Josh. I'm Meri."

"Merry? Do you have sisters named Joy and Gaye?"

"Ha ha! It's M-E-R-I, though. Short for Meredith. But, you know, our old neighbors had triplets named Faith, Hope, and Charity."

"Ugh! You're kidding."

"Yup," she said, applying blush to my cheeks. "I'm kidding."

I laughed. Until then, Rhonda Lelch had been the only girl I knew who made decent jokes.

"Some people just call me Mer. Actually, I don't have any sisters. Just one brother. He's in the show—Louis."

"Louis is your brother?" I looked at her and immediately saw the resemblance; fine, high cheekbones, soulful green eyes. My thoughts tangled for a moment. "Um, hey, I have a brother Lewis, too. Different spelling, I think."

"Yeah, he's in my class. I mean sophomore year. I've never really been in a class with him."

"I bet you're in all Honors courses, right?"

"Mm-hmm. OK, I'm going to do your eyes now."

"I hate this," I said, squinting. "I don't like anyone touching me there." I always imagined an accident, mascara or shadow somehow slipping, damaging my vision.

"Relax," Meri cooed, kneading the back of my neck with one hand as she gently went about her work. "I'm not going to hurt you."

"That was painless," I told her when she finished. "Can you do my eyes every show?"

"Every day, if you want."

"Well, I fancy blue shadow for homeroom, and then something in a frosted green at lunch." I made the same campy gestures I used when I goofed with Rhonda.

"My swabs are at the ready," Meri proclaimed with a laugh. "You better go get changed. I watched rehearsal yesterday. You and Lou need to have your whole bodies made-up."

"Listen," I suggested, grabbing the bronzer from her kit. "There are a lot of people waiting. Let me just do myself in the dressing room. Don't worry, you did the important stuff. Eyes are the challenge. Bodies are easy."

As I swung out over the stage that night, drawing laughs in my loincloth, Dad's automatic flash popped in the darkness. Releasing my tether, I presented the contestants with their unanswerable Wild Guess questions: "How many licks does it take to get to the center of a Tootsie Roll Pop?"; "What is the meaning of life?"; "Why do fools fall in love?"

Louis was greeted with wolf whistles upon his entrance. I watched him crouching on his toned, tanned haunches and savored the moment when he pursed his lips around the bamboo blowpipe to execute Evan. "Ooogah, oogah!" he improvised after shooting the suction-tipped dart.

In the dressing room afterward, I scrubbed at my face with cold cream, black mascara smearing from my eyes onto the paper towels.

"Great job, Lou!" I said when his face appeared over my shoulder in the mirror. "Oh, geez! You scared me! I'm sorry. I didn't realize . . . Your brother did a great job."

It was Meri.

"I mean, you did too. The makeup and all. Sorry. It's the guys' changing room, I just mistook— "

"Don't worry about it, Josh," she laughed. "You should see pictures of Lou and I as kids. Ever see those freakshow pictures, a body with two heads? We're like one head with two bodies. Anyway, I didn't come in here to frighten you, I wanted to find out if you were going to the cast party."

"Benjy's parties aren't really my thing," I fudged, not wanting to admit I didn't smoke pot. Her brother had already announced his intention to get plastered in celebration of his seminude stage debut. "Some people are heading over to my house just to hang out. Do you want to come with us?"

"Funny stuff, kiddo!" my dad greeted me as I stepped into our front hall, about ten kids clustered behind me. "Bet the girls will be chasing after Tarzan's banana on Monday."

"Da-ad," I growled, trying not to blush. "You guys promised you would stay upstairs."

"Don't be so sensitive; I just wanted to say hello. Hi, Evan, Rhonda. Good show. So have you seniors decided where you're going next year?"

"Hey, Mr. Royalton," replied Ev. "Acceptances don't arrive until April. I'm pretty sure I'll get into Penn, though."

"Good school," said Dad, always happy to praise his alma mater. "You'll get to stay in Philly that way, too. Well, Josh tells me it's past my bedtime. You kids enjoy yourselves."

"Your dad's cute," said Meri. "I can see the family resemblance."

"C'mon, I don't look like him."

"Sure you do."

She smiled when I told her I'd forgive her, happy asterisks wrinkling at the corners of her emerald eyes. We all sprawled on the living room carpet playing Trivial Pursuit to an MTV backbeat. When the game ended and a hand of gin broke out, Mer and I retreated into conversation on the couch, resting our stockinged feet on the glass-topped coffee table. Evan stretched out, surly, beneath it.

"You're so funny," I said. "I mean humorous funny. Not weird funny. I'm both I guess."

"You're not weird. That's all in your head."

Mer tilted her own head back then, and my eyes traced a line from the hollow of her neck to her emotion-wet eyes. The eyes are the challenge. The body is easy. I dove anxiously into her glowing green, plunging through my own twin reflections and taking her into my arms.

"I want to love you," I gasped under my breath. But I could articulate no further; I ran my tongue along her tongue and sealed my lips against hers. Her embrace aroused and comforted and convinced me. This was where I was supposed to be. Evan stared up at us through the tabletop glass, and I smiled to the ceiling, to my parents, in their bed. I lost myself in romance with Meri. It was wonderful, like a dream.

I gave flowers and candies and a card that Valentine's Day, gliding down the hall with a new surprise every time I knew I'd find her at her locker.

"You're crazy!" Mer exclaimed. "You don't have to do this!"

"I know I'm crazy," I replied. "And I want to do this."

I wanted to assure her of my ardent affection, to make her feel as obligated as I did from the start.

~

To mark our three-month anniversary, I gave Meri a spongey toy bear named Maurice, who I imagined to be my secret surrogate, taking up a permanent place inside her bedroom.

"Look at him," she said with a laugh, squashing Maurice's head down between his legs. "He doesn't need a girlfriend."

"Sure he does," I said. "He can't hibernate down there forever. Besides, who's he gonna play Scrabble with?"

Scrabble had become our favorite recreation. After school and on Saturday nights, we would eagerly take to the board. I loved the straight-edged click of the tiles, their expressive, yet constrained arrangements. Meri laid down the X for a double-letter score. My CHIMERA intersected her PLUMB. She was fiercely competitive, arguing the legitimacy of printers' measures, musical notes, phonetic spellings of letters of the alphabet: EM, EN, EFF, ZEE.

"I know they're in the dictionary," I complained, "but they're just so unpoetic."

"This isn't poetry," she countered, raising an eyebrow and tallying a triple. "It's a game."

Mer lacked no sensitivity to artfulness, she was simply able to divide and categorize better than I was. She had no requirement for everything to connect. On those afternoons and weekend evenings when we were not together, she spent hours at an easel with watercolors and pastels.

I would telephone incessantly and ask what she was painting.

"Joshy!" she laughed. "Do you really think that one night I'm suddenly going to change? I don't want to talk to you about my paintings, babe. It's something I do just for me."

"I bet you've shown your brother."

"Just never mind, OK?"

"See. You have. I knew it."

"Drop it, Josh," she said firmly. "Have a little respect for privacy."

"OK, OK." I pretended to shrug it off. "Anyway, I can always ask Maurice to describe them to me next time I'm over."

She laughed. "You're not pissed at me, are you? I mean, you understand how I feel about this, right?"

Of course I understood. I understood the need to cloak oneself in solitude, to safely shape one's idiosyncratic vision of the world before sharing it with others, even loved ones. But I felt another understanding, too, coiled with the first like a double helix of venomous snakes. I understood the Royalton impulse to knock and enter, the desire to barge right in, share all the secrets, and make sure that everything is under control.

As if my mind was being read, my father's voice suddenly interrupted on the telephone line. "Sorry to break in, but can you two wrap it up? I have to make an important call."

I wondered how long he'd been listening.

"All right, Mer. Gotta go. So the plan is movies tomorrow night, right? And Saturday the zoo. And next Friday we have that party."

I liked to have things planned out for us.


Unlike Meri's folks, my parents didn't make us sneak about sex. In fact, when Mer was at our house, my father pointedly kept his distance from my room, careful not to discourage us.

One Saturday, the four of us were sharing a pizza. Lew had declined to join us. "Remember how we had to make out in the car before I dropped you off at night, Bec?" Dad asked.

"Sure I do. And even then, we were scared about neighbors seeing us through the car windows. Uptight fifties parents!" laughed my mother, the psychologist. "It's ridiculous. Teenagers are full of hormones. It's completely natural for you to want to be physical together."

"OK, Mom. Let's not go into details, huh?"

"Oh, she won't. You know that's my department," joked Dad, elbowing me and turning to Meri. "You should have seen how embarrassed Josh and Lew would get when I used to tell them the facts of life."

"That's because you made it sound like *Debbie Does Dallas*."

My father was invigorated by the presence of teenage passion under his roof. It was as if Meri and I carried atomizers of secret formula, spritzing them throughout his domain. When Mer and I repaired to my room, he would lose himself in our vapors, playing decades-old songs on the stereo and urging my mother to dance.

We rolled, naked in my bed, body over body, limbs around limbs. I ground against thighs and belly and breasts, losing track of her body in the friction, feeling only the rush of my own. I nosed and licked and ran my fingers wherever she would let me.

"Please, just try it. I know you'll like it."

In everything I'd read, the boy had to beg the girl to take him in her mouth. But Meri had done that for months, with no hesitation. She loved to inflict the agonizing pleasure of tongue under purpling ridge, tugging sharp little pinchfuls of the hair on my belly. But I found myself begging to return the favor. It was supposed to be the hallmark of a masterful, sensitive lover.

"You have what it takes," read an article I'd read on the subject, "to drive women crazy."

"No, baby," she embraced me, placing her mouth over my ear. "I don't want you to. Not that and no fucking."

And so we kissed and we tickled, grappled and grinded.

"Skin is skin," I would think to the rhythm. "Friction is friction is friction."

I would glance to the mirror and moan, "Take me home."

Always then, in a spill of liquid moonlight, I would tell her that I loved her. And I did, as much as I possibly could.

One night, near the end, as she dressed by the window, I thought for a moment about Raphy Cleyskil, about friction.

"Gotta go," she cut in.

"I know," I nodded, and took her home.

While taking great stock in the occasional evenings Meri and I spent with my parents, I also envied my brother, who would shake his head at the four of us, gathered round the Scrabble board.

"You kids have a swell night, now!" Lewis mocked as he slipped out the kitchen door.

"You, too, honey!" my mother chimed back, oblivious to his disdain. "Drive carefully."

He would lock the house behind him, turn another key in the ignition, and rumble off into the night. Distracted from the game at hand, I trained my ears on the sound of the Oldsmobile. I followed Lewis all the way to silence, when he crossed the horizon in my mind. Piecing together words from the tiles, I puzzled over Lewis' destinations. There were rumors that he'd gotten back together with Jen Dulcey, then others that they'd broken up again.

"Ask around," I coaxed Meri. "Lew's in your class. Someone must know something."

"Joshua," she'd chastised. "It's none of our business."

"I'm worried about your brother," my father said to us one night, after laying down JURIST with a double letter under J. "Has he told you what he's up to?"

"Afraid not."

"He says he's giving up baseball. I've been going to every game for years, helping him with his strategy. The kid is terrific. He'd be varsity, you know. In his junior year. Looks awfully good on the college applications. But he's going to quit. Says he wants to row crew instead."

"I'm sure it'll work out, Dad. Lewis will be great at crew, too."

But he was worried as much for himself as for Lew. Dad had taught my brother soccer only to see him abandon it for lacrosse. Dad knew baseball like the back of his hand; now, Lew would drop it for another unfamiliar sport. Dad failed to recognize that my brother had grown into a master strategist. Lew loved athletics as much as our father did, but he sought out games to which Harris did not know the rules.

"Josh says you're trying to go to college early, Mer." My mother tried to move the conversation to more comfortable topics.

"Sarah Lawrence," Meri replied. "They have a special program you can enter right from junior year."

"Just outside of New York—that's not too far a drive," my father offered. "You two will be able to get together on the weekends."

"You're assuming, as usual, that I'm going to Penn," I said, rolling my eyes at the thought of attending my parents' hometown alma mater.

"Great school," he said. "Great law school, too. And it sure doesn't hurt that you're legacy."

"I'm not going to Penn. I'm not going to law school. And I'm not going anywhere just because you've got connections."

"Josh," Mer set her palm on the back of my hand after playing the last of her tiles. "Calm down. Your dad just wants the best for you."

"The only thing I agree with him about is that I'll go somewhere near enough to see you on the weekends."

"There's plenty of time to think about all of this," interjected my mother. "It's all a long way off."

"The future is now!" bellowed my father.

Mom ignored him. "Congratulations, Meri!" she cheered, totaling up our scores. "As Lewis would say, you kick butt!"

Two weeks before school let out for the summer, Mer and I sat on my bedroom floor, playing hearts.

"You know how Lewis is dropping baseball? I'm thinking about changing sports, too." I said.

"What are you talking about?"

"I don't think I want to act anymore. Do you think my dad will be pissed?"

"It's not up to your dad, Joshy. But why?"

"When you paint, you have a palette, right? You dip in with your brush and you apply a little red, a little yellow. You control everything. Well, when I act, I feel like red paint. Like I'm just one color in a picture in somebody else's head. Well, last winter, for Rock-A-Rama, I wrote this skit called 'Wild Guess'— "

"Uh, golly gee." She gave me an idiot's grin. "I vaguely remember something like that!"

"Duh, I'm a spaceman. Sorry. Anyway, when I wrote that script, I felt like you do at your easel. I had control of the whole picture. I loved that. I want to write."

"That sounds nice." She leaned in, gently touching her tongue to my earlobe. "You'll be good at it. What do you want to write?"

"Well, there's the *Bugle,* of course. I want to do a lot more reviews for that: movies, records, everything. By the way, there's a little party on Friday, at Ethan's. He's the editor in chief. Could we go? It might help me get more assignments."

"You don't have to prove anything, Josh; they know you're good. Quit underestimating yourself. But let's go anyway. All your drama friends are graduating. Who are you going to hang out with next year?"

"You."

"I'm one person. I'm not your whole life."

"Now it's you who's underestimating yourself," I said, with a flourish. I pulled her down to the carpet and ground my jeans against hers. "You are Princess Leia Orgasma, goddess of my universe."

"Yeah, yeah, yeah. Well, the princess is taking a pottery workshop at night next fall and organic chemistry on Saturdays, so you and your light saber are gonna have a lot of quality time on your hands."

"I know, I know. Hey, maybe I should take pottery, too."

"Joshua! You're going to be the great scribe, remember? Now come on, besides the school paper, what do you want to write?"

"Well, honestly," I confided, pulling a few slim volumes from my shelf. "I'd love to do some of these."

"You want to write children's books?"

"I remember them better than anything else I've ever read. You can make such an impression on a kid."

I pulled out *The Big Book of Safety Fun* and showed her the picture of the boy in the scalding shower.

She flipped through the stick figure images of bent and broken children.

"Can you believe my parents would give us such a nasty thing?"

"Well, they didn't. Not directly." Mer pointed to a tiny ball point inscription inside the front cover that I'd never noticed before: *"Greetings from the road to Harris, world's greatest six-year-old! Happy Birthday 1946! Love, Dad."*

"No way," I whispered. "That's impossible."

"Joshy, just read the writing."

"No," I insisted, shelving our conversation along with the old books. "I can't remember it that way."

~

"Mer! Guess what?" I punched a celebratory fist against her locker door. "You know how your brother loves that Billy Squier song?"

"Oh right, that boy thing," she laughed, proceeding to pump her arm and mimic the singer's randy grunt. "Stroke me, stroke me! Stroke! Stroke!"

"Well, he's coming in concert and guess who scammed four free tickets from the Spectrum?"

"The intrepid *Bugle* reviewer strikes again, huh?"

"I remembered that Louis was into it and figured we could go on a double date." Mer's brother was enrolled at Penn, seeing a girl named Alisha. "Billy Squier's just the opening act. The main band is Queen."

"Oh, gawd! Testosterone overdose," Meri started thrusting her arm and chanting again. "We will, we will, rock you! Rock you!"

Meri ended up having a great time, jumping into the joke of it, shouting and stamping with the best of the metal boys. But despite the exploding flashpots and the licentious massaging of guitar necks on stage, I paid more attention to Louis Lowen, just a few feet away from me in the dark. Alisha and Meri were sandwiched between us and, despite eight months of experience with his sister, I felt compelled to mimic Louis' moves. He nuzzled Alisha's neck, and I followed suit with Meri. He draped his arm over a shoulder and I did the same, our hands practically touching in the narrow breach between our dates.

There was ringing in my ears the whole ride home.

"Have a good time?" Dad asked as I walked in after dropping the Lowens off. "What group was it, again? Any songs I might know?"

He and Lew had been watching a basketball game on TV, and my brother looked up at me, secretly making a face at our father. One of the few things we'd conversed about recently was Dad's pathetic habit of dropping by our rooms for no reason other than to say hello, then idiotically bobbing his head up and down to whatever music we happened to be playing, attempting to demonstrate how in tune with us he was.

"It was hard rock, Dad. Super loud. I feel like my brain is bleeding. It was Mer's brother's idea."

"He's at Penn, isn't he?"

"Yes, Daddy," I groaned. "Louis is one of those prize students who attend the most wonderful college in the world."

It would be a few months until I heard back from schools. In addition to the obligatory Penn application, I had sent my paperwork to Columbia, Berkeley, and, at my father's insistence, Yale. I didn't really stand a chance, but it was the only school that had rejected Dad for a scholarship back in 1958. He either wanted me to serve as his revenge or to provide reassurance that I couldn't surpass his achievements. Assuming the exercise to be altogether pointless, I handwrote directly onto the Yale application form, answering the essay question: "What famous person would you like to meet and why?"

I scribbled the story of a chat with Seymour Glass, the character I'd come to love most in the stories of J. D. Salinger. A teacher, a son, and an adoring brother, Seymour had killed himself during his honeymoon on an utterly imperfect day at the beach. I wanted to invite him back, to convince him his life was worthwhile. Sentimental drivel, I smirked to myself. But my father's bidding was done, the envelope sealed and posted.

I was jolted back into consciousness as Lew cheered aloud at the TV screen. The Sixers had scored in the final second to win the game. My brother stood and started to head upstairs.

"Hold on," said our father. "Sit down with me another minute, Lew. You too, Josh. Did you know this is the first night in almost twenty years that your mom and I haven't slept in the same bed?"

Distracted by the concert, I'd forgotten. He had driven her to the airport that afternoon. After months of nervous, excited contemplation, Mom was flying to the West Coast for a weekend reunion with her sister, Binnie. Our father was clearly anxious.

"What's the big deal? Afraid she'll become one of those California hippies, Dad?" Lew smirked, getting back up and leaving the room.

Dad and I sat silent for a moment, glancing inattentively at the flicker of the eleven o'clock news. My father cleared his throat and turned to me, plaintive.

"You know I love your mother, don't you?"

"Dad. If there's anything I've never doubted, it's that."

"But I've kept her away from her sister all these years."

"It's not your fault," I said, thinking that it might be, just a little. "Siblings don't always get along. I mean, Mom's going to California now, maybe Aunt Binnie will come here sometime. It's OK. They'll be friends again."

"Joshy," he said, choking on his words. "Can I tell you something? Man to man? Something I've never told anyone else?"

I felt an inner cringe. But Dad seemed so fragile, sitting there on the couch with his arm draped around the space my mother usually occupied. I had no choice but to nod.

"You remember her house on Overbrook Circle? What am I thinking? You were never there. But you know the story. How I was riding by on my bicycle one evening, a few days after Mom's father had died? And I saw Becca out on the front porch, putting that puzzle together of the baby in the sailor hat?"

"How could I forget? If there was a radio station for Royalton family stories, that would probably be the number one hit. Played over and over and over."

"Well, the thing is, Josh . . . that's sort of a short version of the song."

"What do you mean?"

"Oh, Jesus, I'm sorry. Don't hate me for this. I was fifteen years old. See, Joshy, I had been biking by that house for weeks. Sometimes with friends, too. Uncle Art, Uncle Howard, some others. I didn't know your mother yet and there normally wasn't anyone sitting outside. But there was a window on the second floor, a bathroom. And every night around 7:30, your Aunt Binnie would take a shower.

There was a little garden in the center of the circle and we would sit there, on a bench, with binoculars. Watching."

"Oh, shit," I gasped. "You were getting off on her older sister before you fell in love with Mom?"

"Shhhh, shhhh!" He lifted a finger to his lips. "I know. It's horrible. I've never said a word about it. And since then, I haven't been able to stand being around Binnie. But it was all a coincidence, Josh. A lucky coincidence, really. I mean, Binnie's probably not as bad as I've made her out to be all these years; I mean, I don't even really know her. All I know is that she got me to Becca, and nobody can hold a candle to Becca. It's still awful though, isn't it? I was led to your mother by Binnie's tits."

"Oh, Dad," I exhaled in a mix of relief and anxiety, his story triggering my own reflections on Meri and Louis Lowen. "It's not that horrible. It's strange and kind of wonderful, too. But cutting Binnie off like that? I mean, it's crazy. You had nothing to really be guilty about. It is romantic, though, I suppose. Going to such extremes."

"Do you think so, son?"

"Absolutely," I confirmed.

"Swear not to tell, though?"

"Secret," I assured him. "Go on up to bed now."

I watched *Carrie* on the late show. There were buckets of blood and the prom exploded.

~

It was not until a week before my own senior prom that I ever attended one of my brother's high school sporting events. Because his games took place on weekday afternoons, I'd usually had the excuse of rehearsals or newspaper meetings to keep me away. Senior year, I claimed to be busily engrossed in my children's-book writing. In fact, I never wrote a word, just sat on the floor of my bedroom staring at the shelves and feeling paralyzed.

Even during the times when we were barely speaking, Lewis always attended my plays, always read my articles in the *Bugle*. He raised a glass to me over dinner at Bookbinder's restaurant, as our family celebrated my acceptance at Yale. I knew I should have gone to some of his games, but Lew never mentioned my absence. And because my brother felt things differently than I did, It was easy for me to forget that he felt things at all.

Time was running out, though. So I packed a picnic lunch with Meri and went to Lew's last crew regatta of my senior year. Mom and Dad sat on their own blanket, a few yards away from us on the sloping bank of the Schuylkill River. Fat geese honked and sauntered down to the water's muddy edge. Children flew kites overhead. There was a festive poignancy in the air, and I thought about things to come: the pink satin dress Mer was sewing for the prom, the long weekend train trips to visit each other next year.

Over by the dock, I saw Jen Dulcey. I waved weakly at her as she flirted with some boys from the Holy Redeemer team. When Lew came out of the boathouse and headed down to the water, he made a point of approaching them, smiling, and saying hello. As he walked away, though, I saw a sharp intake of breath, a pained squint of his eyes.

"We're gonna kick some butt today!" Lew rallied his teammates. "Bowey High rocks!"

I rose to my feet and leaned toward the water as the starting gun announced the final race. Sleek as razor blades, the shells cut the water. My eyes trained on the rowers' synchronized strokes, their muscle-rounded shoulders leaning into their oars as they rushed forward, staring back at their starting point as it slipped into the distance. In the rippling silver of reflected sun, Lew's boat glided out ahead of the others, passing my place on the bank, surging forward to the finish line.

"Beautiful," I sighed, turning from the boys on the river to Meredith. "You're beautiful."

Lewis paced the length of my parents' room like a caged animal. My father helped put the studs in the tuxedo he had lent me for the prom. Mom watched with a smile, hands fluttering in her lap.

"I can't believe you, Joshy. How can I have a son old enough for the senior prom? Ours was just last week, you know."

"Was it that long ago?" joked Dad. "I can still hear the music."

"Lewis," Mom said, distracted as he crossed between us. "You don't have to be in here if you don't want to. Go on, get! If you're so antsy, go watch TV or something."

"The prom! The prom! I don't know why you're all making such a big deal out of it," he grumbled. "It's just for show. It's not like it means anything."

Lew's words echoed the sentiments I'd heard from Meri in recent weeks. I was too excited, she said. It was just a big party, no more, no less. There would be no fairy godmothers, no midnight transformations, no cornball crossings of sexual frontiers.

"Oh, come on, Mer," I'd pleaded. "We've been together for more than a year. We do everything else, so why not already? It's the big night."

"It's so trite, Josh: the life-altering postprom fuck."

"Yeah! Alter me, baby. Take me to the altar."

"Shut up, weird boy," she laughed in exasperation.

"Put out, lover girl."

"C'mon, Josh. Seriously." She leveled her tone. "I don't want to discuss this anymore."

"What is it, Mer?" I asked, hearing the cliché form in my mind but unable to choke it back. "Don't you love me?"

"You know I love you, Joshua," she glanced away, then turned back, achingly quiet. "I just don't feel right about us doing it. But it's just me, OK? It doesn't have anything to do with you."

"Don't worry," I said, guilty at making her doubt herself. "You're fine. I swear. There's nothing wrong with you. We'll have fun, OK? A good time will be had by all."

"This is so stupid," cried Lewis as I smoothed my lapels. "Look at you in that penguin suit, Josh."

Cufflinks in place, I rose from the edge of the bed and stepped up to the mirror on my father's closet door, admiring the satin stripe of my pants and the pink bow tie I'd insisted on renting to match with Meri's dress.

"Your brother looks handsome, Lewis," chided Dad. "Why don't you keep the criticism to yourself?"

"Lew, honey, you're entitled to your own opinion." Mom played diplomat. "But I wouldn't be surprised if you feel differently next year at this time. Don't you think it's just a little bit exciting? Romantic?"

"Romance is bull!" he snarled. "Guys take girls to the prom because they think it'll get them laid."

"Lewis, that's enough!" snapped Mom.

"Screw you, Lewis. I happen to love, Meri, OK? It's not all about sex, you little jerk."

"I wasn't talking about— "

But I never let him finish, unable to hear beyond the roar in my head. There, in the crucible of our parents' bedroom, Lewis brimmed with an anger that went beyond the subject at hand. I crackled with deeper frustrations, as well. Secrets Lewis had kept from my parents, truths I'd barely glimpsed myself, all of our convoluted privacies came crashing in on each other.

"You little asshole!" I snarled, beaming contempt from my eyes, then turning to Mom and Dad. "He's just jealous because I've had a great relationship all this time and he's never had a girlfriend at all."

"Why you— "

"Well, you haven't, Lulu belle, *have you?*"

With a harsh, guttural scream, Lewis flew across the room, ramming me with his shoulder and taking me to the carpet. In the mirror, I saw his hardened fist come down against my face. He went slack as soon as my father grabbed hold of him, pulling him up and marching him down the hall.

"What got into you two?" asked my mother, still trembling in shock as she applied ice to the plum-like swelling beneath my right eye.

"Tell Dad not to ground him, OK? It's my own fault."

"There's no excuse for hitting, Joshua. Words don't do damage like fists do. Look at yourself."

"I can't go to the prom."

"What do you mean? Of course you're going."

"Everyone will be looking at my eye. What am I going to say? That my brother attacked me? It's not right. I shouldn't go."

"Think about Meri," my mother said, unaware of my own date's lack of enthusiasm. "Come into the bathroom. I'll get you all fixed."

Just as I had done backstage, I flinched and squinted as my mother applied the makeup, her closest facsimile to medium bronze.

"I hate this," I winced. "Be careful of my eye."

After the prom, I simply kissed Meri good night. Lew refused to attend my graduation ceremony. And that summer, rejecting my father's offer to get me an internship at a law firm, ad agency, or some other business run by a friend of his, I found a job through the newspaper classifieds: five dollars an hour, boxing and shipping winter coats in the dusty swelter of a warehouse in the city.

It was dull, tiresome labor. All day long, the loading doors clattered up and down. The dim flicker of fluorescent lights made me lose track of time. Everything felt painfully slow, submerged. Less than a dozen of us were spread throughout the warehouse, supervised by lumbering, cigar-smoking Archie O'Bryan. Arch would make the rounds of the floor every hour or so, but mostly he hid out in his plywood paneled office, steadfastly working through his daily six-pack. My co-workers were not there to kill time before college. Just a few years older than me, these men, in their blunt, inarticulate way, seemed far more experienced at life. Out by the lunch truck, I sat on the curb, listening in as they beefed about wives and children, hookers and dealers, credit and debt. I kept Yale to myself and listened in on a world I'd never heard before.

With the exception of the Cleyskils, I'd met few adults who were much different from my parents. Lew and I were raised with the assumption that we would live lives like our father's, commuting between families in the suburbs and professions in the city. We were shown no other options.

Caring parents tell their children, "You can be whoever you want to be!" But there is a tacit understanding. You can be completely different from your parents, as long as you are exactly the same.

Listening to my co-workers in the warehouse that summer was like discovering a foreign country, minutes from home. It made me wonder what other languages were out there to be spoken, what further provinces waited to be explored.

~

"*Fraaaaaaance,* Joshua! I'm going to Paris, Fraance!"

My mother grabbed both of my hands as I stepped in the kitchen door after work one night, pulling me into an exuberant little jig around the kitchen table. I had never seen her so girlish and giddy.

"The Eiffel Tower, the Follies! I've wanted this since I was eight years old."

"What are you talking about, Mom?"

"Dr. Berger, my supervisor at the clinic, was going to a conference at the beginning of August. But a family problem came up, so he's asked me to go instead of him. One week in Paris, and then I'm adding on a week of other places. Can you believe it? I am so excited!"

As the glossy magazines piled in her office attested, my mother fantasized about traveling the world. Dad had always been reluctant to stray from home, only reluctantly agreeing to long weekends in Florida and New England.

"Dad's up for this?"

"Actually, Dad said he doesn't want to go. Impractical, he says. Overindulgent. But I've decided to do it anyway. I mean, I visited Binnie last year without him. You should just hear about all the trips she's taken on her own."

"Won't you be lonely?" I was worried and amazed.

"I don't think so." She spoke dreamily, drifting with her words. "Doesn't it sound like a nice idea to just be with yourself for awhile, to get lost in your own thoughts, keep your own company? I mean, sometimes I get sick of being in a family."

"Mom!"

"Joshua, don't act so shocked. I'm no different than you are. You're not always cheerful about being a member of the fabulous Royalton clown troupe, are you?"

"No. But I'm not just going to abandon it."

"Who said anything about abandoning? I'm going on a two-week vacation. What makes you say that, Josh? Do you feel that you can't be yourself without abandoning our family?"

"Hey! No way, Sherlock Freud! One minute we're talking about your trip to France and the next you're psychoanalyzing me."

"All right then, I'll stop. I'd hate to foist any good advice on you. OK, listen, you're the French club *secrétaire,* teach me some useful phrases."

"So you say you're traveling without your husband, eh, *madame?* Repeat after me: *Voulez-vous couchez avec moi ce soir?*"

"What does that mean?"

"Aw, nothing," I laughed, shimmying my hips and singing a few bars of the old song.

To my great dismay, Meredith was also going to France that summer, on a special three-week scholarship program for painting in Marseilles. I had urged her not to go at first; we would have so little time together the next year.

"We might as well get used to it," she cut me off. "And besides, you don't really want me to pass up this opportunity, do you? Painting is my great love."

"I thought I was."

"Oh, Josh, give the Romeo act a rest. You know what I mean."

"Kiss me, fair maiden," I cried, dropping to my knees.

Smiling down at me, she turned and cracked, "Kiss my ass."

After the few days it took him to realize that my mother really was going ahead with her trip, Dad suddenly developed an adventurous spirit.

"You remember how my father used to spend hours staring at his foreign coins, Bec? Wishing that he could travel to all of those places? Well, I can actually afford to do it. I can do what he never could. I've decided to go with you after all."

I bridled at Dad's invocation of Grandpop Josh. He sounded more bent on one-upsmanship than the surrogate fulfillment of his father's dreams. Reminded of them for the first time in years, I wondered where those shoe boxes full of Grandpop's coins had disappeared to. But I was quickly distracted by my father's comforting suggestion that, since their trips overlapped, he and Mom might drop in on Meri in Marseilles, maybe buy her dinner, let her show them the town.

"I don't think so, Harris," Mom countered. "For the first time in our life, we're going to another country. Why should we turn it into old home week? If you feel compelled to look in on Meredith, you can do it while I'm in my conference."

"That'd be neat if he came down for a day," Meri said when I repeated my Dad's suggestion to her. "You know, I've always thought he was cool. Besides, it'd be interesting to talk to your father without having you there to poison me against whatever he says."

"Geez, Mer, I'm already nervous enough about you and all those seductive French guys. Do I have to be worried about my father, too?"

"Ugh, Josh! Don't be gross. The only thing you should be worrying about is getting your own warped mind under control."

My father stayed with my mother in Paris. They phoned home to speak with Lewis and me every other day. Mer had warned me that she couldn't afford to call. She promised to send postcards, but cautioned me about the vagaries of international mail.

On the first weekend that my parents and Meri were gone, I searched the house for my grandfather's coins. I checked under the bureau and in the closet of baby Cora's empty room; I poked around the basement utility room and behind the central air unit. I rummaged through the downstairs coat closet, stacked with carousels for Dad's slide projector. I found nothing. It was as if, in attaining some mythical family value, the coins had transcended the tangible world, and now existed only in the minds of my father and myself.

Each weeknight, I came home from the coat warehouse with muscle ache and fatigue. I would drop on my bed, into a thick dreamless sleep, waking up again after eight, avoiding Lewis in the halls, lazily microwaving Chung King chow mein and Stouffer's French Bread pizzas. Back in my room, I would read children's books until bedtime, halfheartedly hoping inspiration might strike.

It was a hot August Sunday when I picked Meri up at the airport. I swelled with relief as she emerged from the jetway. The foreign sun had thrown a warm cast of rose over Meri's alabaster skin. Her hair was brightened in its blondeness, pulled back in an artistically untidy ponytail, little tendrils left to curl in golden circlets around her face.

"You look gorgeous," I exclaimed, pulling her into a crushing embrace. She wilted in my arms though, those beloved green eyes unfocused as she looked up at me.

"What's wrong?" I asked. "You ready for some lunch? How does a big American hamburger sound?"

"I'm really beat, Joshua. The time change. The distance. Can you just take me home? We can go out tomorrow."

"I work tomorrow," I groused, offended that she didn't seem to appreciate my picking her up. "How can you be so tired? You just took a three-week vacation."

"Painting isn't being on vacation, Josh. You know that. When you're writing your children's stories, it's hard work, isn't it?"

"I'm sorry," I said. And I was, especially for having lied to her all year long. I'd told Meri that I was feverishly working on four interrelated stories. But I wanted to keep them private, just like she did with her canvases. One legal pad is all I really had, with variations of "Josh sucks" scrawled over every page.

The next night, on a bench in a park at the end of her street, Meri and I got together and she proceeded to pull us apart. We'd had terrific times, she said, but now it was time to move on. We would be in new places soon, surrounded by new people. It was better to start fresh.

"Did you have an affair in France?"

"Joshua, that has nothing to do with this."

"You did! I can't believe this."

"Calm down, Josh, calm down," she put a hand to my hot cheek. "I love you, but it's time now. We're really just kids, you know. It's not like we're married."

"You don't get it!" I shouted, thinking of my teenage parents. "It can work!"

"But I don't want it to work anymore, Josh. We've gone as far as we can go with each other."

"I can go farther!"

"There's nothing else for me to say. I'm sorry to hurt you."

"Forget it," I snapped. "It was crap; it was nothing. Our whole relationship was about a lousy ten-dollar bet."

Meri's eyes teared up at the brutal tone in my voice.

"Stop it, Josh! You sound crazy."

"Bull! Bull! You think I worship you like a princess or something? Well, guess what, Meri. I hooked up with you on a bet, OK? I won ten bucks for snagging you as my girlfriend. That's what we're all about. And it was hardly worth the money."

The last image I recall from our meeting in the park is my reflection in Meri's eyes as she calmly turned away. I see myself, in the tears that silently streamed down her fine-boned cheeks. It was the end of my blissful, submarine year. Forced to reemerge from the green pools of her eyes, I stood alone in a hot summer breeze, shivering all over. I went home to cry. My parents wrapped me in their arms and said they understood how it hurt. But I knew they didn't; they'd never broken up with anyone in their lives.

"You're very special," said my mother. "I know you'll find the right person."

"Just imagine, Josh," coached my father. "In two weeks it's coed cowabunga!"

"Harris, you're ridiculous. Josh is not out to become a lady-killer."

"Me either," he cracked, grabbing her waist. "I likes my lady alive and kicking!"

"Cut it out! Stop it!"

"I can't resist your succulent flesh!"

"Well, I guess I'll go to bed now," I muttered. "Glad my gloomy little life isn't going to put a damper on your party."

"You guys are both too much!" my mother bolted from the couch. "The world doesn't revolve around either of you, you know."

The next day's mail brought a postcard, long in transit, *par avion*. The hand-painted image of boats in a harbor was backed by a brushstroked note.

*The foreign and the familiar, I'm learning to see, are never too far apart. Hope this finds you well. Love, Meri.*

~

The evening before I left for New Haven, I took my father's car for a drive, not sure where I was heading. I found myself pulling up along the sidewalk of my first childhood lawn. The old house looked tiny, and I laughed, imagining six-year-old Lewis bursting out the front door and running up to the car to greet me, naked. I remembered his idea of buttoning ourselves together, and felt a pang of sadness at how unbuttoned we'd become.

I slipped a cassette called *Torch* in the tape deck, classic songs from my grandfather's era, recently covered by Carly Simon. I'd given the vinyl LP to Dad for Father's Day, then, after he'd opened it, taped a copy for myself. My favorite song was "I'll Get Along Without You Very Well." Over a bed of strings, Carly sang 1940s' composer Hoagy Carmichael's original anguished lyrics: "What a guy, what a fool am I . . . "

After all that time, she sang to me once again as a lonely boy.

Just as the tape clicked off, I found myself parking at the foot of a hill. I had kept away from the Cleyskils' house for years, although I'd seen Raph and Rosalie in the high school corridors and heard news of their family through Mom.

Frizz welcomed me in as if I'd been gone but a minute, immediately launching into a demonstration of his new greenhouse sprinkler.

"So, I understand you're going to Yale, Joshua," he mentioned offhandedly, puttering with a hose. "You know they have one of the best abnormal psychology programs in the country."

"Let him alone, Frisbee!" Ellen laughed as she stepped into the room, clapping dust clouds of flour from her hands. "Nothing changes, does it, Josh? I'm sure he doesn't have any idea what you want to study yet. Right, Josh? Come on, sit down for a little. It's nice to have you stop by."

A huge new painting hung over the kitchen table, rectangular, maybe six feet across by three feet high. Twigs, mud, bits of string, and yarn formed a long oval nest that held a dozen eggs, positioned in six matched pairs. Some were starting to hatch, and the tiny glimpses of the emerging creatures that Ellen provided indicated no ordinary chickens. There was a deep purple tentacle, a pair of bloodshot eyes and what appeared to be the edge of a butterfly wing.

"Wow!" I said. "That's different."

"That sounds like praise of sorts. So you like it, Josh?"

"It's cool. Kind of funny and scary at the same time. Is this what you're doing now? No more portraits of your family?"

She laughed. "This is a portrait of my family."

"Don't listen to her, Joshua," said Raphael, suddenly appearing in the doorway in his Oberlin sweatshirt. "Her mind may be scrambled, but I'm no egg."

"Maybe your mom's brain is fried!"

"More like cracked."

"Watch what you say, boys," Ellen cackled, making loony eyes and gripping a heavy metal meat tenderizer. "I have a great recipe for Smart-Ass Omelette."

Raph and I hadn't bantered like this in ages, rarely giving each other more than a polite nod of greeting on those occasions that our paths crossed. It felt good to have him pull up a chair beside me, to hear his excitement about going back to college.

"It's great to get away," he assured me. "You can really be your own person."

An hour later, I said goodbye to Ellen and Frizz. Raph offered to walk me out. By the screen door, in the thick, damp heat of the Cleyskil greenhouse, I felt his palm come down on the back of my neck. I turned to face him. After all those years, I still looked up to his eyes and braced myself for what might happen next.

"So, Josh," he whispered, slyly. "I hear you know my old friend Louis Lowen."

"Yeah," I muttered, swallowing hard, picturing our loincloth-clad jungle scene.

"But he says you know his sister even better," Raph laughed, coarsely, slapping me on the back. "That is one hot-looking girl. How'd you get so lucky, dude? I remember when you were Mister

Shyguy. Damn! Josh Royalton boinking Meri Lowen. That's awesome, man. You're not gonna have any trouble in college at all. You
sure have come a long way."

I ran down the hill and sped off.

At Bell's Pharmacy, I browsed through *Time* and *People*. Remembering the sorry spectacle of Bobby Nizer, caught stealing away with
his desires, I flipped through the latest *Playboy*. Unimpressed with
Miss September, my eyes were drawn to the stationery supplies shelf
and a caramel-colored, leather-bound notebook. It was soft and
brown and warm to the touch, its pages empty expanses of cream, no
margins and no rules. Anything might appear there. I never considered the price tag. I just clasped the blank book in my hand and ran
from the pharmacy.

Sprinting toward the car, I shouted in my head, "Arrest him! Arrest
him!"

~

The great gothic campus of Yale is a fantasy of iron-gated arches
and hovering gargoyle armies. In the steady gray rains of my first
September weeks there, I clung tight to the buildings' stony facades
and crossed courtyards through underground corridors. I frequently
found myself confused in my travels, lost between starting point and
destination, as if trying to follow in the footsteps of a father who had
never walked this way.

Late afternoons, on my narrow dormitory bed, I would drift from
my studies and try to conjure home, occasionally finding myself de-
toured into a garden of coiled vines and ripening tomatoes, pink beginning to blush through their green. Ellen Cleyskil would be painting, Frisbee blowing smoke rings that floated past like vaporous
Rorschachs. Then, from the back of my mind, Raphael would emerge,
thirteen years old in his BVDs, but with the deepened voice of the
greenhouse I'd heard just weeks before.

"It's great to get away," he'd taunt. "You can really be your own
person."

I would squirm, pinned beneath him. I unzipped my jeans and
wrestled with him again, there on my dorm room bed. Then the telephone rang, invading.

"What?" I'd answer with reflexive defensiveness.

"Joshy. It's Dad. Is something wrong?"

"I'm fine. I was kind of napping, that's all. I thought you guys said you'd be calling Sunday night."

"Oh, don't worry; we'll call Sunday. I just had a minute free at the office and thought I'd say hello."

"Oh. I see."

"That's OK, isn't it? For a father to call his son at college?"

"Yeah, Dad. Sure. Fine. How's Lewis?"

"Your mother is just getting busier and busier this fall. New client referrals all the time. Evening patients, too, now. I had to learn how to use the microwave."

"Dad, Mom can tell me on Sunday. How's Lewis?"

"I finally got him to sit down and start on his applications. Like pulling teeth. I had to threaten to ground him to get him to start an essay. You'd think he didn't care about getting into a good school. Josh, why don't you talk to him, give him some encouragement?"

"What would I encourage him to do?" I asked myself as much as my father, nonetheless flattered to be asked for assistance. "I don't really think he wants my advice. He's pretty independent."

"OK, Mr. Yalie. So what's going on with you?"

"Classes. Life," I muttered, unenthusiastically. "Just trying to be my own person."

"Atta boy. You show 'em the Royalton stuff. Listen, I have a meeting. Just needed to hear your voice, OK? Keep doing great. I love you, pal."

I rose and stamped into the living room, growling as if whole diatribes were caught in my throat. Flinging my leg in an angry high kick, I accidentally sent a loosely tied Hush Puppy flying from my foot and out the open window, plummeting three stories down to the quad. My overcast internal weather held me back from my classmates, who cheerfully dotted the lawn on this rare bright day of Indian summer.

I leaned out into the October breeze to find Greg Ervis, my toad-faced, Zen-quoting roommate, twirling my shoe on his forefinger. Greg hugged his eyes up at me, shouting,

"One of the passengers that got off this flight is having a problem with his baggage claim. You know anything about that?"

His lame joke drew a few giggles from the small group of fellow freshmen clustered with him on the stoop of our entryway. I stepped back into the room, slightly unbalanced on my one stockinged foot.

The first thing Greg had done upon his arrival on campus from Cincinnati was to set up a sort of toaster shrine in the corner of our living room; a silver chrome 1950s two-slicer sat atop a tiny, knee-high teakwood table. Alongside the toaster was an incense burner and a little rubber Buddha. When I'd slouched down on the floor after bringing the last of my bags up to our suite, Greg took a loaf of rye bread from the mini-fridge and turned to me.

"Do you want sandalwood or citrus-clove?"

"What are you talking about?"

"Aroma-toast, Josh Royalton, spiritual sustenance. I guess it hasn't reached the less enlightened cities like Philadelphia, huh? Well, anyway, you burn the incense right next to the toaster so some of the smoke settles into the slots and adds some flavor. Well, not flavor really. It just sort of kisses the toast with poetry."

"Listen, Greg, I think I'm going to pass on the snack. Catch you later, OK?"

As the first few weeks of school went by, I worried about suffering perversion by association. It was just my luck to be paired with the amphibian oracle of Ohio. But I also came to hope that, next to Greg's more blatant forms of peculiarity, my own inner strangeness might go safely unnoticed.

Yet, now, on the most beautiful day of autumn, it was weird Greg Ervis who entertained outside with my empty shoe while I hid away indoors. I dropped to the floor in a sprinter's crouch, staring up at the sky-blue square of open window. My classmates' laughter rose up from below, mixing with the breeze rustling the quadrangle's colored leaves. Soon they would all be snapped from their trees, blown to the ground, and faded to the wasted brown of blank parchment.

In my mind, I heard the blast of a starter pistol firing. I lunged from my crouch toward the window.

Three times I banged my head against the white wooden frame, twice to punish myself for having such thoughts, and once more for being too cowardly to follow through on them.

"Will you bring my shoe up when you come in, Greg? I can't come down now. I have a—a lot of work to get done."

I pushed myself to tag along with the other residents of our dormitory, joining them for meals and movies, even initiating a Tuesday night Scrabble game in our living room, beneath the day-glo splendor of Greg's ancient Donovan and Strawberry Alarm Clock concert posters. I made every effort to be charming and witty, to offer my thoughts on whatever the subject at hand. But I felt eerily withdrawn, somehow absent from my own life.

"Just flip it over. You'll be right side up," Kathy Seeton whispered in the dining hall one night, snapping me out of a self-induced trance. I had drifted from the table's heated discussion of fourth-dimensional physics and fixed on my own inverted image, reflected in a silver soup spoon.

"Thanks," I said with an awkward chuckle. "The blood was really rushing to my head, there."

I found myself doing this sort of thing frequently—opening my Swiss Army knife in the middle of a lecture to stare at myself in the biggest blade; stooping to see my translucent face in the windows of cars parked along Elm Street. Every time I appeared, every time I was reflected, the relief was enormous, and the impulse to check again, immediate. It calmed fears that I might somehow be blinked from existence, or that I'd undergo some involuntary transformation when I wasn't paying attention.

After Kathy caught me staring in my spoon, I excused myself and raced back to the dorm room, sweating and nauseated. I stood in front of the mirror, crying.

"This is useless," I chided myself, picking up the phone to call home. There was no answer.

I opened my desk drawer, frantically searching for an envelope of summer snapshots my mother had sent in the mail that week. Before I ever got to them, though, I came across my purloined leather notebook.

I had yet to write a single word in the blank volume I'd stolen from Bell's. Now, I considered scrawling ragged profanities over every page, rendering the book useless for whatever buried purpose had impelled me to steal it in the first place.

But when I touched it there, in the drawer, the soft suede of its cover sent a wave of comfort riding up my fingertips and radiating through my body, a warm blanket in the blood. I curled on my bed, then, pressing the sweet-smelling volume to my cheek. I remembered how Lew and I would clutch Orangey and Rhino, relaxing ourselves through difficult evenings, creating heroic adventures that transcended our minor traumas. As I lay there, drifting in and out of sleep, my mind crackled with the imagined voice of another childhood hero, a confident voice I thought I might borrow to begin articulating myself.

~

"Check this out," I swept my arm dramatically, pointing out the decor of the Jade Pagoda restaurant to my friends at dinner the next night. The room was simple: blond wood, drop ceiling, bushy green potted ferns, wooden floor, and plain Formica tables. "This style is really retro."

"It's nothing special," commented Greg.

"Exactly!" I replied. "That's how Chinese restaurants were before the big decorating boom of the fifties. Spare, functional, just the basics. Thank goodness Americans have finally developed a taste for real Asian cooking. No need for much of the monkey business that used to go on."

"What monkey business are you talking about, man?" asked Greg.

Nick and Tina and Kathy looked expectant as well, their dipping arrested, fried noodles gripped in an expectant hover over the little white dish of duck sauce.

"They called my grandfather the Chinese Box Man, " I started to speak, launching a grand improvisational experiment. With a slender thread of family and skeins of vision all my own, I began spinning a man to life. "My grandfather worked for his cousin in the restaurant supply business. They convinced bar and restaurant owners that they needed a ridiculous variety of shit. Not one kind of toothpick, no way. You had to have your cellophane frilly-tops for club sandwiches, your plastic swashbuckler pirate swords, your standard woody for olives and pearl onions, and your individually wrapped minted variety for the actual postprandial picking of teeth.

"At swankier places they sold special forks for Caesar salads! Pre-crumpled tinfoil swans to shovel full of leftovers! Those rotating jobbers that cut potatoes into Slinkies!"

"Like on TV?!" Greg chuckled in recognition. "Get two free garnish kits when you buy the Ginsu knife set?"

"Exactly!" I commended him. "But disposable so you could sell 'em by the caseful."

"Well, the grand slam of restaurant scams came in the early 1950s. Grandpop Josh started a trend that swept the country and made a solid American living for thousands of Chinese in the mid-Atlantic states. Difference was, this scheme was actually good for the restaurant owners; it was the customers who were the suckers.

"Starting in about '48, there were floodtides of Chinese from the province of Guelin rushing into America. Now, normally, my grand-father and his cousins didn't try to sell much to small ethnic restau-rants. They had low budgets and built-in clientele who the owners didn't need to impress. This was certainly true in Baltimore's Chi-nese neighborhood. The new immigrants had spent most of their sav-ings on their ocean passage and left money behind with relatives; they had just enough left over to start up some basic businesses.

"Anyhow, the two businesses with the best return on the least over-head turned out to be barbering and running a restaurant. All you needed was a plain little shell of a store front and minimal equipment. As a show of solidarity in their new homeland, the Chinese barbers' families would eat out every night and the restaurateurs would go in for at least one good combing every day. Obviously, not a lot of cash floating around for frivolous supplies.

"But whenever Grandpop Josh went to Baltimore, he made a beeline for the stark and homely Woo Dinette. He didn't try to sell a thing. He loved foreign cultures and had a taste for the exotic. John and Milly Woo's razor clams in sizzling black bean sauce was about as exotic as dinner got in '50s Baltimore. As he sopped up every last drop of fiery sauce with his rice once a month, Grandpop Josh couldn't help but begin to scheme. But for all his schtick and swagger, my grandfather looked for win-win situations. He knew the Woo's cook-ing deserved to be appreciated beyond their small Chinese enclave and suspected there was profit to be made in serving that cause. Over the course of several years, he established a genuine rapport with John and Milly, all the while compiling a secret project binder, full of photographs and drawings clipped from theater magazines, Buddhist religious tracts, and tree nursery catalogs."

I paused for a moment as our waitress set several steaming dishes onto the table and we began to serve ourselves.

"Greg, would you please pass the ginger tofu?" asked Tina.

My roommate responded with a vigorous set of facial calisthenics.

"Oh my God! Are you all right?" Tina gasped, reaching across the table to offer him a glass of ice water, assuming he'd bit into a pepper.

Greg pulled his shoulders taut and pursed his lips. The veins in his temples writhed like just-salted slugs. One would have been within reason to expect dazzling feats of telekinesis to ensue: the lazy Susan rotating itself right off the big round table, the squeeze bottles of hot sauce ejaculating hither and yon. But Greg simply made a dramatic, full-headed nod in my direction, indicating that I should provide an explanation.

The ginger tofu was Greg's dominion. All of the group but Tina had been to Jade Pagoda the previous week. It was the first time any of us had eaten Chinese food together, but we were in general agreement to order family style. It was how we had all eaten Chinese growing up: after determining whether any ingredients were forbidden by any member of the party, a sufficient number and variety of agreeable dishes were ordered, along with a large communal bowl of white rice from which the group would serve itself. Excepting the occasional personal accessorizing via spring roll or wonton soup, all was merrily shared. Everyone chatted and chewed and passed the pork, please. And everyone was happy.

Not Greg. The very concept made him unhappy. Hunan Anathema.

"That's not how we do it in Cincinnati," he'd declared with matter-of-fact oddness. "We each order our own."

"When you go out with your parents and your sisters, you don't share the food?" asked an incredulous Kathy.

"My sisters don't go out to Chinese with us. But my parents and I order for ourselves. If my Dad gets Grandfather Chicken, I might ask him for a taste because I like it. But, generally, I like snow pea things and tofu things—for myself."

The little research librarian in my soul tempted me to ask what his mother ate, but I resisted.

"So the ginger tofu stays here, if you don't mind," Greg told Tina as he caught our waitress's eye. "Miss, could you please bring me my own little bowl of rice?"

Noticing Kathy seething, about to launch into an inquisition over Greg's little rice privatization, I took the opportunity to diffuse the tension by resuming to the tale of the Chinese Box Man.

"In October of 1956, Grandpop Josh was finally ready to unveil his proposal for the Royalton-Woo Collaborative Venture. He waited until the last diners, a young barber named Yashi and his wife, settled their check just after nine. John Woo stepped out of the kitchen, drying his hands on his apron.

"'Lemme take your plate away, Josh.'

"'Thanks, Johnny,' said Grandpop, who had licked every bit of pungent sauce from the pile of clam shells now heaped before him like a memorial to a brilliant meal.

"He felt extraordinarily lucky. My grandfather had always collected foreign currency. And now, here he was, talking shop with a man who just two years before rode an ox through the mist-shrouded hills of China.

"'The Chinese coins, they have a hole in the center, isn't that right, John?'

"'Yes, Josh. That is to carry them neatly on a string and keep from losing them.'

"'It's not just money; it's a little machine. It's a gadget!'

"'You want some Chinese coin, Josh? Remind me to give you some before you go. You give them to your grandchildren someday.'

"'So, Josh, what's this big plan you got for me? We gonna get rich, fly to Las Vegas?'

"'Well, not exactly, but here, take a look.' Grandpop began opening his binders and file folders. 'John, why don't you bring Milly in here, your daughters, too, if you want? You've got a family business here, so it only seems right for them to be in on it.'

"'As I see it, John, you're losing thousands of dollars in business by only catering to your Chinese neighbors. I mean, God bless 'em, they've stuck together through hard times and you'd never want to be without 'em. But why not get all of Baltimore in here?'

"'Baltimore people don't want Chinese food,' said Milly.

"'Maybe not. Maybe just not yet. Look around at this place: it's a plain white box, drop ceiling. Nothing special. Well, every corner in Baltimore has got its own nothing-special diner. And—here's where you're onto something, Milly—they all serve burgers and franks and egg salad sandwiches and whatever your Joe American diner wants to eat.'

"'But what if we were to turn this plain white box into a Chinese box? What if we doll it up with stuff like this?' Excited, Grandpop pointed out favorite pictures in his binder. 'Look at this, remnant sets from the road show of *King and I*. You know, Rodgers and Hammerstein—played three months in DC at seven dollars a head! It was Siam, I know, but your average Joe don't know Chinese from Siamese, right? The point is, they'll start coming to the Woo Dinette because they *don't* want to have burgers and franks; they'll come be world explorers, to have a one-night vacation.'

"'It won't really look anything like Guelin,' laughed Joe, 'But it sure wouldn't be just another dinette.'

"'In fact,' exulted Grandpop Josh, 'I think we'll need to change the name. How about Woo Palace?'

"'Heck,' enthused Milly, 'Why not Woo Hoo Palace?!'

"In moments, they began to pick and choose from the merchandise: Porky little Buddha statues, garish paper lanterns, gilded dragon tapestries, wishing wells with live goldfish. If you've seen it in a Chinese restaurant between Bangor and Charleston, odds are that it was first demo'd and sold out of Baltimore's own red-neon-trimmed and golden-tasseled Woo Hoo Palace. In exchange for his splitting their initial decorating costs and giving them a small cut of each sale he made from bringing other clients to see their restaurant, Grandpop Josh turned the Woo Hoo Palace into an ever-changing showroom of ersatz Orientalia and a B-list Baltimore tourist attraction.

"Lightning crackled in the rainy autumn air as Grandpop, John, and Milly had a tea toast to their future success together. Then, as John Woo walked Grandpop Josh back out to his car on that stormy Baltimore night, lightning struck again. That's when my grandfather came up with the concept of the little paper drink umbrella."

"That is an insane story!" declared Nick, as the waitress approached with our check at the plain white box called Jade Pagoda. "It's not true, though, is it? I mean, your grandfather didn't invent Mai Tai parasols, did he?"

"Of course not," laughed Kathy. "Think of how many billions of those things have sold. His family would be loaded. There would be a whole dorm here named Royalton. But who cares if it's true. You're amazing, Grandson Josh."

Hours later, at nearly 1:00 a.m., I emerged from the library where I'd been studying for a marketing exam. I was in dire trouble gradewise; the class was all number crunching and demographic analysis, not at all what I'd expected. But although the thought of my father seeing a C on my transcript normally made me faint, I was still humming with excitement from my earlier performance; I'd plucked my father right out of the lineage. It was as if Grandpop Josh and I were directly connected. So what if I couldn't derive the optimum formula for bringing widgets to the marketplace? I could always sell toothpicks and paper umbrellas. I could always sell a story.

I had spun myself out to the wiggiest distances, witnessed by friends I'd known only a few short months. Gasping, laughing, and encouraging my passionate display, they'd seemed willing, even eager, to let me be.

Back at the dorm, Greg sat Indian style in the middle of our living room rug, his toaster glowing beside him.

"That was pretty good tonight, Josh. Really true stuff."

I sat down on the floor next to him, both because I sensed his sincerity and because I'd begun to realize that I had little justification writing anyone off on account of eccentricity.

"Listen, Greg, I'm sorry if I was too hard on you about the sharing deal."

"It's OK."

"I mean, I guess there's something to be said for private dishes. There have been times when I got pissed because all of my favorite thing was eaten before I ever got to it. Couldn't complain though. Such are the perils of family style, right?"

"Some families might even take the concept a step further," Greg mused. "Everyone picks a dish and then you just mash them together into a giant kettle with a couple quarts of rice."

"Actually, that sounds like it might taste good."

"Come on! Everyone's rice and everyone's sauce all intermingling like that? It sounds like a disaster."

"Thus sayeth Mister Picky."

Greg laughed to himself as the toaster bell chimed. Then, flashing his mischievous Zen-master grin, he generously tore a corner from his slice of Wonder and offered to share.

"Here, Josh, have a piece."

Anything could be imagined.

~

*"Not Freedy Langton,"* I screeched at my reflection in the cloudy rectangular mirror that hung above the dresser. *"Totally unimaginable."*

It was a nightmare. I blotted my stomach with my top-sheet, then jumped down from the upper bunk. I wrapped a thick red towel around my waist and rushed to the hallway bathroom that Freedy, my sophomore roommate, and I shared with two other dorm rooms, rushing to get my head under the water and scrub away sleep's unpleasant visions.

It was a Tuesday, late November, and, as had become involuntary custom, I'd awakened ahead of the clock's metallic buzz. Every morning, my eyes popped open around 6:30, sometimes spurred by sudden wetness on my belly, but more often by some internal alarm system that delivered me into an hour and a half of racing thoughts and restless tossing in my constraining cocoon of semen-stained linens. I lay there, watching my blurred reflection in the mirror above the dresser, turning my eyes away, then turning back to question myself.

I tried to remember the articles I'd read, the ones that reassured me that it was perfectly normal for adolescent males to have passing homoerotic fantasies. I was nineteen. Still an adolescent, right? Plenty of time for passing fantasies to pass.

After mulling over such thoughts for an anxious hour in bed each morning, I leapt naked to the floor, as if fleeing a burning building. Overheated and afraid, I would stand and observe my head in the mirror, floating disembodied above the dresser drawers.

Freedy Langton normally woke up as early as I did, the roosters of his rural North Carolina home permanently cooped in his subconscious. He bounced up from his bed the minute he awakened, reaching awkwardly for his thick, brown plastic eyeglasses on the dresser top. His gangly six-foot-four-inch pipe-cleaner frame was clad in baby blue pajamas which he shed, to reveal a hairless, skim-milk torso, wet spaghetti arms, and the incongruously expansive pom-pom of pubic hair that puffed around his skinny dangle of chalk-white penis. Twisting about in my own morning torments, I feigned half-sleep to avoid conversation, and Freedy, always as polite as he was bland, silently slipped into his tattered brown bathrobe and rubber flip-flops, uttering not a sound until he shut the door behind him.

"Up and at 'em, Frederick Langton!" I heard him cheer himself in the living room. "It's another beautiful day on God's earth!"

Freedy greeted each morning with an optimism as cockeyed as my recent sexual fantasies. I laid there in my bed, teeth on edge, thinking about strangling both him and the smiley-faced God he saluted every dawn. Freedy's was not so much a religious deity as a sort of bland mayonnaisey balm that could be spread over anything unpleasant or less than upbeat. He was a computer science major, his brain miraculously hot-wired when it came to formulaic logic. But this high-powered thinking machine was encased in a soul of sugar-sweetened mashed potatoes.

Freedy loved *Battlestar Galactica* and James Bond movies. He had a ridiculous crush on Sheena Easton. He volunteered as a "hugger" at the New Haven animal shelter, dropping in twice a week to cuddle abandoned puppies and kittens. My roommate was not a man of shades or nuances. He was annoyingly content.

On the morning of my nightmare, I locked the bathroom door behind me. The smell of Freedy's Old Spice aftershave lingered in the condensation that hung in the air and glistened on the tile walls. He was doubtless already in the dining hall, spooning up his daily serving of Crunch Berries, then tipping the bowl to his impossibly stubble-free face and drinking the sweet, pinkened milk. Even awake, I still felt my nightmare. It was uncontrolled and unbearable; Freedy Daddy Longlegs, crawling all over my mind, pushing me to the breaking point.

Remembering the Nit-Wit from *The Big Book of Safety Fun*, his ass lobster red in a scalding shower, I cranked the hot water as high as I could bear, taking a washcloth to my body like sandpaper, scouring especially hard at the gluey patch of hair below my navel. Through foaming shampoo, I raked at my scalp, digging in with my fingernails as if I might somehow scrape right through my skull, flooding my head with cleansing lather. Goddamn Freedy Langton, what was I doing with him?

It was by my own perverse invitation that Freedy Langton had become my sophomore roommate. Each entering class at Yale is subdivided into a dozen groups of about 100 students, creating more intimate dormitory communities within the larger campus population. Freshman roomies are randomly assigned, but from then on, students make their own matches. After initiating my series of Grandpop Josh

routines at the Jade Pagoda, I became a minor celebrity in our freshman dorm, sweeping into late night study breaks to present fabulous
tales of invented nostalgia over the steady percussion of a hot air popcorn maker.

"When we were little, my brother thought his penis could talk . . .
My friend Robby's father would scrape Rob's teeth with a fingernail.
Now his dad has a new family—and a missing index finger. Robby
became a vegetarian . . . Our next door neighbor was insane. He named
his infant son Lisa and then tickled the baby to death . . . "

Although not among the ringleaders of these gatherings, Freedy
Langton was usually present because, thanks to his cranial circuitry,
he was quick to pick up the arcane strategies of draw-bridge, whist,
and the other archaic card games that Kathy, Tina, and Lloyd had
been raised with in their Central Park high-rises. Freedy served as a
convenient fourth, generally keeping focus on his hand, stumbling
awkwardly whenever he tried to participate in the group's sophisticated banter. His fellow players were caviar at the Ritz, while Freedy
was Skippy on a Ritz. When everyone laughed uproariously at my tall
tales, Freedy turned quizzically to whoever sat beside him, wondering whether the stories were true.

"Relax, Freedy," Nick jibed. "That's not the point, OK? Everything's postmodern now, dude."

"Oh, uh, I get it," Freedy forced a small laugh, adjusting his glasses
on his nose. Despite his unnervingly simple innocence, Freedy became a regular staple of our nightly lounge group, only rarely replaced at the card table by Vincent Oglio, a quiet physics major who
roomed with Nick and occasionally showed up to play a hand or two.

During the spring semester, I continued my efforts to win friends
and craft a persona. I sported a bright red fedora everywhere I went
on campus, a maraschino cherry of hinted pimpdom atop my conservative Oxford shirts, sweater vests, khakis, and loafers. But this flash
of haberdashery and the lunatic lure of my evening yarns were as
much a buffer I placed between myself and my classmates as a genuine connection between us. I knew how to work the crowd but faltered
at individual friendships. I avoided one-on-one situations, as if har-
boring some secret identity I wanted no one to detect. Only Greg had
seen the opposite extreme of my public performances, the almost
daily hours of blackness, when I would curl on my bed with the blank
leather book, lights out and staring at the ceiling, concluding phone

calls to my parents crying, "I love you, too, but I don't know what's wrong with me."

"I'm pathetic," I would tell Greg, blowing my nose in the bathroom. "I'm a mess."

"You're depressed," he replied. "It happens to me sometimes, too. Roshi Sanku writes that we must not waste energy hating the demon. It will go away on its own."

"I know it will. That's what sucks. I'll probably be fine by tonight, I'll be Mister Entertainment, as usual. It's like there's weather inside of me: storm, then sunshine, storm, then sunshine. It's my head, goddammit; I should be able to control what goes on in there."

"You might want to take a psychology class, Josh. It could help you figure things out. That or Buddhism. Have you read *Big Sky, Empty Mind*? Anyway, right now, why don't you just lie down again? Maybe you can fall asleep. I'm going to make a snack. Do you want any?"

"Sure, Mommy, some transcendental toast with shrunken head paté would really hit the spot," I grumbled, heading back to the bedroom. "Forget it, OK? Just try not to make too much noise."

I rued my inability to simply accept Greg's quirky kindnesses. But I could never quite shake the sneaking feeling that his empathy toward me must indicate weaknesses of his own. And the fact that he had seen me at my darkest, tangled in the telephone cord that connected me to my parents, made me want to get away from him. To leave Greg Ervis, along with all the needs he'd witnessed.

In March, when it came time to make new rooming arrangements, I wasted a week, nervously flirting with the notion of asking Nick or Lloyd or one of several other smart, articulate guys from the card game to bunk with me sophomore year. It was a ridiculous hope though; these were popular guys and, although they seemed to like hearing my stories, they didn't really know me very well. If we did live together, and they did get to know me, they might not like me. It was pointless. Besides, Nick was in my contemporary lit class that semester; he could pick apart a text and tease out hidden meanings almost as well as I could. Not feeling I was fully built, I could hardly risk my own deconstruction.

I figured I would make do with Greg again.

"Sorry, Josh," he said, when I finally approached him after dinner one evening. "I mean, ten days went by and you didn't say anything. I figured you didn't want to stick together. I'm rooming with Vince O."

"No way. You're kidding."

"I didn't mean to hurt your feelings. It would have been cool to stay with you. It just seemed like you wanted to change."

"How do you even know Vince?"

"Intramural soccer. He's one of the best on the team. I have lunch with him and his boyfriend sometimes."

"His what?"

"You know, Lex Abbott. That senior, who works in Durfee Sweet Shop some nights?"

"I know him, I reviewed his play in the *Daily*. You mean they're gay? Vince the soccer jock and Lex the ice cream guy are, like, blowing each other?"

"How should I know what they do in bed, man? I just know they're together. When you think about Tina and Lloyd, do you imagine them having sex? There's a koan that goes 'When looking at the landscape, do not be distracted by the occasional passing breeze.'"

"Gosh darn it, Greg, that little bit of sacred wisdom had slipped my mind for a minute there. Thanks for bringing me back into the plane of serenity."

"You don't have to be so sarcastic."

"You don't have to be so goody-goody."

"What's so goody-goody in not giving a damn about Vincent's favorite sexual positions? What I know is that he's a fun guy, he's going to be a fine roommate, and, goddammit," Greg started to laugh, "he's sure as shit getting more action than either of us are."

"But he must have been lying to Nick all year. Nick's never said a word about it. Do you want to live with someone deceptive like that?"

"Vince told Nick an hour after they first met. He also asked him not to gab. Didn't want people making a big thing of it."

"But it is a big thing," I snapped, yanking open our door and stepping out into the stairwell. "It's the biggest damn thing about him, isn't it?"

I paced across the darkened campus on that frigid March night, desperately trying to reconcile my image of the handsome, lantern-jawed boy who sat in on the occasional hand of bridge with this new information. Vincent was an athlete. He roomed with Nicholas Trotter. He studied physics, for chrissakes. How did all of this add up to being gay?

My bleak wonderment was fed by my deepest misapprehensions. I'd always sensed that announcing oneself to be gay would set an opaque, monochrome bell jar over one's uniqueness, like getting publicly branded as Child Genius, Mentally Ill, or His Father's Son. I imagined you would forever be known only for that single, somehow all-encompassing trait. Shivering as I walked beneath two grinning stone gorgons that chilly evening, I was too shocked for logic.

Disoriented and suddenly homeless for next year, I made my way back to the dorm, hastily knocking on the door of the least complicated, least challenging, and most obsequious person I knew.

"Hey, Freedy," I said, affecting a generous tone. "I hear you're still looking for a sophomore roommate."

Ten months later, two days before Thanksgiving, naked and dripping amid billows of bathroom steam, I felt an inevitable coalescence. Some things, I was beginning to understand, were never meant to be washed away. And besides, if I was gay, I surely deserved more than a gross wet dream of Freedy Langton.

I skipped breakfast that morning and telephoned Philadelphia. I was coming home early, I said to my parents, gravely. There was something urgent I needed to tell them.

~

"Joshy's home! Joshy's home!"

Hearing the key in the door, my father rushed into the front hall from his den, embracing me as I arrived at Roslyn Avenue that night.

"Good to have you here for an extra day, pal. Are you hungry? Do you need anything to eat?"

I held up a huge, twine-wrapped box of Mrs. Fields' cookies I'd purchased at the train station, hoping to sweeten the awkward conversation I anticipated going long into the night.

"Mmm. Got any of those chocolate chip macadamias in there?"

It was as if my father was so glad to have me in the house that he'd forgotten I had rushed home to break important news. As I poured two glasses of milk in the kitchen, my mother emerged from her office.

"Hi, honey! So, what brings you home so soon?" she asked. "What's the matter?"

"He just got in, Bec. He'll get to that when he's ready. Just let him relax a bit. He hasn't been home in months. Here, sit down with us. Have a cookie, Cookie. Tomorrow night Lew will get in we'll have the whole family home, just like old times."

"I think Mom's right; we really should talk now."

All through that sophomore fall, I'd lowered my resistance to imaginary erotic encounters with the International Male catalog models, with Vincent Oglio, and even with the activists and scientists who were now regularly appearing in *Time* and *Newsweek* as the AIDS epidemic emerged.

Yet the most liberating fantasies I'd indulged didn't really have to do with being gay at all but with the reaction it might provoke at home. I suppose I never really believed that I would be cut off or disowned, like Vince said had happened to a lesbian girl from his high school. But there was a part of me that secretly wished for just such anger, such outrage, such a throwing up of barriers. Maybe I could turn my parents' fury into an excuse to put some distance between us.

They were more accepting than I'd ever wished for.

"It's strange," said Dad. "We were discussing this just last night."

"What do you mean? I didn't even call you until today."

"I woke up from a dream at two in the morning and I asked your mother if she thought you might be gay."

"Jesus! What did you say, Mom?"

"Well, you know, Joshy, I've been curious for years. I just didn't want to push you. Remember Darren Arblum?"

I sat there, dumbfounded. Having hoped to create some kind of separation, I found that my parents had practically taken up residence inside of my head, reading my thoughts before I understood them myself.

"Well, what about Meri, then?" I was questioning myself as much as my parents.

"What about her?" Dad asked.

"I mean, it wasn't some kind of trick. I really did love her, you know."

"Of course you did, sweetie," Mom said softly. "Anyone could see how much you two cared. I don't think it really matters who you choose to be with, so long as you have that strength of feeling for each other."

"Here, here!" agreed my father, laying an arm around her shoulders. "Just don't cut us off because of this, Josh. We always want to be part of your life."

An hour later, as I brushed my teeth in a daze, Dad pushed open the bathroom door. "Maybe I can relate to you even better than you think, honey. This was just kids' play, of course, but, when Uncle Howard and I were eleven or twelve, we once tried some stuff—homosexual stuff—with each other. You know, oral sex."

"Christ, Dad! Spare me!" I spat a mouthful of foam, both appalled at the image and irked that my father had done more with guys than I had.

On Wednesday morning, my mother awkwardly confessed that she was worried about "health issues."

"You mean AIDS?" I put a point on it for her.

"Well, yes," she said. "Are you being careful?"

"Look, Mom," I said, improvising a credo that has served me well ever since. "It seems to me that I have two choices: I can worry about AIDS every single second of every single day, or I can do what needs to be done and not worry about it at all." I knew that if I took on one more set of anxieties, I'd dissolve into a helpless puddle.

When my father came home from town that evening, he handed my mother a plastic bag from Robin's Bookstore. "I thought Mom and I might read these to help get a handle on what you're going through, Josh. I know we may have seemed clairvoyant last night, but we're hardly experts on this subject."

I quickly glanced at my father's purchases. The titles, *Loving Someone Gay* and *The Best Little Boy in the World,* seemed saccharine and generic. I was mainly relieved not to find a fresh new copy of *Everything You Always Wanted to Know About Sex.*

"Whatever," I muttered, at once grateful for their interest and, at the same time, wishing that they were a bit less curious. "Just don't think you can figure me out by reading a book."

After dinner, my father followed me up to my room.

"I feel a little remiss, Josh. We didn't even ask whether you were dating or if you had somebody special."

I suspected that my mother had warned him not to pry.

"C'mon, Dad, I don't want to get into this."

"Look, I don't care if you like women or men, Josh. But I know that the most important part of my life has been to have a family. To enjoy things with," his voice cracked, "and to get through the rough times, too."

"I'm not going to have kids." I glared at him. "I know I'd drive them crazy."

"Look, you may not want to have kids, but two people can be a family; I checked it in the dictionary. And besides, it won't just be two of you. Anyone you love, we're all going to love, too. He'll become another member of the Royalton family."

I wanted to recoil, yet at some resounding depth, my father's longings were my own. Still, as drawn as I was to his sentiments, I could not allow myself to be drawn by them. Even if my story might end up having much in common with my father's, I still needed to write it myself. I could not take his emotional dictation. I would not be a pale violet carbon copy.

"Listen, Dad," I snapped. "Why don't you let me map out my own life before you start annexing it?"

"Joshua, Joshua," he touched fingertips to my cheeks. "I'm just trying to be helpful."

"I want to help myself," I whimpered inaudibly as he left.

Lewis got in from Walden College, near Boston, at about eleven o'clock that night. My father grinned contentedly as he headed off to bed, all four Royaltons back under one roof. Although I had quietly hoped my revelation would create more of a division between myself and my parents, I was terrified of widening the gap between Lew and me. The palpable tensions of our high school years had yielded to blank, detached courtesy. When he walked in the door that night, I opened my arms to hug him. He offered a handshake instead.

"So how's freshman life?" I asked, breaking the awkward silence as we sat in the living room absently watching a late night horror movie, the flesh eating zombies occasionally interrupted by commercials for diet Nutri-Shakes.

"It sucks. If I can't pick up my grades, I'm going to have to drop off the crew team. And that's the only thing I really like there."

"But Mom and Dad always tell me you're fine when they call."

"You know how they get all worked up if they think something's wrong. So I just don't tell them. I don't need them trying to solve my problems for me. It's my life. Anyhow, what about you? Everything nice and spiffy in the Ivy League?"

"There's something I need to tell you, Lew. I already spoke with Mom and Dad . . . "

A reflexive wrinkle of his nose suggested mild distaste, but, on the whole, my brother seemed nonplussed by my news.

"It's no weirder than anything else about you," Lew joked good-naturedly, socking me in the shoulder. "You were never exactly a regular guy, were you? Afraid of crow feathers. Turned on by men. Go figure."

"I can't believe you remember those feathers," I laughed, recalling another Thanksgiving, so many years before. There was a welcome warmth to our banter.

"Actually, I've had the whole antiprejudice training," Lew explained. "One of the captains of our crew team is like you."

"He may be gay," I cracked, "but, for his sake, let's hope he's not like me."

"You're right, Josh, he isn't. Bryan has a much cuter butt than you."

I blushed at my brother's joke.

"So, how long have your friends known?" Lewis asked.

"Well, I figured I'd start telling them as soon as I get back on Sunday."

He froze for a moment.

"Hold on now, Josh. You're telling me that you came out of the closet to Mom and Dad before you told your own friends? Even I know that's backward."

"What do you mean? They're my parents. They had a right to know first."

"This is classic, Josh. Share everything with them. Get the Good Housekeeping Seal of Approval," Lewis hissed, scowling at me. "You think they had a *right*? We're allowed to lead our own lives, you know. If you bought a house, you'd invite them to visit, not to move in with you, for god's sake. How often do they call you at school? Every night?"

"Who says my way is so bad, Lewis? I feel close to them; what's wrong with that?"

"But when you let Dad get close, he tries to take over."

"Sometimes I just think he loves us too much. That's a hard thing to punish someone for."

"Wanting a little privacy is not punishing anyone," Lewis sneered, shaking his head and turning toward the staircase. "Nothing's ever going to change around here is it? Later, Josh; I'm crashing."

I focused intently on the television. On the late show, the town schoolmaster helped the sole surviving zombie escape a torchbearing mob. At the end of a splintering wooden dock, the young man guided the misunderstood creature into a rowboat and pushed him off toward the rippling, moonlit horizon.

I was embarrassed to find myself dabbing at my eyes as three dramatic organ chords brought the film to its conclusion. My melancholy fugue was broken by a charismatic knife salesman shouting, "Don't hesitate! Do it today! It's soooo eaaaasy!"

In the morning, Mom hollered that bagels and lox were on the table. Brunch quickly devolved into a sort of Homosexual Hints from Heloise.

"It says in the book that the great Greek philosophers were advocates of gay life," offered Dad. "Now there's something for you to be proud of."

"You know, Marge who works at the deli is a lesbian," Mom piped in. "I'm sure it would be fine for you to call her."

This made them feel supportive, made me feel embarrassed, and made Lewis flare his nostrils and make retching gestures whenever they weren't looking.

"Hey Josh," cracked Lew, finally unable to control himself, "remember in *The Big Book of Safety Fun,* where the Lubricant Nit-Wit accidentally uses Krazy Glue and gets stuck up another guy's big red butt?" Mom gasped and Dad flushed with fury. But I inadvertently preempted our father's harangue by laughing so hard that orange juice came out of my nose.

"I'm OK—I'm OK," I sputtered through my coughs as Mom scurried around the table, ready to slap me between the shoulder blades. "No harm done. It just went down the wrong way."

"Now you listen to me, young man," I heard my father holler at Lew as I walked down the hall after excusing myself. "I'm sure this is all plenty difficult for Josh as it is. We're his family, and I expect you to be supportive. You have no right to torment your brother for being gay."

"Torment him? You've got to be kidding. Doesn't bother me at all. What bothers me is that he needs to run home and kiss your ass before he even finds a guy's ass that he *really* wants to kiss."

"Lewis," Mom clicked her tongue. "There's no need for graphics."

"Oh, come on, Ma, I thought we didn't have any problems with homosexuality here. How many times did Josh and I have to sit at this table and listen to the Harris and Becca porno show?"

"That was your father," she muttered. "That wasn't me."

"I didn't hear you telling Dad to can the graphics," Lew snapped.

"I'm sorry Lewis, I never should have let—"

"Never mind that, Becca," Dad cut in, agitated. "It's beside the point. Look, Lewis, Josh isn't a little boy anymore. We don't force him to share things with us. He's doing what he wants to do."

"Well, a psychologist might see it differently, Harris," Mom interjected, skirting the fact that she was a psychologist. "People can't just change at will, always doing what they'd most like to do. You and I were just kids when we met. And how much has our relationship really changed in twenty-six years?"

"But Becca Royalton, love of my life, why on earth would we tamper with perfection?" He reached for her.

"Harris! Cut it out!"

Lew took Dad's amorous maneuvers as an opportunity to slip out of the kitchen. Walking by my eavesdropping spot at the foot of the steps, he shook his head. "You know I'm right," he said, zapping on the living room TV for the first of the day's football games.

"In some ways, you are right. But it's complicated, Lew. Everything's all tangled up. Why do you need to boil it down to winning an argument? You should be a lawyer like Dad."

"Oh, that'd be rich, wouldn't it? The loser son makes good."

"Lewis, you're driving me crazy! Crazier."

"Any time, big bro. Happy to oblige."

"Who's playing?" I asked, not caring, but wanting to linger at my brother's side.

"Penn State."

"Ah, the Nittany Lions. Or the Nit-Witty Lions. That was funny as hell in there, Lewis. I didn't realize you remembered that old book."

"It's kind of hard to forget. The kid sticking his finger in the socket and shocking himself. The one suffocating in a plastic bag. I still test my shower water three times because of that picture of the boiled butt."

"Me too," I confessed. "It's amazing how stuff sticks."

"So what happened to the kids' book you were always threatening to write? You have such wild ideas; it'd probably be pretty cool. You could do an antidote to *The Big Book of Safety Fun*."

"Yeah, *The Big Book of Safe Sex Fun,* right?"

We smiled silently at each other for a moment, then I grew nervous, afraid of losing him. "Lew? Do you really think I'm wrong for coming out to Mom and Dad first?"

"Come on, Josh, enough of this stuff for today." My brother could control the flow of his emotions like water in a system of locks, but I remained awash in flood tides of sensitivity. "Lewis, I want to talk about this. Don't you think everyone is right, in a way?"

"Game's starting," he cut me off, turning to face the set.

"No," I thought to myself, "the game is ongoing."

I headed upstairs, wondering if we'd ever reach the joys of the final championship buzzer: the boys of Team Royalton, allied and victorious, leaping into a hard-earned, exhausted embrace.

Encouraged by Lew's interest in my long-dormant writing fantasies, I retreated to my room and dug to the bottom of my overnight bag to retrieve the stolen book. I kept it with me at all times now, toting it around campus in my knapsack, slipping it under my pillow at night. Despite my many efforts to begin, the pages were still blank, kept clean by some prophylactic force field every time I tried to write. Once again, that afternoon, as the nutmeg and cinnamon of my mother's pumpkin pie floated up through the house in a warm, sleepy cloud of tradition, I opened the leather cover and gripped my pen above the first page. But inside of me, there was a gripping, too. A familiar seizure kept me from setting point to paper, as though protecting us all from the stories I might write.

I turned instead to my childhood bookcases, flipping through *The Story of Ferdinand* and *Babar.* Over the past two years, I had become a frequent visitor to the children's sections of New Haven's bookstores and libraries, sneaking off after classes and eagerly paging through thousands of bright-colored volumes. While daunted by the works of Roald Dahl, Ezra Jack Keats, and other geniuses in the field, I found my confidence bolstered by newer books, condescending tripe like *Marigold Jones and the Gangsta Squirrels,* so painstakingly hip and utterly disrespectful of the dreamlike way that children perceive the world. "I can do better," I thought to myself. But the fact was, I didn't even try. I suppose my secret hope in all of that searching was that, one day, I would find a book on the shelves, already written and perfectly expressed, that said everything I needed to say. That way, I would never end up having to do it myself.

My father and brother hollered all afternoon.

"You jackass!"

"You moron!"

Their yells were not directed at each other but delivered in fervent unison. The Philadelphia Eagles were on TV. I felt jealous of Dad and Lew, able to set their own entanglements aside for the make-believe world of the field. For a few escapist hours, conflict had clear-cut rules. The home team was made up of good guys, and the enemies came from somewhere else.

"Thanksgiving dinner, l'il pilgrim." Dad rapped on my bedroom door and summoned me with his lame John Wayne imitation. "See, I didn't barge in, like you guys are always complaining. I knocked."

I flipped off the radio, which was playing "Wake Me Up Before You Go-Go" for the hundredth time that day.

"Who sings this song?" Dad asked. "It's really catchy."

"They're called Wham!" I sniffed. "They're superfaggy."

"And, um, help me out here, Josh. Is that a good thing or a bad thing?"

"Never mind!" I shooed him out of my room. "Let's go be thankful, OK?"

The Royaltons gathered in the dining room, with tablecloth, candlesticks, and a twig basket piled with miniature pumpkins. It was just the four of us at our holiday dinner, although my mother had cooked for an army nonetheless. This was the first year both Lewis and I had been living away from home, and my father had insisted on no guests, a tight-knit family occasion. So tight-knit, it felt to me, that we might suddenly find ourselves sprung loose, unraveled.

Like refugees among riches, we huddled together at the center of a long oak table designed to comfortably seat twelve. I took the Balloon Man down from the breakfront and set him down in front of my plate. We managed only the smallest of small talk: praise for the excellent corn pudding; quick rundowns of our college course work; an anecdote about one of Mom's new patients, a man with multiple personality disorder. There were awkward, weighted lulls in the conversation, and we ate more and more to get through them, our minds as painfully overstuffed as our bellies.

My mother attempted to leaven the atmosphere, presenting Lewis and me with the wishbone. But the game we'd played since we were little boys now seemed fraught with adult dangers.

Lew dropped the bone to the table. "Don't feel like it," he said sternly, a hint of panic in his eyes.

"Me either," I concurred, unwilling to pit my desires against my brother's.

I pushed the bone across the table. Dad picked it up reached toward Mom, who quickly looked away. Everyone had wishes. No one deserved to lose.

We fell back into complicated silence and ate too much pumpkin pie.

That night, in my room, I turned to *Bartleby the Scrivener,* the week's assignment for my Melville seminar. I began marking pink neon highlights over the text, dense with multiple meanings. "I'd prefer not to," Bartleby chanted his mantra. "I'd prefer not to."

Just as I began to get lost in my studies, an old reflex came kicking in. My head snapped up from the pages and I swiveled to look in the bedroom mirror. There was Joshua Royalton, sitting at his childhood desk. He sat at home, on Roslyn Avenue, where he lived with his parents and his brother Lew. There was the boy, simple and familiar, who I'd so often searched for, who I'd summoned to soothe me in knife blades and the windows of empty cars. But, that Thanksgiving, I found no solace in this old reflection. The image struck me as hollow consolation, neither a portrait of myself at that moment nor anyone I was happy to have been in the past. With no small regret, I turned back to my assignment.

Riding the currents of Melville's ocean late into the night, I felt waves of meaning come crashing down. Submerged messages floated to the surface, eddying through my mind. In quicksilver words flashing round a whirlpool, I glimpsed reflections truer and more elusive than mirrors had ever offered. At two in the morning I laughed, exhausted, my pages and my fingertips all solid, screaming pink. Having tried to highlight every significant detail, I had drenched the entire story in phosphorescent ink.

~

I caught Vincent Oglio on his way to the lounge, classmates beginning to trickle back in at the end of the holiday weekend.

"No way!" he blurted, as if my news bore some threat. "You're not one of these gay pride nuts, are you?"

"Huh? No. I don't . . . I mean, I'm not really anyone yet."

"Oh man, sorry for jumping on you there, Josh. It's just—this guy Lex—who I hooked up with last year—he wanted to make our sex life some big political statement. I mean, they may be the same size, but my dick is just my dick, not the Washington Monument, thank you. There are things that should be dealt with in private, right?"

He winked and slugged my shoulder.

"So c'mon, Josh. Let's go for a walk, huh?"

There were a million questions tumbling through my head, but, striding up Chapel Street at Vince's side, I fell into silence, grateful for his companionship. Vincent led me up to the crest of Science Hill, sporting his typical chilly weather attire: cabled fisherman's sweater, long snowflake-print scarf, and his ubiquitous year-round soccer shorts. Although Vince had classes on Science Hill every day, I had studiously avoided this outpost of campus.

"You know," I confessed, as we sat on the thinning grass of the slope, nobody else in sight. "I've never taken physics; I stopped after chem in high school."

"Really?" he asked, with a look of surprise. "Physics is the instruction manual for the operation of the universe."

"Why do I need to understand stuff that's working automatically? Like gravity. It's doing great on its own. If it starts messing up, shit starts floating around the dorm room, maybe then I'll take an interest in physics. I like to study stuff that needs interpretation."

"Oh, yeah, you're a Lit Boy, aren't you?" Vince scoffed. "Analyzing a paragraph seven different ways without ever deciding that any of them is better or worse than the others. You just go on and on without ever reaching a definite conclusion. That drives me crazy."

"I love it. It's like my own feelings count as much as any predetermined facts."

"I guess so, Wordsworth," he said with a grin, leaning over to press a shoulder against me. "But you while you sit around, endlessly mulling things over, I can come up with an answer, then set my work aside and go have some fun. That's the beauty of physics, when push comes to shove."

Push did come to shove, then, and charged with desire, I tried to set my inner gravity aside. Vincent Oglio was straddling me on the ground, rubbing at my flannel shirt. His forceful kisses covered my mouth, and my tongue reached up to pull him in. Stunned but aroused,

I gnawed at his shoulder, then gripped the bare gooseflesh of his thighs in my hands.

I let Vincent pin me, grabbing my wrists, pressing my back to the cold, hard earth. I stared beyond him, into the violet dusk sky, where sharp-edged streaks of cloud overlapped like phantom Chinese characters. My thoughts drifted up and away from Science Hill toward dim light, Johnny Mathis records, glasses of wine, Vincent and I in gentler embraces yet to come. And then, as I remembered my first romantic plunge into the liquid green of Meri's eyes, I saw Vince's own glazed blue orbs roll back, his face contorting with a grunt as he grinded against me one more time. He quickly stood and brushed himself off, leaving me with aching blue orbs of my own.

Bowlegged the whole walk back to the dormitory, I barely got in a word. Vince rattled on about dining hall food, rooming with Greg, and intramural soccer. His steady stream of chatter prevented real conversation. And though we passed hardly anyone along our route, Vince adjusted his snowflake scarf every few seconds, making sure it draped over the stain on his shorts.

The telephone was ringing as I stepped into my dorm room, a black and blue mark appearing on my forearm.

"Welcome back!" Freedy shouted, oblivious to the phone, drumming his arms to the crappy Rush tape he was always blasting through his Walkman.

"Greetings," I said into the receiver. "Be this friend or foe?"

"This be your mother, Mr. Wiseguy. Was the trip back OK, honey?"

"Yeah, Mom. It was fine. When I went to the snack bar on the train, I wore a condom in your honor."

"You sound out of breath; are you all right?"

"Geez, I took a long walk, Ma. It's cold out, that's all. Why are you calling? I just left home. Did I leave something behind?"

"I'm sorry. I really don't want to intrude. I just need to say something, though. Lewis made me think a lot this weekend. Look, sometimes your brother gets a little strident. It makes your father furious, when Lew throws these walls up around himself. But your brother has a lot of good sense in him, too. God only knows where he gets it from.

"Listen, honey, Dad and I adore you, and we're proud that you were able to talk to us about—about all this. But what Lewis says is also right: I don't expect you to be an open book. You have every right to privacy, to conduct a life of your own."

"Then why is it that you're calling me, Mom? To share a warm moment of my privacy together?"

"Please, Josh, why do you have to be so nasty?" her voice strained with sadness. "I just want us to understand each other. I want you to know how I feel."

"I'm sorry," I winced, pain flaring in my shoulder blades from banging around with Vincent. "Something else is bugging me a little."

"Well, do you want to talk about—" She caught herself, and we both laughed aloud.

"Look, Mom, I'm gonna go now. Don't worry. I'll be fine."

"I know you will," she muttered softly. "So will I."

I wiped my eyes with one of the bunny-print Puffs that Freedy kept on the end table.

"Who was it?" Freedy asked me with a look of concern, lifting off his headphones as I set the phone in its cradle.

"Vincent Oglio," I replied, collapsing on the couch and feeling like one giant bruise. "We're getting together later on."

I knew I should break the gay news to Freedy promptly, but I was stumped as to how to go about it. I wasn't afraid that he'd reject me, but that he'd demonstrate his loving acceptance with an hour-long ecumenical run-on sentence.

"So, how was your gobble-gobble day, Freedy, old pal? Do some serious damage to a genuine Carolina wildfowl?"

"Well, you know," he grinned. "We had turkey meat loaf. It's easier for Grampa to chew. Truth is, I like it better than the real thing. Mom mixes cranberries right into the ground meat, so the slices all have little red polka dots."

"Recalls how the white man brought smallpox to the Indians."

"Ewww, Josh. Cut it out. Why are you always so sick?"

"Sick? Sick? You're calling me sick? Are you saying I'm sick because I'm a homosexual?"

"I'm not a bigot!" exclaimed my resident rainbow hugger. "And wait! You're not a homosexual!"

"Not only am I a homosexual, Freedy, I also get off on watching your Grampa gum his meat loaf."

"Jo-o-sh! Do you have to be so disgusting? Now seriously, are you saying you're really gay or what?"

"Yeah, Freedy, I am. I told my folks over the holiday."

"Well, you know that's just fine, right? As long as you respect yourself."

"I do! I swear!" I stepped to the door. "Hey, I'm starved Freed, gotta hit the chow line. Thanks for making it so easy to tell you."

"Wait a sec," he called after me. "Do you know about the meetings in Fellowship Hall?"

"No Nukes. Save the Whales. All your groups. What about them?"

"Brother Anson has started a gay students' coffee hour. Maybe you want to check it out. It's every Thurs— "

"See ya Freedy! See ya!"

I ran across the courtyard to Greg and Vincent's room. This school year, facing Greg's strangeness voluntarily rather than through force of proximity, I had elevated him in my esteem. His toast fetish had come to seem more whimsical than disturbed, and his incessant play-ing of his hippie sister's scratchy old Donovan records now struck me as quaint, rather than creepy. Acceptance seemed a virtue, and his friendship an odd comfort. There was another ameliorating factor in my perception of Greg, of course: visiting him allowed me to spend time in Vincent's presence. For months prior to our walk that after-noon, I had secretly admired Vince as I hung out with Greg in their room. Donovan cheerfully serenaded, "I love my shirt, I love my shirt, my shirt is so naturally lovely" as I surreptitiously observed Vincent, bare-chested, stretching those, thick-calved soccer legs and smoking a joint.

"You want some?" he'd ask, mimicking the Sistine Chapel poster that hung over his corduroy beanbag chair as he offered the joint with a graceful outstretched arm. Despite being a science major, Vince was Catholic. Whenever I looked at that Michelangelo image, though, I thought less of the original in Rome than of Steven Spielberg's rein-terpretation on the posters for *E.T.,* the boy and the alien touching fin-gertips.

After sprinting over to escape Freedy that day after Thanksgiving break, I gave a perfunctory knock and stepped through Greg and Vince's unlocked door.

"Hey, give me a chance to answer," said Greg. "What if I was in the midst of a Tantric love session with the truly transcendent Kathy Seeton?"

"Oh, sure. In your lucid dreams, Castaneda." I teased, smugly. While Science Hill with Vince hadn't exactly been a romantic smorgasbord, I'd at long last been tossed some simulacrum of sex, and was feeling a bit superior.

"I'm dying of hunger. You guys want to go to the dining hall with me?"

"Vincent's already split. He ran in, showered, and took off. I think maybe he's got a date."

I was dumbfounded. The guy had just humped me an hour ago.

"You mean he has a boyfriend?"

"Oh, no way. I guess date's the wrong word. Vincent claims religious exemption from actual gay relationships. But sex is another story for him. Just physical necessity, he says. And believe me, it's frustrating how much he can get. Did you know there are all these places where gay guys can just hook up and go at it? Certain carrels in the library, men's rooms on Science Hill?"

"You sound like you think this is good."

"Well, man, it's so easy for him to get off."

"But what's the point if you don't have any connection to the other guy? It's like masturbation using a person as a prop. I mean, I'm coming out so I can find something more substantial than jerking off—"

"What? Are you gay now, Josh?"

"Yeah, I told my family over break. My mom brought the turkey to the table on Thursday and I burst out of the cavity in a Carmen Miranda outfit."

"Come on, be serious. Are you?"

"Yeah, Greg," I exhaled. "I am. And you can tell anyone; I don't want it to be some secret. It was a secret from me for too long. I'm tired of feeling like I'm crazy."

"What does one have to do with the other? Maybe you're gay and crazy. They can both be cool, you know. Roshi Sanku says that normality cuts off the sixth finger of your hand." Greg gave a brisk bow to his toaster shrine and we walked to the dining hall.

~

"And then, oh my God, Brother Anson said it was time for—"

I burst out laughing before I could finish, full-body chortles flopping me around the floor like a fish.

"Time for what?" Greg urged me on. "Did they want you to say a homosexual prayer or something?"

"There is no such thing as a homosexual prayer," Vincent seethed from his beanbag. "Come on, Josh, now that you've gone to this stupid thing, I want to know what happened."

"OK, OK," I said with a wheeze, the muscles in my sides still aching. "He said it was time for The Rings of Brotherhood."

"What is that? Some New Age circle jerk?" Vince scowled. "Does he tell you that your cum is the milk of human kindness? Jesus, Josh, I told you to skip this gay pride bullshit. You know the same thing goes on without the flowery language in steam room at the gym every Thursday at nine."

"Well, it wasn't quite that porny, Vince, but it was still way too intimate for my taste. We had to stand in two circles, one inside the other. The guys on the inside rotated clockwise and you were supposed to hug each one as he passed you. And some of these guys weren't even students. There were skeevy fifty-year-old townies who would squeeze really tight. I mean guys older than my father. This one cowboy dude with a white mustache and a stupid turquoise string tie just reached down and grabbed my butt."

"Well, you do have a nice butt," said Vince, arching an eyebrow.

"Maybe so," I retorted, "but unlike your Catholic bum, my ass is not available to the masses."

"Elitist," he grumbled, averting his eyes.

"You better believe it. Just call me Donald Rump. Surely you've heard of my Tower? It's also only accessible to exclusive clientele."

"Shut up!" Vincent tried to stifle a chuckle.

"Honeychild," I joked, "mine *is* shut up. It's yours that's always dangling out like a bait worm."

As a strategic counter to Vincent's furtive sexual exploits, I took to being flamboyantly catty when we hung out together. This knack for dishy attitude surprised everyone, myself included. All of a sudden, one night, just after Christmas break, I opened my mouth and Bette Davis came out. It was sort of like a burp: bad taste accompanied by a good feeling. For years, I'd been subconsciously taking notes on gay humor and now, having acknowledged my sexuality, I was free to display my scholarship. Campy vamps supplanted my improvised Grandpop Josh stories.

"Cut it out. That's so embarrassing," Vincent would complain throughout my monologues, suppressed laughter setting his temples aquiver, belying his handsome straight face. Once, he actually clapped a hand over my mouth; I poked my tongue into his palm.

"You have a very long and tasty lifeline," I quipped in mock-geisha as he recoiled.

"It's not funny!" Vince shouted in frustration, stomping into his bedroom and pulling the door shut behind him.

"Oh, come on back out, Vincent. I'll stop it, OK? Please."

"I think I'm gonna take off now," Greg said, getting up. "Hope you two can work this out."

He winked at me and was gone.

Leaning against the dark varnish of Vince's door, I pressed hard against his silence. I found myself wishing I could pass through the wood, filling his space like some ever-present ghost. My parries of rapier bitchiness were meant as a tickle torture for Vincent, pleasure and pain inflicted in tandem. It was just another version of what he constantly did to me, gracing my days with his presence, but refusing to open his heart.

When he opened his door, swiftly and suddenly, I lost balance and fell in. Vincent had already stripped to his briefs, and I did the same in seconds. He drew me into an animal tangle, pulling us down on the bed. We clawed and pawed and pounded. But we never kissed. Vincent wouldn't allow it, not on that day or any of the dozens that had preceded it. He would twist his neck when my lips approached. He'd burrow between my legs to avoid the light in my eyes.

"Admit it," he'd taunt between bobs of his head, tugging at himself all the while. "You love it when I do this. You're a bad boy, aren't you?"

"Kiss me," I begged.

"Just fuck my face."

I did, and it made my nerve endings raw with pleasure. But as he hid down there, endlessly ravenous, I ran my fingertips through his close-cropped hair, aching to place an overlay of tenderness on his fervor. Secretly, Vincent Oglio felt it too. Sometimes, as we stood in the dining hall line, or walked across campus on a crisp green day, I would see him glance from side to side, making sure that nobody was looking. Then he would gently touch the small of my back, or wipe a cowlick from my forehead.

Once, Vince appeared unexpectedly as I stepped out the arched cathedral doors of the Sterling Library, where I often studied, and slumbered, in the oversized burgundy leather chairs.

"Hey, Joshy!" he greeted me, throwing an arm across my back. We walked a good twenty yards that way, the warm press of Vincent's hand on my shoulder conveying knowledge more important to me than all the books I revered in that library. As it turned out, Vince had just completed an anonymous tryst in Fagonomics—a notorious men's room hidden away in the library's econ stacks. Despite his constant insistence that sex be divorced from affection, I saw his embracing me as an attempt to gain equilibrium. I clung to the possibility that Vincent's scales might someday tip in my direction. But when we eventually agreed to room together as juniors, Vincent took great pains to define our arrangement.

"I don't want to have a boyfriend, OK? I don't want to have a relationship." But every Saturday night that junior autumn, loosened by liquor after making the rounds of campus parties, we would throw off our clothes and crash onto Vincent's bed together. I would make love; he would do whatever it was that he did.

Though Vincent insisted that we weren't dating each other, neither of us wanted to date anyone else. He carried on with his anonymous encounters, but dismissed them alternately as vexation and sport. While gritting my teeth at Vincent's forays, some strange sense of fidelity led me to resist my own curiosity about the Primo Homos, a university-sanctioned group of impossibly attractive, sharp-dressed and quick-witted gay students who sponsored weekly cocktail colloquia and the occasional dance. The Primos were more glamorous than I ever wanted to be, but I admired their handsome bravery nonetheless. Once during sophomore year, I'd suggested that Vincent and I check out one of their dances.

"They're obsessed with homosexuality!" Vince sneered.

"So are you," I'd wanted to snap back at him. But I didn't, because I too was obsessed, not with sex, but with forcing the bloom of romance. We stayed in that night and played Scrabble. My heart welled each time he dipped into the bag to draw new letters.

Greg and Kathy and even Freedy would show happy smiles whenever Vince and I entered a room together. From the moment I'd let them know I was gay, I'd made little secret of my ardor for Vincent. Now that the two of us were living together, now that neither of us was courting anyone else, everything appeared quite clear. We even went to Pepe's Pizza with Lowell and Tina once. Just the four of us, like a double date.

All of this was a great pleasure for me, and it made me a nervous wreck. Vincent could have put an end to our friends' presumptions. But he didn't. And every time he smiled back at them, every moment he didn't say "No," a part of me hoped that he was coming around to my side. Perhaps, as in his physics, there were immutable laws of love. I theorized a righteous gravity, pulling him inexorably toward me. Stumbling into our living room, late one Saturday night, just before Thanksgiving break, I placed my hands on his waist from behind. I leaned in and whispered drunkenly, hopefully, into his ear.

"Why don't you tell them that we aren't a couple?"

He turned and faced me in a pool of dim lamplight.

"Because I care about you, Joshua."

This was it. I gasped. Suddenly, it was all beginning.

"Because I care about you and I don't want to embarrass you in front of our friends. They can believe whatever they want. But I wish *you* would stop believing it, Josh."

Just as suddenly, it seemed to be over.

"Come on, Joshua! You're my best friend, OK? That sounds dopey to me, but I'll admit it. I never even knew what a best friend was before I met you. I love to talk with you and laugh with you and, yeah, to fool around with you. But it doesn't go any farther than that. I don't want it to. Not with anyone. Ever. Best friend is the best I can do, Josh."

"But Vincent, you're— "

"I know you probably think it's because I'm Catholic or because I don't want to hurt my parents or some other analytical literary explanation. And you're probably right. But who cares? Who cares about why? It's who I am, Josh, and I'm ok with it. So you be ok with it, too, OK?"

With a conclusive yet open-hearted nod and a gentle press of his palm to my cheek, Vincent stepped into his bedroom and shut the door.

His clarity filled me with amazement and envy. Somehow, amid all my earnest longing, he'd been more honest with me than I'd been with him. I hated the tangled knot of my feelings, my pulsing emotional radioactivity. Then again, I suspected that these were the very things that Vincent admired about me.

After I cried, before I slept, I spoke to the darkness.

"I love you, too."

~

I can still hear the scrape of shovel against stone. It was Thanksgiving again, a dark, cold afternoon. That autumn had been unusually chilly, but the endless scrim of snow unfurling over suburbia still struck me with icy, stinging surprise. Even the ominous weather forecast on the news the night before failed to convince me. It was just November, after all. Still too early, I hoped, for storms.

But soon enough, I was out there, anxiously struggling to clear the walkway to our house. Each stooped-over shove of the broad gray blade was quickly rendered futile by the unrelenting sky. I'd uncover a section of the flagstone path, then watch it disappear in a matter of minutes.

In frustration, I kicked at the two decrepit plaster lions. Over the years, my father had come to call them 'Losh and Jewis,' never specifying which was which. He'd insisted that they remain flanking the front door despite Mom's recent pleas for their removal.

"Who else will protect us," he'd ask half seriously, "while the boys are away at school?"

"Let them go," she'd argue. "Look at them, Harris. Look how beat up they are."

When Lew and I arrived home for the holiday the day before, Mom showed us that the statues' noses had broken off.

"Maybe this will finally convince your father."

"No way," I teased. "He'll just think of them as sphinxes."

"The sphincter and his sphinxes," cracked Lewis.

Mom let out a wondrous cackle, then quickly composed herself.

"That's not nice," she chided halfheartedly.

As the snow rushed down on that stormy Thanksgiving, my father's crumbling little pride at my feet, I was numbed by the wind. My eyes filled with cold tears as I shoveled. Lewis stuck his head out the door, encouraging me to come inside.

"It's useless; just let it go. C'mon, I'll make you hot chocolate, big bro. And Mom can probably use help with dinner."

I walked down the driveway, put the shovel in the shed and entered through the kitchen door. Lewis was pouring Hershey's syrup into a saucepan and Mom sat at the table, chopping walnuts for the cranberry relish. Prying off the heavy boots I had borrowed from Dad, I hoped that the snow would stop soon. It wouldn't though, I somehow knew, despite my yearning to clear the way before nightfall. It would taper as we slept and then freeze over, bringing a taunting, fantastic sight with the morning: the yard sheathed in perfect, shining armor. But there would be no path, and with every new step we took, the dreamlike surface of the world would shatter.

Lewis drew me out of my funk with his peculiar good cheer. Usually, he grumped his way through these obligatory homecomings, but now, he was upbeat and solicitous, buzzing about the kitchen, joking and grinning and happily doing any little errand our mother requested.

"Why," she wondered, "after nineteen years, are you suddenly passing up the ballgames on TV and taking an interest in holiday entertaining?"

"Just because I love you, Ma." He gave her a big, playful smooch.

She rolled her eyes but didn't persist with her questioning; there was lots to be done. While the prior year's intimate gathering came at Dad's insistence, Mom had opted to surround herself with a crowd this time: two single psychologist friends, five Cleyskils (minus Raphy and Rosalie, whose schools were too far away for Thanksgiving trips home), and, last but not least, our infamous Aunt Binnie.

"What's wrong with the guest room?" Lewis wondered when Mom mentioned that our long lost aunt wouldn't be staying with us. "Is Dad still giving you a hassle about her?"

"I think she just wants to have a little distance."

"I hear you," Lew said. "I hear you."

"What hotel is she at?" I quickly asked. I thought I might send flowers ahead to welcome the mythic exile.

"The Marriott," Mom said, accidentally tipping over a carton of cream.

"What Marriott?"

"You know, on City Line."

She scrambled for paper towels to clean the spill.

"Mom, they tore that place down five years ago."

"Well, I don't know. I thought she said the Marriott. It hardly matters."

"How are we? How are we?" Dad strode into the room and pulled all three of us into his arms. He seemed intent on making the best of the weekend, but his cheer was as forced as Lew's was inexplicable.

"Let go, Harris," Mom withdrew from his embrace. "I've got to finish this pie crust."

"And how's my turkey-lurky?" he asked, yanking open the oven to peek at the enormous bird.

"Leave it alone for God's sake, Harris. It's the same as it was when you looked five minutes ago. If you keep on opening the door, it's never going to get done."

In the past, we'd had a routine little Butterball, the bird little more than a bland centerpiece amidst the savory array of cornbread stuffing, mashed yams, and other so-called side dishes that are, in fact, Thanksgiving's central pleasures. This year, though, as he'd dramatically explained to us, our father had twice made the forty-mile trip to Perkin's Turkey Farm out in Chester County, once to choose the perfect thirty-pound bird and once to collect its plucked carcass.

"He's really tremendous, don't you think? Wait until the crowd gets a load of this guy. A Royalton family monument."

"I can't wait for Mom's pumpkin pie," Lew said sharply.

"It's all great," I mediated. "Everything's going to be just great."

I kept checking my watch, waiting for Aunt Binnie. I wondered what she would be like. I'd begun to think of her as something of a miracle worker, able to break away from her family, live a fiercely independent life, and then, all these years later, to reestablish ties. Ever since Mom had visited her in California, she'd spoken of her sister to me in hushed, admiring tones.

"It turns out that all the distance didn't really come between us. In some ways, I think, It's allowed us to be closer. When Binnie met me at the airport, she called me Rebecca Micklin. I hadn't heard that in years. I've been so caught up in Becca Royalton. She's something, that Binnie. She's something else."

The Cleyskils arrived first, snow and sleet blowing in behind them. Ellen juggled a dish of rice pudding and a baked squash casserole. Frisbee's arms were loaded with arrangements of dried flowers and gourds.

"So how's the weather in your gourd, Joshy?" he reached up and rapped on my forehead. "Managing to keep everything together in there?"

Essex and Avi, the Cleyskils' middle boys, now fifteen and thirteen, stormed past their parents to greet Dad with high fives.

"Harris, dude!" Essex blurted. "You got the game on?"

"Do Pilgrims pray? So who do you pick, Avi? Is Notre Dame gonna romp? Come on into the living room; we don't want to miss the kickoff."

"Now, here's a great Dad," Essex teased Frisbee. "He doesn't hog up the TV watching the opera and Julia Child."

Lewis and I swapped sardonic smiles as our father stepped away with the two younger boys. Then, I noticed their sister, Ulana, quietly leaning against the banister in a smart black jersey dress. She was quite sophisticated for a twelve-year-old. She looked remarkably like Raphy.

"Hello, Joshua," she said, with an impish grin.

"Well, hey, U. Looking good there."

"Do you still have that tree room?"

"Well, the room's still there, but the tree's cut down."

"No! I loved that tree when I was little," she cocked her head and stroked her hair. "You probably still think I'm little, don't you?"

"You seem pretty old to me. So, um, what kind of denture cream do you recommend, Granny?"

"Can I see your room anyway? I remember how Mom would bring me along when she came to see Becca. You were always so nice to me. My brothers never let me in their rooms."

"Well, I'm a big Cleyskil fan, U. C'mon, let's take a look."

Ulana looked out of my bedroom windows, into the falling snow. She smiled. "I can still see it," she said, laying a finger on my elbow. "In my mind, the tree's still there."

"I know what you mean. You're a pretty smart kid."

"I'm not a kid," she pouted stagily. "I'm a lot smarter than Essex, and he's fifteen." Pronouncing her brother's name with coy emphasis on the second syllable, Ulana had casually slipped off a shoe. Raph's baby sister was flirting with me.

"Oh, man!" I laughed. "We've got to get downstairs. Someone special is going to get here any minute."

"I'm special," she sighed.

I chummily brushed a hand across the scruff of her neck.

"Sure are, Ulana. You make me feel pretty special, too."

She blushed happily and we headed down the hall.

I answered the doorbell and Binnie stepped in, a tower of fox fur on ticking heels. Framed, for a moment by the arched front door, she stood before a backdrop of the floodlit storm. The snow swirled chaotically against the slate gray sky, like characters on a blackboard, refusing to stay still and allow me to read them. As I closed the door behind her, Binnie whipped the red silk scarf from her neck, imperiously shrugging her coat off into my father's waiting hands.

"Well, well. It's been a long time." He offered a halfhearted embrace, buffered by the fur draped between them.

"Too long, Harris. Too long."

He hurried off to hang her coat, shouting, "Becca, your guest of honor's here."

She was tall and taut and utterly in charge. I wondered it would be like to have such confidence, to walk into a house as if you possessed some inherent right of ownership. The resemblance was remarkable, much more than in the childhood photographs I'd seen; chic, worldly Binnie looked as exactly as my mother would if, well, if she wasn't my mother.

"Hello there, Joshua," she said with a smile, embracing me in long silk-sheathed arms.

"I wasn't sure that you knew who I was."

"Well, I'm not sure that you know who I am. I'm afraid someone may have told you I'm the new Cruella De Vil."

"Actually," I confided. "He prefers 'The Joan Crawford of Family Values.' But don't worry, we homosexuals are rumored to adore Joan Crawford."

As soon as I heard the words come out of my mouth, I wondered why I was so quick to mention that I was gay to this virtual stranger. No doubt she already knew through Mom, but I'd felt some compulsion to create an intimacy between us. Binnie chuckled.

"Well, you're as clever as Becca says you are. She tells me you're winning prizes in the literature department. Do you want to be a professor? A writer?"

"Oh man, I don't think I could ever teach. I never feel like I really understand anything thoroughly. There's always another way to look at it all. I'd feel like a fake teaching. And writing? My friend Kathy says I have an unusual perspective, she always tells me I should do a novel. But I can't imagine it. I don't know enough. Actually, for years, I've been dying to do a kids' book." I laughed nervously, and turned toward the kitchen. "Geez, I can't believe Mom's not rushing out here to see you."

"Well, we spent some time at the apartment yesterday."

"What apartment? I thought you just got in this afternoon."

"Oh, the hotel room, I mean," she said, dismissively flipping the back of her hand and turning to look at my parents' framed wedding photo on the wall.

My mother was teary-eyed when she emerged through the double doors from the kitchen a minute later, followed by Ellen and Frizz.

"What's got all the onions, Ma? The stuffing?"

"Where's my sister Binnie?" she asked me, wiping her face with a sleeve.

My aunt was in the living room, casually avoiding Dad and winning over the rest of the crowd. She chatted knowledgeably about football, shocking the Cleyskil boys, and talked real estate with Leslie and Gerald, Mom's friends from her psychology review group.

"Oh, man," I heard Essex gush to Avi later, "She's like a cross between Joan Collins and John Madden. Ask Mom where she's staying. I bet she likes to seduce young studs."

Only Lewis resisted Aunt Binnie's charms.

"She's driving Dad crazy," he complained to me in the hall.

"What, you've got some monopoly on irritating him?"

"It's just that this is a bad weekend for her to be around. He's going to have enough . . . Look Josh, I wasn't going to tell you until later, but— "

He was cut off by an exuberant Ulana.

"Joshy," she rushed to me. "Now I know where you get your personality. Binnie is soooo nice and smart. Look what she gave me."

From the depths of her little black clutch, Binnie had presented Ulana with an Yves St. Laurent lipstick. It was a strange, pale puce.

"Lovely," I said, withholding my observation that the gift bore a remarkable resemblance to her eldest brother's penis at fourteen.

As my mother added final garnishes, Lewis and I escorted the procession of dishes from the kitchen to the dining room table. Everyone settled into their chairs, spread navy blue napkins on their laps, and watched in a state of amazement as my father ushered us in through the doors, the Royalton boys bringing on the abundance: string beans with mushrooms and almonds, buttery corn pudding, sweet potatoes topped by brown-edged marshmallows, mountainous quantities of stuffing. On and on it went, Dad taking snapshots of the food and the guests.

My father walked to his end of the table, straightened the front of his white shirt and addressed the group.

"I am thankful to have such a wonderful wife and sons. And to be able to share their love with all of you. It's particularly nice to have Becca's sister, Binnie, here with us. We've had our differences in the past, but tonight, let's let bygones be bygones. You're all family here. Cheers."

He didn't even look over at Binnie, who wore a disbelieving smirk. Instead, his eyes blinked at my mother's empty place at the opposite head of the table. She was still in the kitchen.

"Oh shit." He muttered. "Hey, Bec! Everything looks gorgeous. Come on in here and take a bow."

"Here, here," toasted Frizz as she stepped in. "Hail to the chef."

"There's a little problem," she whispered to Dad through gritted teeth. "Actually, a big problem. Thirty pounds big."

"Why doesn't everyone start helping themselves. We'll be right back in with the *pièce de résistance*."

I followed my parents into the kitchen. My mother and I had already removed the Godzilla of poultry from the oven. His skin was crisp and golden, his aroma mouthwatering.

"I told you not to get this show-off turkey, Harris. It's not like we don't have enough food."

"Come on, Bec. It's the symbol of the holiday. What's the problem?"

"It looks great, but it's stuck. It's stuck in the roasting pan. See where his big fat wings hang out over the edge? Well, they've baked right on. The bottom, too. What a mess."

"Cooked to perfection but trapped in his nest," I mused.

"I guess we'll just hack him up in here and bring the pieces out on the platter," suggested Mom.

"No way, Becca. Everyone's got to see this guy. He's Mr. Thanksgiving. I've got to get pictures of their reactions to this baby. Come on, Josh, grab the other end of the pan."

The two of us carried it through the swinging doors, a naked emperor in an oven-blackened sedan chair.

"Holy shit!" cried Avi. "That turkey's on steroids."

"It's a free-range, natural-fed Perkin's farm turkey," Dad boasted as we set the pan down on the sideboard. "The most perfect you can find."

"He's the unattainable ideal," I joked. "We can't get him out of his cooking pan."

"Damn it! It's the perfect Thanksgiving picture, this big guy on a silver platter in the center of this beautiful table. There's got to be a way."

Lewis, who had an appreciation for engineering, joined Dad in pushing and prodding at the bird, even trying to reach in with a knife blade and surgically sever it.

"It's useless, Dad," he said after a few minutes. "Give it up. Everyone's hungry. It's carnage time."

"Josh, I've got it!" Dad shouted. "Help me put this pan on the floor."

A moment later, at my father's bidding, I was crossing the icy driveway to the shed. I hadn't put on my coat for the quick dash, and by the time I made it back through the kitchen door, my nipples felt like bottle caps. I felt weird about noticing this in the midst of a family dinner. Kneeling on the hardwood dining room floor, I held the pan steady as my father wedged the snow shovel under the turkey's belly, I looked up at our table of astonished guests. Their eyes were wide, their brows furrowed, like spectators at some esoteric sporting event.

It was Rockwell gone amok, simultaneously wholesome and perverse. My father pressed down hard on the red shovel handle and, with a quick ripping sound, the bird broke free. It thumped clumsily onto the floor and, propelled by Dad's force, proceeded to skid four feet, slamming through the double doors and into the kitchen. The room erupted in laughter as the doors swung shut, punctuating Big Bird's dramatic exit.

"He'll be back," joked Frisbee. "I think he just went into the kitchen to get something to eat."

"I thought turkeys were supposed to be flightless birds," Binnie added.

"Too bad he couldn't run like that before they caught him and killed him," cracked Lew.

I chuckled along until I turned and saw my father. Surrounded by laughing friends and relatives, he stood frozen, his eyes moving back and forth from the empty pan to the threshold his precious quarry had carried itself across. The turkey's route was memorialized by a wide streak of grease on the floorboards.

"Don't worry, Dad. I'll clean that up," I said. Something much more was bothering him, but I didn't know what. My mother rose from her place and led my father toward the kitchen. Ellen and Frisbee glanced at each other. Binnie shook her head.

"It's OK," Mom assured. "Go on, help yourselves. Lewis, I know you're starving. Set an example. Your father and I will get the turkey on a tray and be right back out."

As everyone else reluctantly dug in, I knelt on the floor by the double doors, trying to rub away the bird's greasy track with paper towels. It reminded me of the terrarium snails in third grade, carrying their houses and leaving trails behind. Over the dining room chatter, I tried to make out the faint strands of my parents conversation I could hear from the kitchen.

"Come on, Harris. Pick it up already. Let's get back out there."

"Forget about it. You hated it anyway."

"I didn't hate it, Harris. I just thought it was too much. Please don't act like a child. We agreed to get through this holiday. We've got to behave like adults if . . . "

"Kiss me, Bec. Please kiss me."

Most of Mom and Dad's words were lost to me. Even the tone of their voices was hard to pin down, veering from flinty anger to melancholy to warm nostalgia. It was an excruciatingly intimate mix. For a few minutes more, I scrubbed in frustration.

That night, I crept downstairs after everyone was asleep and worked at the wood with Murphy's Oil Soap. The turkey had left a faint but indelible stain, a permanent presence in the place from which it escaped. Outside, the snow still tumbled down, illuminated in great speckled cones by the street lamps. Climbing back up to bed, I felt overlapping waves of sadness and confusion. I had struggled to make one path that day, and struggled to remove another. Gazing out my bedroom window, I tried to see the tree that used to hold me aloft.

In the morning, Lew's duffel sat packed by the front door.

"Hey," I said finding him in the kitchen. "What's with your bag?"

"Sit down, Josh. I'll make you breakfast before I take off."

"What do you mean, take off? It's only Friday. You've got the whole weekend."

Lewis cracked four eggs in a bowl, puncturing the yellow yolks and scrambling them with a fork. He cooked like an athlete, every motion pointed and deliberate.

"I would have told you sooner, Josh. But I didn't want Mom and Dad to know. I was afraid—"

"You were afraid I'd tell them and then they'd try to guilt you into staying." I paused. "It's OK, Lew. I understand why you'd think that. I've thought a lot about what you said last Thanksgiving. You know, sometimes I feel like there's this whole family amoeba and all I am is a pseudopod; maybe I branch out a little, but I'm always totally connected. You're more like your own separate organism, Lew. I wish I was more like that myself."

"That's pretty cool," he laughed. "I'm a free cell and you're in a jail cell."

"Don't be so cocky, Lew. Where do you think your lame humor comes from? It's built in, baby. A Royalton legacy. No way you'll ever completely escape."

He emptied the bowl into a hot skillet, breaking up the egg batter as soon as it began to set. One jab of a saltshaker, one crank of the pepper mill, two sweeps of a spatula and breakfast was served.

"So Josh, where'd you come up with that amoeba stuff, anyway? You don't even like science."

"Actually, a friend of mine thought of it. I was telling him about our family, and he made it up."

"This is that Vincent guy, right? The physics major? How come you've never told me about him, Josh? I had to hear you had a boyfriend from Mom and Dad. Man, something major like that, I can't believe you didn't tell me. I'm your brother, Josh. I want to know this stuff."

"I didn't tell you because it's not true."

Lewis was crestfallen.

"What? Dad said— "

"Since when do you believe what Dad says?" I lashed. "I've been trying to take a bit of your advice, OK, Lew? He's always asking me about dating, and I just wanted to get him off my back. I lied to him, OK? I lied. Vincent and I are just friends." This confession tasted bitter on my tongue, less honest, somehow, than the wishful dream I'd presented to my father as fact.

"Oh shit, Josh. I'm sorry. I was mad because I thought you didn't tell me, but I was glad that you had a boyfriend."

"I shouldn't keep secrets from you, huh? You want to know about my love life? Guess you're not as different from Dad as you think."

"Gimme a break. We have zip in common. You're my brother; he's my father. There's a big difference."

"I don't know if there's a big difference between any of us, Lew. It's like the Royalton amoeba has a life of its own. Even if you break away, the original still exists. You may think you've cut loose, but you're still a part of it. And it's a part of you, too."

I looked away, then turned back.

"So what about you, Mister Jocko? Dad says you're like some cloistered monk. There really hasn't been anybody since Jen Dulcey?"

"Josh, Dad never knew about Jen, remember? You and Meri were the celebrity couple. Now it's the same old fake out: you're pretending to be with Vincent for Dad's benefit."

"That's wrong, Lewis. I never fake anything. I didn't exactly lie about Vincent. You don't understand. Jesus, you're the one who pretended that Jen didn't exist. You're the faker, Lew."

"I don't want to fight you, Josh. We're both going to do what we need to. But I want to be honest with you, now. OK?" I nodded in silence. "I do have a girlfriend. A serious one. For more than a year we've been together. It's the only thing in life that makes me feel like my own person. Me and Erin, it's like a whole private universe. She's so cool, Josh. She looks a little like Rosalie Cleyskil, even plays the saxophone."

He drew a deep breath.

"They say you become independent by going away to college, right, Josh? But when Dad basically picks the school and Dad pays the tuition and Dad wants to lecture on the phone about my grades and what classes I should take, I don't feel like I've ever left home. It's like my whole life is a haunted house and Harris is the ghost.

"When we were kids, my guy friends always thought he was such a cool father, always paying so much attention to us. I just couldn't risk it with Jen, or now with Erin. You know how Dad would be. He'd start charming her and pulling her into the family, when all I want is a chance to get out. I've wanted to tell you about this for so long, Josh. But it's like me taking off this morning. You said you understood. I wasn't sure you could keep it from Dad." Lew glanced at his watch, a nervous tremor crossing his face. He stood and slipped on his long wool coat. "It's the same with Mom. You have no idea how much I've wanted to tell her about Erin. I think they'd get along great. But she tells Dad everything; she can't keep anything separate."

Lewis dug a hand in the back pocket of his jeans. My brother seemed to know exactly what he wanted. I was struck by his confident organization: the train schedules, the timed disclosures, the letter he handed me as he gripped my shoulder.

"This is something important, Josh," he tapped a finger on the envelope. "I wanted to give it to you first. Mom and Dad will get a copy in the mail on Monday. Please don't read it until you're on the train back to school. Don't tempt yourself to tell him, Josh. I need you to be on my side now."

"They're going to wonder why you left. Will you be back at Walden tonight? You know they're going to call you."

"Tell them I'm going to a friend's for the weekend. Tell them I'll be in touch on Monday."

"OK, Lewis. Whatever you need."

I felt nervous but unwaveringly committed to keeping his confidence. It felt as if, after all our years together, we were setting genetic happenstance aside and agreeing to participate in a higher form of brotherhood. Lewis slung his duffel bag over his broad shoulders and, together, we stepped out the front door.

"Thanks for helping me, Joshy." My brother's voice quavered. "If I had time, I'd run naked through the neighborhood in your honor."

I gave him one of those concentrated grins intended to bombard its recipient with particles of pure goodwill and affection. He flashed it right back and then, clumsily, leaned forward to wrap me in an uncharacteristic bear hug. We held that embrace, staring over each other's shoulders, and Lewis whispered in my ear.

"That Vincent must have a screw loose, Josh. You're a totally lovable guy."

He let go of me, then, and with a shiver of embarassment, Lewis turned and headed toward the station. Resisting the impulse to follow him with my eyes, I bent down and busied myself brushing off Losh and Jewis. A small white object jutted from the snow.

"Hey!" I shouted, scooping it up. "Lewis, wait up!"

I ran down the driveway and twenty yards up the street, my chest heaving from the cold. I shoved the small chunk of plaster into my brother's coat pocket, saying it would bring him luck.

"What is it?" Lew asked.

"A lion nose."

Not giving him a chance to refuse me, nor myself a chance to try changing his mind about leaving, I raced back to the house, icy fissures cracking at my feet. Closing the door as I stepped inside, I resisted the urge to look out through the diamond-paned window. I couldn't watch him walk away.

~

The news of Lew's departure distressed my father, but somehow Mom's announcement that she was going to the mall rattled him much more.

"There's tons of stuff I need to get," she said.

"Don't go," he urged her. "Stay home. It's a family day."

"I'm going with Binnie. She's my family. Do you want to come with us, Josh?"

Though I longed to spend more time with my aunt, I declined the invitation, choosing to stay with Dad. I wondered if I could possibly make him feel any better.

"Black Friday. Black Friday," my father muttered. "Everyone thinks they need to run around. The roads are slippery out there, Josh. What if she gets in an accident?"

"She'll be fine, Dad. So will Lewis. Now what are you and I going to do?"

At my coaxing, we retreated to his den, sprawling on the carpet with the old Scrabble set. More concerned with maximizing wordplay than tallying high scores, we quickly found ourselves jockeying to outpun each other. Gagging and feigning nausea at each other's silly gambits, we fell away from the morning's worries, discovering simple pleasure in each other's company. It was like a rare moment from my childhood.

"I'd suggest turkey salad sandwiches for lunch," he managed to joke about the night before. "But they're only available to go."

We tuned the stereo to his favorite oldies station. The music from his teenage years worked on Dad like a balm: Elvis pleaded "Don't

Be Cruel," The Platters offered "My Prayer," and Pat Boone crooned "I Almost Lost My Mind." Then "American Pie" came on. It reminded me of that afternoon years before, my father and I driving in his Chevy. But as the song drew to its melancholy close, I found myself slightly disoriented. I could recall when this song was first a hit. How had it ended up on the oldies station so soon? My father's music was mixing with my own.

Dad led me on a raid of his bedroom closet. The cedar smell reminded me of Grandpop Josh's old lairs and, despite the lack of glimmering coins and goblets of plastic exotica, It held its own simpler, masculine charms. There were cherrywood shoe trees, rubber-banded bundles of stiff white collar stays, and a shallow leather box full of cuff links and money clips.

The trinkets and treasures in Grandpop Josh's closet had always struck me as landmarks along a road I was bound to travel, while my father displayed totems of a land from which I felt uncomfortably exiled. Still, I eagerly accepted Dad's offer of some slightly threadbare dress shirts; where he'd tucked them into Brooks Brothers suits, I would sport them tails out, flapping over blue jeans. I spotted a gray cardigan sweater that dated back to his own college days. There was a moth-eaten hole in the right elbow, he protested. He'd planned to give it to Goodwill.

I persuaded him to let me keep it, though, complete with the secret fantasy it inspired. I imagined walking into a Primo Homo dance, wearing a whole outfit of my father's comfortable old clothes. Vincent would be with me, and I would hand him a small pewter whistle. When he blew it, a cloud of silvery moths would fly in, devouring every stitch of clothing from my body. I'd stand there, naked except for my Converse high tops and nerdy wire rims, in front of all those self-consciously trendy boys in their chic, but moth-inedible synthetics. Vincent would grab me and we'd make out like crazy.

"I've got suits for you, too, pal." My father broke the spell. "You're almost my size now. Just a few alterations."

"I'm never going to wear a suit."

"Law school interviews next year, Joshy."

"I'm not like you, Dad. I'm not going to law school."

We'd performed this bit of dialogue over and over by phone for the past few months, like bratty toddlers refusing to let go of a nursery rhyme's jangling refrain.

"Well, you'd better plan on something productive," he'd say next. "I'm not going to support you just drifting about."

"I can support myself," I'd snap back. "I'm looking forward to a little independence."

Fortunately, just as our singsong routine was threatening to teeter into genuine argument, I heard my mother pull in the driveway.

"The stuff is great, Dad. I can't wait to wear it. Lemme go help Ma with her packages, OK?"

"Sure, Josh, go on. I think I need a little nap. Nice spending time with you. Say hello to Becca for me."

"I thought you needed tons of stuff." I teased my mother, who carried a single overstuffed Macy's bag in her arms. "This is the result of a full day's shopping?"

"It's for you." She handed the bag to me. There were shiny, band-collared rayon shirts inside, overpriced underpants with hot boys on the boxes, droopy-ankled eggplant- and mustard-colored socks. Primo Homo clothes.

"Geez, Mom, did the Gap burn down?"

"Binnie said these were in with the hip kids."

"I'm gay, Mom, but I'm not even verging on hip."

"Well, I can return them. I'll be back at the mall next week. I have lots more shopping to do. I just thought I'd get you a little gift, that's all."

"Thanks anyway," I said, fingering an underwear box. "I appreciate the thought."

The next morning, I almost collided with my mother at the top of the stairs. I was barreling down the hall with my suitcase, hurrying to catch the early train.

"Joshua, what's the hurry? We're not going to leave until noon."

"What do you mean, Mom? I'm walking to the station now."

"What? Didn't your father tell you? We're driving you back to New Haven."

"I didn't tell him," said my father, materializing at the bottom of the stairs with a grin. "Josh is a big boy. He can take the train to New Haven just fine. We need a nice a day to ourselves, Becca. Just you and me."

He withdrew an arm from behind his back, clutching two spears of Mom's favorite yellow freesia. With his other hand he clicked the stereo remote, string-sweetened music mingling with the flowers' perfume.

*Look at me, I'm as helpless as a kitten up a tree, and I feel like I'm clinging to a cloud . . .*

"We shouldn't go anywhere, Bec."

There was a frantic, reedy edge to his voice, not harmonizing well at all with Johnny Mathis, who had segued from "Misty" into "Too Much, Too Little, Too Late." Dad stood, muscles tense, with his back to the front door.

"Harris, please. Enough already. Are you going to blockade us in? Let's all take this trip together, OK? Let's do this like we discussed."

"Don't go," he pleaded with both of us now. "The roads are slippery out there. What if you get in an accident?"

"I'm going, Harris. Whether we drive Josh to school or not, I'm going."

Everything collapsed then. Everything fell into place. The meaning of the past few days now seared me with painful clarity. I understood that there had been no simple drive to the mall, no simple visit from a long lost sister. There was no hotel room awaiting my aunt, but an empty apartment that she was helping to furnish. I understood that my mother was leaving home.

Dumbstruck, I shouted something truly dumb.

"Binnie made you do this, Ma! You don't have to listen to her."

But when I saw my father brusquely nodding in assent, I felt a pang of guilt. I wanted to grab hold of my mother and beg her forgiveness. I wanted to tell her that I understood the things she felt, the things that her sister and my brother felt, too. I suppose I wanted to feel them for myself. But, in that moment, the sound of my father's anguished weeping drove all these notions from my head.

The great romance of my life was my parents'. And it tumbled that morning like a house of cards. A flush of hearts, you might call it. A good hand held too tightly. Lewis, it turned out, had an ace up his sleeve. I tore open his letter on the train back to New Haven and learned that my brother was not returning to college at all. He and Erin had lit off for unknown territories. He intended their location to remain a secret from our parents for the far foreseeable future. Once settled, though, he would fill me in; he would trust me. Lew regretted cutting off Mom like this, but there was no way around it, he wrote, no way around *them*. Would I please take care of her?

Had my brother stuck around for a couple more days, he'd have seen that she could take care of herself. He'd have seen her loading her last suitcase into the car, while I stumbled off to the train, half in shock, refusing to accept her repeated offer to drive me up to school.

Compared to our mother's quiet, unsettling courage, Lew's grand escape struck me as melodramatic in the extreme, less like real life than a boy's adventure story; it made me smile deliriously for forty-five minutes, all the way from Philly to Trenton. I was grateful for my brother's letter and even more for the photo enclosed: Lewis stood with a sweetly lascivious grin, hands protectively set on Erin's shoulders. A jungle of black ringlets tumbled round her Cleyskil face. The perfect couple, I thought. A familiar dream come true.

~

When Vincent and I had moved into our dorm room that September, I'd suggested that we share one big memo board. But, intent on clear divisions between us, he'd insisted on separate boards: one for messages from me to him, another for those from him to me.

"It'll keep things from getting mixed up," he'd predicted.

My board was completely covered when I returned that Sunday afternoon, Vince's Magic Marker letters growing tinier and tinier as they reached the bottom:

Hi! Man, are my relatives boring! Welcome back, bud! No hard feelings, I hope. We're OK again, right?

10:40   Your Dad. Call home as soon as you get in.

12:15   Your Mom. Call as soon as you get in. 215-555-4759.

 1:00   Dad again.

 1:15   Dad again. (Does he think I'm withholding messages?)

 1:30   Dad: "Are you *sure* he's not there yet?" (Josh, did you tell him I spurned you or something?)

1:35     Aaargh! You've got to get this guy under control! Going to gym. See you later.

I had missed Vince by ten minutes and, without him around to hear my weekend's sad story, I was faced with returning calls from the tale's other characters, who would surely twist and reinterpret its plot. Just the decision of whom to call first seemed a minefield of explosive hidden meanings. In childhood, whenever our family configured into opposing teams, there was still an underlying sense of the whole, always more important than the moment's battling parts. Now, I stared at the phone, wondering who I belonged to.

I was saved by the squeak of ink on vinyl: it was the third memo board, outside our hallway door, for friends to leave messages when neither Vince nor I were home.

"Hey! Don't go! I'm here! Come in!"

Greg popped his head in the door.

"So how's small town life here in Homo Corners?"

Having once been the focus of all my anxieties, Greg had evolved into a source of constant comfort. I didn't subscribe to any of his mystical weirdness, but admired his acceptance of his own peculiarity.

"Hey, I just ran into Freedy. His grandfather died last summer, you know. So they finally got to have a real turkey instead of speckled meatloaf. Freedy said he almost started to cry when he sank his teeth into a drumstick."

"That's our Little Boy Hallmark." I attempted to sound cheerful. "So what's up?"

"What's down, Josh? What's down? You've got a majorly gloomy aura. Something wrong? Want to talk about it?"

"Jesus, Kreskin, you dive right in, don't you? As usual, though, you're right. But before I spill my guts, my proper upbringing demands that I ask if you had a nice turkey day."

"Actually, we never have turkey. All that ugly butchering and then the arguing over who gets which meat color. Forget it. We each have our own peaceful little Cornish hen. That's *my* proper family upbringing."

"Well, my upbringing has just been upended, man. Take a walk with me?" As we stood in the hall and I locked the door, the telephone started to ring inside. "Never mind it. Let's just go."

When we met up with Vincent in the dining hall a few hours later, Greg patiently listened to my weekend all over again. I heard myself describing everything a second time, using the same words as before. It was as if the crumbling lions, the sharp icy snow, and my mother's powder blue suitcase had all been painfully tattooed on the tip of my tongue.

Back at our room, Vincent strode directly to the phone jack and popped the cord from the wall. "Anyone else who needs me can wait until the morning. And you might as well just wait until your folks get Lewis' letter tomorrow before you call them. You need to take a break from this. Jesus, Josh, I mean, I can't imagine my parents . . . I don't even know what else to say."

So he didn't say anything, just sat there beside me on the couch. We shared a joint he'd bought from Greg, put Joe Jackson's *Night and Day* on the turntable and played a strangely soothing game of Othello. The tiles flipped from white to black and back again in haphazard, random patterns. I felt incapable of strategy, only reaction. And Vincent—whose head for algorithms had made him the Othello champion of our dorm—wasn't trying to win, either, just keeping the game moving along, watching the mosaic shift with me. After flipping the album to side two, though, I began slipping out of our game, into the scratchy gaps between the tunes: "Breaking Us in Two," "Cancer," "Real Men," "A Slow Song." I shifted uneasily to the cynical, yet somehow hopeful, music. I wondered if maybe I should go ahead and call home after all, and I berated myself for wishing Vincent's arm would slip along the sofa back and drop around my shoulders.

"Vince," I turned to catch his eyes. "Just for tonight . . . could we?"

"Josh, it won't help anything. I'm just your friend. They're your family."

"That family is over!" I spat, anger rising unexpectedly. "That family is over, and I need a new one, goddammit. Dad's stuck in a re-run of "Father Knows Best," Mom's in "Sister Knows Best," Lewis is off to fucking Timbuktu, and I'm left alone with little replicas all of them crawling around inside my head like fire ants. Come on, cut me a break, Vince."

"I'm here, Josh, same as I've ever been." He put the game board back in its box. "I'm still me, though, not some spare part that can replace what's broken in your family."

"But you— "

"And don't twist this around so you can see me as a bad guy here. I'm not the villain; your father is." He breathed in sharply. "I'm sorry, I'm sorry. That's not for me to judge. I didn't mean to say that."

"It's OK," I muttered, getting up and distractedly combing my hair in the mirror by the door. "He is a screw up. He always claimed to be so open-minded, but he kept trying to fit everything into these picture-perfect scenarios. And when it ends up exploding on him, we all take the shrapnel. Sometimes I really hate him."

"Hey, try not to be so harsh." Vincent's face appeared over my shoulder in the mirror. "He's always meant well, hasn't he?"

"But he wants to control everyone else's feelings." I shook my head in frustration. "Why can't I make him understand that's impossible?"

A half-smile crawled over Vince's face, but he kept himself from speaking, and I remained oblivious to the irony of my desires.

"I need to sack out, bud," he said. "I've got eight-thirty lab on the hill. You gonna be OK for tonight?"

"Yeah, I'm all right. Until I talk to them, at least. Vince? Thanks. Thanks a lot for helping. You know I wasn't really mad at you, right? You know—"

"It's OK," he nodded, slipping into his bedroom. "I understand."

I lay awake late into that night, trying to make sense of my long holiday weekend. On the other side of the wall, Vincent slept, untouchable. And I realized that I was glad to have him there, glad that someone beyond my control would choose to care for me nonetheless.

"You've got to come home, Josh. You've got to."

For months, my father's phone calls all ended with variations on this refrain. I spoke with him almost daily. His distressed hectoring gave me painful indigestion. But if he didn't phone, I worried and called him, clutching my gut as we talked. He bemoaned his intolerable solitude, retelling family anecdotes in dismissive, acid tones, as if all the happy moments of his past had just been part of the setup for the huge, cruel joke that he felt his life had become. Although I rejected his entreaties to come home and be with him, guilt led me to turn myself over to him in conversation. The mundane details of my life were recounted for almost an hour each night in a ridiculously meticulous verbal diary: classes, articles I was writing for the *Daily*, meals, friends.

After these quotidian litanies, I would share whatever scant details of Lew's life that my brother had given me permission to pass along. "He has a job," I told my father. "He's working for one of Erin's second cousins. He writes that he really likes it."

Lew and Erin were living in a California town called Tiburon at the base of a mountain, on the edge of a bay. I'd found it in an atlas in the reading room at Sterling. My brother's occupation negated everything my father ever expected our jobs would require: no degree, no desk, and no paperwork (unless, of course, you counted wrapping mackerel). Lew worked on a fishing boat, the *Lisbon Kiss,* casting off into silent waters at two in the morning and selling the catch over steaming mugs of coffee by seven, at the very wharf I'd seen on a hundred television shows. By ten, their work was done and they'd motor back to Marin, late morning sun illuminating the rippling line they cut between Alcatraz Island and the streets of San Francisco.

"I've never even met this Erin," my father complained. "How can I know what to think about her?"

"I've never met her either, Dad; just saw a picture. But I know how Lewis feels. And I know where his feelings come from. It's the same place mine come from. You know what I mean? In spite of everything that's happening now, you and Mom really did show us a lot about how to care for people."

"Well, great for me," my father sputtered. "Everyone's learned their love lessons, so now there's Lewis and Erin, Josh and Vincent, Becca and, God, who knows, Phil Donahue or Mister Rogers, one of those touchy-feely, shrinky-dink types."

"Do you really think so, Dad?" I held back a chuckle. "Maybe Fred Rogers will adopt me away from you and I'll open a gay disco with X the Owl in the Neighborhood of Make-Believe."

He laughed, ruefully.

"C'mon, Dad. You know dating is the last thing on Mom's mind."

While I tried to make him see my mother's situation clearly, I could never make myself come clean with my father about Vincent. My parents put in nearly twenty-five years together before they fell apart. I was ashamed that my own effort at romance had sputtered out almost before it had gotten started.

There was also this undeniable, guilt-ridden truth: It felt good to make my father believe I could possess the very thing he had lost forever.

Of course, the real friendship that Vincent and I been struggling to build would have been completely wrecked had he known I was letting my father believe we were a couple. But even this risk didn't stop me. As many times as Vince had drawn his lines in the sand, something in me still believed that a wave of love would eventually come crashing down to wash over them. When I tried to imagine myself as just Josh, alone, I saw an endless plummet into inky, obliterating darkness. To spare myself, I had to cling to Vincent in my mind or else fall back into my father's arms.

"You'll be home for winter break?" Dad had nervously half asked at the end of our very first phone call, that Monday after I'd returned from Thanksgiving.

"I don't think so. Not so soon. I'm going to spend some time with friends in New York and Boston."

"You've got to come home," he'd insisted again before spring break.

I went to Kathy Seeton's country house in Maine.

"You've got to come home for the summer," he'd pleaded. "It's been too long since we've spent any time together."

I explained that Professor Paterson, my academic advisor, had offered me a three-month research position. I would even get a credit in the monograph he was writing. *Paint It Black: An Interdisciplinary Meditation on Mark Rothko and Holden Caulfield* would draw important sociocultural links between the depressive modern artist who crafted a fictive persona to help him deal with the world, and the depressive fictional character who incessantly complained about the world being phony.

"Well, I expect you to come home for at least a few weekends, Joshua. Do you understand me?" his voice took on a strange, serrated edge in these conversations, cutting from insistent demand to desperate need. "We'll have fun. I promise. Just you and me."

"But Dad," I responded, playing my trump card. "Vincent's going to be working in New York, and weekends are the only time I'll be able to see him. I know you can understand that."

"I see," he exhaled. "Well, I guess he's a kind of family to you now."

In fact, Vincent was going home to Wisconsin for the summer.

"Josh? Did you know I asked your mother to see me on the weekends."

"Really?"

"She said no."

"Sorry about that," I replied with forced nonchalance.

This bit of news upset me profoundly. Not because I harbored any real hope that my parents would reunite, but because of the ache and panic in my father's voice. Harris Royalton was a family man. Now, for the first time in his life, he found himself alone. He found himself lost. Behind that arched oak door, he was slowly becoming unhinged.

I almost proposed that he take the train up and visit me someday, but I knew that such a suggestion would be unduly cruel, like dangling a licorice whip just beyond a hungry child's reach. As incapable as I'd begun to feel about ever passing between those desiccated lions and entering our house on Roslyn Road again, my father was just as incapable of leaving it. Each day he rushed back from his office in the city, stopping as briefly as possible to pick up cold cuts or drop off dry cleaning, then closed himself into a bunker of wishful memories. He sat in the dark, '50s tunes on the radio, projecting carousels of Kodak slides. Sometimes, the images filled him with a sense of joy and justification, but, at other moments, he could only see them as frail translucent castoffs—our family's skin, shed and left behind.

"Damn it, Joshua. Why won't she come home? Why won't any of you come home? I told your mother she could keep her office, you know. Her patients were used to seeing her here; why did she have to rent a new space? She loves that office, Josh. Remember the day I decided to have it made for her? The puzzles all falling?"

"Not really," I said. "It was a long time ago. Life goes on, right? I don't keep track of all these little details of our past."

"The point is," he went on in frustration, not even hearing my remarks, "she has a private entryway to the office. She wouldn't even have to see me."

"Why does it matter to you then, Dad?"

"Joshy," he choked up, "I just want to have her close to me sometimes. To sit in the kitchen and know that she was on the other side of that wall would make me feel better, even if she won't love me like I love her. Even if I can't touch her or talk to her. I just want to have her nearby. I can fill in the blanks. Oh Jesus, I'm sorry. I must sound completely crazy."

"It's OK. It's OK," I said, staring at Vince's bedroom door. "I don't think you're crazy, Dad."

"Thanks. Thanks for listening to me, son. You know I love you, right?"

"Yeah, Dad. I know. Me too. OK?"

"All right then, pal. I'll talk you again soon. I'm sure we'll be able to work something out, won't we, Josh? You'll come home sometime soon, right?"

"Good niiiight, Daddy," I enunciated with sugared annoyance and hung up. I swigged Maalox from the bottle and stared at the framed M. C. Escher poster on our living room wall, two pencil-wielding hands drawing each other.

"You've got to come," he wrote me.

It was a long, exuberant letter from Lewis.

"All these amazingly different places linked by tremendous bridges. Men died building the Golden Gate, Josh. Don't let their deaths be in vain! There's lots of available gay guys here, you know—Duh! You could live in the city and write great children's books, and we'd visit back and forth so easily. It's so different from Philadelphia. You know how downtown and the suburbs were entirely different places? Well, in my town of Tiburon and in San Francisco, you look out your window and see miles of mountains and water connecting everything and you realize that everyone's in the same place. Our tiny apartment is as big as the sky. Everywhere Erin and I go, we feel at home."

With the exception of required school compositions, endlessly redrafted under our father's vigilant scrutiny, Lewis had never voluntarily written more than a brief kitchen table scrawl—"Out. Will be late. Don't wait up.—L."—so the rhapsodic missives that began arriving every few weeks after his escape took me by surprise. Spotting California postmarks when I picked up my mail at my campus post box, I would tear the envelopes open and read them standing there, immersing myself in my brother's words, oblivious to the bustle of my classmates swarming around me with their outstretched hands and glinting metal keys, their hopes for care packages or love letters or *Playboy* magazines.

Back at the dorm, I would hand the letters to Vincent, who would sprawl on our threadbare brown corduroy couch and read them to me again, aloud, dramatically enunciating Lew's evocative descriptions of Chinatown— "chickens in cages and old ladies spitting on the sidewalk with no shame" —and the Castro district— "Nipple ring-o-rama! It's not exactly romantic, all these guys gawking at each other, practically drooling. Talk about obsessive. I mean, I have no problem with the fact that the world is full of people who just happen to be gay, but in the Castro, it's more like gays who just happen to be people."

"This is Lewis!" I marveled. "Where did he learn to write like this? When did he learn to think like this?"

"It's a family thing," Vince theorized. "You were the brain boy. He was the jock. Now he's far enough away to be whatever he wants."

I agreed, but there was something more. As far away as he'd managed to get from us all, Lewis kept inviting me to join him. "You've got to come," he enthused. "You'll love it. We want to show you everything."

My feverish Yale apprenticeship in the picking apart of prose—all the syntactical hairsplitting, nuance-swatting, and disinterment of subtext with which I'd fairly successfully distracted myself from the need to lead a real life—finally revealed itself to have a practical use. Not in some epiphanic understanding of Melville or Shakespeare or Nabokov, but in the quiet moment one night, alone at my desk with Lew's fifth or sixth letter, when I realized that—without ever writing the exact words down—my brother was telling me that he missed me. He'd found Erin, who he loved and planned to marry. He'd filled his days on the water with a shimmering contentment. And still, Lewis missed me.

My eyes spilled over because he was so far away. Because I thought he had grown so different from me. Because I doubted my own ability to travel such a distance, to ever reach that place where my brother urged me to join him. In the midst of this tear-streaked meditation, I reached in my desk drawer and took out the leather-bound book, the dream I'd abandoned as futile nearly a year ago, despite my brother's persistent encouragement. But as I sat there that night with Lew's letter, I opened the book and printed neatly in the center of the first blank page.

"I miss you, too, Josh."

Then I shoved the book to the back of the drawer again, burying it in syllabi, schedules, and the mini-fridge warranty, resisting it as much as I clung to it.

~~~

In a sort of penance for rejecting Lew's constant exhortations to work on my kids' book, the articles I wrote for the *Yale Daily News* that spring semester clearly bore my brother's influence. I fashioned myself the paper's newest sportswriter in a column called "Game of the Week." Each piece spotlighted a relatively obscure sport ignored by most of the world but preserved and cherished by die-hard aficionados in the Yale environs.

Fencing, croquet, curling, badminton, Australian volleyball, and duckpin bowling all got their moments of glory. The players of these games had mastered sets of rules that the rest of us didn't even know existed. Scribbling down the lovingly described details of their pastimes, I remembered my father's frustration when Lew abruptly abandoned baseball for the unfamiliarities of crew. Even back then, my brother was running away from home, pushing off to the peace of the water. No shouts from the sidelines can be heard by a rower, neither disparagement nor good wishes. Pulling hard against the river's mirrored surface, he makes his own momentum. It is all breath and heartbeat and distance from the shore.

Of all my subjects that semester, it was jai alai that changed me. Originally played in the mountaintop villages of the Pyrenees, between France and Spain, jai alai is a sort of adrenalized, round-robin handball. The players use scoop-like wicker baskets—*cestas*—to fling and catch the rock-hard rubber ball, called a *pelota*. Spectators gamble on the players, like horses at a track, betting on which of the eight men will place first, second, and third. In the United States, the sport is played in only a few arenas, called *frontons,* mainly in Florida and Nevada. But there was also a *fronton* in Milford, Connecticut, only ten miles from Yale.

Like all of my series' topics, I was initially drawn to jai alai not because of any real interest in the game itself, but because I saw its players and fans standing in quirky, stark relief against the televised American landscape of Monday Night Football and wide-smiling Wheaties boxes. I imagined them to have found a deep sense of pride and comfort in their arcane, unfashionable devotions. But as it turned out, jai alai was a blast. Long after my story had been filed, I returned week after week. I loved the wicked thwack of *pelota* against concrete, the impossible diving catches, the sweaty players' grunts as they released each throw in a graceful scythe blade arc. For the first time in my life, I was a sports fan. In the Basque language of its native players, jai alai means merry festival. That's not exactly how it felt on the evening I introduced my mother to the fine points of the game.

It was a Saturday toward the end of May. Virtually the entire student body had left campus, and I was spending twelve to sixteen hours a day on Professor Paterson's project, holed up in a library carrel rereading *The Catcher in the Rye* and ferreting through the university's Rothko archive (which held everything from the painter's recipe cards to his suicide note). "It's like theater, Ma!" I enthused, announcing our evening plan when she arrived. Indeed, from the raked bank of seats that sloped down to the three-sided playing court, I found it easy to ignore the incessant electric rattle from the cashiers' windows and the caustic haze of cigarette smoke and imagine myself sitting in a velvet upholstered box. The court's transparent mesh front was an open curtain on endless evenings of my new favorite drama: the small, intense cast, dashing and leaping, each player straining to catch the caroming ball, then sending it back with his own spin, his personal English. My mother had surely been expecting something different for our reunion, reservations at some quiet restaurant where we might share a bottle of wine with dinner and, in the flickering peace of candlelight, talk about the six months we'd just spent not talking.

"I'd do anything in the world to make you feel better," she had insisted in our one, brief phone call two days after that fateful Thanks-but-no-Thanksgiving weekend. "But there isn't anything I can do, really, is there? You're a grown man, Josh. You're a grown man, and you're entitled to whatever feelings you have right now. I can understand if you're pissed off at me."

"*Pissed off,* Mom? What, are you adapting your youthful patient's speech patterns, Ms. Therapist?"

I regretted the venom in my tone. I knew my mother had meant no condescension. But I had little interest in the rational conversation she offered. I didn't want us to be two intelligent adults. I wanted to bawl and scream until everything was taken care of.

"Listen, honey, I don't want to fight with you."

I heard her swallow. "I love you, Joshua Royalton. As much as one person can possibly love another, I love you. And that's how I love Lewis. And that's how I love Harris. I can't be with your father anymore, Josh, but I still love him, if that makes any sense at all."

"How can you leave him?"

My voice retained its accusatory bitterness, but below the surface, the question was a practical one. I envied my mother. I had no idea how to do what she'd done. How could *I* leave him?

He trespassed in my mind; he ran in my blood.

How could I get him to leave me?

"Listen, Joshua," she ignored my invective. "You have my new number. Whenever you're ready to have a real conversation, I'm ready, too. We don't have to discuss family things if you don't want. Just call me and tell me about school or what movies you've seen or anything in the world. And Lewis! Oh Josh, just leave messages on my machine if you don't want to talk to me, but let me know when you hear from your brother, all right?"

"Sure, Ma. I will." I tried to sound conciliatory. "Lew felt really bad about not letting you know what was going on with him."

"Well, we all have a right to keep things private, Josh. Even if it makes other people feel bad sometimes. You tell Lew not to worry. I'll just have to get over it."

"OK, Mom." I wavered between respect and resentment. Every day, dark emotion welled up inside of me, settling into viscous pools. I was a waterlogged man, bogged down and swamped by sentiment: Son of the Creature from the Black Lagoon. Somehow my mother had learned to let her emotions pass on after she felt them.

"So, Joshy? You'll call me, OK? When you're feeling a little less shaky. I know its tough, honey. Just take the time you need. It's OK. I love you no matter what."

So matter of fact, she loved me. So undemanding. What about possession and obsession and dreaming and drowning?

"All right, Ma," I said. "I'll talk to you soon."

But I didn't. Not for more than six months. I was scared. Listening to my mother, I wondered if my whole way of feeling was wrong.

Vincent had packed his bags and headed home to Wisconsin the day before my mother finally phoned me again at the end of April. The call jolted me from the half-sleep of an afternoon nap, and I jumped up from the stripped mattress in Vince's empty room to take her call. I eagerly accepted her proposal of a visit, my discomfort with our differences overwhelmed by my desire for her company. While I took heart in Lew and Erin's California letters and even in my father's phoned-in neuroses, it was not enough to hold my family as words in my head. I missed hugging them tight, however awkwardly. And so I encouraged my mother to come up the next month.

As her visit approached, I grew uneasier, wishing I could somehow have the comforts of her closeness without the challenge of her perspective. And so I took my mother to Milford Jai Alai, where I could sit beside her in the midst of a noisy crowd, impress her with my expertise on a subject she knew nothing of, and keep her feelings unspoken, though they hung between us in a palpable cloud.

She offered to ante up at the bettors' window, but I explained that I'd never been interested in the gambling. While everyone else in the crowd bet on their favorite players and rooted for their opponents to miss the speeding *pelota,* I throve on the perfect tension of scoreless volleys. When each man stayed alive, catching every throw that came his way, ball and bodies ricocheting through the court in elegant spontaneous webwork, I held my breath, awed by a beauty that transcended competition.

I slumped forward in my seat at the break of a long, excruciatingly gorgeous stalemate. My mother spoke to me then, and I realized that while I saw the game differently than most of the crowd, she had her own viewpoint, as distinctive as mine.

"This reminds me of dinnertime when you were growing up, Josh. You and Lewis and your father all flinging jokes and insults around the table and me stuck on the other side of a transparent wall, not invited to play along."

I was astounded that she could discern this strange, subtle echo. I'd assumed the ability to read such hidden patterns was my private purview, the result of immersion in literature at Yale, a viewfinder that let me see beyond the realm of my family and into someplace altogether my own. But maybe, at least in part, it was a gift from Becca. Having spent so much life in emotional battle with my father, it had rarely occurred to me that I was also my mother's son.

"Come on," I said, rising from the orange plastic seat and extending a hand to her. "Let's get out of here."

I took her to a quiet restaurant after all. DeMarco's, one of precious few establishments in sleepy New Haven that had evolved to even the cursory elegance of "Care for some freshly ground pepper, ma'am?"

"Far cry from your noodle kugel," I said, forking up another mouthful of leaden spinach lasagna. She smiled at me as the over-eager, bow-tied waiter asked if everything was all right.

"Just fine," I said while he shakily refilled our glasses with the house Merlot, spattering the tablecloth with crimson flecks.

"If Grandpop Josh were here, he'd sell this guy an ultradeluxe, spill-guard wine funnel," I joked.

Even without the distractions of jai alai, some nascent conversation seemed to hover between the two of us, unarticulated. We chatted in warm, blank tones about my schoolwork, the latest news from Lewis, my mother's caseload.

"It's nice to be with you, sweetie," she said, stirring a packet of Equal into black coffee. "I wasn't sure you would even want me to come up."

"Me either," I confessed, glancing down into my napkin.

"Well, I'm glad you invited me, Josh. There's some news I really wanted to tell you face to face." She reached into her purse and slipped out an ivory business card. She handed it across the table.

REBECCA MICKLIN, M.Ed.
Licensed Psychologist

"Who's thi— " I caught myself, then responded with indignant alarm. "Wait, this is your maiden name, Mom! Why the hell — "

"It's just for professional purposes, Josh. No big deal. That's not what I was trying to show you, honey."

"Jesus. There's more?"

My mother reached across the table to touch my cheek. I flinched.

"The address," she said.

In a moment's elation, I convinced myself that she had returned home, to her office at 801 Roslyn Avenue. Then I looked at the card again.

Wagner Therapeutic Associates
37 Gaebler Boulevard
Los Angeles, California 90052

She retained her composure in my silent, bug-eyed glare.

"It's an incredibly respected practice, Joshua. I still can't believe that I'm going to be working at this level. But they made me a terrific offer, honey. Such a lucky coincidence, too. Binnie's dating one of the docs there; she got the whole ball rolling."

The silverware clattered as my palms slapped the table.

"Motherfucker," I gasped.

"I'll just take that as 'Congratulations'," she said, shutting her eyes for a moment. "Joshua, I wish you could be happy for me. I knew this would be startling after not speaking for all these months. But not calling was your choice."

"Are you sure about this, Ma? You've never lived anywhere but home."

"I'm going," she said. "Next month. El and Frizz are throwing me a little bon voyage party, If you want to come down."

"And how are we doing?" asked the waiter.

I emitted a sharp, impulsive dog bark that sent him scurrying. My mother laughed. In the midst of everything, I took pride in accidentally giving her some small pleasure.

"Does Daddy know?" I asked anxiously.

"Tomorrow night," she said. "I wanted to tell you first. You'll call Lewis? Maybe this will finally convince him it's OK to get in touch with me. That I'm really not going to turn him over to your father."

"He's in California, too," I confessed. "I guess that's where we're all supposed to go, huh? Manifest destiny. Royaltons, ho!"

"Maybe so," she said with a wink. "Graduation's just a year away. You know you've got a home wherever I am."

~

The very first listing in the New Haven phone book is AAA CON Auto Transport. People moving long distances on short notice pay to have their cars sent after them with volunteer drivers. If your schedule is flexible and your driving record checks out, all you need is a $100 security deposit and the price of gas to get you someplace somebody else needed to go.

The day before my own class's commencement ceremonies, I rolled out of New Haven in a pea-green AAA CON Volkswagen Rabbit. It belonged to a General Electric engineer who'd been transferred from Hartford to San Francisco. According to the paperwork, his name was Dave Zippel. His license plate, to my chagrin, was ZIPPY.

I actually could have waited another day before leaving, but I told Vincent and Greg that it would be easier for my parents this way. If I had to take off before the ceremonies, Mom wouldn't feel obliged to fly east and Dad could be spared the upset of leaving home. I told him I would have my diploma sent to Roslyn Avenue, to his attention.

In fact, graduation was too frightening for me to bear. Throughout our senior year, my classmates had buzzed through interviews with corporate recruiters, taken LSATs and MCATs and signed on for the Peace Corps. Greg had been accepted at a school of Chinese reflexology in Taos, New Mexico. Vincent had arranged to remain at Yale for a few years longer, continuing on for a doctorate in physics. Amid all the outward bound optimism surrounding me, I made no future plans, receding deeper into the texts and images of my studies, stubbornly bent on decoding shaded meanings for every word in every novel I read, every painted gesture hidden in Rothko's blackest fields.

Professor Paterson actually laughed at me during our last afternoon meeting in his office. "You've done marvelous work, Mr. Royalton. My paper—*our* paper—will no doubt make a big stir on the conference circuit next year. But you can stop with the research now. I've got everything I need. I don't have time to incorporate anything more."

"But I don't think we have the cigarette symbolism right yet. I've almost got it all down for you, but not quite— "

"Joshua, what we have is just fine. It isn't as if there are correct answers to be found. Please don't think that, my boy. You'll drive yourself mad. You mustn't try to solve the world like a puzzle. It must be read like a poem."

Without the clarity I believed my classmates had somehow come by, I felt ill equipped to be formally declared a graduate. It seemed fraudulent to attend the ceremonies. And so, the day before, I zipped away.

Every pop radio station in America had an annoyingly infectious jingle by the all-girl trio Exposé in heavy rotation that spring. "You're takin' me!" they swooned over a rapid, throbbing synthesizer beat, "to the point of no return!"

The song was omnipresent, across 3,000 miles of America. Wheeling, Columbus, Chicago, Kansas City. I couldn't get away from it. Crashing at a Motel 6 on the outskirts of Indianapolis at the end of my first day on the road, I flipped on the television and there was Exposé in a music video, three hyperactively slinky vixens writhing beneath the cardboard easel advertising in-room pizza delivery.

I gave in, ordering a small pepperoni and bouncing on the queen-sized bed in time to the music. "You're taking me!" I sang along. "To the point of no return! Ooooo-oooo!"

While it would be untrue to say that anything seemed a certainty in the four days I took to push the East Coast behind me, I tried to convince myself that San Francisco was the place for me, my own point of no return and new beginnings. Lew and Erin had urged me to hurry out and stay with them in Tiburon until I found work in the city. For months, sneaking breaks from Rothko and Salinger, I had pored through the Yale library's volumes on Baghdad by the Bay, imagining as my brother did that I might find a home amid the free thinkers, artists, homosexuals, and Chinese restaurants. Maybe I could be like Lewis after all, put some distance between myself and our past and start a different kind of life.

"Can't you get here quicker?" he'd asked me when I called before leaving New Haven. "Hammer it and you can make it in three days."

"I don't want to kill myself, bro. What's the big rush?"

"Just hurry, OK? This is going to be great."

Waiting for Lew to pick me up after I dropped the Rabbit at AAA CON's San Francisco garage, I wandered around the intersection of Broadway and Columbus, taking in the city's unpredictable hiccuping rhythms. The famous hilly streets seemed so absurdly steep, so quick and prolific in their ups and downs that, rather than momentous drama, they projected a sense of quirky humor. Amid the tiny winding side streets of North Beach, there was a dizzy polyglot bustle. Italian and English and Mandarin mixed in my ears. Cappuccino foam hissed and caramel-sheened ducks swung from ropes in restaurant windows. Everyone was a foreigner; everyone seemed at home.

Under the blinking electric nipples of the Condor club's burlesque show billboard, I grinned at the city. It seemed so vibrant with possibilities, completely different from Philadelphia. I wondered what it would have been like to grow up in a place like this. I wondered if, perhaps, it was not too late to start.

"Hey, sailor, wanna bellyfight?"

I felt Lew's arms around me and laughed with tears in my eyes as he lifted me from the sidewalk in a bear hug. His showy college weight room physique had been transformed to a fisherman's natural sinew. The face I'd last seen taut and determined eighteen months ago now relaxed beneath a couple days' stubble.

"Well, where the hell's my future sister-in-law?" I greeted him, the words out of my mouth before I recognized the rotund young woman standing a couple feet behind him. Through all of our brief phone conversations, I'd stared at the single snapshot Lewis had given me before they took off, Erin slim and sporty in the Walden dorm.

"Thar she blows!" Erin chuckled at my confusion and waved her arms above her head, as if I was a mile away. "Whale watchers alert!"

"Honey. I don't think it's a good idea for you to jump around like that."

"Oh, Lewis, don't be such a worrywart." She gyrated in her egg-plant-colored muumuu, pointing both index fingers at her gut. "So, welcome to San Francisco, Uncle Josh."

I gasped in joyful speechlessness.

"Any minute now," said Lew, glancing at his watch. "We're three days overdue. See why I wanted you to hurry, bro?"

"This is going to be the happiest kid in the world," Lew turned to me in the backseat, steering with his left hand and patting Erin's belly with his right as we crossed the Golden Gate out of the city in their mud-flecked, beat-up Honda.

"Would you keep your eyes on the road, Big Daddy?" she ribbed him. "If you don't leave the baby alone, you're going to drive it into the bay before it's even born."

"I'm going to do this right, Josh. I'm going to make sure every-thing goes perfect for this little one."

Now Erin looked back at me, raising her eyebrows in mock con-spiracy.

"And I, of course, will just sit back, relax, and watch the miracle of paternity unfold."

I laughed, reaching forward and affectionately mussing the backs of their heads.

"We're gonna have a big house right down there someday."

From the tiny deck of their apartment, on the low-rent outskirts of upscale Tiburon, Lew pointed down into the town. "The big boss,

Erin's cousin, Nick Apostos, he owns six boats and five fish markets. He likes me, Josh. He's gonna bring me into the business someday."

"Don't count your chickens, honey," said Erin. "Anyway, we've got everything we need to be happy now. Don't we?"

"I got you, baby," he grinned. "And you, baby!" he dropped to his knees, gripped her butt, and mashed his face against her swollen belly, grunting with primal pleasure.

"Lewis!" she scolded, blushing. "Your brother!"

"Believe me, Erin," I laughed. "It's nothing I haven't seen before."

I fumbled with the alphabet magnets decorating their refrigerator door. Tucked under a bright orange R was a single baseball ticket Lew had bought for next month at Candlestick Park. The Phillies were playing the Giants.

Erin stepped into the bathroom, and Lewis sat down next to me on their small thrift-store couch. A fishbowl lined with bright green gravel rested on the windowsill just above our heads. Two black mollies chased each other in and out the archway of a gold ceramic castle.

"Josh," my brother said awkwardly, "you know I'm not good at this stuff. But I want to tell you . . . "

"You don't need to say anything. You and Erin have kept me alive for the past two years."

Lewis looked over to the bathroom door and cracked an ear-to-ear smile.

"I love her so fucking much, bro."

He slapped a palm on the coffee table.

"Welcome to California. Welcome to the all-new Royaltons."

"Hey, Lew!" Erin suddenly hollered from the bathroom, "either start the car or declare me a water slide and sell tickets."

Just like the last time I'd seen him, my brother had planned his great life change like clockwork. He tossed me an extra Honda key wrapped in a page of handwritten notes.

"Go on, Josh, pull it up front. I'll get out Erin's suitcase and call Mom with the shuttle schedule."

"Mom?" I was amazed. "You're talking to her?"

"A bit. Since she got to LA. Just on the phone. But she doesn't know about the baby. I guess it's time to tell her, huh?"

"Boys! Con-trac-tions! Could you save the reunion chit-chat until I've got a little anesthesia happening?"

I dropped them at the hospital in San Rafael and then, following Lew's detailed instructions, stopped at a bayside bed-and-breakfast in Tiburon to reserve a room for my mother through the weekend. I'd suggested that I take the room and Mom stay with Lew and Erin, but my brother wouldn't hear a word of it.

"She does have some experience raising babies," I pressed.

"Yeah?" he glared at me. "How successfully?"

He bit his lower lip.

"Look, I'm inviting her, Josh. I'm allowed to keep a little distance."

"I'm sorry; you're right. She won't have any problem with it."

"Of course she won't. And neither should you."

Following Lew's precise directions, I drove south along the freeway to the airport. Forty minutes before Mom's flight was scheduled to arrive, I settled into a hard plastic seat and tried to imagine the art of raising a child. No matter what you did right, you would always do something wrong. Time must have a way of diluting the pain generations cause each other. But somewhere, within even the vastest sea of filial love, there would always be that eyedropped tincture of hatred. I didn't know if I could take that. I didn't know if I could bear the imperfection.

"Hiya, sweetie!"

Mom stepped through the crowd of disembarking businesspeople wearing a cream silk suit and a new short haircut. She was forty-two years old and she didn't look like my mother at all. She looked like a real person.

"Hi, Granny!"

"Button your lip!" she laughed. "Holy shit, Joshy! Can you believe this is happening? When's Harris getting in?"

I stopped and set her bag down on the corridor floor.

"Dad's coming?"

"Well, of course. Joshua, this is your father we're talking about. He's going to be dying to see this baby! I'm sure he caught the first flight out."

"Mom," I caught her eye and fell silent for a moment. "I don't think he's invited. I don't think he even knows."

"Oh, Jesus," she shook her head. "Can your brother be that stubborn? Takes after someone else we know."

"So, you'll try to convince him to let Dad— "

"That's not for me to do, Josh. I'll call Harris with the news, but the rest is between the two of them. And the grandbaby."

Erin had delivered by the time Mom and I reached the hospital. A boy. A nephew. A firstborn grandchild.

"He's a perfect little dude," beamed Erin. "Healthy as they come."

Eyes glistening with love, Lew handed his tiny, cotton-swaddled son to our mother.

"Ma," he said, his whisper trembling, "We named him after someone very special. Meet Cory. Little Cory Royalton."

Mom pressed the baby's cheek against her own.

"Hey, Cory!" my brother cooed. "Hey, Cory boy! Your Uncle Josh is gonna write you a storybook."

I told them how much I loved them all, how much I appreciated their welcoming me to California along with the new baby. After midnight when everyone had settled in, I crept out and caught the red-eye to Philadelphia.

~~~

I had not been to my father's office since I was eight years old. I made my way down the dark paneled hall and found the brass name plate that read HARRIS ROYALTON. His secretary was out to lunch and, through a crack in the door, I saw that my father was not at his desk. I crept inside and pored over his things. His bookshelves were arrayed with crystal-framed photographs, a truncated timeline of the lives of Lew and me, beginning with baby pictures and ending with high school graduation shots. Alone, on the center shelf, was my parents' wedding portrait.

The vast mahogany surface of my father's desk was a sprawl of yellow legal pads and documents, all of their margins swarming with the same ball-point doodle, a compulsive gridwork of tiny repeating squares. An amber pill bottle sat by the telephone.

CLONAZEPAM 1.0 MG
1 TABLET EVERY 6 HOURS AS NEEDED TO RELIEVE ANXIETY

The prescribing physician was Frisbee Cleyskil. In the wake of my mother's departure, my father had somehow permitted himself to ask her friends for help. I lifted the bottle and rattled the pale yellow discs against the plastic. The telephone bleated, and I jumped, startled, as if caught in the midst of a crime. I jammed my hands in my pockets and took off for the elevator. I didn't leave a note.

Rushing out the lobby door, I accidentally bumped into a tall, expensive-haired woman who stood on the sidewalk, smoking.

"Pardon me," I apologized.

"That's OK, hon." She pointed at me with a vampire fang fingernail. "Hey, you're Harris Royalton's son, aren't you? I've seen your picture on his desk. What's your name again? Something biblical, right? Noah? Jonah?"

"It's Josh," I said, "Joshua."

I stared at her two-tone lip gloss—frosty mauve with a dark maroon outline—and wondered if the blue vapors of her Kool didn't ruin the flavor of the gum bobbing around her mouth.

Years ago, my father had done dead-on imitations of secretaries like this one over the dinner table, describing them as alien creatures or exotic animals spotted on safari. I would laugh myself into wheezing speechlessness, as he mimicked the cocky bob of their heads, their sweeping hand gestures, and honking South Philadelphia accents.

"So, what's your name?" I asked the smoking woman, relieved that I could suppress my inbred disdain.

"Monica," she said, offering her hand—five fire-orange talons and one cockroach-sized hunk of zirconium. "Mrs. Monica Goodman."

"Goodman?" I asked, incredulous, remembering Dad's snapshots of his partner's second family. "Like Uncle—I mean Howard Goodman?"

"Yep, that's the one." She pointed up the building's granite face. "Tenth Floor. Sweet Howie G., Legal Quarterback for the biggest names in the NFL and, as of March, my own number-one draft pick."

"Well, congratulations," I said, resisting the impulse to mention that she was his third-string wife. "I didn't realize about the wedding. My dad must have forgot to mention it."

"Yeah. I'll bet," she said, shaking her head, blowing a dismissive stream of smoke from one corner of her painted mouth.

"Did I say something wrong?"

"Hey, you seem like a good kid and this may be a little out of line, but you know what? I'm a big-mouth South Philly pisser, Mr. Joshua Royalton, and I feel just fine out of line. So here's the deal. I can handle your father not respecting me. I mean, I don't have your mom's education, but I was never the sleaze-bag, man-hunting, paralegal on the prowl that Harris seems to think I was. But your pop can believe what he wants about me. Am I different from him? You bet. That's a point of pride."

"What really gets me is how your dad hurts Howard. I mean, to hear Howie tell it, they were best friends once. When Howie got divorced from shrew number two, your dad just cut him off, like he's some monster. Like nobody ever splits up in this world. Like you're nothing if you don't happen to have a perfect happy family like the famous Royaltons."

I said nothing.

"I told Howie that Harris can't let bygones be bygones. But Howie can't either! He says it's too important a part of his past, his childhood, his college. Harris is one of his oldest friends. So in January, right after we decide to get hitched, Howie asks your dad to lunch. He has to let on that it's business for Harris to even sit down with him. So he tells your dad that we're planning a tiny little wedding on this beautiful island, St. Lucia. We're going to stay for five days. We're bringing my sister Theresa and her husband and we'd like to bring your dad and mom, too. It's time to mend fences. Rekindle the old friendship."

"But my parents— "

"But your parents are selfish jerks if you ask me, kid!" She tugged a pale blue tissue from her Louis Vuitton purse and blotted a fat tear as it crested her cheekbone. "'Becca and I just wouldn't feel comfortable with that,' your dad tells Howard. Howie *still* wouldn't let go, asked him to think it over. But your dad never says another word. Not even a thanks for asking."

"Well, for what it's worth," I said, looking straight into her eyes, where real emotion pooled under the fake lashes, "I'm really sorry about what's happened. I feel bad. About my father and all."

"Aw, hon," she said, making the gesture of patting my face from a scratch-resistant distance. "Don't worry. What's past is past, right? I was just letting off some steam. It's your pop's problem, not yours."

"Look, it was really nice to meet you," I said, sincerely. "Please give the groom my regards, OK?"

"Sure will." She smiled.

"Man, it's been ages since I've seen Uncle Howard." Hearing myself blurt that old nickname, I laughed uneasily, a memory suddenly flashing in my head. I stepped toward the corner, then wheeled back around with a smile. "Tell your husband that Weeping Flower sends his best."

"C'n I help you w'sumpin?" asked fat Frankie at the newsstand around the corner from the office. He was another character I recognized from my father's stories, a man of Paul Prudhomme proportions, fingers blackened from handing out the daily papers. His colossal bottom spread over the edges of his wooden stool, threatening to collapse it into a pile of tinder.

"I can just imagine his wife removing those splinters," Dad had joked, years before.

As I stood there, about a half dozen customers came and went, cheerfully exchanging greetings, bemoaning the Phillies' losing streak, asking Frankie about his new baby daughter.

"She's perfect. My apple dumpling!" He shook his jowls and slapped his gut. "Just keep your fingers crossed that she doesn't take after her father in too many ways!"

"Don't be so hard on yourself, hon," said a woman in a custodian's uniform, paying for a Find-A-Word puzzle book.

"Y'need somethin, Mister?" Frankie spoke to me again,

"No, no, I'm OK," I stammered, embarrassed to be caught staring at him. "No, wait; I'll take these." I lifted a roll of peppermint Life Savers from the box and dropped thirty-five cents into Frankie's palm. Stepping away, I pressed the familiar blue and silver cylinder between my palms and rolled it back and forth. Shoving the unopened package into my pants pocket, I realized I had taken my father's pill bottle. I had no idea where I wanted to go.

There were pungent homeless people all around me. There were makeup-caked women drenched in Obsession. Lanky black kids shouldering boom boxes made the pavement pulse as they passed. Crew-cut FedEx men sporting short pants and special deliveries. Green- and purple-haired punks with safety pins glinting in their sweet baby faces. Arab incense vendors and Korean fruit-salad ladies. There were businessmen in suits, rushing to catch the next train out.

I was dazzled and terrified. I felt homeless myself.

Hunger knotted my stomach, and I bought a clammy plank of four soft pretzels for a dollar outside the Academy of Music. I tore off two and slathered them with dark mustard from the old man's squeeze bottle and shoved the brown paper bag in my backpack. I wolfed them down under the old man's silent eye, willing away the complexity of the city around me, trying to concentrate on bland, simple sustenance.

Next to his battered steel steamer cart, the vendor—all sad eyes and bony-elbowed psoriasis—had a small display of inflatable children's toys hanging from thin wooden sticks, like the ones they sell outside the zoo or along parade routes. He had big-eared dogs, out-of-season snowmen, and unlicensed Pink Panther knockoffs. One shiny cluster of gold Mylar helium balloons bobbed in the exhaust from a grate on the sidewalk beside him. I stared at my cloudy reflection in their gilt surfaces, peering out the corner of my eye and rocking on the balls of my feet, trying to center my profile in a single circle of gold. I thought of myself as buried treasure. I dreamed of being engraved.

"You see heads," I heard a voice from behind me as a hand grabbed my butt. "I see tails!"

I was being mugged. I spun, panicked.

"Long time no see," chirped a woman with white face powder, jet black bangs, and deep green, unforgettable eyes. There, with a dye job and fashionably gothic pallor, was Meredith. Failing to connect with my father, I had stumbled onto her, after four long years. I felt dizzy. It was as if we were all spinning, circulating, the blood of each other's dreams.

"What are you doing here?!" I whooped, pulling her into a giddy embrace, then quickly dropped my arms, backing up two steps, nervous, afraid of misinterpretation.

"Meri, I, uh, I'm sorry— " I dug a hand in my front pocket. "Would you like a mint?"

"Oh, Joshua, don't worry. A girl can always use a friendly squeeze." She grabbed my butt again, wiggling her painted eyebrows. Taking my elbow, Meri started leading me across Broad Street, charging along with friendly energy.

"Slow down, Mer, there's some stuff I should tell you— "

"Like you're sorry about being out of touch for all these years? Like I really meant more to you than a ten-dollar bet?"

"Well, yeah, and— "

"Like you turned out to be the kind of scout who gets his sparks by rubbing two sticks together? So what? Who cares? Glug, glug, glug. Hear that, Josh? It's the sound of water under the bridge." She grabbed my chin in her hand. "Geez, it's great to see you!"

She hugged me again, right there in the middle of Broad Street. The light changed mid-clinch, and a man leaned out of his shiny Suburban and honked.

"Get outta my way, goddammit!" he yelled.

"Get outta our city!" Meri barked back at him.

Safe on the opposite sidewalk, I looked up at City Hall clock tower, crowned by the statue of William Penn. The city's patriarch stood frozen as the crowds and the second hand kept sweeping along beneath him.

"Did you hear the rule's been broken?" Meri asked.

"The William Penn rule? No way."

Since City Hall was first erected in the nineteenth century, there had been a law that no building could climb taller than William Penn's hat.

"Believe it, Joshy. Five years from now, Billy Boy is going to be surrounded by skyscrapers. The old guy is going to be nothing but a birdhouse for the pigeons."

"I've always had a fondness for pigeons," I replied. Pulling my two remaining pretzels from my pack, I tore them up and scattered the pieces on the pavement with a flourish. Pedestrians swung a wide arc around us, giving me strange glances as a cooing clan of street birds gathered at our feet.

"You're still crazy," Meri laughed. "Same as ever."

But, in fact, I felt different than I had in ages—brand new, freshly minted, and out of my head. I was in a buzzing city of car horns and dirty feathers, a world of sounds and sights and possibility. I'd caught a glimpse of Philadelphia through San Francisco eyes.

"Hey, Mer, are we near Chinatown?" I wondered.

"My god, Josh, where are you from again? You're going to have to learn this whole town from scratch."

I followed her from the bustle of Locust Street onto bleak, pothole-scarred Juniper, lined by a peep show shanty, a nameless bar, and the service entrances to buildings with addresses on other streets. Two stubble-faced men slept propped against a wall, sweat stains ringing the armpits of their T-shirts. Suddenly, I was scared again. This was the kind of place I could end up if I made the wrong choices. I looked up, trying to see my father's building, but the alley was too narrow. The reek of piss simmered from the sidewalk.

"Juniper," I spoke reflexively, backing out of the world and into abstraction. "It has urine in its scent and urine in its name. U-R-I-N-E. All the letters are also in Juniper."

"Come on, Joshua!"

I blinked and saw Meri, a half block ahead of me. I had hoped she'd express amazement at my anagrams, maybe call me a poet or say something else reassuring. But she hadn't heard me at all. I rushed to her.

"If you keep getting lost in your thoughts, you're going to get *really* lost, Josh."

"Yeah, and wind up someplace like this." Another sleeping man issued a raspy belch. "I think maybe I should go back—"

I faltered. There was no place to go back to.

"What? You don't appreciate the glamorous big city life of Juniper Street?"

"Well, it's not exactly the Liberty Bell."

"No bell, but these guys can score you some crack."

"Ring-a-ding-ding!" I laughed, my fear subsiding in her confident company. "Oh man, Mer. I'm so sorry I avoided you all this time. I didn't think we'd ever get along again. It's like I pieced together this idea in my mind about how you must feel about me after high school and just assumed it would never change."

"Just like those glued-together jigsaw puzzles you used to bitch about," she challenged, gently shaking her once-blonde head. "Pretty lame."

I didn't say anything.

"I think that what goes on in our heads is more like playing Scrabble than building puzzles," offered Meri. "It's like your mind is the little tray, your thoughts and memories are the letter tiles, and the board is the real world. Every set of tiles you draw can be rearranged to make all different meanings. But the moves that other players make affect what you can do with your letters. Just because you have an idea doesn't mean there's a place for it on the board just then. Love. Solve. Evolve."

Now Meri was making anagrams, turning everything inside out.

She led me down a tiny side street, not even wide enough for a car. A few paces more and we turned again, then once more, into a webwork of crooked cobblestone alleyways. Spindly green trees, like leaf-bedecked toothpicks, poked from barrels packed with soil in front of impossibly narrow row houses. Some of the alleys were less than twenty yards long, not even marked with street signs. The others boasted bric-a-brac names—Ink Street, Egg Row, Pennypack Way. They zigzagged and doubled back and led only to each other, weaving together with off-kilter logic, interlacing and overlapping like twigs in a nest.

Meri stopped in front of one of the row houses, its crumbling brick front countered by carefully tended marigolds in bright blue window boxes decorated with white abstract figures, like Matisse collages. They echoed a giant, cheerful wraith on the door.

"Ghost dancers," Meri explained, seeing me take note of them. "So, finally, you get to see my paintings."

Before I could respond, a boy came bumping around a corner on a wide banana-colored skateboard. Knee patches of cartoon turtles decorated his tattered thigh-length jeans and a candy-striped nightcap hung down to the small of his back.

"Yo yo, Meredith!" he called in greeting, wheels clattering over the cobblestones as he careened down another alley. A window creaked open, and a whiskey voice rasped out.

"Hey, was that Timmy's jalopy I just heard roll by?" The street was so narrow, I had to tilt my head all the way back to see the slender Indian girl who leaned from a third-floor window across the way. She had impossibly high cheekbones, a caramel complexion, and a clean-shaved head. She looked nothing like her voice.

"That little fuckwad owes me twenty bucks," she snarled.

"You and the rest of us, Persis," Meri shouted up. "He always pays up, eventually. Just make him give you free shiatsu as interest. That boy can massage like nobody's business."

"I'll see you later? At the Copa?"

"Where else?"

"You'll have to tell me about your new escort," Persis winked down at me before closing her window.

"Oh, please. Tell us, too," a seductively reedy voice piped in.

A pair of identical twins stood on the corner in matching blue satin shorts, golden hair, silver hoop earrings, and '70s replica Quisp and Quake T-shirts. They ran their eyes over me from head to toe. They were probably just a year or two younger than I, but they had the smooth skin, wet pink lips, and bratty attitude of the perpetually boyish. Just being in their presence made me feel inept, my button-down Oxford, khakis, and loafers suddenly taking on the weight of medieval armor. I was a rhinoceros confronted by otters.

"Do make the proper introductions," said the second, with the same prankish tone as the first. "Is there any chance he's one of ours?"

"It's getting to be such a snooze in this neighborhood," the first elaborated, carelessly stroking his Adam's apple. "All the glammy little art school Qs get so the same, don't they? I mean, look at us," he gestured flamboyantly at their running togs, "We *are* snoringly boring, aren't we, Jase?"

"You know it, Jared," Jason snapped back, stepping forward and running a finger down my shirt front.

"But this one looks like a *serious* piece of work. This upstanding young gentleman could be the No-Doz of homos."

I was, in fact, upstanding by then. I leaned forward, trying to obscure the evidence.

"Meet the Tyler twins," said Meri, with an exasperated sigh, "as if they need anyone else to introduce them. Jason, Jared, this is Joshua Royalton. We were the proverbial high school sweethearts— "

"Another one bites the dust."

"Alas and alack!"

"I'm the only lass with a lack, here, you dweebs. Josh plays on your team now."

"I hate that expression," I said. "It's not like there's a competition, Mer. I mean, I still love you, just in a different way." I extended an ingratiating arm to the twins. "We're all on the same team, right?"

Jason and Jared snorted simultaneously, then broke into a chorus of "We Are the World."

"Re*lax*, Josh," urged Meri, squeezing my hand. "Don't take everything so seriously."

"We dig the Daddy drag," said Jason, tapping the bridge of my wire rims. "But don't let it go to your head."

"And don't forget," added Jared with a shimmy, "even on the same team, everyone has his own position!"

He slapped the satin-sheathed ovals of his brother's bottom.

"See you grown-ups tonight at the Copa, Miss Meredith?"

"Well, I suppose it's bound to happen. Now get out of here already, you guys!" She turned to me as they left. "Fair warning. All their flirting's just for show. They're perversely wholesome. Never date at all. They watch over each other like mother hens. Everyone wonders if they sleep with each other."

As the twins disappeared down the next alley, three drummers in papier mâché monster masks marched out, banging and chanting through the crooked streets. I watched in amazement as they turned another corner and disappeared.

"Welcome to the Elbow Bends," said Meri. "This is where we live."

The houses in the Elbow Bends were over a hundred years old, tiny, three-storied buildings, known as trinities. Most of them were shared by pairs of art students, struggling writers, retail wage slaves, or other aspiring adults. Meri was the rare solo resident, paying $500 to have an entire house for herself. She had her own car, too, a classic old Caddy with hot pink fins. She'd graduated with a computer science degree six months before and taken a well-paying day job on the surface of the city, slipping down into this rabbit-hole neighborhood by night, where she painted in her third-floor studio.

"I'm going to save up all that corporate money and go back to Marseilles. This is my real life," she said, sweeping her arm past several canvases in progress, emerging dreamscapes of orange and turquoise.

Brushes stood at angle in an empty salsa jar. Fat, half-used paint tubes lined a windowsill: larvae awaiting metamorphosis. I remembered my long-ago fascination with Ellen Cleyskil's studio, and, as I breathed the sweet chill of turpentine fumes, Ellen and Meri and Raphael whorled together in my head. Past and present chased tails, time and memory blending in a potent vapor.

"You could get high up here," I remarked, slightly dizzy.

"That's what art will do to you, isn't it?" Meri quipped as she slid a large painting out from the corner. "Look. My family."

It really did look like them. It felt like them. Her parents, standing in the background, seemed as crotchety as ever to me, but there was no doubt that this was a happy painting. They were all smiling, bathed in yellow light. In the foreground, Meri and her Louis linked arms.

"How's your brother?" We asked each other simultaneously, then laughed.

"Jinx!" I cried.

"Lou's great. He's in grad school at MIT."

"My brother's a father."

"No way. You're kidding. The grandpop didn't mention a thing. I didn't even know Lewis was married."

"He was just born a week ago. Wait. What do you mean, the grandpop?"

"Harris. Your dad. I must bump into him three times a week. My office is right down the block from his. He buys me a beer every once in awhile on the way home. I always tell him to send you my love. How do you think I knew you were gay and all, Josh?"

"You mean my dad told you that!?"

"He said you told them it was no big deal."

"It isn't!"

"Well, you're sure reacting like it is."

"The big deal isn't that I like guys. The big deal is that my father has secret conversations with my old girlfriend."

"I didn't know there was any secret. He said he talks to you all the time and I just figured—Anyway, I had no idea. We usually don't say much. He'll ask me about my job, tell me how much he and your mom are looking forward to having you back in town when law school starts—this fall, right?—but mostly he just tells me silly stories about when you and Lewis were kids. It's a little boring but kind of sweet, don't you think? So, I indulge him a bit. He was always really nice to us, Josh, back in high school. So anyway, tell me this news about your brother."

After filling her in on Lew and Erin and Cory, I stepped over and picked up Meri's sunlit family portrait. I rocked it back and forth, like a boat. I turned it upside down and gently shook it. They all remained in their places. I could not imagine such a painting of the Royaltons. The fumes were beginning to make me queasy. The making of art could be toxic.

"Hey, are you all right?" Meri noticed my sickened expression. "I really wouldn't have spent the time with your dad if I thought it was some kind of a problem for you. He just—I don't know—he seemed lonely. He's looked really beat lately. I'm sure he's glad that you're back."

"I'm not back. I'm here."

"What do you mean?"

"I'm not going to law school. Dad doesn't even know I'm in town. And as far as he's concerned, this neighborhood is not part of his home," I gestured out the window to the alleys below. "It's a foreign country, some alien parallel universe."

"A perpendicular universe, actually," she corrected. "Parallel universes never intersect."

"Clever as ever, aren't we? I guess that hair dye hasn't affected your brain."

She bit her lower lip to stifle a laugh.

"What?"

"You don't want to know."

"Sure I do."

"The first time I bumped into your father on Walnut Street, he made the same stupid hair joke."

Nauseated and dizzy, I felt the blood drain from my face.

She gave my hand a squeeze, then pulled the light cord. The colors of her artwork were changed in an instant, dreams left to vibrate in alternate shades. I had an urge to tug the light back on. Everything seemed so unfixed.

The long day had begun to wear on me. I'd traveled from Tiburon to the Elbow Bends; I was anxious, still not knowing where my journey would end. Down the stairs, in Meri's unkempt bedroom, I collapsed on her rumpled white futon.

"I'm sure you'll want to go stay with your dad soon, but you can stick around here for awhile if you need. With me or with somebody else in the Bends." Looking down at me, Meri's face took on a sudden softness. "It will all work out with you and Harris, you know."

Glancing up at her window, I saw a squirrel scampering along a branch, backlit in lavender by the late summer dusk. I relaxed and let my eyes slip shut.

I heard the sound of rushing water. The bathroom door was half open, steamy condensation filling the wedge of light. I feel my father's old insistence. Paint-spattered jeans and a work shirt at the foot of the stairs let me know that I was awake, that this was Meri in the shower.

I stood up from the futon and stepped toward the bathroom, unbuttoning my shirt. In my head, the smell of herbal shampoo bloomed into an image of Meri's dye washing clean. She would step out of the shower with golden high school hair. Back in my room at 801 Roslyn, we'd clutched and lapped like insatiable bears. Afterward, we would lie there quietly, speaking kind words and meaning them.

But there were images I'd constantly deflected as we embraced—Raphy, her brother, Christopher Atkins in *The Blue Lagoon*. "Friction is friction," I'd chanted to myself. It made me sad to recall, because Mer and I had been so close to right. And because I'd never really made love with anyone since.

I laid back down on the futon, unzipped my khakis, and conjured naked pictures of Vincent. I gripped tight, to make the skin hurt. "Friction is friction," I thought ruefully, "and fiction is fiction."

"Are you ready to have a good time, Mister Serioso?" Meri hollered from the bathroom just after I'd accidentally spattered her bedside bookshelf. I was frantically trying to wipe off her art history book collection before she emerged.

"It's midnight. I thought you were getting ready for bed."

"I'm just getting going, Josh. Persis called while you were napping. She's at the Copa. There's somebody there you should meet."

"What do you mean?" I said, nervous. "Who?"

"E. O. Jennio, the guy who owns it. Sometimes he needs help. I thought you might be looking."

She emerged from the bathroom in a pink T-shirt and black overalls festooned with buttons touting Planned Parenthood, NOW, Dead or Alive, and the Philadelphia Orchestra. "Whoa—what's that smell? Have you been cleaning with ammonia out here or just fantasizing about the Tyler twins?"

I stammered, embarrassed.

"Would you relax, already? I don't give a shit. Just zip up your pants and let's get out of here!"

I ran a comb through my hair, splashed some water on my face, and took my father's pill bottle from my pocket, tucking it away in Meri's medicine cabinet behind a messy jumble of sample packets.

Outside, the Bends glittered in the darkness. Timmy McGinty had shimmied up the lampposts one evening and removed the coconut-sized city-issue bulbs that blasted the narrow houses with unwanted all-night glare. Now, the streets shimmered gently under strings of colored bulbs that hung beneath everyone's second floor windows. They were simple Christmas lights for the most part, punctuated here and there by novelty lanterns shaped like chili peppers and geckos and cowboy boots.

"That's Jared and Jason's place," Meri pointed up at their lights, colors ordered like the stripes of the gay rainbow flag.

"Neat," I said.

"They used to have the bulbs coiled around a giant dildo, but Jase was drunk one night and banged on the front door so hard that it fell down on his head. Knocked him out. Talk about unsafe."

As we headed around the corner, I heard the hiss and pop of an old phonograph record. A young man's voice sang a plaintive ballad over a gently strummed guitar. I couldn't understand the words, but they sounded Spanish. The singer's tone seemed to glide between pleasure and loss.

"Here we are."

The music crackled from a small speaker, mounted next to a simple placard with wood-burned letters: *Copa Mà*.

It was really just another little trinity, a father, son, and holy ghost house with a public space instead of a living room. It opened onto a ragged corner where a half dozen little byways spilled together. Three curved cement stairs rose to a green-framed screen door. Persis sat on the bottom step with an elaborately pierced woman she introduced as Irie. They rolled cigarettes and played jacks with a neon pink Superball.

"Josh is a dear old friend," Meri purred, hooking an arm around my waist and raising a conspiratorial eyebrow at her friends. "You think E. O. Jennio might have something for him?"

"Could be," said Persis. "And I've definitely got something for you, Mer. That guy, Cole, from the party last week—he's around the corner on Rectory Way. Practicing on a stoop. Just him, a mandolin, and a big beeswax candle."

"Cole Wexler," Meri said, turning to me, with a sigh. "Last Saturday night I saw the trailer, Josh, and I'm starting to think he's my long-awaited sequel to you."

"This girl's the choosiest bitch I've ever met," Persis cracked. "Whatever you did to her in high school, you sure did good."

"He loved me, Miss Cat-Scratch. I hope you have the pleasure someday."

"Oh, *looove*. I hear such good things about it."

The women laughed together, but Meri cast me a sidelong smile.

"You better go find him, Mer," I joked. "Wouldn't want to miss out on a big beeswax candle."

"Well, well, chivalry is not dead," remarked Irie. "I'd scoop you up for myself, Mr. Josh, if I didn't know that your candle burned at the other end."

"You sure you're OK, Joshy? You seemed shaky this afternoon. I can catch up with Cole another time."

I caught a strangely appealing scent wafting through the screen door and looked up at the tinny speaker, pouring forth its sweet, sorrow-flecked melody.

"You can catch up with me another time, too. I don't think I'm going anywhere for awhile."

Persis led me inside the dimly lit room, just a handful of wrought-iron tables topped with flickering votives and terra-cotta pots of geraniums. The music was louder—a turntable and two speakers propped on a window ledge. Small groups chatted quietly, drinking mugs of black coffee and pouring red wine from paper bags. One table of boys squinted its way through hands of pinochle until Jason Tyler leaned in too far and accidentally set the jack of diamonds on fire.

"Jack didn't quite make it over the candlestick," he sang with a shrug as he rose from the table. "Guess that's a sign I better be getting back to work."

"You guys should really order something," he said to his friends. "You think E. O. Jennio's running this place for his health?"

"OK—fair is fair," said a crooked-toothed fellow wearing Buddy Holly glasses. "Platters for everyone, Jason. Don't worry, guys; it's on me."

"Awesome. I'm starving. I just had Ramen today."

"Excellent. You're a pal, Myron. I owe you one."

"Hey there, queen of hearts," Jason greeted me with a wink. "How 'bout a plate for you, too, huh? It's only three bucks."

He came back down bearing pie tins piled with glistening grilled sardines. That's what I'd smelled through the screen, the scent of their shining oil blending with curls of coffee steam. It was a warm silver scent, complex beyond imagination. I breathed in deep, closed my eyes, and listened to the strumming of the guitar.

There was whispered heat at my ear, a single accented word.

"Fathers?" I echoed, pulling back from the voice, alarmed.

"No, no. *Fados*. Is the name of this kind of music. I see you like it. It's Portuguese. I am E. O. Jennio."

Setting a plate of sardines and a coffee mug on my table, he reached through their rough perfume, extending a work-worn hand to me. He seemed to be around thirty, but all I could notice at first was his color; tousled hair, liquid eyes, broad lips, and smooth skin, all shifting variations of brass, the kind of evanescent hues that can only be seen for a moment, like the light that catches a spinning coin or glints off a ring of keys.

"I'm Josh," I said, loosening my grip slowly, fearing he might disappear on release. "Pleased to meet you, E. O."

He furrowed his brow in confusion as he sat down in the chair across from me.

"E. O. That's your initials, isn't it? E. O. Jennio? What do they stand for?"

He laughed and rapped a palm on the table.

"We are having trouble with translation, some misunderstanding," he said, grinning. "You have some paper?"

From my pack, I pulled a Bic and my leather-covered book.

"This is too nice; you don't want my scratches in here. Let me get some scrap from— "

"No, please," I interrupted. "Go ahead."

"*Fados*," he wrote first, saying it aloud. "That is the Portuguese music. The songs, they are romantic, but they are full of pain. The singer, he wears a black cape."

"And my name," he laughed again, then wrote and spoke, "Eugenio."

I laughed, too. It was so exotic on the ear, but little more than Eugene on paper. I wondered how glamorous "Myron" might sound in Portuguese.

"I think we've got something going here," I said. "*The Big Book of Misunderstanding*. Meri would love it. It's even more like life than Scrabble."

"Ugh. I cannot stand that stuff. Isn't American hamburger meat loaf bad enough without being made from the lips and snouts and guts of pigs? Some of you Philadelphians think my sardines are disgusting, and then you eat that garbage for breakfast."

"Now it's my turn," I laughed, opening the book again to sketch the distinctions between Scrabble and scrapple.

For eight weeks, I pressed myself into foreign territory. His armpits. His belly. The folds of his scrotum. Coffee and fish oil and sweat met my nose, mixed on my tongue, rushed through my head like a brand new fuel. I raked Eugenio's back with my fingers. He teethed on the soft flesh of my neck, and licked tenderly at the hollow. It felt like luck, and magic, and something I deserved.

By day, I helped out in the café, and several nights a week we were together. I stayed over when Cole was at Meri's. The tiny third-floor bedroom above the Copa Mà was pitch black. The cafe closed at 2 a.m. and opened at noon, so Eugenio took cautions against the morning sun. Green woolen blankets hung over the windows to keep the light out. His alarm clock ticked beneath the bed. "When the bell rings, I'm ready to go," he said. "Until then, it doesn't matter what time it is. It's my time."

He would click off the beaded floor lamp and pull me into velvet blackness. There was no sight and no insight when we slept together, just hard breath and our bodies' braid. I always wanted to ask about his love life, his history, to tell him I hoped this was more than a fling. But whenever I began to speak, Eugenio sealed my mouth with his broad lips and pressed my tongue into silence with his own.

In the deep of a sweaty July night, we sat on the bed panting, our legs curled around each other. I took our cocks together in my right hand, their twinned firmness as comforting as it was arousing. I tried to close my fist around them, full circle.

"Too much to handle," I joked, "in a good way, of course. Not like everything else . . . "

I drifted into thought. Despite Meri's constant urgings these past months, I'd made every effort to avoid my father, pulling away from the world and cloistering myself with Eugenio, in this neighborhood I'd come to love.

"You'd never even have discovered the Elbow Bends if you hadn't flown back to make things right with Harris," Meri insisted. "Come on, Josh, if that's the excuse it takes for you to see him, then use it. It's not fair for me to have to see him on the street and play dumb while he's worried sick about you. I will, Josh—I will if you keep insisting. Because I love you. But Harris loves you too, Josh. Forever. No matter what he's done wrong, he loves you in a way that I can never come close to."

Still, the most I'd been able to bring myself to do was leave occasional messages on my father's machine from Meri's untraceable cell phone, telling him I was alive and well but leaving my whereabouts as secret as my stubborn, unfair brother's.

"Joshua. Hello? Joshua?" I was brought back to consciousness by an irritated Eugenio, waving a hand in front of my face on the bed. "Joshua. You always say that you don't like flings that are just sex or one-night stands, right?"

"Yes," I said warily, sensing that I was finally about to be evicted from our temporary romance.

"Me either. I think you know by now."

"Oh, man, Eugenio. That's great," I sighed with relief. "I was afraid you were about to send me off to write a depressing new entry in *The Big Book of Misunderstanding.*"

"But there is misunderstanding, Joshua. What is much worse to me than a fling or a one-night stand is a one-minute stand or a one-second stand. I would very much like to be in this room, in this bed with you for this night and for many more nights. But every other minute, your mind keeps going away. In your eyes, I see you talking to other people. You should talk just to me. It is only us here."

Eugenio offered the prospect of unthinking bliss, a truly private place for two, no hidden meanings, no wider world.

I didn't know if it was possible. I didn't know if I would want it anyway.

"I'm sorry," I said, tears welling uncontrollably as series of gorgeous images burst across my eyes, exploding like flashbulbs: perfect memories of Vincent, Meri, the Cleyskils, Lewis, my parents. "Please E. O., I do want to be with you, it's just—"

"No, no. Don't cry, Joshua," he wiped my cheek, then massaged the back of my neck with his fingertips. "You are like the *fados,* so much passion and sadness all mixed. Maybe you are secretly Portuguese, not American, huh? That would be something for the *Big Book,* wouldn't it?"

We sat quietly for a moment, at ease, if unresolved.

"You are the kindest man in the world," I said, coaxing him back onto the mattress and slipping down between his legs. "So, you think it's time for me to get out of my thoughts and get into my head?" I ran my tongue over his hard warmth, and he growled with contented forgiveness. A perfect sound.

In my mind, though, it was echoed by my nephew Cory's sleepy gurgles, a continent away. Eugenio didn't seem to notice, wriggling happy on his own back. I heard a whole party of familiar voices join in then, chattering in celebration, happy for my romance.

*It's only us here,* I heard Eugenio say again.

I laughed with my mouth full, in that noisy intersection.

It was not the alarm that woke me the next morning but a telephone in my dream, ringing and ringing in my dorm room: Harris, desperate to speak with me. I would have to call him. I bolted up in the bed, Eugenio's smooth chest rising and falling in steady, contented rhythm beside me.

It felt like hours, sitting there alone, noting each minuscule gradation of gray as light seeped around the blanket covering the window and the objects in Eugenio's room were born into the morning. I looked around, waiting in vain for the phone to appear.

The poster of Eugenio's hometown gradually revealed itself on the wall: a seaside Portuguese panorama of the ancient coastal village called Sessimbra. Wooden boats painted in the bright greens, reds, and blues of children's toys bobbed on the waves, tethered to dockside pilings by lengths of rope. A net of sardines sprawled open on the planks of the dock. Most of the catch was bound for the wooden barrels lining the pier, but some fish seemed to be wriggling to the dock's edge and dropping back into the water. I imagined them being caught and then escaping, day after day, their whole lives.

Eugenio sprung up with the alarm's first electric cries, swiftly reaching under the bed to turn off the clock.

"Good morning, Joshua!" he crowed, flipping like a switch from deep slumber to wakefulness, distracting me from my ruminations.

As I sat on the edge of the mattress, rubbing the filmy residue of sleep from my eye, Eugenio put his hands on either side of my waist and pulled me up toward him.

"How long can this last?" I wondered aloud.

"I don't know," he laughed, kneading my shoulders. "Today for sure. And then tomorrow we will see again."

In the shower, Eugenio came with a sigh, his erection sliding against the sweaty porcelain tiles as I sprayed the small of his back.

Only after we toweled off, got dressed, and sat down to plan the day over mugs of coffee in the kitchen did I allow myself to return to my waking thoughts.

"There's a coin phone around the corner on Ink Street," he said, frowning as he flipped me a quarter across the wobbly table.

"You're kidding. You don't have a telephone? I've never noticed that you don't have a phone."

"You see, we have everything we need right here in the Bends, Josh. All our friends come here every afternoon and night. They tell us everything we need to know."

"Don't you feel kind of disconnected? What about your family in Portugal?"

"Hurry if you have to make this call," he said, abruptly rising and stepping to the sink, his back to me. "I need you to walk down to the fish man in South Philly. Order has to be picked up by ten."

"OK, sure," I paused. He scrubbed hard at a plate with a scouring pad. "Hey, did I say something wrong?"

"No, no problem. Come here."

He pulled me close and kissed me again.

"This is now," he said, his eyes full of sincerity and light. "This is pure."

But there is a difference between purity and permanence in love. One is an unexpected flash of magic, the other a painstaking work of art. I walked around the corner that morning and called my father at his office.

Ten days later, after a series of awkward conversations held hunched in the phone booth on Ink Street and curled on Mer's over-stuffed couch, I saw Harris for the first time in nearly a year.

Even when I'd left Eugenio to run grocery errands at the Italian market in South Philadelphia, every moment outside the Bends felt like walking in a minefield. So as I emerged from Juniper Street and crossed back over Broad for the first time since my reunion with Meredith, the pit of my stomach quivered with anxiety. I noticed that the vendor and his balloons were gone.

I met my father for lunch at Bookbinder's, a legendary Philadelphia fish house, just down the block from his office. He looked trim, composed, better than I'd expected. We leaned in to kiss each other outside the front door, but somehow ended up just shaking hands.

Having worked a few doors down for over twenty years, my father was acquainted with much of the lunchtime crowd. He offered curt hellos and handshakes as we made our way to a table in the back.

I was wearing the same khakis and blue pinpoint Oxford shirt that had seemed so conservative my first day in the Elbow Bends. But in Bookbinder's clubby, wood-paneled dining room, I felt distinctly underdressed.

"Try the bouillabaisse," my father urged, adjusting his tie. "They only make it on Fridays."

All around us, men in navy blue suits spooned up the brick red stew.

"I'll try the bouillabaisse," I said quietly to our waitress. "It comes highly recommended."

"That was easy," my father remarked, raising an eyebrow. "So, can I interest you in a suit?"

"I swear, Dad, I'll walk out if you get started on this stuff . . ."

"I'm just joking, Josh. Please relax. I'm trying to be relaxed, OK?"

"OK," I said.

Then we glanced down to the tablecloth, silent.

There was a large brandy snifter filled with oyster crackers in the center of the table. Our eyes locked as we reached for them simultaneously, then again as we both went for the jar of chopped horseradish.

"Go ahead," he said. "I didn't know you liked the hot stuff."

"Grandpop Josh always used it."

"He did indeed. It's nice that you remember that. You hardly knew him. He was quite a character, your grandfather."

I smeared the hard round biscuit with white paste and placed it, heat side down, on my tongue.

"Ouch," said my father, watching me. He applied just a tiny dot of horseradish to his cracker then noisily crunched it up, blending the heat into a floury mash.

I imagined mine was Eugenio's testicle, my father forced to observe politely as I slowly sucked it. Then I felt the back of my eyes begin to burn.

"Are you all right?" He offered a glass to me as my face reddened.

I gulped down the water and spit the soggy cracker into a napkin. "Can I have yours, too?" I gasped.

"Sure, sure."

I drank it down and wiped my sweating forehead with a napkin. He turned and gestured for the waitress, who brought a full pitcher. He poured another glassful for me.

"I'm sorry," I muttered, embarrassed. "I forgot how intense that stuff is."

"Don't worry, Josh. Just relax. Let's enjoy our lunch. It's so nice to see you. I wasn't sure you'd come. It was so good to find out you're so near." He reached across the table laid a hand over mine. "Tell me what's going on again, son. I know you've told me on the phone but forgive me. I get so caught up in the sound of your voice, I'm afraid I lose track of the words."

I gave him a scantily detailed sketch of life in the Elbow Bends, told him Meri had found me a job at the Copa Mà. "The owner is a Portuguese guy, Eugenio. He rents me a room upstairs."

"A room with no phone. Isn't that peculiar?"

"Lay off!" I snapped. Then I backed off of my reflex. "No, you're right. It is a bit strange. But he's different. A very good guy though, a good friend. And it's a decent deal, between the work and the room."

"Insurance?" my father asked.

"Huh?"

"Health insurance, Josh. Does he give you good insurance?"

I laughed, there in the middle of the blue suits, and thought about the flea-market economy of the Bends: there were constant out-of-pocket loans, shared suppers, used and useless housewares sold from neighbor to neighbor whenever someone was short on cash. I thought about Eugenio's ever-extending line of credit with DiSalvo, the fish man.

"It's not like that, Dad. He doesn't offer those kinds of benefits."

"What kind of legitimate businessman— "

My father stopped short, quickly checking his criticism. He looked up at me, suddenly ashen.

"What's wrong? Are you OK?"

"I'm OK," he said, setting his spoon down in his empty bowl. "I don't mean to snap at you. Please. I don't want to chase you away. I'm frightened, Josh. Do you think we could talk about—"

"About what?"

"Everything." His voice dropped to a prayer-like whisper. "My grandson. Cory. I'd like to see him."

In my father's voice, I heard the same gnawing hunger for completeness that had first sent me hurtling back to Philadelphia.

"Lew sent some photos," I offered weakly. "I'll bring them next time."

"Not pictures, Josh. Not stories. Real life."

I nodded silently.

"I don't want to be some mythical monster. I don't want this little boy's whole experience of me to come through Lewis. I don't want to be hated. I don't think I deserve to be hated."

"Please. Nobody hates anyone, Dad. We just love strangely. Maybe we love too much."

"I don't think that's possible, Josh. And love aside, you know, if they give him the chance, the kid might find something to *like* about the Wicked Grandfather of the East."

"I believe it, Dad." I gave him a quick smile. "Grandpop Harris."

We fell hushed, together, for a moment.

"Joshua?"

"Yes."

"I'm just asking. I'm not being pushy. How about coming out to the house one night? We could order Chinese. You can stay over if you want, of course."

During the last of the calls in preparation for this meeting, I had made my father promise not to raise certain issues over lunch. I needed a certain degree of control. We would just try to enjoy each other's company: no law school, no long range plans, no going home. I had been as clear as I could with him. If he broached these subjects, I would get up and leave. My life in the Elbow Bends would be farther away from him than California or Portugal or the secret worlds of his own father's coin collection.

I surprised myself by remaining seated.

"I'd be more comfortable talking about things at home." He glanced around the room. "Not surrounded by strangers like this."

He had boiled the world down to family and strangers.

"We're talking just fine," I said. "But we're not talking about home, remember?"

I stayed in my chair but cocked my head toward the doorway, indicating that I was prepared to leave at a moment's notice.

"But Joshua . . . "

"Cut it out, Dad." I turned away from him. "Oh, Miss—Miss, could we please have some coffee here?"

"I know I agreed," he whispered as she stepped away. "But I can't help wishing."

"You're wishing for something that's already over and done. You're wishing for the past to come back."

"A family is never over and done, Joshua." He sighed. "I suppose you're right, though. I would like to have the past back. But I'd also like my future back. Until you called, I felt as if I'd been removed from the loop altogether."

"Well, I'm glad I called, then."

I set my jaw and slid my chair from the table, wanting to stay with him but needing to stay apart. From my head to my heart, there was a ripping sensation.

"I'll call again."

"Are you leaving?" He was distraught.

"It's two o'clock already." I bent and kissed his forehead. "Eugenio is waiting for me."

His eyes blinked in a way that suggested he'd never heard me mention Eugenio's name.

"Give a hello to my girl Meredith," Harris said, trying to sound composed. He refolded his linen napkin on the table in front of him. "I used to run into her all the time, Josh, but I haven't seen her in a few weeks."

He raised his eyebrows at me. I shrugged.

"Tell her I've got a big bottle of peroxide waiting for her in my briefcase. Why is she doing that with her hair, Josh?"

"See ya, Dad," I said, laughing a little in spite of myself.

I took a wooden toothpick from a shallow dish by the register and chewed hard on it as I walked back into the Bends. Passing Meri's door, with its friendly painted phantoms, I had an urge to let myself in. She kept a spare key under the window box. Up in the studio, I picked up a blue pastel and wrote in big, childlike letters on a blank sheet of her sketch pad:

M—HARRIS SAYS HELLO. I SAW HIM.
—Love J

Then I picked up her phone and called him at his office.

Every Friday afternoon for two months, I met my father for lunch at Bookbinder's.

The most basic elements of the universe have their place in *The Big Book of Misunderstanding*.

"My father makes quarks," is what I thought Eugenio whispered in bed on the night of my last Bookbinder's lunch with Dad. We had closed the Copa early and were curling on top of the comforter, legs folded into each other like the panels of a paper fan. Eugenio's power had gone out unexpectedly, the coffee machine blinking off, the music dropping away. Eugenio had rushed his customers out. Cole Wexler gave me a playful punch in the shoulder as he and Meri departed.

"Night, Josh-o-rama!" I liked him. They made a handsome couple.

Eugenio took my hand and led me up the rickety stairs to the bedroom.

"Shouldn't we find the fuse box? Try to see what's wrong?"

"If it is still wrong tomorrow, we can see to fix it. Now it's dark. We'll enjoy the dark now."

But that night, as we held each other, it was Eugenio who seemed unable to take pleasure in the moment. He rolled onto his back and fell strangely silent. The rattle of Timmy McGinty's skateboard in the alley below reminded me that it was still early.

"I wonder what's wrong with the electricity?"

"Shhhh."

A minute later, Jared Tyler wandered down the sidewalk, offering up a song in his campy diva falsetto.

"We are fa-mi-ly!"

And Jason snapped back.

"I got my big old bitch queen sistah with me!"

Irie bellowed from her window.

"Some people are trying to sleep, you bloody eunuchs!"

"We are fa-mi-ly!"

I laughed at the friendly sound of the Elbow Bends, then yawned, and wrapped my arms around Eugenio.

"I have to go," he said, wriggling away, sitting up on the bed, then walking to the bathroom and pulling the door shut behind him. I must have fallen asleep to the sound of running water. The next thing I knew was a dreamy whisper in my ear. His breath, in the dark.

"My father makes quarks."

I felt a shock of pleasure at this revelation. In nearly five months, Eugenio had never spoken of his family. Disoriented in half sleep and not remembering his odd mood, my reaction was celebratory.

"The fundamental unit of existence!" I muttered, smiling and cupping his chin in my hands. "The basic building block of all time and space. Everything flows together; everything is one." I recalled Vincent Oglio's preachings about the sovereignty of science. His theories flowed themselves, now, into the very sort of romance that Vince had pitted them against. Nirvana. Proof positive. All mysteries would soon be solved.

Eugenio scowled, pulling away from my hands.

"Sorry to get so goofy, but I'm happy. I'm grateful, E. O. I've always wanted to know this stuff about you. A guess you could call this a quantum leap in intimacy, huh? So, your dad's a physicist. Is there a university in Sessimbra?"

"My father is a businessman, Joshua."

He spoke in a taut, telegraphic staccato, as if channeling his words from a great distance and trying not to feel them as they emerged in sound.

"A very proper Portuguese businessman. He is a national finance minister and a councilman in Sessimbra . . . "

"Didn't you say he made— "

"His company makes corks, Joshua. C-O-R-K-S."

His voice grew feverish, violent.

"You take a knife to a living tree and scrape away the bark. You cut it to pieces, boil it, jam it in bottles, so nothing can spill out." Eugenio's muscles tightened and sharp bursts of hyperventilated breath pushed through his gritted teeth. I reached across the mattress to lay my hand atop his trembling clenched fist.

"When I finish school, eighteen years old, I am working for my father," he spoke in strained tones. "In the evening, I go into the town for coffee at Copa Mà."

"Copa Mà? Same name as here?"

He didn't respond, continuing to speak, as if in a trance.

"Mario Beralho is the son of the owners. Seventeen. Part Arab, part Indian, part Basque. The whole world in one boy. To me, he is everything."

In the spill of Eugenio's memory, in the wake of my exaltation, I was filled with unexpected regret that his past had finally opened to me. He could no longer be a magical emanation of bronze light and warm heart. Pure love has no tales to tell.

I listened, in knotted anguish, to Eugenio's story.

"When I tell my father about Mario and me, he forbids me to see him again. But I will not stop. I do not stop." His speech slipped to a tremulous, sobbing shorthand, English more broken than ever before. "One night, after two days' business with my father's exporter in Lisboa, I walk down to the Copa Mà. There is a sign on the window that it is closed. I pound on the door. I cannot think what is going on."

He winced, each recalled moment hitting him like a blow.

"What is going on is the town council. Restaurant license inspection. The Copa has been shut down on violations. It is a small place, Sessimbra. My father has the power to do this. The whole family is gone, that sudden.

"It is no secret for my father. He is waiting when I come home. 'You will not hear from Mario Baralho,' he says, as if he is proud. 'The boy's parents and I have a very clear understanding. And you'd better understand, too, young man, no son of mine is a *bicha*. My father looked me straight in the eye and told me I was not the person who had been with Mario: 'That Eugenio is not here anymore. He does not exist.'"

"So, what did you say back to him then?"

"There is nothing to say, Joshua. It is not like Philadelphia in Sessimbra. The Tyler twins are not singing in the streets. And you do not argue back and forth with your father. There is no discussion to be had. I was silent. For three years. And then I left. Through a man who worked for the exporter, I found my first American job, at a hotel in Washington where many Portuguese stay."

"Your father let you go?"

He gave a bitter snort of a laugh.

"I left a note in his office one morning and walked out the door. I was gone. I still am."

Eugenio heaved a long sigh. He wiped his eyes and kissed me softly, then stretched his arm into the dark room, pointing toward his poster of the dock at Sessimbra, as though the image were somehow illuminated in the heart of the night.

As we drifted to sleep, his voice played on in my head.

"When I was a boy, I would hide in those little wooden boats. The fishing was over by early afternoon. The men went up the hill to the bars. I would run to the beach alone after school, strip my clothes, and set them under a rock. I would dive into the sea, swim out, and pull myself into a boat."

He pointed his toes and flattened his back to the mattress.

"I am lying on the bottom and looking up at the sky. I cannot see the shore or the horizon, just the clouds, always changing. The sun is warm, and the waves rock the boat. I am the baby in the cradle, but nobody can see me. Nobody knows I am here."

When my watch read 8:01 a.m. I gently roused Eugenio.

"Come on, E. O. I know it was a rough night, but we'd better get up. We have to figure out what's going on. No alarm today. The power is still out."

"Good morning, Joshua!" He leapt from the bed with unexpected energy. Turning to me with a grin, he presented his testicles cupped in both hands. "Shower time, Mr. Royalton?"

He hooked his thumbs into my armpits.

"Eugenio! What about getting the lights on? What about last night? Are you OK?"

"Last night is last night, Joshua," he touched a finger to the tip of his tongue, then pressed it against my nipple.

I stepped back.

"Aren't you upset?"

"Last night I was upset. Not now. The lights went out because I did not pay the bill. You know I am not good with the bills. This makes me think I am a bad businessman. And so I got upset. But that is stupid. I am not a bad businessman. I am not a businessman at all. And I will not close down the Copa Mà.

"This morning I will go to Timmy and others who owe me money and collect enough to go pay the electric. Don't worry, Josh. There is an office on Market Street. It will work out. This has happened before . . ."

His levelheaded explanation struck me as perverse. Could he be so oblivious to the drama of his own life? I expected him to be overwhelmed with emotion.

"But what about everything else you told me last night? Your father? Mario? Portugal?"

"It's OK. That's over now, Josh. It's another day." He tilted his head and gave a sheepish smile, as if to apologize for his revelations. "I'm fine."

He really was. I could see it.

It was me who could not let go of the night. I didn't want to.

Somehow, Eugenio had learned to cultivate his memories. They bloomed to life only in their telling, then retracted, safe and harmless, tucked away in their buds. My memories were a weave of vines. They grew in thorny lushness, entangling all they touched.

"I am here now, Joshua. It is just me and you."

He took me in his arms. I felt like a foreigner.

Resisting a welling sense of unease, I tagged along with Eugenio through the alleys. Rapping on doors yielded cheerful Sunday morning donations, paybacks of past debts and undocumented new loans. The denizens of the Elbow Bends lounged about in their least glamorous private attire, ratty bathrobes, fuzzy leg warmers, and cut-off sweatpants. They happily dug loose change from their couch cushions and dumped Mason jars of pennies into Eugenio's canvas sack.

Jared and Jason Tyler ushered us in, their cream-colored flannel pajamas printed with lassos and ten-gallon hats. An array of cobalt blue glassware graced their mantle, alongside a collage of Kate Bush and Billy Idol pinups. The oatmeal voice of Charles Kuralt burbled from a television upstairs.

"Trick or treat for UNICEF." I greeted the twins. "Did you know that only forty-two cents a day can provide enough electrical light to illuminate the pinochle games in a third world café, such as the Elbow Bends' own Copa Mà? Did you know that thirty dollars a week can keep DiSalvo the fish man from having his cousin, DiSalvo the hit man, lop off E. O.'s lovely fingers and turn them into frozen fish sticks?"

"Eugenio, are you behind again?" shrieked Jason, feigning a horrified scowl. "When will you ever learn to budget? Spreadsheets! Spreadsheets! When I say those words to you, does it make you think of anything besides bedtime fun with Mr. Royalton here?"

"He's spending too much on the sardines, Joshua," Jared scolded with mock consternation. "He throws half of them away every day, you know. You're too caught up in this Portugal thing, Eugenio. It's great as a stage set, but I'm telling you, if you want some serious sales, microwave some overpriced nachos and bake up some Otis Spunkmeyer cookies, man."

Eugenio laughed. "I don't care about sales. I care about the Copa Mà."

Jason sang, "You like to live in A-mer-i-ca! Sardines a joke in A-mer-i-ca! Cheez Whiz is king in A-mer-i-ca! Please don't go broke in Amer-eek-a!"

"Arriba, arriba!" Jared capered in his cowboy pj's, fingers snapping.

"But, Eugenio, dear friend," declared Jason, "because you are so devastatingly hunkular, because you know the difference—*you are the difference!*—between the European and the merely Euro, and, above all, because you're so very much entranced with this crooked little quarter of our hometown, we will dip into the emergency fund and save your sweet caramel-colored heinie."

Jason lifted the ceramic yellow comb feathers from a Woodstock cookie jar.

"Fig Newtons and a fifty? Will that get you through, Captain E. O.?"

"Jase and I are on a roll," Jared blurted. "We sold three thousand dollars' of our new photo collages to one of the trustees at the Academy last week. Can you believe it?" The twins, savvy and sensitive beneath their ditzy veneer, were simultaneouly celebrating their success and expiating the twinge of bohemian guilt that accompanied it.

"So, you'll have a little extra," Jared shrugged, urging Eugenio to take the money. "It's a donation to an essential nonprofit cultural institution as far as I'm concerned. Either accept this or you'll have to find a practical way to survive: like a rack of Doritos and dollar cans of Coke."

"But if you do that," warned Jason, with a synchronized wag of butt and forefinger. "I'm resigning from my Friday night sardine-slinging gig."

"It hardly sounds like you need to work at the Copa," I congratulated him. "You guys are really raking it in, huh?"

"Money has about as much to do with my working at the Copa as it does with your boy here running the whole shebang," replied Jason, dropping his customary irony for a rare moment, his voice filling with delicate marvel, as if addressing a butterfly, tentatively perched on his fingertip.

"Four hours a week, I'm on a trip, faraway. Eugenio doesn't call himself an artist, but the Copa might be the best piece of art in the neighborhood. Step inside and you're gone from the rest of the world. The tiny votive flames, those sad, scratchy records. Time stops, and we're all in some perfect secret family. Everyone helplessly, hopelessly in love with each other. If you tried to make sense of it, the whole place would just collapse. It's dreamland."

Jason nestled a fine-boned cheek against Eugenio's broad shoulder. E. O. responded with a contented grin.

Stepping forward, in a trance, as if to find a place for myself within their handsome counterpoise, I placed open palms atop their heads, Eugenio's rough straw and Jared's soft cornsilk. An electrical rush surged through me then, and I yanked my hands away, afraid of blacking out or blazing up.

"Josh! Are you OK?" Jared grabbed my elbow. "Is something wrong?"

"No. No. I'm sorry. It's just—I'm having—" I fumbled to make sense of a headful of overlapping thoughts. Eugenio stepped over and set his hands on my hips. I had learned to calm myself by locking into his tight, focused stare, but that morning it couldn't hold me. Peripheral vision rushed in.

"Just give me the electric bill and some of the cash, E. O." I urged, reaching for the canvas sack with a trembling hand. "I'll run it up to the office on Market Street. I'll go, OK? Just stay here, Eugenio. You can stay here."

I lost my sense of threshold that morning.

There was no magical crossing between the Bends and Philadelphia. All fell together, enormous and miraculous and terrifying. In my mind, the alleys flowed seamlessly into the wide city streets, then rolled onward, outward, across the city line, and into my childhood's suburbs. They became highways, ribboning west, climbing mountains, bridging continents. By night, they passed harbor towns, where luminous fish swam through dark waters. In the dawn, they drifted as delicate mist through the ancient hills of China's Guelin province.

Was I in the world or the world in me? I was everywhere at once, with no idea where I belonged.

I was at the electric company office on Market Street. The sign on the door said "Closed." It was Sunday.

On the sidewalk outside my father's building, I wept. Staring up at William Penn's clock tower, I clasped my hands, as if begging the yellow dial to open beyond its sweeping second-hand moments, to tell all time at once. I gave a dollar to the homeless man and peered into the bank, through a black iron security gate pulled across its entrance. Staring through my reflection in the window, I saw the chairs upturned on the tables at Bookbinder's. I lingered beneath the restaurant's awning, feeling desperately unbound.

I ran back frantically to the Elbow Bends. I pounded, pleading, on the painted ghosts of Meri's door. I let myself in with the window box key, ran upstairs to the bathroom, and turned the shower on, scalding hot. Stripping to my briefs as the room closed in with steam, I had a fleeting urge to telephone Lewis in California.

WAKE THE BABY, I wrote in the fog on the mirror, then watched the words fade away as I opened the medicine chest.

Meri found me sprawled, half-conscious, on a drop cloth in her studio. I had wandered in from the bathroom, the empty amber pill vial still clutched in my hand.

"Oh my God. Josh!" She hollered down the stairs. "Cole! Call 911! Get an ambulance."

Meri fell to the floor beside me.

"Tell me you didn't," she wept. "Tell me you didn't do this, Josh."

Drawn out of my daze by her sobbing, I slowly reached over and took her hand.

"I didn't," I muttered. "I couldn't. Flushed them. Guess the old turtles will be getting mellow in heaven tonight."

"Jesus, Joshua," she laughed and cried all at once. "You seem so lost lately. You've got to pull things together. I don't know how to help anymore."

"Just one thing you can do now, Mer," I smiled up at her, trying to contain my fear. "Same thing I wouldn't let you do all along. Can you give me a ride, Mer? Will you take me home?"

~~~

I awoke on my mother's office couch. I'd scrawled with abandon for three days and nights, crying and laughing and shivering with joyful release as I filled the blank pages of *The Big Book of Misunderstanding*. Now, I emerged from my fever dream. I looked up to the window and saw the old Balloon Man, resting on the inside sill, all weary face and floating colors in the morning sun.

I suppose I'd known that Meri would call my father, that she would tell him about his pills and my confusion, that he would discover me holed up in this long-abandoned room.

I was amazed at his restraint.

It was hard to imagine him, sitting on the other side of the wall, in the kitchen, struggling to be satisfied with the knowledge of my presence without barging in, all tears and embraces. My father had set the figurine by my side as I slept, offering me comforts he could not feel himself.

In the old man's sad eyes, I saw the Elbow Bends, a small town hidden in the folds of the city. My father's office was less than a quarter mile from the Bends. For almost twenty-five years, he had been just that close to where I had found myself. He had been that close without ever walking down the alleys that led away from the life he knew so well, the life he'd wanted to raise me into, with love.

There was a halting, tentative rap on the office door.

"Come on in," I said.

"You sure it's OK, Josh?" my father stepped halfway into the room. I managed a nervous smile as he came cautiously toward me. "I'm so glad you're here, son. But I don't—I'm afraid you'll run out the minute I say a word. I don't want to do the wrong thing, Josh. I'm walking on eggshells."

"Red, blue, or plain old yellow eggs, Dad?" I replied, sharpness rising in my voice. Standing up from the couch and turning away from him, I rested a finger on the Balloon Man's tiny black fedora.

"You're not Grandpop Josh," I muttered.

"What did you say, honey?" my father leaned forward.

"You're not like your father," I realized, speaking my thoughts aloud, engaging in two conversations at once.

"You make it sound like that's a disappointment, Josh."

"He wasn't afraid, was he? He wanted to have a life full of experience. He wanted to go places."

"But he always wanted to go someplace *else,* Josh. Not where I was, not with the people who needed him most. He was out on the road or hiding away with his collections. Or running around with all those women, all those women he didn't love."

I blinked.

"At least he had imagination."

"No, Josh. Not much of one. That's you. That's yours. Somehow, in your head, you've passed it back on up the family tree. You've got a generous heart, Josh. I'd like to think that comes partly from my little tree branch, gnarled as it may be." He laughed softly and put a hand on my shoulder. We sat together on my mother's couch. "I did love my father, you know. But I always wanted to be different from him. And I was. I am. I just went overboard, I guess. And then I couldn't figure how to keep myself from drowning.

"But for all the mess I've made, Josh, I can't really say I regret anything. It hurts. But that's me. I love you all, as honestly as I can."

"But who are we supposed to love back, Dad?" I tensed with frustration. "It's like trying to enter a reflection. Besides being our father and Mom's husband—or whatever—who are you in this world? What do you imagine? What adventures do you want to go on? Do you ever have a dream that we're not a part of?" I pounded my fist against the wall, hollering. "Because if you don't, then your love doesn't have any substance. Then your sacred Royalton family is just a trick done with mirrors. Forget the fucking pills! I want broken glass! I'm sick of looking at you looking at me looking at you. I'm sick, I'm sick, I'm sick."

I stopped myself, weeping and gasping for air.

"Oh, Dad, I didn't mean—I'm sorry."

He laid a hand on my forehead. "Let me be the one who's sorry. Let me be the one who's sick. You need to get well, Josh. You need to have those adventures for yourself."

He stood then, and handed me the Balloon Man from the windowsill. I clutched it in my arms like an old stuffed toy. "I treasure you, Josh. And I trust you. I'm going to trust you not to hurt yourself. That's the only thing you could do that would really hurt me now. Do whatever you need to get back on your feet, Josh. I'd like you to stay here for a while, of course, but you've got to do what's best for you."

As he stepped out of the room he'd built for my mother, Harris Royalton cast a wistful glance to the ceiling, to the spot where the old laundry chute was sealed shut.

I never peeled away the duct tape that sealed those long lost shoe boxes filled with Grandpop Josh's coins. I just pulled them out of the chute and hefted them out of the house. Out from between my father and me. He'd gone to work. I took the keys to the Oldsmobile and drove downtown as well. I parked on Broad Street, in William Penn's shadow. In the bank next door to my father's office, I filled out the papers and left the boxes behind.

I slipped the tiny silver safe deposit key into my pocket and listened to my own cool footfall as I crossed the bank's marble floor. As I stepped back out into the morning, I swung my arms, amazed at their lightness.

Eugenio was getting ready to open the Copa as I arrived, setting fresh geraniums in the mason jars on the tables. I watched him from the doorway. He still took my breath away.

"Joshua!" He ran over and kissed me on both cheeks. "It is so good to see you. Meredith said you have gone to stay with your father for awhile."

"Yes," I said, with a slow nod. "I just came to get the rest of my stuff."

"Don't worry, Joshua. I will wait for you—" he stopped short. "Or I will let you know where I am."

"I won't worry, E. O. I wish I knew how to thank you." I pulled him tight to me, one last time. He was beautiful. He was as beautiful as he could be.

I didn't hear my father come in the front door early that evening. I didn't hear him wander back to my mother's office. I had moved my things upstairs. Not to my old room, but the guest room. I sat at the desk there, in lamplight, filling the pages of my notebook with memories, pulling them out of my bloodstream and setting them down in ink. I wrestled with them and sculpted them and, someday, I would slide them into the bookshelf of my childhood.

I would always be able to visit when I wished to leaf through the stories, but at last they would be set aside, written out of my life. The funny parts. The sad parts. The parts about love. No neat and happy ending would be necessary. The telling itself had begun to set me free.

From downstairs, I heard the sudden panic, my father shouting my name and running down the hallway. I sat there, waiting as he tore through the house. His face flushed when he finally reached the top of the stairs and saw me through the open guest room door.

"Oh, God, Joshua." He heaved a sigh of relief. "I thought you'd run away."

Calmly, I raised my eyes from my notebook and turned to offer him a smile over my shoulder.

"No," I said, setting pen back to paper. "I've been here all along."

# ABOUT THE AUTHOR

**Jim Gladstone** is a creative consultant and writer. His wide-ranging cultural commentary and criticism have appeared in publications including *The New York Times Book Review, SPIN, Lambda Book Report,* and a host of major daily newspapers. His writing has also graced tampon packages, encouraged the consumption of fresh turkey products, and been declaimed by the world's most popular red and yellow spokescandies. Educated at Yale College and the University of Pennsylvania, Gladstone's checkered past includes stints as a devoted bookseller, library staff member, radio commentator, writing teacher, and leotard-clad Playboy Club dancer. He currently resides in Philadelphia and Paris but will happily show up anywhere given a good excuse. *The Big Book of Misunderstanding* is his first novel.

## *Order Your Own Copy of*
## *This Important Book for Your Personal Library!*

# THE BIG BOOK OF MISUNDERSTANDING

_____in hardbound at $27.95 (ISBN: 1-56023-383-4)
_____in softbound at $17.95 (ISBN: 1-56023-382-6)

COST OF BOOKS_____

OUTSIDE USA/CANADA/
MEXICO: ADD 20%____

POSTAGE & HANDLING_____
*(US: $4.00 for first book & $1.50*
*for each additional book)*
*Outside US: $5.00 for first book*
*& $2.00 for each additional book)*

SUBTOTAL_____

in Canada: add 7% GST____

STATE TAX____
*(NY, OH & MIN residents, please*
*add appropriate local sales tax)*

**FINAL TOTAL____**
*(If paying in Canadian funds,*
*convert using the current*
*exchange rate, UNESCO*
*coupons welcome.)*

❏ **BILL ME LATER:** ($5 service charge will be added)
(Bill-me option is good on US/Canada/Mexico orders only;
not good to jobbers, wholesalers, or subscription agencies.)

❏ Check here if billing address is different from
shipping address and attach purchase order and
billing address information.

Signature_____

❏ **PAYMENT ENCLOSED: $_____**

❏ **PLEASE CHARGE TO MY CREDIT CARD.**

❏ Visa  ❏ MasterCard  ❏ AmEx  ❏ Discover
❏ Diner'c Club  ❏ Eurocard  ❏ JCD

Account # _____

Exp. Date_____

Signature_____

Prices in US dollars and subject to change without notice.

NAME_____
INSTITUTION_____
ADDRESS_____
CITY_____
STATE/ZIP_____
COUNTRY_____ COUNTY (NY residents only)_____
TEL_____ FAX_____
E-MAIL_____

May we use your e-mail address for confirmations and other types of information? ❏ Yes ❏ No
We appreciate receiving your e-mail address and fax number. Haworth would like to e-mail or fax special
discount offers to you, as a preferred customer. **We will never share, rent, or exchange your e-mail address
or fax number.** We regard such actions as an invasion of your privacy.

### *Order From Your Local Bookstore or Directly From*
### **The Haworth Press, Inc.**
10 Alice Street, Binghamton, New York 13904-1580 • USA
TELEPHONE: 1-800-HAWORTH (1-800-429-6784) / Outside US/Canada: (607) 722-5857
FAX: 1-800-895-0582 / Outside US/Canada: (607) 722-6362
E-mail: getinfo@haworthpressinc.com
PLEASE PHOTOCOPY THIS FORM FOR YOUR PERSONAL USE.
www.HaworthPress.com

BOF00